PRAISE FOR THE GRIPPING SNIPER ELITE SERIES FROM THE COAUTHOR OF THE #1 *NEW YORK TIMES* BESTSELLER *AMERICAN SNIPER*

THE SNIPER AND THE WOLF

"[A] military series that just keeps getting better."

—*Booklist*

"[A] white-knuckle realistic military thriller . . . Gil Shannon is a man to be reckoned with, delivering nonstop energy, vivid imagery, and intense scenes of combat making it simply impossible to put down."

—*Military Press*

TARGET AMERICA

"Gil Shannon is the most addictive thriller character alive today. Pick up *Target America* and you will see why—rapid-fire action, unforgettable characters, and explosive scenes."

—Richard Miniter, author of *Losing Bin Laden*, *Shadow War*, and *Leading from Behind*

"*Target America* delivers the goods. The harsh reality is that McEwen's fiction isn't far from the truth. Few writers I know would have the guts to go there. McEwen does, and so should you."

—Brandon Webb, former Navy SEAL, editor of SOFREP.com, and author of *The Red Circle*

"... As good as any fictional battle scene in recent memory. Readers will want to see a lot more of SEAL Team Black."
— *Publishers Weekly*, starred review

ONE-WAY TRIP

"An unfiltered portrayal of modern warfare backed by complex yet compelling storytelling, this one hits the target."
— *Publishers Weekly*

"*Sniper Elite* is a gripping, fast-paced adventure. Packed with action, it takes the reader into the shadow world of real military operations. A great read—don't miss it!"
— Dan Hampton, author of *Viper Pilot* and *The Mercenary*

Also by Scott McEwen with Thomas Koloniar

Sniper Elite: One-Way Trip

Target America: A Sniper Elite Novel

SCOTT McEWEN

WITH THOMAS KOLONIAR

THE SNIPER AND THE WOLF

A SNIPER ELITE NOVEL

Pocket Books

New York   London   Toronto   Sydney   New Delhi

Pocket Books
An Imprint of Simon & Schuster, Inc.
1230 Avenue of the Americas
New York, NY 10020

First Pocket Books paperback edition February 2016

POCKET and colophon are registered trademarks of Simon & Schuster, Inc.

For information about special discounts for bulk purchases, please contact Simon & Schuster Special Sales at 1-866-506-1949 or business@simonandschuster.com

The Simon & Schuster Speakers Bureau can bring authors to your live event. For more information or to book an event contact the Simon & Schuster Speakers Bureau at 1-866-248-3049 or visit our website at www.simonspeakers.com.

Cover design by Jae Song
Cover images © tudor antonel adrian/Shutterstock (soldier); © SJ Travel Photo and Video/Shutterstock (Istanbul sunset); © Alan Wilson/Wikimedia Commons (helicopter)

Printed and bound by CPI Group (UK) Ltd, Croydon, CR0 4YY

10 9 8 7 6 5 4 3 2 1

ISBN 978-1-5011-4252-9
ISBN 978-1-4767-8728-2 (ebook)

This book is dedicated to the men and women whose lives have been lost in fighting the War on Terrorism worldwide.

"Only God can judge whether the terrorists are right or wrong. It is our job to arrange the meeting."

—*Unknown US Navy SEAL*

THE
SNIPER
AND THE WOLF

A SNIPER ELITE NOVEL

On April 8, 2014, the director of the Russian Federal Security Service confirmed the death of Dokka Umarov, the Chechen Islamist militant responsible for Moscow Metro bombings in 2010. Though the exact date and place of his death remain unknown, his demise has been confirmed by the United States government, and he was removed from the US State Department's Rewards for Justice list in April 2014.

PROLOGUE

CANCÚN,
Mexico

Former White House chief of staff Tim Hagen sat beside the pool at his Cancún hotel on the tip of the Yucatán Peninsula sipping a piña colada and skimming a paperback copy of *The Art of War* by Sun Tzu. Though he knew each of the twenty-seven concepts backward and forward, he enjoyed studying the printed words, searching them for insight into the mind that had written them. He was particularly interested in the concepts covered in chapter thirteen, "The Use of Spies."

Up until six months earlier, Hagen had been chief military adviser to the president of the United States, but that had changed abruptly upon the president's asking for his resignation mere minutes after San Diego was nearly destroyed by a Soviet-era suitcase nuke. Of course, Hagen's ego wouldn't permit him to see that he'd brought the dismissal upon himself through his constant manipulation of the president to serve his own ambitions. Instead, he blamed Gil Shannon and Robert Pope for undermining his influence.

Now Hagen was waiting to hear that the indefatigable Navy SEAL was either dead or on his way to a French prison. Upon hearing the news, he would return to Washington, DC, with his honor restored to him and begin anew his ambitious pursuits of power and influence. He intended to offer his strategic services to a rising new political star: a handsome, young senator named Steve Grieves from New York, who, with the right *guidance*, might one day make a successful run at the White House.

A hotel concierge approached from across the patio. "Señor Hagen?"

Hagen looked up from the book. "Yeah, I'm Hagen."

"There is a call for you, señor, at the front desk."

Hagen glanced at his phone sitting silent beside his drink on the table. "For a *Tim* Hagen?"

"Sí, señor."

Wondering if something had gone wrong, Hagen picked up his phone and left the book on the table. "Show me the way."

"This way, señor." The concierge guided him to the hotel lobby, and they stopped at the front desk, where a young woman handed Hagen the landline.

"This is Hagen," he said, taking the receiver.

"Tim?"

"This is Tim Hagen," he said impatiently. "To whom am I speaking?"

"Tim, it's Bob Pope. How are you enjoying the sunshine down there?"

Hagen's heart skipped a beat, and his sandaled feet felt suddenly cold. "Well enough," he said, clearing his throat. "What can I do for you, Robert?"

"I'm calling to tell you that Gil Shannon has run into some serious trouble in Paris."

"I'm awfully sorry to hear that," Hagen said, a thin smile coming to his lips as the blood began to flow again. "But I'm no longer with the White House. Why would I be interested in anything having to do with Chief Shannon?"

Pope chuckled. "Well, I know how closely you and Lerher have been following his career."

Pope's cheerful demeanor sent a chill down Hagen's spine. "I don't know what you've been told, Robert, but I—"

"Gil's out of France," Pope said, his tone suddenly icy. "So if I were you, I'd start looking for a cave to hide in."

Hagen's mouth went dry. "Listen, you don't—who the hell is Lerher?"

"You should be running," Pope answered, "instead of standing there in the lobby wearing that ridiculous hat."

The line went dead, and Hagen turned around, searching the lobby for anyone resembling Robert Pope. He spotted a security camera on the wall above the desk. "Is your security system connected to the internet in any way?"

The concierge glanced up at the camera, a puzzled look on his face. "I don't know, señor. I don't think so. Why, is something wrong?"

"No," Hagen said, his paranoia increasing by the moment. "I'll be checking out within the half hour. Please send someone to the room for my bags."

"Sí, señor." The concierge smiled curiously at the young woman as Hagen hurried off across the lobby, watching him drop his Panama hat into a hotel trash container on his way to the elevator, wondering why the caller had asked him to describe what Mr. Hagen was wearing before bringing him to the phone.

1

PARIS,
France

The hour was closing in on three o'clock in the morning, and Master Chief Gil Shannon lay prone atop an empty freight car on the outskirts of Paris, a Remington Modular Sniper Rifle pulled tight into his shoulder, eye to the Barska nightscope, its illuminated green reticle highly visible in the darkness. He studied the blacked-out warehouse one hundred meters across the rail yard to the east. The April night was cool, and there hung on the breeze the distant whine of a locomotive as Gil adjusted his posture carefully, needing to urinate, waiting for Dokka Umarov to show himself. His right foot ached dully where he'd been shot the year before during a combat jump over Montana— much of the metatarsal bone having been replaced with an experimental titanium implant—and his chest tightened with anxiety that nowadays seemed to haunt him whenever things got too quiet for too long.

He drew a deep breath, slowly letting it back out, taking his hand from the grip to flex his fingers.

"Are you tensing up?" asked the voice of his overwatch, an earpiece nestled comfortably in his ear.

Gil smiled in the darkness. "Are you watching me or the target area?"

The voice chuckled softly. "I see all."

"You see too much," Gil muttered good-naturedly. "How about you get off my nuts and watch if Umarov slips out the back."

Again the chuckle.

A few minutes later, Gil said, "This little meet and greet's takin' longer than it should. I wonder if—"

"Heat signature! Sniper on the roof!"

Gil didn't so much as twitch, but kept his eye to the scope. "North or south?"

"North side," the voice said. "He's been hiding under an awning of some sort . . . no, I think it's a proper hide. He's sliding back under now. Umarov must have anticipated satellite surveillance."

"Can you see the rifle barrel?"

"Enhancing resolution now . . . Yeah, I can see six or eight inches of it—the suppressor."

"Which way is it pointing?"

A slight pause. "About twenty degrees to your right . . . south of your position."

"He hasn't seen me, then," Gil said. "But that's obvious." He let his eye scan back and forth across the flat roof of the three-story structure, cluttered with water tanks and air-conditioning units, ventilation ducts, and enclosed observation platforms once used by train spotters. "I can't find him. You didn't get a look at his optics by any chance, did you?"

"Yeah," the voice said. "Big scope."

"Shit," Gil muttered. "That means infrared. Sounds like maybe I brought a knife to a gunfight. What was he doing out of the hide?"

"Stretching his back, I think."

"At least he's careless. That's something." Gil relaxed and proceeded to piss his pants to solve that nagging issue. This was more difficult to accomplish while remaining stock still than most people might have imagined, but Gil had more or less mastered the art by this point in his career. An operative had to drink a lot of water in Afghanistan to stay alive and alert, and a sniper couldn't be jumping up to hit the head every ten minutes.

Now he was ready to engage. "I need to eliminate this guy before Umarov comes out. Guide me to him."

"Find the northern water tank."

"Got it."

"He's beneath a hide made of plywood and debris thirty feet south of— Look sharp! He's shifting his aim!"

Gil adjusted his own aim ten degrees right. His blood froze when he saw the enemy sniper, perfectly visible beneath the hide, silhouetted in the greenish-black field of vision.

"Shit!" He flinched away from the scope a mere instant before it shattered, the enemy round passing directly through the optic tube without touching the sides. Splinters of glass stung the flesh of Gil's neck as the deadly bullet streaked past his ear. He let go of the Remington, rolling across the roof of the railcar to drop off the far side just as the enemy's second round grazed his hip. He twisted midfall to land feetfirst like a cat in the gravel, ducking for cover behind one of the great steel wheels of the railcar.

"Christ Jesus, that was close!"

"Are you hit?" the overwatch asked, slightly unsettled.

Gil took a moment to pull down his jeans partway for a look at the wound. "He nicked my hip. Nothing serious."

"Good," the voice said grimly, "because you're about to be hip deep in shit. You've got a few dozen French gendarmes converging on your position from the north and west. Two hundred yards distant. They've got a pair of German shepherds."

Gil didn't want any part of German shepherds. He might handle one if he was willing to take damage, but a pair of them would drag him down and rip him apart. He took off at a dead run to the south, running parallel to the train through the loose gravel. "What's the fuckin' sniper doing?"

"Forget him," the voice said, slightly distracted now. "He's pulling back."

Gil adjusted the earpiece as he ran. "Is it possible the gendarmes are here for Umarov?"

"They're not moving toward the warehouse. Hold on a second." Another pause. "Umarov and his people are leaving out the back. You must've been set up, Gil."

"Goddamnit, by who?" Gil demanded, running through the darkness with the shouts of the pursuing gendarmes drifting down on the wind.

"The dogs are loose," the voice said. "Closing fast at a hundred yards."

"Fuck!" Gil leapt onto the ladder of a railcar and scrambled to the roof, sprinting along the tops of the cars, jumping the gaps between them as he made toward the locomotive still a half mile ahead at the front of the train.

"They're going to see you up there."

"Well, if you got a better idea, Bob, I'm all ears." The dogs were barking, catching up fast, the hollow thudding of Gil's footfalls clearly audible; the microdroplets of his perspiration heavy in the air and impossible for canines to miss.

"Widening the angle for a look ahead," was the response from his overwatch.

Gil could feel the titanium implant in his right foot beginning to bite into the muscle tissue, and he wondered how long before something inside the foot broke loose. He wasn't exactly built for escape and evasion anymore, and the fact became more evident with each leap from one railcar to the next. The German shepherds were directly below now, barking their asses off to let their handlers know they had caught up to the suspect.

A pistol shot rang out, and Gil cut a glance over his shoulder to see a gendarme fifteen cars back, also running along the rooftops.

"What happened to 'Thou shalt not shoot a fleeing felon'?" Gil muttered aloud.

"You're in France," the voice reminded him. "They don't have that law over there."

"Bob. I'm running out of train, and that gung-ho prick back there is faster than I am." Another pistol shot. "I'm pretty sure they aim to kill me."

"They do. Somebody called a tip into the Sûreté about a terrorist in the train yard." The Sûreté Nationale was the French national police force.

"You're channel surfing?" Gil leapt a gap between cars, almost stumbling upon landing.

"I have to find out what you're up against," the voice said calmly, the faint sound of fingers running over a keyboard. "Okay, you're in luck. The tracks span a wide canal about ten cars ahead. The dogs won't be able to follow you across, so you can hit the ground and do some open-field running."

Gil jumped another span and stumbled, expertly sum-mersaulting back to his feet, the footfalls of his pursuer growing ever closer. "I have to shake Carl Lewis back there."

"Run, Gil. If you're captured alive, you'll do life in a French prison."

"Thanks, Bob, no shit!" Gil ran across the car that spanned the canal way, leaving the dogs barking at the edge and scrambling down a ladder to the ground. A quick glance, and he saw the gendarme only six cars back, closing fast with pistol in hand. He disappeared into the shadows of a stockyard full of shipping containers stacked two high. The shouts of more gendarmes became audible as they gathered at the canal's edge, the beams of their flashlights flickering wildly.

Gil pulled up around the corner of the nearest ship-ping container to wait for the gendarme. As the younger man rounded the corner in the darkness at full speed, Gil delivered him a vicious strike to the throat with the V of his forefinger and thumb, temporarily collapsing the esophagus and taking him off his feet.

The pistol fell to the ground, and Gil snatched it up. He didn't want to kill anyone, but the possibility of life in prison was not acceptable to him, so he would have to play this fucked-up mission as close to the edge as it came, dancing along the razor until he finally escaped or was forced into making some fatal decision. He jammed the pistol into his waistband and kept moving, leaving the gendarme choking in the dirt.

"Find me a way outta this fuckin' rat maze!" It was moments like this that Gil was relieved that he and his wife were separated, and that she wasn't at home worrying about him.

"Keep moving straight down the row until it dead-ends, then break right. A few of them are crossing the canal over the train now. The rest are moving west with the dogs toward a footbridge."

"Where am I in relation to the embassy?" Gil asked.

"You can forget the embassy," the voice answered. "It's being cordoned off as we speak. Somebody knows you're an American, and they're expecting you to head that way."

Gil dashed down a narrow passage between the containers. "Where is Umarov?"

"Never mind him. We have to find you a place to hole up."

"Fuck that!" Gil snapped. "Vector me back toward Umarov!"

"Gil, no. It's—"

"Bob, your Paris contacts are compromised. I'm completely on my own down here. So vectoring me toward Umarov is as good a direction as any—and it's the last thing he's gonna expect!"

The overwatch remained silent, so Gil kept moving toward the end of the row, reaching the dead end. He looked up into the starry night sky. "So what the fuck up there? Am I turning left or right?"

"Oh, hell," the voice said. "Break left!"

Gil took off down the row. "Did Umarov go far?"

"He stopped and entered an apartment building about two miles away."

"What about the gendarmes?"

"They've crossed the footbridge to the west, and the dogs are looking for your scent. You don't have more than a minute before they're back on your trail."

Gil reached the end of the row and dashed across the open rail yard toward the warehouses.

"Step on it," the voice urged. "You're entirely exposed."

"I'm worried I'll blow out this damn implant."

"If you don't make it to cover within the next the thirty seconds, you'll be spotted by the gendarmes. They've got night vision."

Gil stepped up the pace and made it to cover behind a line of six lone tanker cars parked on a sidetrack, ducking behind another wheel.

"Hold there a minute," the overwatch said. "They're scanning up and down the rail yard."

"What are their orders?" Gil knew that his overwatch spoke fluent French. "Are you listening to their traffic in real time?"

"Their orders are to not let you escape."

"Okay, so dicey at best," Gil muttered. "I could use a smoke." He sat on his haunches with his head tilted back against the wheel, sucking air deep into his lungs. "I can't run like this much longer. You have to find me a ride."

"The dogs will pick up your scent any second now," said the overwatch. "Get up and move out exactly perpendicular to the tracks. You need to keep the wheels between you and the men on the far side. If you can make it to the warehouses without being spotted, you've got a chance."

Gil ran and made it to the nearest warehouse, running down the far side to get out of sight.

"Oh, Christ," said the overwatch. "Do you hear any shooting down there?"

Gil froze. "No—why?"

"Someone's shooting the gendarmes. Two of them are down on the tracks, and the rest are falling back under cover. They just set the dogs loose again."

Gil broke a window and climbed into the warehouse. "I'm inside now." He made his way toward the back of the building, winding among the crates and quickly getting disoriented in the darkness. He came to a dead end and had to turn around. "Who stacked these fucking things?"

"What things?"

"Crates," Gil said. "Who's shooting at the gendarmes? Is it that damn sniper?"

"I don't know. Gil, you have to find a way out of there right now. The dogs are jumping in through the window— they're inside!"

Seconds later, Gil heard the dogs' claws on the concrete as they scurried unerringly through the inky dark, following his exact path through the maze of crates. He came to a steel staircase and ran two stories to the top, where he stood overlooking the warehouse floor. He ran to the end of the catwalk and came to a locked steel door.

Both German shepherds scampered to the top of the stairs, and he saw their faint silhouettes at the far end of the catwalk, moving toward him shoulder to shoulder, each growling low in the throat.

Gil's own dog came to mind, a Chesapeake Bay retriever, as he took the Beretta from his pants, preparing to shoot them. The German shepherds snarled and charged. In the glow of a vapor light mounted outside the window, he saw a series of conduit pipes running down the wall, leading to a door at the bottom. On the spur of the moment, he dropped the pistol, swung his legs over the railing, and stretched to grab on to the conduit, bracing his feet against the wall. The dogs snarled furiously as he clung to the wall less than a foot beyond their reach. Glimpsing their white fangs, he shinnied down the conduit to the floor two stories below. The dogs backtracked to the stairs.

Gil made it to the floor only to find that this door, too, was locked. "Can I get a fuckin' break?"

"What's the matter now?" asked the overwatch.

"*Dogs* are the matter!"

He ran along the wall toward what he hoped was the back of the warehouse as the shepherds scrambled down the stairs. Gil broke into a locked office and quickly jammed a desk up against the door, snatching a pack of French cigarettes from the desk and stuffing them into his pocket. Within seconds, the dogs were scratching around outside, whining in frustration. He forced open another door at the back of the office and ran down a blind hallway toward a dim glow at the far end.

"You still up there?"

"Yeah, I've been making some calls," the voice said. "Trying to find you a place to hide. How close are you to finding your way out of there?"

"Let you know in a second." Gil put his hand against a pane of grime-covered glass. "I think this leads out."

He groped about in the darkness for a chair or a trash can to break out the window.

Without warning, a German shepherd slammed into him at full tilt, sinking its teeth into his left forearm.

"Holy shit!" he shouted, completely unprepared for the suddenness of the impact. He struggled to keep his feet with the dog whipping him from side to side, not quite like a rag doll but close.

"What's happening?" the overwatch asked anxiously.

The animal was unbelievably strong and took Gil down in seconds. He sensed more than heard the second dog's arrival, and so he kicked out in the dark to ward it off. The animal latched onto his boot, savagely ripping it back and forth, its fangs easily penetrating both the leather upper and the instep of Gil's already damaged right foot.

Fortunately, the narrow hall limited the dogs' room to

maneuver enough that Gil was able to pin the first one in the corner, bracing his free foot against a wall and using his forearm to jam the dog's head against the floor, transitioning to the top position. The second dog still had hold of his foot, and though painful, it posed no immediate threat to life or limb.

Gil was about to jam his thumb into the dog's eye socket when he smacked his head against a fire extinguisher sitting on the floor against the wall. He grabbed it with his free hand and thrust the plastic nozzle into the dog's mouth, squeezing the lever to emit a large blast of CO_2. The dog howled, immediately releasing Gil's arm, flailing insanely to get back on its feet. Gil rolled off and gave the second dog a blast in the face, causing it to let go of his foot. He sprang into a crouch and used the extinguisher to haze both animals back down the hall. Then he wheeled around and hurled the extinguisher through the window. The glass fell away, and he leapt out into the night, landing in a steel dumpster half full of garbage.

One of the German shepherds landed beside him a second later, sinking its teeth into his thigh with a snarl. "You motherfucker!" Gil busted the dog in the side of the head with his fist hard enough to make let it go. He kicked the animal away and threw a leg over the side of the dumpster as the second shepherd was leaping down from the window. Gil turned to slam the steel lid down on one of the dogs with such force that it was knocked out cold. The other dog continued barking inside the steel box as Gil trotted off down the alley.

"Christ Almighty." He leaned against a wall, flexing his fingers to check the extent of the damage to his left arm. Gil looked up into the sky again. "How do I get outta here?"

"Keep an easterly heading," the voice said quietly. "If you move fast, I'm pretty sure you'll have time to hail a cab half a mile from there."

"What about the cops?"

"Three more got shot down while you were having it out with the dogs. They're under cover now and calling for medevac."

"Did you see which way the shooter went?"

"No, but whoever he is, he sure as hell put the bloody finger on you."

Gil took a second to light up a smoke, tossing the match to the ground. "Make sure you find out who ghosted this operation. I'm gonna cut his fuckin' heart out."

"We'll be lucky to get you out of France."

Gil drew from the cigarette. "Then killing Umarov is still my number one priority. Which way to that cabstand?"

2

PARIS,
France

Gil caught a cab a half mile from the target area. The over-watch told him which words to use in French, and though Gil's accent was terrible, the cabbie understood him well enough to follow his directions along the outskirts of Paris. The cabbie saw how badly his passenger was bleeding, and it soon became apparent to him that Gil was getting his directions from someone speaking to him through an ear-piece. He began jabbering away over the back of the seat in hurried French.

"He thinks you're CIA," the overwatch said with a chuckle.

"You've seen too many movies," Gil told the cabbie. "Just drive." He was betting the cabbie spoke at least some English, as did most Parisians, though they usually pre-tended not to when dealing with American tourists.

The cab driver pulled to the curb. "Get out. I don't need your trouble."

Gil wasn't in the mood for games. He lunged forward over the back of the seat, punching the cabbie in the face Indiana Jones style. "Now, you either drive this cab, or I will! I don't have time for your shit! *Comprendre, mon ami?*"

The cab driver leaned against the door, holding the side of his face where Gil had struck him, his eyes full of anger. "You *are* CIA."

"You're damn right I am," Gil grumbled. "Now drive!"

The driver sullenly shifted into gear and pulled away from the curb. "Why are you bleeding?" he asked a couple minutes later.

"I was attacked by a werewolf." Gil sat listening to the overwatch, who was monitoring the cab from above in infrared via satellite locked in geosynchronous orbit two hundred miles up.

"Make a right up here," he told the driver. "We're close."

A minute later, they pulled to the curb, and Gil got out in a Muslim section of Paris, shoving three hundred dollars' worth of euros into the cabbie's hand. "Keep it." He shut the door, and the cab pulled quickly away up the street.

Gil stood in the shadows, eyeing the three-story apartment building on the far corner. There was a light on in one of the apartments on the top floor. "I don't suppose you know which floor Umarov is on," he said to the overwatch.

"Not a clue, but the SUV on the corner is the one he arrived in. It's probably got an alarm."

Gil rooted around in a trash can on the corner until he found a glass bottle. He hurled the bottle across the street, and it shattered against the windshield of the SUV, causing the car alarm to start blaring and the headlights to flash on and off.

"I guess that's one way of doing it," the overwatch said in amusement.

Gil stepped into the shadows. The curtains in the lighted room parted, and a man stood looking down at the SUV for a moment before closing the curtains again.

"It worked." Gil slipped across the street, where he hopped a waist-high stone wall and took cover in the darkness beyond the amber light of the streetlamp.

The car alarm fell silent after a minute, and the man from the window came out the front door of the building. He stood staring at the fractured window of the SUV in the light of the lamp, his visage at once discerning and predatory. He watched hawkishly up and down in all directions from the intersection, with a hand inside his jacket.

Gil lowered himself into a crouch, keeping low as he made his way along the stone wall toward the corner. The man reset the car alarm and turned to go back into the building. As he passed the end of the wall, Gil pounced like a cougar, delivering him a deadly strike to the cerebellum and knocking him forward off his feet. Even as the man fell face-first onto the sidewalk, Gil followed through with his attack, bringing down the heel of his boot on the back of his neck fast and hard to break the spinal cord.

He immediately dragged the body into the shadows by the head, searching it for weapons and intel. Gil found a ring of three keys—one of which went to the SUV—and a Glock 39 subcompact .45 with a six-round magazine. He made sure a round was chambered and moved out around the back of the building. One of the keys fit the rear door, so he slipped inside easily. He was casual about mounting the staircase, keeping the pistol gripped in his right hand but concealed behind his thigh. The halls of the ancient building were dimly lit, and the wooden stairs creaked with every step.

He reached the top floor and stood watching the door to the apartment. A light shone beneath it, and Gil could hear at least two men speaking in Chechen. Their voices were anxious, and he assumed it had to do with the car alarm, but there was no way to be sure. He looked at the third key on the ring, guessing it would fit the knob, but he didn't know if the Chechens used some sort of secret knock before keying into the room. There was no telling how many hostile Muslims might be living in the building, and six rounds wouldn't last long in a protracted firefight. Not to mention he didn't fancy another encounter with the French police.

Deciding to keep the initiative, Gil pocketed the keys and stalked forward, kicking in the door to the room and shooting the first man he saw. The wide-eyed Chechen grabbed his throat and fell backward over a coffee table. Gil's original target, the bearded Dokka Umarov, leapt up from the couch, grabbing for a Glock 39 tucked into the waistband of his trousers, and Gil shot him through the top of the forehead. Most of the skullcap disappeared in a spray of bone and blood as Gil pivoted left to shoot the last remaining man in the room.

He froze a mere fraction of an instant before squeezing the trigger, finding himself face-to-face with agent Trent Lerher of the CIA, formerly attached to Joint Special Operations Command, or JSOC. "What the fuck are *you* doin' here?"

Lerher was tall and slender, and highly experienced in the world of espionage. "Take it easy, Gil. This isn't what it looks like."

"Answer the question!"

Gil had worked with Lerher on two separate occasions during his time with SEAL Team VI. Once in Indonesia years earlier, and once more recently in Afghanistan when Lerher had sent Gil into Iran to eliminate an Al Qaeda bomb maker and his pregnant wife. Gil had refused to kill the wife, instead bringing her back alive to Afghanistan and making a stink about Lerher's mishandling of the operation. The CIA agent's controversial order to assassinate a pregnant woman hadn't sat well with his superiors at headquarters in Langley, Virginia, and as a result, Lerher had been demoted from JSOC and returned to regular field operations.

"Who's there?" the overwatch asked in Gil's ear.

"It's Lerher!"

Lerher spotted the earpiece. "Tell Pope that I'm—"

"How the fuck do you know it's Pope?" Gil demanded. "Get those hands back up!"

Lerher lifted his hands higher. "We don't have time to do this here, Gil. Let's go, and I'll explain on the way."

"Gil!" said Bob Pope into Gil's ear.

"I'm listening."

"He's the one who fed you to the wolves. Take him out."

"You're sure?"

"Listen!" Lerher said, realizing he was losing the initiative. "This isn't what it looks like! Pope doesn't know what the fuck he's talking about!"

"Gil, kill him and get the hell out of there. You don't have much time."

"Goddamnit. You're sure?"

"I'm an American!" Lerher shouted.

"Kill 'im, Gil! The police are on the way."

Lerher grabbed for the inside of his jacket, and Gil

shot him through the face. Lerher stumbled backward, twitching and blinking, making a sickening strangling sound, and Gil shot him again in the chest. The agent went down, and Gil jumped forward to search him. All he found was the same model pistol that the Chechens were carrying, so he grabbed up the spare magazines and dashed out of the room, running down three flights of stairs to the street and getting into the black SUV. European high-low sirens were approaching from the north, so he sped off south.

"What the fuck is going on, Bob? Lerher isn't even attached to JSOC anymore!"

"He's not really attached to anything anymore," Pope deadpanned.

Gil stopped for a red light. "That's not funny."

"You said you wanted him dead. You got what you wanted."

"I want to know what the fuck he's doing in Paris with Dokka Umarov."

"I'll get to the bottom of it," Pope promised. "Right now you have to head for the Russian Embassy."

The light turned green, but Gil didn't notice. "What the fuck am I gonna do at the Russian Embassy?"

"Get yourself stitched up, for one thing. Maybe even a shot of penicillin. Those dog bites are going to fester."

"You're saying the *Russians* have agreed to take me in?"

"You just killed Russia's bin Laden," Pope said, referring to the Chechen Islamist warlord Umarov. "It's the least they can do for you. Now make a left, and try not to drive like you're fleeing the scene of a multiple homicide, will ya?"

3

PARIS,
France

Security at the Russian Embassy was expecting Gil when he arrived, and he was immediately admitted through a side entrance to the garish-looking building. Four hulking soldiers escorted him to a conference room with a one-way mirror set into the wall.

"If you have weapons, put them on the table," one of the stone-faced soldiers said in good English. On his shoulders, he wore the rank insignia of a sergeant major—or a *starshina*, as they were called in the Russian army, a rank roughly similar to that of a US Navy master chief.

Gil slowly took the Glock 39 from beneath his jacket, placing it on the table along with three extra six-round magazines and the cigarettes. "That's everything," he said, his blue eyes smiling.

The *starshina* pointed at Gil's earpiece. "That too."

"They're making me sign off, Bob."

"That's to be expected," Pope replied. "Good luck, Gil. There isn't much more I can do for you."

"Just find out what Lerher was up to." Gil took the earpiece from his ear and tossed it onto the table.

"Passport?" the *starshina* asked.

Gil was almost six feet tall, lean and wiry, and with brown hair cut high and tight. He took the passport from his jacket and handed it to the sergeant.

The Russian looked it over. "You're Canadian?"

Gil shook his head.

"CIA?"

"I guess that sorta depends on who you ask. 'CIA' don't mean what it used to."

The sergeant stood eyeing him and then pointed to a steel chair against the wall. "Sit there."

Gil did as he was told, and the solider gathered his possessions into a leather attaché case, which he took with him when he left the room. The other three guards, a junior sergeant and two *efreitors* (similar to corporals), stood at three different points around the room watching Gil with their arms folded across their broad chests.

"I don't suppose you guys have any—"

The door opened, and a doctor in his late twenties came into the room carrying a large red case of medical equipment. "Take off your clothes, please." He set the case down on the table. "There is not a lot of time."

Gil got to his feet, stripped to his skivvies, and retook his seat. He was bleeding from wounds to his left forearm, left thigh, left hip, and his right foot. There was also a two-inch gash in his scalp that he couldn't explain.

Seeing Gil's many battle scars on his legs, torso, and head, the three soldiers exchanged glances of what might have been approval.

"This is from dog?" the doctor asked, examining Gil's ripped-up forearm.

"Yes."

"And this?" the doctor asked a moment later, carefully probing the bite marks to Gil's thigh.

"Along with my foot, yeah. This here on my hip is a bullet wound. And I don't know why the fuck my head is bleeding."

The doctor looked over at the youngest soldier, one of the *efreitors*, speaking at length in Russian. When he finished, the *efreitor* gathered up all of Gil's clothes, including his boots and socks, and left the room.

"I am going to treat your wounds now," the doctor said, taking a syringe and a small bottle of lidocaine from the medical case. His fingers were deft, and he had all of Gil's wounds neatly stitched within a half hour.

The stone-faced sergeant returned with a new set of street clothes the same moment the doctor finished, and this was when Gil fully took in that he must be under observation through the one-way mirror.

Gil got dressed and wasn't a little impressed to find that the new shoes were his exact size. He smiled at the soldier. "Well done, *Starshina*. You guys are pretty good."

The Russian allowed a thin smile.

The doctor left the room, and a photographer came in immediately after with a digital camera.

"Sit," the sergeant said. "Don't smile."

Gil sat back down, and the photographer took his photo, disappearing again almost as fast as he had appeared.

"So what now?" Gil asked.

The sergeant motioned the other two soldiers to leave and followed them out. Gil was alone in the room for forty-five minutes before the door opened again, and a healthy-looking man in his early seventies came in. He offered Gil his hand, and Gil stood up from his chair to take it.

"My name is Vladimir Federov," the old man said.

"Good to meet you, sir. I'm—"

"I know who you are. Come sit at the table. We'll have a talk."

They sat across from each other, and Gil waited to hear what the man had to say.

Federov laced his fingers in front of him. "I was captured in Berlin in 1973 by the CIA," he began. "I was a young KGB agent then, and, luckily for me, a CIA agent had been captured in East Berlin the day before. After twenty-four hours, it was agreed we would be exchanged at Checkpoint Charlie." Checkpoint C had been the most famous crossing point in the Berlin Wall during the Cold War, and many spies were exchanged there during that period. After the final collapse of the Soviet Union and the reunification of Germany in the 1990s, the location became a tourist attraction.

"I hope you were well treated," Gil said, meaning it.

"Oh, I was very well treated," Federov replied. "I was captured by a young agent named Robert Pope. I understand you know him quite well."

Gil smiled. "Pretty well, yeah, but I didn't know he'd ever captured himself a genuine KGB agent."

Federov grinned. "The son of a bitch used a woman to dupe me."

Gil was hard pressed to conceal his amusement. "Well, knowing Pope's taste in women, I doubt you stood much of a chance."

"I was young and foolish," Federov admitted. "But Robert treated me well, and he saw to it that I was exchanged quickly, something I have always been grateful for.

In those days, the families of captured KGB agents were treated with suspicion by the Soviet government, and their lives were often made difficult. Robert understood that, and my quick return spared my parents those humiliations."

"I understand." Gil knew the pleasantries were out of the way and that it was time to get down to business.

"Dokka Umarov is dead?" Federov asked.

"Very," Gil answered.

"He has been mistaken for dead many times," Federov said. "I need to know every detail of your mission leading up to this moment. This is a condition which has already been agreed to by your superior."

Gil knew it didn't much matter whether Pope had agreed to the condition or not—though he believed he probably had—so he told Federov every detail of the mission, from the moment he had set up on top of the railcar to his arrival at the embassy gate.

Federov appeared slightly surprised that Gil had killed Agent Lerher. "Did Lerher truly reach for his weapon? Or is that the story you plan to tell your people? Don't worry, your secret will be safe with us."

"He really did go for his weapon," Gil replied, "but I would have shot him regardless."

Federov glanced at the one-way mirror before returning his attention to Gil. "And you have no idea who shot the French gendarmes?"

"If I had to guess," Gil said, "I'd say it was the same sniper covering the Umarov meeting, but that's speculation. Pope lost sight of him after he displaced."

"Who was Umarov meeting with?"

"Our intelligence had him meeting with members of Al Qaeda to discuss infiltrating Al Qaeda fighters into Georgia to help him with his war against Russia."

"Where in Georgia? South Ossetia?" South Ossetia, the northern part of the Republic of Georgia, had attempted to claim independence in 1990. Georgia had refused to recognize its autonomy, however, and civil war erupted soon after. Battles were fought in 1991, 1992, and then again in 2004. Still more fighting broke out in 2008, and Russia finally invaded northern Georgia in support of South Ossetia. The region had been completely reliant upon Russian military and economic support ever since.

Gil shook his head. "South of Tbilisi, the Georgian capital. Intel indicates Umarov wanted to coordinate a series of attacks along the Baku-Tbilisi-Ceyhan pipeline."

The BTC pipeline was 1,100 miles long, running northwest from Baku, Azerbaijan, on the Caspian Sea, to Tbilisi, and then southwest to Ceyhan, Turkey, on the coast of the Mediterranean Sea. It afforded Western powers access to oil fields in the Caspian Sea without having to deal with Russian or Iranian interference, and though operated by British Petroleum, the pipeline was owned by a consortium of eleven different oil companies around the world, including Chevron and ConocoPhillips.

"Tell me," Federov said, "did you not find it strange for Umarov to take a meeting so far from the Caucasus?" The North Caucasus was Dokka Umarov's home territory, a mountainous region of European Russia located between the Caspian and the Black Sea.

"Well, he was observed boarding a Grecian tanker in Athens, and then again transshipping to a private yacht off the coast of Sicily thirty-six hours later. He landed at Marseille the next day, and from there made his way north to Paris."

Federov rested his chin on his fist. "The CIA tracked him?"

"One of their people in Athens made the initial identification, yes. It was just dumb luck, really. Once he boarded the tanker, it was easy to keep tabs."

"I see." Federov sat back in his chair with a sigh. "Agent Shannon, you did not—"

"Master chief," Gil said good-naturedly. "I'm retired navy, not CIA."

Federal smiled dryly. "Mr. Shannon, you did not kill Dokka Umarov tonight. You killed a GRU operative named Andrei Yeshevsky." The GRU was the Chief Intelligence Directorate, Russia's version of the CIA.

Gil dominated the nausea that immediately rose up in his gut. "How is that possible?"

"The GRU sent Yeshevsky into North Ossetia six weeks ago as an imposter to undermine the real Dokka Umarov's credibility in the Caucasus. He made speeches in small towns where his face was not well known, renouncing Chechen terrorist attacks on Russian military targets and urging Chechen Muslims to accept Russian authority." Federov smiled blandly. "Now, of course the GRU did not expect this to stop the attacks. What was hoped was that the real Dokka Umarov would be forced to show himself and create an opportunity for our Spetsnaz to finally eliminate him." Spetsnaz were Russian Special Forces, basically Russia's version of the US Navy SEALs.

Gil was not amused. "So what the hell is this Yeshevsky doing here in France?"

Federov sat back scratching his chin. "To be honest, we have no idea. We thought he was dead. He disappeared two weeks after he was sent into North Ossetia along with his entire Spetsnaz team. It wasn't until Robert called me this evening for help with *your* predicament that we had any idea Yeshevsky might still be alive."

"That means it's possible I killed the real Umarov."

Federov shook his head. "Yeshevsky has a tattoo of a woman on his chest. One of our informants with the French police has verified the body to have such a tattoo. What's more, we believe the sniper who was shooting the French gendarmes to be a Spetsnaz operative named Sasha Kovalenko. Kovalenko was attached to Yeshevsky's security team, and he has always been somewhat—shall we say—unstable?"

"An entire Spetsnaz team went off the reservation?"

There was a knock at the door, and the sergeant stepped into the room, speaking briefly to Federov in Russian and stepping back out again.

Federov turned back to Gil. "It's been verified the other two men you killed at the apartment were also members of Yeshevsky's Spetsnaz team."

Gil sucked his teeth. "I don't suppose one of them was this Kovolenka fella."

"Kov*a*lenk*o*," Federov said, correcting Gil's pronunciation. "No, his body was not found—and that is very unfortunate."

Gil rubbed his face, feeling the fatigue catching up to him. "I'm going to need to fill Pope in on this. There's a good chance he'll be able to piece some of it together."

"Was it him who tracked Yeshevsky from Athens?"

"No." Gil shook his head. "The Mediterranean chief of station did that. The intel wasn't passed on to Pope until after Umarov's—*Yeshevsky's*—arrival here in Paris. He's in charge of a top-secret antiterrorism unit now, and there wasn't time to vet the intel properly before moving on it. Things are bit disorganized within the CIA at the moment. There's been a huge shake-up since the September nuke attacks six months ago."

Federov nodded, obviously aware of the CIA's internal problems. "That is always the trouble when there are too few competent men to go around."

Another knock. The sergeant stepped in, handed Federov a dark red passport, and left, failing to close the door behind him.

Federov examined the passport briefly before sliding it across the table to Gil. "This document is one hundred percent authentic. You are no longer Gil Shannon of the United States of America. You are Vassili Vatilievich Siyanovich of the Russian Federation."

"You're shitting me." Gil opened the slightly weathered-looking passport to see the photo they had taken of him less than two hours before. He noted that the passport had been issued the previous year and that many of the back pages had apparently been stamped in a number of different European countries.

"You'll need that to get out of France."

Gil looked up from the passport. "But I don't speak Russian."

Federov chuckled. "Neither do the French. So don't worry. We'll teach you a few words to mumble at the customs agent." He offered his hand across the table. "Good luck to you, Vassili. You're going to need it."

Gil took his hand. "What the hell does that mean?"

"It means you're coming with me," said a gruff-looking Russian who'd appeared in the doorway. He spoke in a gravelly voice and wore the blue-and-white-striped shirt of the Spetsnaz. His head was shaved, and he had pale, merciless blue eyes with a thick five o'clock shadow. Standing an inch or so taller than Gil, he appeared to be in his mid to late thirties and looked like he'd been carved from black oak. His face cracked into a grin as he stepped into the room.

Gil noted the lower part of the Spetsnaz wolf tattoo protruding beneath the sleeve, glanced briefly at Federov and then back to the Russian. "You're the man behind the mirror?"

"This is Major Ivan Dragunov of the Tenth Independent Spetsnaz Brigade," Federov said. "His grandfather was Yevgeny Dragunov—the inventor of the Dragunov rifle, which I understand you're well acquainted with."

Gil looked at Dragunov. "If you're with the Tenth, that means you're assigned to the Southern Military District—the Caucasus?"

Dragunov was noticeably impressed by Gil's immediate knowledge of the Tenth ISB. "I've also served with the Black Sea Fleet."

"Where exactly do you think *we're* going?"

Dragunov shrugged. "Where else but to kill Kovalenko and the rest of the Chechen traitors you fought with tonight?"

Gil looked to Federov for an explanation.

Federov put his hands into his pockets. "Yeshevsky and his Spetsnaz team were all ethnic Chechens from the Vostok Battalion. They were born in South Ossetia. For whatever reason, they've gone rogue."

"How many are left?"

"Ten—counting Sasha Kovalenko."

Gil crossed his arms. "And I suppose it's purely a coincidence that a Spetsnaz major from the Tenth ISB happens to be here in Paris on the same night Mr. Yeshevsky gets himself killed during a meeting with a crooked CIA agent."

Federov deferred to Dragunov.

Dragunov stretched and let out a long yawn. "No coincidence," he said, his eyes watering with fatigue. "We thought Kovalenko murdered Yeshevsky in Ossetia, and I've been tracking him for a month. All Spetsnaz traitors have to be hunted down and killed. That's our creed."

"Well, then you don't need me," Gil said. "My job here is done."

Dragunov took Gil's Canadian passport from his own back pocket and tossed it onto the table. "Good luck at the airport. Hopefully there are no CIA traitors waiting there to point you out to the gendarmes. Life in a French prison would be a sad way to end such a career as yours."

Gil looked at the two passports on the table, chewing the inside of his cheek.

Federov cleared his throat. "If you're going with Major Dragunov, Master Chief, now would be a good time to leave. It's a diplomatic flight, so the French shouldn't be overly vigilant, but the moment they discover Yeshevsky and the others to be Russian citizens, that will change."

Gil eyed them both, glancing briefly over his shoulder at the mirror. "You fuckers," he muttered, smirking as he grabbed the red passport from the table and tucked it into his jacket. "Okay, Ivan. But when this is over, I get one of those ugly fucking T-shirts."

Dragunov laughed. "When this is over, comrade, we'll both probably be dead. Kovalenko is the best. We call him the *Wolf*."

Gil cocked an eyebrow. "I got news for you: the Wolf hesitates. Otherwise I'd be dead already."

"That was not hesitation," the Russian replied. "He probably just wanted you to see it coming."

4

BERN,
Switzerland

"It was Hagen?" Gil said in disbelief, talking to Pope on a satellite phone from the tarmac in Bern, Switzerland, where he had just deplaned from an Aeroflot DC-10. "Chief of Staff Hagen?"

"*Ex*–chief of staff," Pope reminded him.

"I knew Lerher had a hard-on for me, but what the fuck did I ever do to Hagen? He burned *me* after Earnest Endeavor. Remember?" Operation Earnest Endeavor was the rescue of a female POW in Afghanistan, which Gil had orchestrated against the president's specific orders to the contrary. As a means of "punishment" for acting without authorization, then–White House Chief of Staff Hagen suggested that the president award both Gil and his fellow operative, Green Beret Daniel Crosswhite, the Medal of Honor. The public award ceremony—while an effective political gambit for the president—had revealed

Gil's identity to the entire world. Not only did this end his career as a SEAL Team VI operator, but soon it led a band of Muslim assassins directly to his Montana doorstep, very nearly costing both him and his wife their lives.

"Hagen's a sociopath," Pope said. "An egomaniacal power junkie, and he blames you and me for his dismissal from the White House."

"But how'd he get hooked up with Lerher? Lerher wasn't stupid enough to throw in with a jerk-off like Hagen."

"I don't think they were directly linked," Pope said. "I tracked Hagen down by phone a little while ago, and when I dropped Lerher's name, it genuinely confused him."

"You talked to Hagen?"

"Yeah. I told him you're coming after him. Hopefully that'll keep him out of our hair long enough for us to get things figured out."

"How did you know it was Hagen who ghosted the op?"

"I didn't, but he seemed a logical suspect. Have the Russians told you anything more about what Yeshevsky was doing in Paris?"

Gil glanced over at Dragunov, who stood near the nose gear of the DC-10, also talking on a satellite phone. Five rough-looking Russians in street clothes stood off in a tight group, smoking and talking. "If they know, they're not telling me, but they definitely want to find this Kovalenko and punch his ticket."

"What's their next move?"

"I'm waiting to find that out now. Dragunov's on the phone with the GRU. His team is standing by here."

"Spetsnaz?"

"Yeah, and one look at these guys," Gil said, "tells you they're heavy pipe hitters. Dragunov says they've seen a lot of combat against the Chechens." "Pipe hitter" was a Special Forces term referring to an operator willing to do whatever it took to accomplish a mission.

"I've done some research on Dragunov," Pope added. "It looks like he killed one of his own men a few years ago for lagging behind on a mission in Chechnya. And he's not your run-of-the-mill Spetsnaz operator; he's a member of Spetsgruppa A—the Alpha Group. He doesn't mess about, this one." Spetsgruppa A, an elite subunit of the Spetsnaz, often operated quite separately from the rest of Russian Special Forces, answering directly to the Kremlin.

"Well, I don't intend to hang around long enough to get to know him. He's got his team here, so he's not going to need me."

"Hanging around might be the best way to find out what the hell Lerher was up to, Gil. I checked, and the agency has him listed as being on vacation all this month."

"That's doesn't mean shit. They take their people off the books all the time."

"But that's not what this is," Pope insisted. "The personnel office genuinely believes Lerher's on vacation, which means he was either acting independently, or he was part of an unsanctioned operation. If there's a shadow cell operating inside the CIA, we have to expose it."

Gil glanced again at the Spetsnaz men. "These guys are all wired for sound, Bob—chain-smoking and hyper-vigilant. I don't like it."

"Is Dragunov chain-smoking?"

"No. He seems to have his shit mostly together."

"Well, maybe that's why he wants you along. Maybe he needs another level head."

Gil chuckled. "Don't piss down my back and tell me it's rainin', old man."

Pope laughed. "I wouldn't do that, but we need to figure out what Lerher was doing in that apartment with the Chechens."

"I don't like operating in the blind, Bob. I'm not an espionage guy. I need a well-defined target."

"Suppose I can give you one."

"What, a target?"

"The yacht that Yeshevsky took to Marseille is slowly making its way back to Athens. It's called the *Palinouros*, currently anchored at Malta. It belongs to a Turkish banker with loose financial ties to Chechen terrorists, but the owner's not aboard. He's at his home in Istanbul."

"So who's aboard?" Gil asked.

"Good question. Maybe your Spetsnaz friends would be interested in helping us find that out. The GRU has resources in Rome they can bring to bear on a seaborne operation of this nature. And Dragunov has operated with the Black Sea Fleet."

"Yeah," Gil said dryly. "He mentioned that."

"If you're not interested, Gil, you can ditch the Russians and head for our embassy. I'll make sure you're brought home ASAP. It's your call."

Gil glanced over at the Spetsnaz men. One of them caught his gaze and grinned mischievously.

"You there?" Pope asked.

"I'm thinking, damn it."

The grinning Russian came over, shaking an unfiltered Russian cigarette from a crinkled pack and offering it to Gil. "Brody," he said pointing at himself.

"I'm Gil."

"*Vassili*," Brody said with a chuckle. He had pale blue eyes and a narrow face, the youngest of Dragunov's men at twenty-five. Gil accepted the smoke, and Brody lit it for

him from the end of his own cigarette. Gil took a deep
drag, and the unrefined tobacco hit his central nervous
system like a truck. Brody saw his eyes start to drift and
laughed, clapping him on the arm, saying something over
his shoulder that made the other four men laugh with him.

"Are you there, Gil?"

"Yeah, I'm here," he said, letting the dizziness pass.
"Go ahead and upload the intel on the *Palinouros* to my
phone. I'll have a talk with Dragunov and see what he can
put together. If his people are game, we'll take the yacht
and gather whatever intel there is. But after that, I'm done.
I'm not chasing all over Eastern Europe so these yahoos
can get me killed."

5

MARIGNANE,
France

Though Sasha Kovalenko was an ethnic Chechen, he too was a member of the Spetsnaz Spetsgruppa A, and he was no stranger to violent combat. His years as a sniper in the Chechen wars had left him with a frazzled nervous system and a supernatural ability to sense danger over long distance. It was this sixth sense that had allowed him to pull the trigger on Gil in the rail yard a split second before being shot himself.

When the French gendarmes had first appeared in the rail yard, he'd concluded that Agent Lerher must have betrayed their cause. This sent him into a rage, causing him to shoot down as many of the encroaching French as he dared before leaving for the agreed-upon rally point where he was to rendezvous with Yeshevsky. But owing to trouble avoiding the police en route to the apartment, he had not arrived until a full minute after Gil had cleared the scene.

The sight of his friend Yeshevsky's body on the floor had enraged him further, but seeing Lerher's body had given him pause to reconsider his assessment of a CIA double cross. There were too many possible scenarios to bother speculating, but one thing was for sure: he and his team needed to tie up loose ends and find a place to lie low until they could figure out what was going on.

"I'm taking three men with me to Malta," Kovalenko said, coming out of the bathroom and tossing his cellular onto the hotel bed. "Use the French credit cards to buy the plane tickets. The ones we were given by the CIA may be compromised."

"Why Malta?" asked his second-in-command, Eli Vitsin. "It's an island. You could be trapped there."

Kovalenko took him by the shoulder. He was a tall, muscular man with greenish eyes and black hair. Vitsin was a head shorter, dark complexioned with a thick mustache. "We can't risk being backtracked. Someone told the French we were in that warehouse. There's no way to guess how soon they were on to us, but if Yeshevsky was spotted in Athens or seen coming ashore in Marseille, the *Palinouros* could be their next target. We can't allow the crew to be questioned—especially Miller, the CIA captain."

"Moscow has sent Dragunov to track us down," Vitsin warned. "He's been seen at the embassy in Paris, and where he goes, his men are sure to follow. We need to get back home to our mountains, where it's safe."

"Don't worry about Dragunov," Kovalenko said, stepping into the kitchenette. "I can handle him. The trouble is the CIA. Whoever killed Yeshevsky also killed Lerher, and that could mean that Lerher's people have been found out. If that's happened, we're entirely on our own, so we have to wait to see if they make contact before we can head home. In the meantime, I'm going to Malta."

Kovalenko took a loaf of bread and some lunch meat from the refrigerator and stood in the kitchenette eating a sandwich while Vitsin sat at the computer scheduling the Malta flight for Kovalenko and three other Spetsnaz operators.

"You're sure about this, Sasha?" Vitsin closed the laptop and pushed it aside. "Moscow may have submitted our photos to Interpol. You could be taken into custody at the airport."

Kovalenko shook his head. "Moscow wants us for themselves. They can't risk us telling what we know to anyone else. That's why they've sent Dragunov: to make sure we don't talk to anyone—ever." He took a bottle of vodka from the freezer and unscrewed the lid, taking a drink and passing the bottle to Vitsin. "After we've taken care of the crew of the *Palinouros*, we'll lay a trap for Dragunov somewhere; lure him in for the kill."

"Bad idea." Vitsin took a pull from the bottle and set it down on the table, shaking his head. "He'll absolutely expect a trap."

"Of course he will," Kovalenko said, capping the bottle and putting it back in the freezer. "That's why it's going to work. He's arrogant enough to think he can outsmart me."

They stood in silence for a while, each lost in his own thoughts, until Vitsin said at last, "Who was the sniper on the railcar? He *wasn't* French."

Kovalenko looked at him, nodding pensively. "I was just thinking the same thing."

6

MALTA

The nation of Malta is an archipelago located roughly fifty miles south of Sicily in the eastern basin of the Mediterranean Sea and is home to almost a half million people. Only the three largest islands are inhabited, the largest being the island of Malta, around which there are no less than nine sizeable bays providing safe harbor from the open seas, making Malta a highly popular maritime destination for both tourism and commercial shipping.

Anchored in the darkness, not far from St. Paul's Island near the mouth of Xemxija Bay on the north coast of Malta, the *Palinouros* was a 223-foot Kismet yacht manufactured by the German company Lürssen in 2007. She featured six staterooms, both a formal and an informal dining salon, a Jacuzzi deck, a disco, a galley to rival the kitchens of most restaurants, separate crew quarters, a laundry service, various lounges, and a state-of-the-art navigational system. Fully crewed, she carried twenty-two hands, and her twin 1,957-horsepower Caterpillar diesel engines gave her a cruising range of 5,000 miles, boasting a top speed of 15 knots. Brand-new, she had cost her Turkish owner well over $100 million.

Gil stood beside Dragunov on the rocky shore of the uninhabited island of St. Paul, studying the starboard beam of the vessel through a pair of Russian binoculars. The night was calm, and the *Palinouros* rested easily at anchor, having fallen off slightly to the north with the current. "The lights are on," he muttered, "but nobody seems to be home."

Dragunov grunted as he studied the vessel through his own binoculars. "Aye, they're bedded down for the night."

Gil scanned the decks. "There doesn't seem to be anyone on the bridge, either. That's odd. Our intel says she has a Greek crew. Greeks know better than to leave the bridge unattended at night."

Dragunov lowered the binoculars. "She's at anchor." He clapped Gil on the shoulder, a bit more roughly than Gil considered customary. "Whoever's on the bridge is probably lying down." Pope had emailed them the schematics of the yacht, so they knew her precise layout, and the bridge was fitted with a pair of built-in sofas.

"I reckon we'll board at the stern. Eh, Ivan?"

"Aye, Vassili, we'll board at the stern."

As Dragunov walked off in his wet suit to ready his men, Gil grinned after him, thinking the word *aye* made him sound like some kind of incongruous pirate.

The *Palinouros* was anchored a cable's length from the shore, or approximately two hundred yards. While this distance would be no trouble for Gil—a leisurely swim—he wasn't so sure about the Spetsnaz operators, who almost never stopped smoking. Even now they stood in the darkness with their glowing cherries dangerously visible for hundreds of yards over the open water.

The Russians dropped their smokes as Dragunov approached, stepping on them and double-checking their brand-new suppressed Arsenal Firearms Strike One pistols. The Strike One was a Russian-made semiautomatic. It operated on the same Browning recoil system as the M1911 and could be chambered in three different cartridges: 9 mm, .40 Smith & Wesson, and .357 Sig Sauer. The weapons the GRU had supplied them in Rome were chambered in .40 caliber. Gil had never fired the Strike One before—called the *Strizh* in Russian—but he liked that it had a much lower profile than most other pistols.

They moved into the water as a unit and were about knee-deep when Brody let out with a gut-wrenching groan, grabbing his groin.

Gil saw the spout of water kicked up by the rifle bullet after it passed through Brody's genitals. "Sniper!" He grabbed Brody and dove forward with him into the water.

"It's Kovalenko!" one of the Russians called out. A bullet tore through his throat, and he went down thrashing in the shallows.

Everyone else was already stroking for the *Palinouros*. Gil rolled to his back, keeping Brody's head out of the water as he kicked hard for the yacht. There was no place else to go. St. Paul's Island was entirely flat, with no cover except for a statue of the island's namesake on the far side. Brody moaned in Gil's arms, unable to swim because his hands were locked onto his mangled privates.

Dragunov and the other three men swam as fast as they could, porpoising like dolphins to make themselves as difficult to hit as possible. Gil was unable to drop below the surface because of Brody, so he concentrated on making as little wake as possible as he kicked his feet, stroking with one arm. He couldn't hear the incoming rounds, but from the angle they were striking the water, he could tell that they were coming from the Maltese shoreline to the south.

"The only easy day was yesterday," he muttered, certain he would never make it out of the water alive.

Another of Dragunov's men cried out and began to flounder, shot through both lungs. Within a few seconds, he sank beneath the water and did not resurface as Gil stroked steadily past the point where he'd gone down.

Gil watched the stars to keep his heading, estimating that they had probably covered half the distance to the *Palinouros*, and glad that shark attacks in the Mediterranean were basically unheard of. The way Brody was gushing blood would have been bad news in most other seas.

Another Spetsnaz man cried out, hit in the leg, but he kept swimming as best he could. Unable to continue porpoising, he was quickly zeroed for a second shot and hit through the torso. He made no sound at all this time, but sank at once and did not return to the surface.

With fifty yards to go, the firing stopped inexplicably, and they made it to the stern of the *Palinouros* without taking any more casualties. There were four of them left alive, but by the time Gil and Dragunov managed to haul Brody from the water and onto the low-riding stern of the yacht, Gil could see the young man was nearly bled out.

Dragunov's only other remaining team member, a Russian Mongol named Terbish, provided cover with his pistol as Gil and Dragunov tended to the quickly dying Brody.

Dragunov hissed, "He could have gotten you killed. You should have left him."

"That's not how SEALs operate," Gil said, unzipping Brody's wet suit for a look at the wound and finding that the young man's penis and most of the scrotum were completely shot away. Aggravated that the man was going to die, he looked at Dragunov, the two of them able to see each other clearly in the yacht's stern lights. "And we don't shoot our own men for falling behind on a mission, either."

Dragunov smirked. "Then you don't have what it takes to be Spetsnaz."

"You got that right." Gil zipped Brody's wet suit closed. There was nothing to be done for him. He was dead a few moments later, and the three of them formed up to move forward with Dragunov at the head of the column.

The sight of a dead middy sprawled out in the lower passageway stopped them in their tracks. She had once been a pretty young woman with long blond hair, but she'd been shot in the head, and one of her eyes was now badly distended in an eight-ball hemorrhage, indicating that she had not died instantly.

"We're too late," Dragunov whispered. He mumbled something to Terbish in Russian and then looked back at Gil, who covered the rear. "Kovalenko and his men have already been aboard."

Gil had begun to suspect as much by the time they reached the vessel without taking any fire from the crew. He nodded, gripping his pistol. As they began to move forward again, a furious firefight erupted near the Maltese shore some five hundred yards away. The shooting reached a murderous crescendo and then died off after ten seconds of constant firing.

Gil locked eyes with Dragunov. "We'd better hurry the fuck up if we're gonna do this!"

7

MALTA

Prone on the deck of a small charter boat, the frustrated Kovalenko couldn't see the swimmers well enough by the riding lights of the *Palinouros* to make them out in their black wet suits, so he was firing at the white froth of their wake. The rifle was a quality weapon, an Accuracy International AWS (Arctic Warfare Suppressed) in .308 Winchester bought on the Italian black market—very probably having been stolen from the Ninth Parachute Assault Regiment—but the Zeiss scope did not have night vision capabilities.

Kovalenko and his men had chartered the fishing boat earlier that day, killing the Maltese owner and stuffing the small man's body into the fish cooler at the stern. After boarding the *Palinouros* and murdering her entire crew shortly after midnight, it was their intention to take the charter boat to Pachino on the southern tip of Sicily and then later catch the ferry from Messina to the Italian mainland. Problems with the charter's carburetor, however, delayed their departure, forcing them back to shore.

With the carburetor fixed an hour later, they were in the process of casting off when one of Kovalenko's men spotted the tight group of glowing cigarettes over on St. Paul's Island two hundred yards away. He knew the island was supposed to be deserted, so the sight looked odd to him. He pointed it out to Kovalenko, who immediately took the AWS from its case and had a look through the scope.

"Spetsnaz!" he'd hissed, dropping to the deck and setting up the rifle's bipod. By the time he was ready to fire a few seconds later, Dragunov's men had stepped on their cigarettes and waded into the water. His first shot to Brody's groin had not been accidental, wanting to inflict as much psychological damage to the enemy Spetsnaz team as possible. His second shot was to the throat of the man who had chosen to shout a warning rather than stay alive.

By the time the swimmers drew within fifty yards of the *Palinouros*, he believed he had killed two more but couldn't be sure. It was possible they were swimming beneath the surface.

"Start the motor!" he ordered, getting to his feet. "We'll finish them as they try to board the yacht."

At this moment, they saw a Maltese P21, a seventy-foot inshore patrol boat, coming toward them from the southern rim of the bay. Its spotlight snapped on, and the charter craft was bathed in light. Kovalenko left the rifle on the deck, where it couldn't be seen immediately.

"Ready yourselves," he said to the other three. "If they attempt to board us, we kill them all."

As the P21 approached off the starboard beam, Kovalenko and his men spaced themselves apart.

"Boris, switch on the riding lights. That's why they're approaching—because we're dark. And put smiles on your faces!"

Boris went into the wheelhouse to switch on the riding lights, and Kovalenko waved at the crew of the P21, smiling and shielding his eyes from the spotlight with the opposite hand. He could see that the Browning .50 caliber machine gun on the foredeck was manned and trained directly on their vessel as they came alongside. "Boris, stay in the cabin until I call. Then kill the gunner on the foredeck."

"Right!" Boris called from inside the wheelhouse.

The P21 had an eight-man crew. There were three men on the foredeck besides the .50 gunner, one on the quarterdeck behind the wheelhouse, two manning the portside rail, and one at the con. Five of them were armed with Heckler & Koch MP5 submachine guns, but only the man on the .50 caliber appeared ready to fire.

The P21 shifted into reverse, backwatering until the vessel came to a stop alongside. The only unarmed man on the foredeck, the officer, threw a line to Kovalenko, signaling that they intended to board.

Kovalenko waved, making like he was going to tie the line to one of the bow cleats. "Now, Boris."

Boris sprang from the wheelhouse with an AK-47, firing a perfect six-round burst that struck the .50 gunner in the chest, knocking him backward and clean over the starboard rail into the water. He continued to fire until the magazine ran dry, killing the officer and both MP5 gunners on the foredeck before ducking back inside to reload.

The remaining three MP5 gunners opened up on the wheelhouse with blazing fire, killing Boris instantly but leaving Kovalenko's other two men free to pull Glock pistols from behind their backs, picking off the gunners in quick succession along the portside rail.

Even as the MP5 gunners were dropping, Kovalenko was pulling the line to haul the P21 in close, jumping aboard and scrambling into the wheelhouse where the first mate was grabbing for the radio. He shot him in the back of the head with a 9 mm, and the bullet exited through the first mate's face, hitting the radio and causing sparks to fly.

"Get aboard!" he shouted. "We have to run for Sicily."

One of the two remaining Spetsnaz grabbed up the AWS sniper rifle, and the other took a moment to put a bullet into Boris's head, making absolutely sure he could never be interrogated. Both of them leapt aboard the P21, and Kovalenko applied the throttle, motoring steadily away from the shattered fishing charter.

"Take their jackets and toss the bodies overboard," he ordered. "Then man the machine gun. We have to look like Maltese navy." The radio was destroyed, but that didn't matter. Kovalenko's English wasn't good enough to convince anyone that he was from Malta, where all they spoke was English and Maltese. Their best hope was to make it to Sicily before anyone in the Maltese military could piece together what had happened and give pursuit.

He increased speed toward the *Palinouros* as one of his men came into the wheelhouse to hand him the AWS. "Take the con," Kovalenko told him. "I'm going to kill as many aboard that pig yacht as I can on the way past."

8

MALTA

Gil continued to cover the rear as Dragunov led the hurried search of the *Palinouros*, finding no one alive. In one of the smaller state rooms, they came across a couple shot to death in the midst of lovemaking, a single 9 mm hole in each of their heads. Judging from the white uniforms on the floor beside the bed, Gil guessed there was no one aboard other than crew.

Making their way below decks to the crew quarters, they found a veritable slaughterhouse, eleven of the crew knifed in their sleep and two more bodies littering the passageway, one with a vicious wound under the jaw where a blade had been rammed upward into the brain stem. They found another pair of bodies sprawled in the engine room, blood pooled on the otherwise spotless white deck beneath their heads.

"They went through these people like shit through a goose," Gil muttered.

They accounted for nineteen dead crew members by the time they arrived at the bridge, where they found two more bodies. The first mate's throat was cut, and the captain, a man of about fifty, lay faceup on the deck with a single bullet through the forehead. Gil recognized him at once.

"This asshole's ex-CIA." He holstered the pistol and took a knee beside the body.

Dragunov stood over him. "How do you know?"

Gil rolled the dead man onto his belly to search his back pockets. "I worked a mission with him when he was attached to SOG." There was no need to tell Dragunov what SOG was. Spetsnaz operators knew more about the Special Operations Group of the CIA than 98 percent of Americans. Nor did Gil see any need to mention that the dead man was also a former navy destroyer captain who'd been kicked out of the CIA three years earlier for malfeasance. He found an unusually long key in the bottom of the captain's back pocket and tucked it into a zipper pouch on his wet suit.

"Hate to tell you this, partner, but I'm pretty sure shit's about to get complicated. Covert elements of the CIA are working with covert elements of the GRU."

Dragunov leveled his gaze. "The GRU is clean."

"So's my ass, Ivan." Gil got to his feet and put his foot on the body. "This sorry motherfucker here was thrown out of the CIA for raping a fourteen-year-old girl in Thailand three years ago. He only escaped prison because the girl disappeared before she could testify. And now he's here— *on this boat*—working for a Russian Spetsnaz team that turned back around and shot him in the head. Somebody's tying up loose ends, and they're not gonna—"

One of the windows shattered, and Terbish's head blew apart, splattering gore all over Gil and Dragunov, who both hit the deck.

"You were saying about the GRU being clean?" Gil said, wiping the gore from his eyes.

Dragunov's blood-spattered face split into a malicious grin. "Are you going to help me kill these *sukiny dyeti*—or run home like a little girl?"

Gil drew the Strike One, unscrewing the suppressor. "Oh, we're definitely gonna kill 'em." He got into a combat crouch, moving to the hatchway leading from the bridge to the gangway. He could see that the P21 was already out of pistol range, heading north at her top speed of twenty-six knots, almost double that of the *Palinouros*.

"Well, that's why God made radar." He stood up and went to the satellite phone on the console. "Get ready to weigh anchor, Ivan."

Dragunov went to the window, easily making out the wake of the P21, but the patrol boat itself was scarcely more than a silhouette. "Can you pilot this thing?"

"Sorta," Gil said, punching numbers into the phone. "We'll need a little help."

A few seconds later, Pope was on the line. "Bob, we've taken the *Palinouros*. The entire crew's dead. The skipper was Paul Miller, an ex-CIA man with the Thailand office. I need you to patch me through to a yacht in Auckland called *Frieda's Joy*. I'll explain what's going on while you work your magic."

"Stand by," Pope said. "I'll put Midori to work while you bring me up to speed."

Within eight minutes, Gil had Pope completely updated, and the satellite phone was ringing aboard *Frieda's Joy* in Auckland, New Zealand.

"This is the *Frieda's Joy*," answered a female voice with an Australian accent. "First Mate Dana Keener speaking."

"Keener, my name is Master Chief Gil Shannon. I

need to speak with Wild Bill ASAP." "Wild Bill" Watkins was a retired Navy SEAL from the West Coast teams who now captained a yacht similar to the *Palinouros* for an Australian millionaire.

"I'm sorry, Master Chief, but Captain Watkins is ashore at this time. May I be of assistance?"

"I sure hope so. Listen, Keener, I'm stuck in the Med aboard an anchored Lürssen Kismet with her engines at dead stop. I'm only semi familiar with the controls, and I need to get her under way fast. All I got for crew is a grumpy Russian, so if you could keep your instructions simple-stupid, I'd appreciate it."

First Mate Keener chuckled. "I'll try and keep it fairly dinkum for you," she said, her lilting voice sounding suddenly sexy. "Where in the Med are you, Master Chief?"

"North coast of Malta."

"So you've got slightly rocky bottom."

"Yeah, I believe so."

"And I assume she's fallen off with the current?"

"Yes, ma'am. To the north."

"Then you'll need to ease off the cables before you weigh anchor. Are you at the con?"

"Roger that," Gil said. "And the computers are all up. I just need to start the engines and get this tub turned around."

With Keener's help, it took Gil and Dragunov fifteen minutes to get the *Palinouros* under way and headed north in pursuit of the P21 at her normal cruising speed of twelve knots. Anything faster might have looked suspicious on Maltese military radar. Keener helped them figure out which blip on their own radar was the P21, and judging from the heading, Kovalenko and his men were heading directly for Sicily. Keener remained on the line in case they needed further assistance conning the vessel.

9

MEXICO CITY,
Mexico

Tim Hagen, sitting in the lounge of a third-rate hotel, gaped across a roughly hewn table at Ken Peterson, whose jolly demeanor was starting to annoy the shit out of him.

"So who the *fuck* sent this Lerher guy in there?" Hagen wanted to know. "I mean, whose bright *fucking* idea was it to send someone that Shannon knew, for fuck's sake, you fucking imp?"

Peterson looked at him, wishing he could leave Hagen to the wolves, but the pen was a long arm from the grave, and there was no telling what Hagen had left with his attorneys. "They were never supposed to come into contact," he said. "The French authorities were supposed to grab him without the meeting ever being affected. It's like I told you, there are too many variables to contend with in operations of this sort."

"You're not answering my fucking question!" Hagen flared, his face red. "Why Lerher?"

Peterson's patience suddenly evaporated. "This was a shadow op, you overeducated moron, and there aren't a lot of men qualified for that kind of job! Lerher had worked with Shannon in the past, so he was the logical choice! Now stop casting aspersions—you don't even know what the hell happened yet!"

"I know that Shannon is coming after my ass!" The fear was visible in Hagen's eyes. "And when that crazy bastard gets going, he doesn't stop until there's nobody left standing!"

Peterson made a face. "How can you possibly know that?"

"I've seen his fucking handiwork!"

"No," Peterson said, his patience returning as suddenly as it had gone. "I mean, how can you know he's coming after you?"

"That maniac Pope!" Hagen picked up his drink, taking a gulp.

Peterson suppressed a smile. "Pope contacted you? Here in Mexico?"

Hagen set down the glass hard. "Well, I sure as hell didn't call *him*, Ken!"

"And he told you that Shannon was coming after you?"

"In so many fucking words, yes!"

Peterson began to chortle. "And that's why you're hiding here in this shitty hotel?"

"What's so fucking funny about that?"

"Oh, I don't know," Peterson said with a shrug. "Maybe I can't believe you're that damn stupid."

Hagen's face clouded over.

"Think about it, Tim." Peterson signaled the barman

for another beer. "If you're Pope, and you've just discovered your entire operation has been compromised by persons unknown, what are you going to do?"

Hagen increased his grip on the glass. "Why don't you spare me the pop quiz and tell me what the fuck you're talking about?"

"I'm saying Pope couldn't possibly have *known* you were involved. He probably suspected, sure. It's no secret you hate him—but so do five hundred other people in DC. He called to see if you'd panic. And you did. Now he's waiting to see if you'll do something else stupid. Hopefully, you didn't just compromise me."

Hagen dared to believe he might actually survive. "Is Shannon still in France?"

Peterson shook his head. "No, he got out—the Russians helped him—but you can believe that *Tim Hagen* is the last thing on his long list of shit to do. Pope's gonna run him all over Eastern Europe trying to figure what the hell is going on." He chuckled. "And you can bet the old bastard's up there in Langley laughing his ass off, knowing he's got you down here scared shitless."

"How soon can you verify Shannon's location?"

Peterson brushed a small cockroach off the table. "He'll be almost impossible to track in real time. The best we can do is watch for anomalies within the theater."

"What kinds of anomalies?"

"Unexplained chaos. If one of our people—or one of the GRU's people—gets killed, it'll be a safe bet Shannon was there. In the meantime, I suggest you get yourself checked into a better hotel. You're more likely to get killed by a hooker in this city than you are by Gil Shannon."

"Have you heard from our friends in the GRU since the Paris meeting fell apart?"

Peterson noticed that Hagen was in no way acknowledging that it was his backwater op that had caused things to go wrong in Paris. "Our people in Rome tell us that Kovalenko went to Malta to eliminate the crew of the *Palinouros*. We're still waiting to hear how it went."

Hagen gulped the remainder of his drink. "Let's hope he took out Captain Miller while he was there. We sure as hell don't need that fucking pedophile coming back to bite us in the ass."

"I'm sure Kovalenko was thorough."

Hagen sat back, clearing his throat. "Can we get at Pope?"

Peterson pursed his lips, thinking it over. "Anyone can be gotten to. Depends on how bad you want to get at him."

"I want him dead. Is that bad enough?"

"Hitting Pope is a risky move, but I've got an ex-Delta operator on standby for domestic ops. Now that I think about it, it might actually be a worthwhile investment . . . considering."

"Considering what?"

"Well, Pope took a meeting with the president a while back, and it's still making people nervous up in Langley because nobody—and I mean *nobody*—has been able to find out what was discussed." Peterson saw an opportunity to rub salt in Hagen's ever-festering wound: "And who knows better than you how odd it is for Pope to be seen around the White House?"

Hagen let the baiting remark pass, some of his confidence returning. "I can control the president's reaction if Pope is taken out. I was with him on the campaign trail during his first run for office, and there's a lot the first lady doesn't know about his nighttime campaign activities."

"So the rumors are true?"

"I've got the footage to prove it."

"Does he know?"

Hagen leaned into the table. "He had his drunken face so far up that Korean hooker's snatch, he couldn't even see daylight."

Peterson snorted. "You think that's enough to blackmail him?"

"Not into starting World War Three," Hagen said, "but more than enough to make him look the other way on the demise of a pain in the ass like Bob Pope. Very few people know what the first lady's like when she's pissed, and, trust me, you do *not* want to be there when that storm hits."

10

SICILY

Gil and Dragunov arrived on the Sicilian coast near the small town of Sampieri about twenty-five minutes behind Kovalenko and his men. The Maltese P21 patrol boat was already sinking by the stern in thirty feet of water and would disappear long before the sun came up.

Gil killed the engines on the *Palinouros* and dropped both bow anchors. "You up for another swim? If we leave the skiff on the beach, it'll be obvious somebody came ashore."

Dragunov pulled on the hood to his wet suit, saying grimly, "Let's get wet, Vassili. In two hours the sun rises."

They weighted Brody's body with a scuba tank and watched him sink beneath the surface at the stern before stepping into the water and swimming the hundred yards to land. The two of them came ashore on a stretch of empty beach concealed from an adjacent village by a long wood running the length of the cove. They ditched their wet suits and moved east through the trees parallel to the road.

"Will they move inland on a direct route to Messina?" Gil asked. "Or stick to the coastal road?"

"They will steal the first car they can and take the coast road. We'll have to do the same if we want to catch them before they make it to Italy. Are you prepared to kill Sicilians?"

"Only to stay alive and out of prison," Gil answered. "Not to steal a car."

"What if stealing a car is the only way to stay alive and out of prison?"

"We'll burn that bridge when we get to it."

They moved into the village and found a small black Fiat with the keys in the ignition. Dragunov slipped behind the wheel, and Gil pushed it down the dirt road away from the house before Dragunov started it up. Soon they were riding along the coastal road, headed east.

"I think they'd take the highway inland," Gil said. "It's a lot faster to Messina that way."

"Oh, you are Spetsnaz?" Dragunov asked in his gravelly voice, shifting gears, his eyes glued to the winding road. "You know how they were trained?"

Gil chuckled. "Well, maybe we could take the highway and get to Messina ahead of them. We could cover the ferry."

"And do what?" Dragunov said, stealing a glance. "Shoot them in front of everyone?"

"Hey, I'm just thinkin' out loud here."

"Think quiet," Dragunov said. "Your thoughts give me a headache."

Twenty minutes later, they rounded a bend and saw, in the taillights of another black car pulled off to the right, a man just finishing up with changing the left rear tire. Dragunov gunned the engine and swerved toward the car.

"Watch it, Ivan, you're gonna hit the fuckin' guy!"

"Blyat!" Dragunov snarled, slamming the front right fender of the Fiat into the man as he jumped too late to get out of the way. The body flew up over the top of the car and landed in the road behind them as Dragunov slammed on the brakes and the car skidded to a stop in the dirt. "That was Lesnichy—one of Kovalenko's men!"

Gil pulled his pistol and dove from the vehicle, rolling into a shallow depression at the side of the road. Dragunov disappeared in the darkness on the far side.

Both the black car and the badly broken—but not dead—Lesnichy were faintly visible in the taillights of the still idling Fiat. Lesnichy's right leg was folded grotesquely beneath him, the other leg twitching involuntarily.

Gil heard the faint sound of a suppressed pistol shot, and Lesnichy's leg stopped moving. Two more whispered pistol shots took out the taillights of their Fiat in quick succession, throwing the road into almost total darkness. Screwing the suppressor back onto his Strike One, Gil knew they were all equally pressed for time by the coming of dawn.

The red dot of a laser sight glinted off the chrome fender of the Fiat, and Gil grabbed a handful a dust from the road, throwing it into the air behind the car. The powder instantly formed a cloud, illuminating the beam of the laser. The laser disappeared in that same instant, but it was too late. Gil had been shooting azimuths by eye for too long. His brain worked with computerlike speed to trace the angle of the beam back to its source through the darkness. He fired three shots from the Strike One on pure instinct.

A man grunted.

Hearing him scramble to displace, Gil fired two more

shots, and the man cried out, swearing in Russian. Gil could tell by the sound of the voice that he'd struck vital organs, so there was no reason to fire again.

A suppressed rifle shot hissed through the air, and a chunk of flesh the size of a quarter was torn from Gil's right shoulder. Recoiling from the suddenness of the impact, he rolled back into the road against all prudence, hoping the sniper would expect him to roll the opposite way. Another shot hissed through the air, striking the ground three feet to his left, and Gil froze, knowing the sniper would now be listening for the faintest hint to his location.

"Comrade Dragunov!" someone called out from behind the enemy car.

"Kovalenko!" Dragunov called back.

Gil used this noise as cover, inching his way backward around the front of the car. He listened as the two Spetsnaz men exchanged brief insults in Russian, sitting against the front bumper of the Fiat, probing the wound. It wasn't life threatening, but it was bleeding and would be difficult to conceal without a proper field dressing and a change of clothes.

"It will be light soon," Kovalenko was telling Dragunov. "We should finish this another time. Otherwise we may spend the rest of our lives washing one another's backs in an Italian prison."

"You'll wash *my* back, traitor!"

Kovalenko laughed uproariously from the far side of the car. "Even so, there will soon be light enough to see."

"You're the one with your back to the water!" Dragunov shouted. "I have all day!"

"Do you, comrade? We both know I am the man with the rifle."

Dragunov thought that over, believing Gil dead and

realizing he'd be no match for Kovalenko's rifle once the sun came up. "What do you propose, traitor?"

"You in your car, me in mine—now! While it's still too dark to see one another. I reverse, you go forward, and we both live to fight another day."

Dragunov decided to let discretion be the better part of valor. "On three?"

"We count together!"

Together they counted: "*One . . . two . . . three!*" Then each man darted for his car.

With no idea what the hell had been said, Gil heard Dragunov come scrambling from the rocks. When Dragunov jumped into the car, he reasoned what must be going on and moved quickly around to the passenger side where the door still hung open.

Dragunov nearly shot him when he appeared. "Get in! I thought you were dead!"

Gil got in, and Dragunov gunned the motor before he even had a chance to close the door.

"What the hell was all that about back there?"

"We called a truce before it got light," Dragunov said. "Kovalenko doesn't want to risk being caught by the police, and I couldn't fight him without a rifle. If I'd known you were still alive, I would not have agreed, but at least this way we can beat him to Messina."

"How do you know he won't change his plan?"

"The rest of his men will be waiting for him in Rome."

In the beam of the headlights, Gil saw clothes hanging on a line in front of a house up ahead. "Stop there. I need a new shirt."

Dragunov pulled to the side and Gil jumped out, grabbing a shirt and some socks to use for bandages. They were under way again a few seconds later.

"Do you guys have a safe house in Italy? Someplace I can get stitched up?"

"Don't you, American?"

Gil shook his head. "Pope still has no idea who we can trust in Europe. I can't risk being tracked."

"I thought you said the GRU was just as bad."

Gil was shrugging out of his shirt. "You said they were clean. Besides, any port in a storm, Ivan. I won't be effective for long unless I get this fixed."

Dragunov shifted gears. "You killed one back there, yes?"

"Yeah."

"Good, Vassili. Maybe you Americans would have given us a fight after all."

Gil wrapped a sock around his wound. "Yeah, well, I'm glad we never had to find out."

"It does not matter," Dragunov remarked a few moments later. "There would have been nothing left for anyone. We always knew that. It was all a stupid waste. War is a stupid waste."

"So why do we love it so damn much?" Gil wondered.

Dragunov smiled in the light of the dash. "That is a good question."

11

TIJUANA,
Mexico

Thirty-eight-year-old Daniel Crosswhite was a former Green Beret captain, former Delta Force operator, and Medal of Honor winner, but since his discharge from the army almost two years earlier, he had devolved into someone less than a model citizen.

Just months after his return to civilian life, he and former Navy SEAL Brett "Conman" Tuckerman formed a two-man vigilante squad, dressing up at night as FBI agents to knock over drug dealers in the cities of Detroit and Chicago, killing a few of the hapless dealers in the process. They were ultimately apprehended in Chicago by the Eighty-Second Airborne Division during that city's brief period under martial law, which had been imposed in response to the menace of nuclear terror then gripping the nation. Only the timely intervention of Robert Pope—director of the Special Activities Division of the CIA—had saved them from life in prison. In exchange for covering their tracks, Pope had required they assist Gil Shannon in his hunt for a Russian RA-115 "suitcase" nuke. Sadly, Tuckerman was killed during the hunt, leaving Crosswhite to carry out further missions alone.

What Pope had never known, however, was that in the moments before Crosswhite's and Tuckerman's apprehension by the Eighty-Second, they managed to hide a half million dollars beneath the foundation of a dilapidated building, and Crosswhite had long since returned to Chicago to retrieve it. Now he lived in relative obscurity back and forth across the California-Mexico border, having fallen off the grid and mostly out of contact with both Shannon and Pope.

However, as an avowed adrenaline junky, he had also made it known in the right circles that his services were available on the international mercenary market—if the price was right.

It was two in the morning, and Crosswhite lay naked on a hotel bed with his arm around an equally naked Mexican prostitute when his cellular chirped on the nightstand. With a curious glance at the clock, he sat up and switched on the lamp. The adrenaline began to pump as he read the lengthy text message, supplying him with names, flight numbers, and the location of a CIA drop box in San Diego, where he would find the money to cover his expenses should he decide to accept the mission.

"You gotta be shittin' me," he muttered.

Crosswhite replied at once, confirming his acceptance and his intention to begin immediately. Setting aside the phone, he reached for a powder-covered mirror on the nightstand. He used a rolled-up hundred-dollar bill to snort a thick line of cocaine and then reached over and gave the girl a sharp slap on her backside. "Up at 'em, baby! We got shit to do!"

The twenty-three-year-old girl woke up pissed, taking a swat at him and missing as he got off the bed. "*Pendejo! Don't fucking hit me when I'm sleeping!*" Her name was Sarahi. She had obsidian eyes and long, raven hair. "*Pinche puto!*"

He stopped short of the bathroom and whipped around, his devil-may-care grin splitting his handsome, dark face. "Hey, you wanna take a fuckin' trip with me, baby?"

She sat up, her gaze narrowing with suspicion. "Where?"

"Fuck you care, where? The fuck outta here! *That's* where!"

"You gonna pay me?"

"Hell, yes. Now get that hot little ass into some jeans. I just got a mission, and the CIA pays fucking *bueno*, baby!"

Her eyes lit up like black fire. "CIA money?"

He laughed. "Yeah, CIA money. Now get your ass moving, you sexy little bitch. We're on the clock!"

She did a couple quick lines of coke and then sprang out of bed, reaching for her jeans. They were dressed and out the door a few minutes later.

Crosswhite fired up his black Jeep Wrangler and sped out of the hotel lot.

"So where we goin'?" she asked, opening her purse.

"San Diego." He lit a cigarette and tossed the lighter onto the dash. "I gotta pick up some *dinero*."

"Can we stop to see my *tía*?" She pulled down the vanity mirror to check her makeup.

"We don't have time to visit your fucking aunt, baby. This is a goddamn mission."

"A mission to do what? What *kind* of mission?"

He stopped at a light and looked at her, his face suddenly serious. "We're gonna kill a motherfucker, baby. We're gonna kill a motherfucker, and it's gonna be the most exciting, most *dangerous* fucking thing you've ever been involved in."

She stared at him, thinking at first that he was joking. When she saw that he was not, she felt her pulse quicken. "Is it legal?"

"Legal!" He laughed again. "Baby, this is the CIA. Whatever you can get away with is legal."

"What if you get caught?"

He took a drag from the cigarette and flicked the ash out the window. "Well, if you get caught, that's just your tough shit."

"Then we ain't getting fucking caught," she said, looking back into the mirror. "How much are we getting paid?"

The light turned green, and he stepped on the gas. "Two hundred grand."

"What?!" She smacked the vanity mirror closed. "Two hundred fucking grand? Shit! My *primo* Migue will kill a guy for fifty bucks!"

He gave her a look, keeping an eye on the road. "This dude we're goin' after, he'd turn your cousin Migue into a fucking piñata. Now get those jeans off and slide over here. That coke's makin' me horny as fuck."

"*I'm* making you horny." She started to undo her pants, then stopped. "Half the money is mine, right?"

"Yeah, it's half yours. Now get over here and straddle this thing, baby. You're killin' me with those eyes!"

She laughed and wriggled out of the jeans. "I knew there was a reason I liked you."

He laughed with her as she climbed aboard. "You ain't

foolin' nobody." He had to look around her to keep from going off the road as she got into position. "What you like are dead presidents."

She grabbed his chin as she slid onto him, looking into his eyes. "That's right, and you'd better not fucking rip me off!"

He clipped the curb, and the Jeep bounced back into the lane. "Don't worry," he chuckled, one hand on the wheel holding the cigarette, the other gripping her ass. "I don't want your *puto* cousin trackin' me down."

12

HOUSTON,
Texas

Twenty-nine-year-old Jason Ryder was not a Medal of Honor recipient, though he had been awarded the Distinguished Service Cross for bravery during the Afghan War. He was lean and wiry at 145 pounds and stood no taller than five foot six. He was fast on his feet and even faster with a gun. Ryder was also a man with a severe case of post-traumatic stress, and since returning home from the war, he had been virtually ignored by the Veterans Administration. "Backlogged" was the official term they used.

It hadn't taken Ryder long to give up on the VA, turning to a private military company (PMC) named Obsidian Optio, where he took a job leading offshore security details. The work was boring and tedious, and it made his nerves hum with anxiety. When he wasn't working, he spent his time drinking and smoking pot, sliding ever deeper into the hole of PTSD until he finally began to consider suicide. It was during a detail in Brazil that Ryder had first met Ken Peterson of the CIA.

Peterson was very coy at first, feeding Ryder's anger at being brushed aside by the VA. He said there were factions within the US government working to change things from the inside out, but key people were standing in the way. It didn't take more than three hours over beers for Peterson to have Ryder talked into accepting a private contractor's role with the agency.

"Sure, it's against our legal charter," Peterson said, "but the agency's been turned upside down since the nuke attacks last year." He went on to exaggerate further the severity of a genuine administrative problem. "Nobody really knows who's in charge of anything, and nobody can get anything done according to policy. So we're operating outside official parameters to keep the ship afloat, fighting a holding action against the old guard back in Langley while Washington decides how it wants us to function in the age of 'nuclear terror.'" He smirked. "Hell, the president can't even get Congress to confirm a new director. It'd be laughable if it wasn't so damn tragic."

Ryder now sat in George Bush Intercontinental Airport, waiting impatiently to catch an early-morning flight to Washington, where he would assassinate Bob Pope, one of the traitors Peterson claimed was standing in the way of a safer, stronger America.

What Ryder did not know—nor did Peterson or Tim Hagen—was that Pope was the director of a newly formed top-secret Special Mission Unit of the CIA called the Anti-Terrorism Response Unit (ATRU). Though the ATRU was similar in concept to other SMUs such as SEAL Team VI and Delta Force, it was much smaller. It did not operate under the auspices of the Special Activities Division. In fact, the ATRU was not even officially part of the CIA. It answered directly to the Office of the President. It did not conduct large-scale operations, it did not gather its own intelligence, and its operations certainly weren't subject to congressional oversight. Operators within the ATRU had one purpose and one purpose only: close with and destroy Muslim terrorists wherever they could be found and do so without leaving a trace of having been there. To use the cliché, they didn't exist.

Ryder sat at the gate and looked at his watch, his leg jiggling up and down. He needed a cigarette, but there was no place to smoke. He'd gone to the restroom to sneak a drag, but there'd been a pair of chubby National Transportation Safety Board cops standing right outside the door, jawing and laughing about some foreign national they'd just denied entrance into the country. So instead, he popped a Xanax and chased it with a swig of water, wondering idly if Peterson understood how close to the edge he really was these days.

Part of him didn't trust Peterson—the guy was a spook, after all—but fifty grand was good money, and if this guy Pope was only half as bad as Peterson made him out to be, the disloyal bastard still deserved what was coming to him. He'd seen much better men killed on the battlefield for a whole lot less. But in the end, it didn't really matter to Ryder. He was itching to take his aggressions out on someone in government, and Pope was probably more deserving than most.

An hour before boarding, he managed to nod off, but a bickering couple sat down across from him. A young Mexican woman was bitching about something in Spanish. She was in her early twenties, accompanied by a man easily fifteen years older, and she had long black hair, dark sunglasses, and jeans so tight they fit her like she'd been poured into them.

"Would you shut the fuck up for five minutes?" the guy said irritably. He was tall with dark features, built like a professional baseball player.

Ryder pulled his black Craft International shooting cap down tighter over his eyes, tuning them out.

"If your mother pulls that shit on me again," the girl said in English, "I'm slapping that bitch right in her fucking mouth!"

"Calm down," he repeated. "We're not the only ones in the airport."

"Hey!" the girl said. "Hey, you."

Ryder lifted the brim of his cap. The girl was looking right at him. She'd taken off her glasses, and he could see the bloodshot drift of her black eyes, the cocaine shine. "You talkin' to me?"

"Would you let your mother call your girlfriend a whore?"

Ryder stole a glance at Crosswhite. "Depends on if she was."

Crosswhite snickered, and Sarahi sat back in the seat. *"Pinches putos,"* she said under her breath.

Ryder pulled the cap back down and drifted off again. He awoke a short time later to the toe of someone's shoe tapping against his. He looked up to see the tall man standing over him.

"This your flight?" Crosswhite asked, drinking from his coffee. "It's boarding."

13

MESSINA,
Sicily

Gil and Dragunov were parked on the side of the road, waiting for Kovalenko to show his face at the ferry crossing to Villa San Giovanni on the far side of the Strait of Messina. It was late in the day, and Gil sat dozing in the passenger seat when Dragunov spotted Eli Vitsin and three other Spetsnaz men driving off the ferry in an old Italian LaForza SUV.

"That's them!" Dragunov said, starting the motor.

Gil looked around. "Who them?"

"Kovalenko's men." Dragunov pointed at the red LaForza. "It looks like they're coming to him."

Gil watched the unusually wide SUV turning north. "Why are they doing that?"

"I don't know." Dragunov pulled out slowly from the side of the road. "Maybe they plan to kill us here on the island." His satellite phone began to ring inside the zipper pouch on his hip as he shifted gears. He answered the phone, saying, *"Da?"* Then he handed the phone to Gil. "It's for you."

Gil took the phone. "Yeah, who's this?"

"Gil, it's Bob. Federov gave me the number."

"Whattaya got?"

"It's definitely a shadow op," Pope said. "Looks like black elements of the CIA and the GRU are planning to disable the BTC pipeline."

"What the hell for?"

"One can only speculate," Pope said. "Listen, Gil, there's something you need to know. Hagen's made a move to have me assassinated. I've scheduled a meeting with the president for tomorrow to brief him on your new mission profile, and I'm going to request permission to bring Acting Director Webb into the loop. That way SOG can take over in the event something happens to me."

Gil was so pissed that he forgot the pain in his festering shoulder wound. "Who does Hagen think he is, Al Pacino?"

"I'll handle him," Pope said easily. "But I want you aware in case the impossible happens. Where are you now?"

"Looks like we just got lucky," Gil said. "Kovalenko's men showed up here at the ferry crossing in Mes—"

The windows of the car shattered in an implosion of flying glass as a second SUV sped past them on the left, a bald gunman in the passenger seat spraying their Fiat with 9 x 18 mm fire from a suppressed Kashtan submachine pistol. Dragunov rammed the SUV to send it careening toward the far side of the road, where it swerved briefly onto the berm and then back onto the street. Another burst from the machine pistol, and the front left tire of the Fiat was blown out.

"Sukiny dyeti!" Dragunov shouted, pounding the steering wheel in a rage as the SUV sped away. Sons of bitches!

"Stop the car!" Gil urged, tossing the shattered satellite phone aside. "Gimme your weapon!" One of the bullets had struck the phone as he was ducking down in the seat. "There are too many people around."

Dragunov pulled off and tossed his pistol into Gil's lap. "What are you going to do?"

Gil jumped out, sliding quickly beneath the car to wedge their pistols between the fuel tank and the chassis. "Now pop the trunk. I'll see if there's a spare."

"You're bleeding again," Dragunov said, pointing at Gil's hand, where he'd been nicked by the bullet.

"What the fuck else is new, Ivan? Come on. Let's get the tire changed before the local— Shit!" A black police car with "Carabinieri" stenciled along the side pulled past them and off the road with two cops inside. "All I got's my Russian passport."

"I'll do the talking," Dragunov said, getting out. "Just mumble what we taught you at the airport—and act stupid. I'll tell them you lived in Chernobyl and that the radiation rotted your brain."

Gil chuckled sardonically, pulling the bloody sock from beneath his shirt to get the shoulder wound bleeding for effect. "And if that doesn't work?"

Dragunov shrugged. "We kill them."

14

PALERMO,
Sicily

Kovalenko would have preferred to stay and finish his enemy while he held the advantage of rifle over pistol. But the real reason the Wolf had struck the truce with Dragunov was that one of Gil's blindly fired .40 caliber rounds had penetrated the back of his right thigh and passed clean through, leaving him with a four-inch-long hole through the femoral biceps muscle. It was late in the day now, and he occupied a cottage on the outskirts of Palermo near the northwestern tip of Sicily, waiting for Vitsin and the rest of his men to arrive from Rome. Kovalenko knew that by now Dragunov or someone else from the GRU would be covering the Messina ferry crossing, so he'd called Vitsin and changed the plan, warning him to watch for the Spetsnaz major as they came ashore. The Wolf's wounds were clean and stuffed with cotton wadding to stanch the blood. The bullet had passed dangerously close to the sciatic nerve, so he counted himself lucky not to need major surgery.

He stood in the kitchen looking down at the bodies of a dead goat farmer and his wife, whom he'd shot in the middle of their breakfast. He took a seat and broke open a couple of cold biscuits, smearing them with marmalade and pouring himself a cup of cold coffee from a tin pot.

Vitsin and the other five Chechen operatives arrived a short time later, sharing the news about their failure to kill Dragunov at the Messina crossing.

Kovalenko was annoyed by their failure, but Dragunov had an uncanny knack for survival, so he wasn't entirely surprised. "Who the hell is the other guy?" he wondered aloud. "I saw him on the bridge of the *Palinouros* but didn't recognize the face."

"It has to be that American operative Gil Shannon," Vitsin said. "The US Navy sniper. Before we left Rome, our CIA contact told us he was spotted at our embassy in Paris."

Kovalenko knew a lot about Shannon. He grunted. "So the GRU is working with the old guard of the CIA." He thought back to the gunfight by the road, remembering how the red laser beam had shone in the dark, and he realized that it was Gil who'd had the immediate presence of mind to toss a handful of dust into the air. "The dot must have reflected off the car," he muttered.

"What dot?"

Kovalenko told them how Dragunov had rammed Lesnichy with the car and how Gil had used the laser beam to accurately place his shots. "That's how Anatoly got himself killed—and very nearly me."

"We have to get back to Georgia," remarked the bald man named Anton, who had failed to kill Dragunov and Gil in Messina.

"*Da!* As soon as possible," seconded one of the others.

"At first I thought so too," Vitsin said, "but now I disagree."

Kovalenko eyed him, waiting for an explanation.

"Dragunov will follow us wherever we go," Vitsin went on. "If we escape back to Georgia, the bastard will surely appear when we least expect him—*like he did in Malta.* And back in Georgia, he will have the close logistical support of the Russian army. So I say it's best to deal with him here on Sicily, where both sides are equal."

"But Dragunov is only one man," Anton protested. "There will be others."

Kovalenko spoke up. "True, there *will* be others—but not like Dragunov. He knows me better than anyone, and like Vitsin says, he's a cagey whoreson."

"And what about the American?" asked another.

"Well," Kovalenko said thoughtfully, "*someone* in the CIA obviously sent him to France, which either means our American friends are not as well informed as they say, or they're lying to us."

Vitsin straightened in his chair. "Regardless, there's no reason to assume Shannon won't accompany Dragunov to Georgia—especially if the Americans know we plan to hit the pipeline."

"That, too, is correct." Kovalenko sat quietly for a moment, trying to see ten moves ahead into his chess match with Dragunov. "In the end, the Americans will do whatever is necessary to protect their oil profits—short of war. And Moscow will do whatever is necessary to avoid provoking them—within reason. So, my friends, the decision is thrust upon us: we deal with Dragunov and Shannon here on Sicilian soil . . . then we go back and help Umarov hit the pipeline."

15

MEXICO CITY,
Mexico

Hagen met with Peterson in the restaurant El Cardenal on the south side of Mexico City in a zone densely populated with hotels and restaurants. It was a quiet place with good food. "So what's going on?" Hagen asked, spreading the linen napkin in his lap. "What couldn't we talk about over the phone?"

"We have an anomaly," Peterson said, opening the wine list. "A number of them, actually. Eight Maltese sailors were killed last night by machine-gun fire, and their patrol boat is still missing. Also, the *Palinouros* was found anchored off the coast of Sicily with her entire crew murdered."

"Miller?" Hagen asked.

"Dead," Peterson said, scanning the wine list. "Shot right between the eyes—or so I'm told."

"Who killed the Maltese sailors?"

Peterson looked up. "Shannon. Who the hell else?"

"It might have been Kovalenko if he was—"

"Kovalenko doesn't exist," Peterson said. "There is no Kovalenko. Only Gil Shannon—*murderer*. Get it?"

Nettled, Hagen spoke through gritted teeth. "Who the fuck killed the Maltese sailors?"

"Quick answer is, *we don't know*," Peterson said. "But it gets pinned on Shannon. I've already put the word out to the right people in Malta, and they're moving on Sicily."

"Well, my first guess for the Maltese sailors wouldn't be Shannon," Hagen said. "So you'd better tell your people not to waste too much time on that lead."

"Why not?"

Hagen sucked on a shrimp cocktail. "Because Shannon's a fucking idealist, Ken. He doesn't like to kill people who don't have it coming. I'd tell you to ask your buddy Lerher about that, but, then, Lerher's already dead, isn't he?" He closed the menu and nudged it aside. "You'd better find a way to kill him, and soon. I'm telling you!"

Peterson reached for a tortilla chip. "You're the one who insisted on fucking the guy."

Hagen's temper flared. "And *you're* the one who said it could be done, no problem!"

"Lower your voice," Peterson warned, cutting him a glance as the waitress approached.

They ordered their food and drinks and sat in strained silence until the other patrons were entirely refocused on their own tables.

"So what about Pope?" Hagen asked, smoothing the table cloth.

"The contract has been accepted. He'll be dead within thirty-six hours."

"Oh, really? And suppose he never comes out of that damn cave of his?"

"He's coming out tomorrow." Peterson wanted to punch Hagen in the face. "There's a meeting scheduled with the president for the afternoon. He'll be exposed all the way from Langley to DC and back."

"It's not exactly going to look like an accident, is it?"

Peterson shook his head. "This isn't TV, Tim. It's war."

"I'm glad you realize that." Hagen took a drink of water. "By the way, I need a security detail. Do you have one you can supply me with?"

Peterson gaped at him.

"What's that look?"

"You can hire your own team—locally."

"You mean Mexicans?"

"No, Chinese!"

"You're the Central America chief of station," Hagen said. "You're telling me you don't have a detail you can spare?"

Peterson made an effort to keep his own voice down. "Any detail I could spare would be made up of indigenous personnel: *Mexicans*. And the allocation could draw attention from within the agency—which we don't need—so hire your own team. There are plenty of private firms here in the city."

Hagen's lips puckered, and he looked almost as though he were pouting.

Now it was Peterson's turn to smirk. "Jesus, it's the money, isn't it? All those millions, and you're too cheap to pay for your own goddamn security."

Hagen sat back so the waitress could pour their wine. "Find me a firm that isn't going to cost me an arm and a leg. I don't think that should be *too* difficult, considering where we are."

Peterson waited for the young woman to leave the table. "Remember, tight-ass, you get what you pay for."

Hagen took umbrage. "It should occur to you that I have money because I know how to manage it."

"You have money because your father left it to you," Peterson retorted. "Speaking of which, you're picking up the tab for this meal. I flew down from Monterrey at my own expense." This was, of course, untrue, but Peterson had learned to enjoy the small victories in his dealings with Tim Hagen.

16

MESSINA,
Sicily

Gil stood with his hands on the hood of the shot-up Fiat while Dragunov explained to the Sicilian police sergeant in very broken English that he and Gil were simple Russian tourists. He said they didn't know who had shot at them or why. The sergeant then asked him if he knew anything about a yacht anchored off the southern coast, and Dragunov pretended not to understand the word *yacht*.

"*Boat!*" the cop said, pointing south. "A rich man's boat. Do you know about it?"

"No, we arrive by car." Dragunov pointed back toward the ferry.

The cop rolled his eyes, growing impatient with the man he believed to be avoiding his questions.

Gil couldn't see the second cop standing right behind him, his hand on Gil's shoulder, but he could tell by the look on the sergeant's face that he and Dragunov were only seconds from being placed under arrest. He adjusted his hips slightly in preparation for the spin move he would use to take the cop off his feet when he reached for Gil's wrist to cuff him.

A hundred yards off, a white van pulled to the side of the road. The side door slid open, and a man appeared with a scoped rifle. Though Gil couldn't make out the weapon at that range, it was a Heckler & Koch G28 in 7.62 mm.

"Ivan, get down!"

Gil ducked behind the car as the cop grabbed for his wrist. There was no report from the suppressed rifle, but the cop flew backward, hit in the chest by an armor-piercing round that easily defeated his thin body armor and exploded his heart before ripping out through his back.

With the speed of a striking cobra, Dragunov hit the sergeant in the throat and dove for cover. The cop stumbled backward, and he too was struck in the chest by a bullet. He crashed to his knees and fell over onto his face. Dragunov grabbed for his sidearm, but a round took off the ring finger on his left hand, and he jerked back behind the car, swearing foully.

It took the pedestrians in the vicinity a few seconds to realize what was happening, but once they did, they ran off up the street. Bullets tore into the car—deadly missiles that made no sound at all until they struck the steel and tore clean through. Gil crawled beneath the car in an effort to retrieve their pistols.

"I can only reach one!"

"They're coming!" Dragunov shouted as the van pulled back into the street, speeding toward them.

Gil slid from the beneath the car and tossed the Russian the pistol, jumping up and running for the police car.

Dragunov got to his feet and fired at the windshield of the oncoming van, but the pistol ran dry after four shots, and he again turned for the dead sergeant's sidearm.

Gil jerked open the passenger door of the police car and opened the glove box, popping the deck lid and scrambling for the trunk, where he found an H&K MP5 submachine gun. He primed the receiver and shouldered the weapon, running out into the street.

Seeing he was about to be machine-gunned, the driver cut the wheel hard to the left, exposing the door gunner on the right side, who was forced to grab the handhold to keep from being thrown from the vehicle. Gil fired on the run, cutting the door gunner to pieces with a sustained thirty-round burst. The van hit a road sign, bounced to a stop, and stalled. Gil dropped the machine gun and leapt aboard through the open door.

The driver fumbled free of his seatbelt and tried to jump out, but Gil caught him by his curly black hair and yanked him back inside, punching him in the face repeatedly until he quit struggling.

"Who sent you?" Gil screamed. He found a compact Colt .45 in the man's waistband and jammed the muzzle into his groin, thumbing back the hammer. "One more time, cocksucker! Who sent you?"

The driver's lips were split and bleeding. "CIA," he sputtered in a British accent. "Malta station."

"Fuck you!" Gil slugged him with the pistol in the side of the head.

Dragunov stood in the street, aiming the sergeant's gun at a blue Nissan rounding the bend, a startled young Italian woman at the wheel. She stopped the car, and Dragunov opened the door, shoving her over. "Come on, Vassili! Let's go!"

Gil grabbed the G28 from the floor of the van and jumped in on the passenger side of the car. Dragunov gunned the motor to spin the car around, and they sped off in the same direction as Kovalenko's men.

"They're CIA!"

"You are surprised?" Dragunov had one eye on the road, the other on the rearview mirror as he ran through the gears, taking the winding road as fast as he dared.

"I'm not surprised—I'm pissed!"

The girl begged in panicked Italian to be let out of the car.

"Sorry, baby, I don't *habla*, so shut up." He stole a look at Dragunov. "Any idea where they'll go?"

"Palermo."

"Why Palermo?"

"Because they're going to need resources, and Kovalenko will want to finish me here before running back to Georgia."

"Please!" the girl begged in English. They were getting blood all over her and her car, and she was completely petrified.

Dragunov downshifted and gunned it through another curve. "What about her?"

"She stays with us." Gil took a moment to check his ammo. The G28 had a dual-magazine clamp, and both ten-round mags were full.

"Please!" the girl bawled into his face. *"Liberatemi!"*

"Listen!" he said, grabbing her arm. "I don't understand what the fuck you're saying—*so shut up!*"

She pulled her arm free, apparently understanding the "shut up" part, and sat sobbing between them.

Dragunov glanced up at the mirror, the hint of a grin on his face. "We could kill her."

"Sure," Gil said, checking the .45 and tucking it into his belly. "Even you're not that cold-blooded."

"We'll have to find a place to treat our wounds soon."

Gil chuckled sardonically. "It was no big deal when it was just me, but you lost a finger, so we suddenly need a corpsman? I don't think so, partner. No stopping before we get to Palermo. I'm gonna kill those Russian bastards."

"Chechen," Dragunov said. "They're *Chechen* bastards."

"I'm gonna kill those *Spetsnaz pricks*. How's that?"

The Russian smiled without taking his eyes off the road, pressing the accelerator and gripping the wheel with his bloody left hand as he grabbed another a gear. "If they already found the *Palinouros*, the island will soon be crawling with carabinieri. We might find Kovalenko in time to kill him, but we'll never make it back to the mainland alive."

"I'll get us off this rock when the time comes," Gil assured him. "You just find Kovalenko." He gripped the G28 resting butt-down between his knees. "I'm gonna reach out and touch that son of a bitch."

17

Ryder woke up slightly hung over in his DC hotel room and took a shower. Then he sat naked on the bed, eating cold pizza from the night before. Pope's meeting at the White House was scheduled for three thirty that afternoon, and it was his job to make sure the meeting never took place. He chased the pizza with a cold beer from the minifridge and got dressed, and then unzipped his bag and took out the USP .45 ACP he had picked up from a CIA contact the night before.

He broke down the brand-new pistol to make sure that it was properly lubricated from the factory. Then Ryder put it back together, loading the twelve-round magazine with 230-grain ammunition. Racking a round into battery, he dumped the mag again to load a thirteenth round and then tossed the readied pistol aside on the bed. Next, he took an SWR HEMS 2 suppressor from the bag and disassembled it, lubricating the internal parts with wire pulling gel. He did this because a "wet" suppressor was slightly more silent than a "dry" one (the lubricant absorbing the heat of the expanding gas), and Ryder wanted there to be as little sound as possible during the hit on Pope.

He put the pistol into the small of his back, slipped the suppressor into his jacket pocket, and then went to the window for a peek through the curtain. What he saw caused every nerve in his body to sing with alarm. The sexy Latina from the airport the day before was walking across the mostly empty parking lot carrying a McDonald's bag. The sky was heavily overcast and threatened rain. He watched her cross to a room on the far side of the lot, knock twice at the door, and then enter. A second later, someone peeked out briefly through the curtains.

He stepped back and took his cellular from his pocket, calling Peterson. "I've been made!" he said.

"I doubt that very seriously," Peterson replied calmly. "I'm the only one in the agency who knows anything about you. What's got you worried?"

Ryder told him about the girl and the military-looking guy who had been on the plane the day before, and that they were now staying at the same cheap hotel. "Which is hell and gone from the airport!"

"Let me see if I understand you," Peterson said. "A pair of travelers are staying at the same hotel as you—and that's got you worked up."

Viewed from that angle, Ryder felt a little silly. "It's not as simple as that. They sat right across from me in the airport."

"And they were on the same flight, were they?"

"Yeah, like I just told you."

"So two people who were on the same flight as you

are staying in the same hotel. Look," Peterson said, "I don't want to get in your business, but it might be time for you to lay off the marijuana. You don't need the paranoia working your nerves, and I don't need you calling me with these kinds of episodes. There's no way you've been made. But ya know what? Let's suppose for a second you had been. What the hell would you expect me to do about it over the goddamn phone?"

Ryder was embarrassed, but his discomfiture quickly morphed into a simmering anger. "Seeing as how you're in command, I thought you'd want to know."

"You're not in the army anymore," Peterson said, "and you're not working for Obsidian Optio. You're a freelance operator, which means you think for yourself. Got it? Now shitcan the dope and call me when the job is done."

"I haven't smoked in three—" Ryder realized that Peterson had already hung up. He threw the phone at the pillow. "Fuckin' asshole!"

CROSSWHITE OPENED THE McDonald's bag and took out a sandwich. "Any movement across the lot?"

Sarahi shook her head and sat down at the table to paint her nails. "Car's still there."

"Yeah, I saw it." He took a bite and continued talking with his mouth full. "So far everything fits the profile. We have to keep a close eye on him now so he doesn't give us the slip."

She looked up at him. "Didn't you put that tracker thingy on his car last night?"

He nodded, sitting down on the bed in his underwear. "But we gotta keep close to him." He looked at the sandwich in disgust. "This must be two hours old. Would you hit the Coke machine so I can wash this shit down?"

She dipped the tiny brush back into the red bottle. "Gimme a sec."

He dropped the sandwich back into the bag and got up. "Gonna get dressed in case he rolls out soon."

She sat blowing on the nail for a moment, and then took a dollar from his wallet and went out the door.

Ryder was watching through a thin crack in the curtains when Sarahi stepped out, looking directly toward his room. "Paranoid, my ass!" he said, taking a folding knife from inside the waistband of his jeans and thumbing open the three-inch black tanto blade.

He watched as she made her way toward the Coke machine in the corner where the hotel made an L shape at the halfway point between their rooms. He waited until she took the can from the machine and started back before slipping out and moving swiftly after her. She was still blowing on her finger when he caught up to her just outside the room.

She glanced back at him and let out a startled gasp, dropping the Coke as he swiped expertly at the side of her neck with the knife. The tip of the scalpel-sharp blade caught her carotid artery, and he swept past her up the walk as though nothing had happened.

At first Sarahi didn't realize she was even cut; she simply stood there with her hand over her beating heart watching Ryder walk away, but then she realized she was gushing blood from the left side of her neck, and she started screaming bloody murder.

Crosswhite jerked open the door to see her standing there spurting blood all over herself. "Holy Jesus!" He pulled her into the room and sat her down in a chair, snatching a towel from the floor and pressing it to the side of her neck. "Hold that tight, baby!"

He grabbed the phone and punched 0 with a bloody finger to get the front desk. "Call 911! Room 14—arterial bleed!"

He dropped the phone and clamped his hand back over the towel, pressing as tightly as he could. "Hang on, baby! They're comin'! They're comin'!"

"Please don't let me die," she begged, her strength beginning to fade. "Please, don't let me die, Danny!"

"Shhh," he said, kissing the top of her head. "Relax, baby, relax. We gotta slow your heart down. You gotta keep calm."

When the paramedics appeared in the doorway fifteen minutes later with their latex gloves and boxes of equipment, he was still standing there beside the chair clutching her lifeless, blood-soaked body against him, a thousand-yard stare in his eyes.

"Jesus," one of the medics murmured.

Crosswhite blinked once, his gaze sliding into focus as he looked at them. "There's nothin' you guys can do here. Never was."

18

CIA HEADQUARTERS,
Langley, Virginia

Pope was getting into the back of a black government sedan at CIA headquarters when he received a text message from Daniel Crosswhite: "Detained by police. Have temporarily lost contact with target." He sighed and slipped the phone into his coat pocket. It had begun to rain, and the air was turning cold.

"Keep your eyes open, Lieutenant," he said casually. "There exists the off chance of an attempt on my life. I wouldn't want you hit in the cross fire."

The marine driver looked at him in the mirror. "We'll deal with it, sir."

Pope was a tall man in his midsixties with soft blue eyes and a head of thick white hair. "Sorry to put you in harm's way."

"That's where marines belong, sir."

Pope settled into the seat as they pulled out of the

parking deck. They drove across the CIA campus, turning onto George Washington Memorial Parkway and heading south along the Potomac River toward the District of Columbia. The GWM was a scenic highway of four lanes with a wide, grassy median separating northbound and southbound traffic. The trees of Fort Marcy National Park were only beginning to bud, and Pope caught glimpses of the river as he rode along, trying to discern in his own mind whether Gil was still alive. There had been no further contact with him since they were cut off the day before, and the murder of the Messina cops was all over the Italian news.

He wondered how much to tell the president. The commander in chief was entitled to a certain degree of plausible deniability, but it was possible that Gil had been killed and that his body might soon be identified. There would be no evidence that Gil was working for the US government, but, regardless, his identification would cause some friction at the executive level.

The satellite phone rang inside his coat, and he answered it quickly, hoping it would be Gil.

"Pope here."

"Hello, Robert." It was Vladimir Federov of the GRU. "Have you heard from your man on Sicily?"

"No," Pope replied. "Have you heard from yours?"

"I'm sorry to say we have not," Federov said. "But there is good news. There have been no arrests, and their bodies have not been found."

"Any word on who killed the Maltese sailors?"

"Our people in Rome have concluded that it was Kovalenko," Federov said. "Also, they have verified that someone in the CIA's Rome office has been helping him with his logistics—someone named Walton."

"Good old Ben Walton," Pope said, a piece of the puzzle falling into place. "That fits." He had recently reviewed a dossier on the now-deceased Captain Miller of the *Palinouros* in which Walton's name was mentioned numerous times. Both men were former US Navy. "Walton's the agent who tipped us on Yeshevsky, the imposter Dokka Umarov, transshipping from the Greek tanker to the *Palinouros*. Which leads me to conclude that our man in Athens—an agent named Max Steiner—must also be working with Kovalenko. It was Steiner who tipped us that Yeshevsky was boarding the tanker."

"How do you plan to deal with them?" Federov asked.

"I'm going to have to give that some thought," Pope said, brushing a speck of lint from the knee of his corduroy slacks. "I'm on my way to meet with the president now."

"Here is something else you may wish to consider," Federov added. "We now have cause to believe the real Dokka Umarov sent Yeshevsky to Paris to meet with Al Qaeda, to strike a deal with them for an insurgency— probably posing as the actual Umarov. Such a display of apparent bravado would be convincing to Al Qaeda— considering the distance between Paris and the safety of the Caucasus."

"Do you think Umarov still intends to hit the pipeline?"

"Personally, I have no doubt."

Pope needed to know exactly what kinds of resources the GRU could put forth in southern Europe. "Do your people have anyone else available to help Shannon and Dragunov while they're stuck in the Med?"

There was a slight pause before Federov replied. "Not immediately; not with the necessary skills and intelligence clearances. Dragunov and his men were brought in special."

"Which leaves the ball in my court," Pope said. "Okay then. But if I can get them off of Sicily and back to mainland Europe, you can cover their transportation to Georgia?"

"That I can do," Federov promised. "But we must first verify they are still alive."

"Well, you said no bodies and no arrests. That's good enough for me. For now, though, you're probably right. We have to wait for one of them to make contact."

Pope was off the line a few moments later, tucking the phone into his coat. "I trust there's no need to tell you that conversation was top secret, Lieutenant?"

The marine never took his eyes from the road. "What conversation, sir?"

Pope nodded. "Good man."

When they arrived at the White House, Pope was admitted into the Oval Office for a meeting with not just the president but also the chairman of the Joint Chiefs of Staff, General William J. Couture, and the new White House chief of staff, Captain Glen Brooks—former commander of the United States Naval Special Warfare Development Group (DEVGRU), aka SEAL Team VI.

These were the only men in Washington who knew about the Antiterrorism Response Unit. Not even the vice president was privy to the ATRU.

Captain Brooks was a broad-shouldered, soft-spoken man with discerning brown eyes, and he carried himself with a calm, military bearing. He'd been chosen to replace Tim Hagen—over dozens of more likely candidates—at Couture's suggestion. Brooks was in no way a qualified political adviser, but his organizational skills and immediate knowledge of foreign intelligence matters was unsurpassed, and his constant presence provided the commander in chief a full-time military adviser who possessed actual hands-on experience—the kind of experience that Hagen had sorely lacked.

Within five days of Brooks's appointment, the White House had begun to function with the same military efficiency as a US aircraft carrier conducting flight operations. With nuclear terror now a bona fide reality, many on Capitol Hill were wondering if the likes of hard-core warrior types like Brooks and Couture might be the future of White House staffers, and well-known journalists were writing ever-critical op-ed pieces speculating on what an increasingly militarized federal government might mean for the future of the United States.

"Bob," the president said, standing to reach across the desk. "Glad you could make it."

"Thank you, sir." Pope turned and shook hands with Couture. "Bill," he said quietly, "good to see you."

General Couture was the only man in the room taller than Pope. He had merciless gray eyes and a wicked scar on the left side of his face, courtesy of an Iraqi RPG-7 grenade launcher. "Bob, you remember Glen."

"Yes, of course," Pope said, matching the firmness of Brooks's grip.

Everyone sat, and the president rocked back in his chair. "Okay, Bob, bring us up to speed on Dokka Umarov and this BTC pipeline business. Is Umarov finally dead?"

Pope pushed his glasses up onto his nose. "No. He's not. But our immediate problems are much bigger than Dokka Umarov." He broke Gil's situation down over the next fifteen minutes, and when he was finished talking, everyone sat waiting to see how the president would react.

If the president was rattled, it didn't show. In fact, he appeared vaguely intrigued. "General?" he said quietly.

Couture looked at Pope. "How badly is Shannon wounded?"

"I have no idea," Pope replied. "As I say, he might even be dead, but there's no reason to assume that yet. My gut tells me he's still alive and combat effective."

Couture shifted his gaze to Brooks. "Glen, you're the navy man. Who do we have in the Med to pluck those two maniacs off that island without the Italians getting wise? We obviously can't involve any of our people at Sigonella—at least not directly." He was referring to US Naval Air Station Sigonella, located on the eastern side of Sicily.

Brooks gave a calm, sly smile, reminding everyone present that silent waters ran deep. "There's a detachment from Group Two aboard the *Whitney*." He was referring to Naval Special Warfare Group Two, which commanded SEAL Teams II, IV, VIII and X. The USS *Mount Whitney* (JCC 20) was the command ship of the US Sixth Fleet, presently on station in the eastern Mediterranean. Brooks turned to the president. "A squad from SEAL Team Eight could be brought to bear rather quickly, sir."

"What do you propose?" the president asked.

"Well, sir, assuming Shannon and Dragunov are still alive . . . and assuming we can reestablish contact . . . our best chance would be a submersible SDV: a SEAL delivery vehicle. It could be used to sneak both Shannon and Dragunov aboard the USS *Ohio*. The *Ohio*'s a ballistic missile sub fitted with a pair of dry dock shelters on her hull." He grinned. "And this is exactly the kind of mission she was fitted out for. I recommend we get a team of SEALs aboard and get her into position ASAP."

The president sat behind his desk feeling for a moment like Captain James T. Kirk at the con of the *Starship Enterprise*. It was good to be in command, but it was even better knowing that you were surrounded, at last, by men who knew how to do their jobs. And he was glad to finally have no one in between himself and Pope.

"I'm glad I never fired him," he thought. "I can't afford to be without him now."

"I'll leave the details to you, General." He knew that Brooks would cut the actual orders to the navy, which was not strictly within the authority of the White House chief of staff, but the White House now ran on a perpetual war footing, for all intents and purposes, and everyone in the Joint Chiefs understood it.

"Now, about this shadow cell you mentioned, Bob. Do you have recommendations?"

Pope didn't need to explain the CIA's troubled state; everyone was acutely aware of how badly the aging intelligence agency was foundering. Many on Capitol Hill were even calling for the CIA to be broken up, its responsibilities distributed across the FBI, the NSA, and the DIA—the Defense Intelligence Agency, which presently handled all military-based espionage operations. It was obvious even to the president that the CIA was in genuine danger of slipping into obsolescence in the post–Cold War era, and he was secretly on the verge of going public with that exact sentiment. The ATRU could easily—and probably should—be placed under the auspices of the DIA.

"First," Pope said, "I'd like to bring Cletus into the fold." Cletus Webb was the acting director of the CIA, his confirmation still on hold in the Senate. "This intelligence coup is happening on his watch, right under his nose."

"Do you suggest making him privy to the ATRU as well?" Couture asked.

"I don't see how we could avoid that."

The president shifted in his seat. "Is Cletus the right man, Bob? Did I make a mistake with his appointment? You can speak frankly."

Pope noted how much more relaxed the president was now that Hagen had left the White House; how much more reasonable and willing he was to ask for advice. "Cletus is not the problem, Mr. President. He's a good man."

The president glanced at Couture. "What do you think, Bill? Is today the day?"

Couture nodded. "I think so, Mr. President."

Pope looked between them. "The day for what?"

"Bob," the president said, "I've given this a lot of thought, and the three of us have spoken about it at length. I'm going to withdraw Webb's appointment."

Pope didn't like the sound of that. Anyone else they brought in to fill Webb's position would have too many scores to settle, and that would serve only to further destabilize the agency.

"Mr. President, in all honesty, I think that would be a mistake."

"I'm going to appoint you as director of operations instead."

Pope sat back, his spine stiffening involuntarily.

"Effective today," the president went on. "When I make the official announcement, I also intend to make it clear that you almost single-handedly saved San Diego from nuclear destruction last September—a necessary minor embellishment." He traded glances with Couture, a smirk coming to his face. "Let Senator Grieves try and delay *this* confirmation."

"Mr. President, I'm not the—"

"I'm sorry, Bob, but I'm leaving you no choice. You'll relieve Cletus of his duties today."

"But, sir, he's—"

The president held up his hand. "Don't worry about Cletus. I agree he's a damn fine man. So if you want him for your DDO, that's entirely fine by me. To be honest, I don't give a damn if you let him run the show—I know how you like to spend your time in private doing whatever it is you do—but I want your name on the goddamn door."

Brooks sat back and chortled. "That's going to set a cat among the pigeons."

The president puffed up his chest, nodding with satisfaction. "It damn well better. If not, I'll close down that entire shop over there—then we'll see how they like it."

"What about the Joint Chiefs?" Pope asked. "I've never exactly been their favorite person."

The president pointed at Couture. "There sits the chairman—and this was his idea."

Pope looked at Couture. "And I haven't exactly been your favorite person, either."

Couture smiled. "I think we've come to understand one another rather well these past couple years. Don't you?"

Pope nodded, sat thoughtfully for a couple of moments, and then looked at the president. "Mr. President, if Shannon is still alive, I intend to send him into the Caucasus to kill Dokka Umarov."

The president exchanged brief glances with each of his military advisers, and then, hearing no objections, said, "There's something you're not telling us, isn't there?"

"Do I have a free hand, sir, to root out the people who exposed Shannon in Paris?"

"It's your agency now, Bob. Do what you have to do to clean it up, or I'll have to throw in with Grieves and the other radicals over there on the Hill, and we *will* shut it down."

"Yes, sir. I understand."

A short time later, as Pope was settling into the back of the sedan in front of the White House, the marine lieutenant asked as a politeness, "Everything go okay, sir?"

Pope met the lieutenant's gaze in the mirror. "Just the way I'd planned, as a matter of fact."

19

During the drive back to Langley, Pope spoke on the phone with Midori, his young Japanese-American assistant, directing her to gather and collate all available intel on the CIA traitors Ben Walton and Max Steiner. He had deliberately not told the president of Hagen's suspected involvement—or that Peterson had hired the assassin Jason Ryder—because it was his intention to have all five men in question terminated, and that was precisely the kind of thing the president of the United States didn't want to know about.

Pope's next call was to agent Mariana Mederos, a CIA analyst in Langley. "Mariana, are you still able to contact Antonio Castañeda?"

Castañeda, a former *Grupo Aeromóvil de Fuerzas Especiales* (GAFE) operator with Mexican special forces, was head of the deadliest drug cartel in Mexico. The tacit deal he had struck with the Mexican and American governments the previous September in exchange for his help in locating the Russian suitcase nuke—along with his promise to cease the violence against civilians—had allowed him to eliminate virtually all of his competition in northern Mexico, with only limited interference from the Mexican army and the American Drug Enforcement Administration.

Mederos knew Pope. She had briefed him on her experiences in Mexico during her time there, but she was not attached to the Special Activities Division, so she was not subordinate to him.

"I can if it becomes necessary," she said. "Why?"

"I need you to fly down there and meet with him as soon as possible," Pope said. "Make sure he understands that his ongoing cooperation will be part of the ongoing truce that has allowed him to become such a wealthy man."

"He won't like that," Mederos said. "Does Mr. Webb know about this?"

Pope decided now was a good time to start letting people know there was a new sheriff in town. "The president has appointed me the new director as of today, so there won't be any need to contact Mr. Webb. Just arrange the meeting with Castañeda, then swing by my office so Midori can fill you in on what I want done."

"Mr. Pope, I'm sorry, but I'll need confirmation of that before I can—"

"Mariana, listen to me very carefully," Pope said, not unkindly. "Do you want to be dismissed the day my appointment becomes official?"

She paused, clearing her throat. "No, sir. No, I don't."

"Then please do as I've asked, and speak of this only to Midori—it's classified top secret. You're one of the few people I trust over there, so keep it that way, and I'll take good care of you. Understood?"

"Yes, sir."

"Thank you." Pope put away the phone.

They crossed the Francis Scott Key Memorial Bridge, and the driver stopped for a red light behind a line of four other cars. Pope noticed a man in street clothes on the far side of the intersection with his hand inside the signal box that controlled the traffic light. The man was very definitely looking in their direction.

"Get us out of here, Lieutenant. We're about to be hit."

The marine didn't hesitate, dropping the shifter into reverse and pressing the accelerator just as Jason Ryder was stepping from the pine trees to their right.

Ryder was dressed in a black North Face rain jacket and black wool cap. He cursed and gave chase, firing twice through the windshield with the suppressed USP .45 and hitting the marine driver center mass. Ryder fired three more times into the backseat as the car continued in reverse, and Pope fell over on the seat. The car slammed into another car coming off the bridge and came to a stop.

The marine managed to open his door, rolling out on the opposite side of the car and drawing a Springfield Armory .45. He sprang into a crouch as Ryder went in to finish Pope. The lieutenant fired a quick shot through the windows of the car and hit Ryder in the side of the neck, knocking him off balance. The marine stood up and fired over the roof three more times in quick succession—*tac-tac-bang!*—hitting Ryder twice in the torso and once in the head to drop him in the street beside the car.

The marine made sure there were no more targets to engage, and then climbed into the backseat and ripped open Pope's coat to find him bleeding from a single hole in the right side of his chest.

Pope was conscious but having trouble breathing.

The marine turned him onto his wounded side to keep the blood from draining into the good lung and yanked a military med kit from beneath the seat, tearing away the green plastic from a combat field dressing. "You should've worn your vest, sir."

Pope was going into shock. "You're right," he croaked. "You okay?"

"Some cracked ribs—nothin' I can't handle." The marine pressed the compress to Pope's wound and held it. "I don't know what tipped you, sir, but you saved both our asses. I thank you for my wife and kids."

"You did all the work," Pope muttered, starting to shiver. "Jesus, this really hurts. I'm getting cold."

"It's just shock, sir." They could hear sirens on the far side of the Potomac now. "You're gonna be fine. I promise."

"Semper fi," Pope said, closing his eyes. "I'm going to have a little nap while we wait."

The marine gave Pope a painful sternal rub with his knuckles to bring him back around. "Sir, I need you stay to awake for me. No sleeping on the job."

Pope opened his eyes wide, the sharp, unexpected pain to his sternum worse than that of the bullet wound. "Good Christ, Lieutenant! I'd rather you not do that again!"

The marine chuckled, patting him on the shoulder. "Just hang in there, sir. Help's almost here."

20

BETHESDA NAVAL HOSPITAL,
Bethesda, Maryland

Flanked by a pair of Secret Service agents, the president of the United States stepped into Bob Pope's hospital room to see Daniel Crosswhite standing beside Pope's bed. The last time he'd seen Crosswhite had been at the White House two years earlier when he'd pinned the Medal of Honor to his chest. Gil Shannon had received the medal at that same ceremony.

Crosswhite stood up straight. "Mr. President."

Pope turned his head. "Hey! Nice of you to stop by." He was slightly loopy from the pain medication—though not as loopy as he intended to make out. "I got shot down over Macho Grande."

The president smiled. "I was going to ask how you're feeling, but that's apparent."

"Haven't felt this good in years." Pope chuckled, his blue eyes glassy from the morphine. "I'm hoping they'll let me stay awhile."

The president nodded, having been told by the doctors that Pope would probably be released in a week or so. He looked at Crosswhite. "Why am I not surprised to find you here, Captain?"

"I'm like a bad penny, Mr. President."

Pope chuckled again. "He came by to see if I needed any nudie magazines."

"That's the morphine talking," Crosswhite said.

"I understand," the president replied, his expression turning serious. "Should I take it the young woman killed at your hotel this morning was not really killed by her pimp?"

Crosswhite exchanged glances with Pope, both of them surprised to learn the president was so up-to-date.

"Dan's one of mine," Pope said, suddenly lucid. "The girl was his cover, and she somehow gave herself away. I think a personal phone call from you to her aunt in San Diego will probably satisfy the family's concerns."

"I'll handle it," the president said reluctantly, signaling his Secret Service agents to wait in the hall. He closed the door after them and turned back toward the bed, his index finger poised peremptorily. "I don't want any more blood on American soil. Is that understood?"

"Yes," Pope said. "But this wasn't our fault. Ryder was hired by someone inside the agency."

"*Who* inside the agency?"

"Someone presently *not* on American soil," Pope said. "Do you require the name?"

The president judiciously allowed the question to go unanswered. "The media already knows Ryder was an ex–Green Beret. That's a possible problem."

"Not really," Pope said. "All the Pentagon has to do is let them know Ryder had a severe case of PTSD—which is documented. It's also true he had a bone to pick with the Veterans Administration. For most Americans, that will be enough to convince them he was certifiably nuts."

"Possibly," the president said.

Pope reached for his hand, and the president awkwardly took it. "You can use this assassination attempt as an excuse to demand more funding for the VA." Pope gave him a wink. "That will help the vets *and* draw attention away from the CIA—two birds with one stone."

The president nodded, half liking the idea and looking at Crosswhite. "So what's next for you?"

Crosswhite was still angry over Sarahi's murder and greatly disappointed at not getting to kill Ryder himself. "I'm the tip of the spear, Mr. President. I go in whichever direction I'm thrust."

The president pursed his lips, releasing Pope's hand. "Robert, I'll send someone to look in on you daily. And you'll have Secret Service protection from now on."

"Has my driver been taken care of?"

"I've spoken with him," the president said. "He's got a cracked sternum, but he's fine otherwise. He suggested that I demote him for allowing you to be shot, but I told him not to be foolish. He credits you for saving both of your lives; says that Ryder would've had you both 'broadside-to-a-barn-door' if you hadn't spoken up when you did. What tipped you off?"

Pope adjusted the oxygen hose beneath his nose. "Ryder had an accomplice on the far side of the intersection with his hand in the signal box . . . making sure the light was red instead of green. He was wearing street clothes, and it looked odd to me. I could just as easily have been wrong, though. The lieutenant deserves all the credit."

"It's partly my fault as well," the president admitted. "I should have seen to it you were issued a sedan with bulletproof glass. Pure oversight on my part. Well, I'll leave you men to it." He shook their hands and left the room abruptly.

"So what now?" Crosswhite asked, relieved to have the president gone.

"Get to Mexico and find Peterson," Pope said. "Check with Midori before you leave. She'll have the latest intel."

"And when I find his ass?"

Pope looked at him, his eyes still glassy. "What do you think?"

Crosswhite chewed the inside of his cheek. "And what about Hagen?"

"We'll play Hagen by ear," Pope said. "What the hell were you thinking bringing that poor girl into this?"

The question brought them back to the point where they'd left off when the president interrupted. Crosswhite still didn't have the courage to admit that he'd been coked out of his mind when he first decided to bring Sarahi along.

"I was stupid," he said. "There's no other explanation. No excuse."

"You'd better get your head screwed on straight," Pope warned. "One more loose-cannon event from you, and you're out of the ATRU. Is that clear?"

"It won't happen again, sir. You've got my word."

Then Pope chuckled, the morphine making it difficult to remain completely serious. "At least not until I *require* you to be a loose cannon. That is, after all, part of what makes you so damn useful." He shook his head. "Poor girl, though. Hell of a way to die."

Crosswhite grimaced, thinking to himself that only a fourteen-karat piece of shit would put a twenty-three-year-old girl into harm's way like he had. "I want Walton and Steiner, too."

"I'll think about them," Pope said. "For now, I want you completely focused on Peterson. You'll have to be careful with him. He must have somebody in the White House feeding him intel—otherwise he could never have gotten Ryder into such a perfect position."

21

SICILY

Night had fallen. Gil and Dragunov were parked behind a crowded shopping mall on the outskirts of Palermo with the young Italian woman—a brunette named Claudina—still crammed between them. Dragunov had wanted to put her in the Nissan's trunk, but Gil had vetoed the idea. Using Claudina's cellular, Gil tried again to reach Pope but had been unable to establish a connection. Dragunov finally managed to contact Federov at the Russian Embassy in Paris, arranging for a GRU doctor from Rome to meet them the next morning.

Both men were in pain from their festering gunshot wounds, and Dragunov—who had never been shot before—was acting even more cantankerous than normal. Both of them were too bloody to risk going into a store for supplies.

"The doctor will bring a pair of satellite phones tomorrow," he said, giving the phone back to Claudina, who had stopped crying hours earlier. She seemed to have figured out they weren't going to hurt her and no longer gave the impression that she was terrified of them.

"Good thinking," Gil said. "Do you think Kovalenko is still on the island?"

"He's still here," Dragunov growled. "I can smell him."

"Well, I was lookin' for somethin' a little more evidentiary than your sense of smell."

Dragunov glanced at him in the dim light. "What the hell are you talking about?"

"Why do you really think he's still on the island? Your nose doesn't tell me shit."

Dragunov turned to face him, pushing the girl back against the seat so they could see one another clearly. "With the Italian navy patrolling the coast, Kovalenko couldn't get back to the mainland in a destroyer. He's as trapped as we are."

"How's the hand?" Gil asked.

"It hurts like hell," Dragunov mumbled. "More than I would have thought."

"You wanna get in back and catch some sleep? I'll keep an eye on Claudina here."

Dragunov shook his head. "You sleep first. You need it more than I do."

"It's too bad we can't trust her to go for food," Gil said. "I'm starved."

"Don't talk about food, Vassili. Get some rest."

Gil opened the door and pushed the seat forward. Then he climbed into the back, where he quickly fell asleep.

He awoke a couple hours later, bleary eyed, to see that Dragunov was out like a light, with his head against the window. Claudina was not there.

He sat rubbing the back of his head. "Ya didn't have to put 'er in the trunk. I said I'd take watch."

Dragunov came awake, looking over the back of the seat. "What did you say?"

"I said you didn't have to put her in the trunk. I offered to take first watch."

Dragunov looked around and sat up straight. "Where did she go?"

"Fuck, Ivan! You fell asleep on watch?"

"I told you we should put her in the fucking trunk!"

"Don't blame your fuckup on me!" Gil shoved the seat forward and opened the door so he could get back into the front. "Christ, man. You'd better get us the fuck outta here. No tellin' how fuckin' long she's been gone."

"Fucking soft Americans," Dragunov grumbled, hitting the key. "That's why you lost in Vietnam. You don't have the heart for war."

Gil smirked. "I don't exactly remember a Russian victory parade in Afghanistan."

They were pulling from behind a large delivery truck when Gil spotted Claudina walking across the lot with a plastic grocery bag in each hand, her long brown hair blowing in the wind.

"No way."

Dragunov hit the brakes. "Go get her!"

"Will you calm down? She went for supplies."

"That makes no sense." Dragunov reversed the car, and the girl came around the front of the delivery truck, walking up on Gil's side of the Nissan and holding up the plastic bags. Gil got out and pushed the seat forward so she could get into the back.

Dragunov killed the motor and immediately grabbed one of the bags. It was full of food and bottles of water. The other was crammed with gauze, bandages, tape, disinfectant, and a bottle of aspirin.

Gil tossed the aspirin to Dragunov. "Swallow a handful of those." He looked at the girl and smiled. "Thank you, Claudina."

She shrugged and turned her head to look out the window.

"Why didn't she call the carabinieri?" Dragunov asked, chewing the aspirin and chasing them with a gulp of water.

"Beats me," Gil said, tearing open a package of bandages. "I guess she decided to take mercy on us."

Claudina helped Gil to dress his shoulder wound properly, and then Gil and Ivan helped each other bandage their hands. A short time later, they sat eating cold hamburgers and French fries, each man feeling much better about his physical condition.

"She's kind of pretty," Dragunov said, watching out the window and stuffing a handful of fries into his mouth. "I'm glad I decided not to put her in the trunk."

Gil bit off a mouthful of hamburger and sat chewing. "You're all heart, Ivan."

"When will you allow me to go?" Claudina asked in heavily accented English, sitting in the back with her arms crossed.

Gil and Dragunov looked at each other. This was the first real English she had spoken.

"I don't want to lose my car," she said. "The police will take it."

Dragunov laughed. "Women!" he said, shaking his head. "The same everywhere."

Gil looked over the back of the seat. "We'll let you go as soon as we can. I promise."

"I call my parents," she said. "I tell them we are south of here near Corleone. That will lead the police away, yes?"

Gil grinned. "You're a good little operator, yeah."

Dragunov swallowed the last of his hamburger and looked at him. "There is something you need to know. Federov told me your man Pope was almost assassinated today. He's in the hospital but going to be okay."

"Why didn't you say somethin' before?" Gil snapped. "How bad is he?"

"He's not too bad, I think. He was only shot once."

"Why didn't you fucking tell me?"

Dragunov shrugged. "We were in rough condition before. I didn't think bad news would be good for your morale."

Gil thought that over. "I guess I can see that."

"In the morning you are supposed to contact Pope's Japanese woman. Federov was not given a name."

"Midori," Gil said. "That means we're still in business. Hell, we might even still have satellite surveillance." He glanced into the back to see Claudina curled up on the seat. "We gotta cut her loose in the morning, Ivan. We can't risk her getting killed in a cross fire with the cops."

Dragunov sat nodding, balling up the burger wrapper and dropping it into the bag. "I know. She's a good girl."

22

PUERTO VALLARTA,
Mexico

It was midday as cartel boss Antonio Castañeda sat down across from agent Mariana Mederos at a street-side café in the tourist section of Puerto Vallarta where the local police had been told to regard Castañeda as nothing more than a harmless apparition. He had first met Mariana during the previous September, shortly after Chechen terrorists had detonated the Russian suitcase nuke in one of Castañeda's tunnels running beneath the Mexican border with New Mexico. Castañeda may have been a ruthless drug lord, but even he wasn't willing to allow the traffic of nuclear weapons on Mexican soil.

Realizing that the Chechen liaison had lied to him about the true nature of the shipment, Castañeda had him tortured, extracting all information about the remaining suitcase nuke before ordering his throat cut. The subsequent assistance that Castañeda provided to the CIA had been instrumental in averting a successful nuclear strike against the home port of the US Pacific Fleet in San Diego Bay. For this reason, both the CIA and the Mexican PFM (Policía Federal Ministerial) had since cultivated a tacit working relationship with the Castañeda cartel.

Castañeda had agreed to cease all violence against civilians and to provide any information he could regarding future Muslim terrorists attempting to operate in Mexico. In exchange, no direct action would be taken against Castañeda's person by either government. Many of his drug shipments were still being interdicted at the border, but that didn't really matter. He continued making millions, and the freedom from having to live as a fugitive more than made up for any such losses.

Castañeda looked at Mariana and smiled, his bulbous eyes protruding slightly. He said in Spanish, "It's good to see you again, Señorita Mederos. You have more curves than I remember. Your new position in Langley must be treating you well."

Mariana smiled dryly, aware that she'd gained a couple of pounds since being given her own office at headquarters along with a significant augmentation in salary. Castañeda's remark, however, caused her to instantly resolve to resume her previous exercise regimen as soon as she returned to the States.

"I have no complaints," she answered in the same language.

"Nor do I. You were shaped like a white woman before, but now you're shaped like a Latina—as you should be."

"We're not here to discuss my anatomy." Mariana was all too aware that Castañeda was a *mujeriego*—a womanizer—and a dangerous one at that.

He signaled the waiter and ordered himself a tequila on the rocks, taking the liberty to order Mariana a gin and tonic. "That is your drink, is it not?" His gaze was level, penetrating.

"A lot of people drink gin," she replied with a smile, hiding her discomfort at his knowledge of her personal tastes and wondering what else he might know.

"So," he said, satisfied to have her guessing, "why are we here? What does the CIA want from me now?"

She set a flash drive on the table. "Everything you'll need is there. We have a traitor on our hands, and he's taken refuge in Mexico City. It can't look like the US government had anything to do with his . . . expulsion."

"Su expulsión!" Castañeda said, chortling. "So now the CIA is hiring me to do their assassinations. Oh, the hypocrisy of life seems to have no limitations."

"We're not *hiring* you do anything. Your assistance in this matter is conditional upon your ongoing truce with the US government."

"And with my own government?"

"The Mexican government is to know nothing about this," she said, sitting back so the waiter could set her drink on the table, and then switching to English. "Your government asks for favors, mine asks for favors, and everyone gets along. There's plenty of precedent for such an arrangement. And you've done a good job of holding up your end: violence is down, tourism is up, and everyone's happy—so far."

He lifted his drink. *"La chingada DEA cerró uno de mis túneles la semana pasada."* The fucking DEA closed one of my tunnels last week.

She shrugged. "The truce protects you—not your tunnels and not your drugs."

He tucked the flash drive into the pocket of his black guayabera shirt. "Do you dance, Mariana?"

She smiled and shook her head. "I'm back on a plane in two hours—but I do appreciate the drink."

23

MEXICO CITY,
Mexico

Ken Peterson sat impatiently on the sofa in Tim Hagen's hotel suite while Hagen finished up with the prostitute he was shagging in the other room. A pair of Mexican security men sat on the far side of the suite playing cards and drinking Tecate beer. They were big men but not burly looking; professionals with a private Mexican firm who were licensed to carry .380 Walther PPK pistols. Larger-caliber bullets were considered military ammunition and therefore were illegal under Mexican law.

Eventually a bleached-blond Mexican girl came out of the bedroom, casting Peterson a benign look on her way to the door.

Hagen emerged a few minutes after taking a shower. "I didn't know you were here already."

"I got that impression," Peterson said. "Listen, we've got a problem."

A menacing shadow crossed Hagen's brow. "I'm getting pretty sick of hearing that, Ken."

Peterson was untouched by Hagen's displeasure. "The hit on Pope went bad. His marine driver blew Ryder's brains out."

"Fuck!" Hagen swore, causing both security men to idly turn their heads in his direction.

"At least this way Ryder can't talk," Peterson remarked.

"But we'll never get to Pope now. The president will surround him with a wall of steel. Does Pope know you sent Ryder?"

"Pope doesn't know anything about me," Peterson said, a droll grin spreading across his face. "But he was already suspicious of you."

Hagen pointed a finger. "You'd better not even *think* of throwing me under the bus! My bases are covered!"

"Which is the only reason you're still alive," Peterson thought to himself.

"Relax," he said. "It gets a little worse. The president's going to withdraw Webb's nomination. He's naming Pope director of operations."

Hagen felt suddenly nauseated, realizing it was the perfect move on the president's part.

"It's that damn Couture advising him! He knows Congress will have to approve the nomination." He ran a hand over his head, looking around as if there might be a solution to their problem somewhere in the suite. "We're fucked."

"No, not yet," Peterson said confidently. "Pope took a bullet to the lung, so he won't be able to take the helm for at least a couple of weeks, and it'll take him another month to thoroughly clean house. That gives us five or six weeks to bury what little evidence there is and generate whatever false documentation we need to cover our asses. Don't worry, there are very few direct links to either of us. We're extremely well insulated, so if the know-it-all-son-of-a-bitch comes after us, we'll go on the offensive. We could tie up the investigation in congressional hearings for years if we needed to, but I don't think the old man will let Pope push it that far. Oh—and there is your phone video, which is a very nice ace in the hole to have. Entire governments have been toppled by less."

Hagen took a chair, reaching for a snubbed-out cigar on the table and relighting it. "What about Shannon?"

"Still on the loose, but still stuck on Sicily. He killed the Malta team we sent after him—along with a couple of Italian cops—and the Italian navy has since blockaded the island, checking all fishing charters, et cetera. It looks like he must have kidnapped an Italian girl when he stole her car, because she managed to contact her parents by cell. The police are searching Corleone now, so I don't think it'll be too long before Master Chief Shannon is either dead or in custody. And if he lands in an Italian prison, we can have him killed at our leisure."

Hagen was long past believing that Gil Shannon could be cornered so easily. He felt his palms begin to sweat and subconsciously began rubbing them together. "I think it's time for me to disappear."

"Tim, you're panicking again. Running will only make you look guilty."

"How do you think I look hiding out down here?"

"Look, you're a respected diplomat around Washington." Peterson realized he needed to calm Hagen down before he did something stupid to put everyone in jeopardy. "You're independently wealthy, and you're allowed to take a vacation to Mexico whenever you want. But going completely off the grid is a bad idea."

"Okay, you're right," Hagen agreed, attempting to buck himself up. But the truth was that he was a nervous wreck with Shannon still on the loose. "Maybe I should take a trip up to DC—or to New York for a meeting with Senator Grieves."

Peterson absolutely didn't want him meeting with Steve Grieves again before the Gil Shannon issue was resolved. Grieves was too closely linked, and he didn't need those two cooking up anything behind his back.

"I think you're fine right here," he said. "Not too close, not too far away. You might look into some kind of a business deal, though. Real estate, maybe, to make it look like you're involved in something lucrative down here."

"That's a thought," Hagen said enthusiastically. "There's a hotel in Cancún looking for American investors. Wouldn't mean a lot of profit, but it would make my visit appear more legitimate . . ."

"And you know what? Screw Pope! Let him speculate all he wants. Once Shannon's dead, he'll have nothing to threaten me with. He'll be the head of the CIA, and he'll have to play by the rules like everybody else."

"Exactly," Peterson said, having intentionally failed to mention something else he'd discovered recently. Peterson's White House spy had reported to him only hours earlier that Pope was now the head of some kind of top-secret Special Mission Unit: an SMU the informant had referred to as a "presidential hit squad." Peterson doubted that Gil Shannon was this mysterious SMU's sole operator, and he doubted equally that Pope would rest until everyone who had participated in the now doomed-to-fail intelligence coup was either jailed or terminated.

With this grim reality in mind, Peterson and Senator Grieves had already agreed that Hagen should be maneuvered into a position to take the fall. Hagen did, after all, have good reason to hold a grudge against the White House, and would make the perfect patsy.

24

"Do you see us now?" Gil asked Midori over a satellite phone. It had been given to him by the Italian GRU doctor who had arrived from Rome shortly after sunrise to treat their wounds.

"I see you," she said. "You're standing next to a blue car."

Gil looked up into the crystal clear morning sky. "Yeah, that's me. Okay, so how long before Pope's out of the hospital?"

"About a week."

"He's gonna be okay?"

"Yes. He said to tell you you're still on for the Georgia operation. JSOC has approved the removal of Dokka Umarov. I'm gathering all the latest intel on him now. Also, the Joint Chiefs have arranged for your exfiltration from Sicily via submersible. An SDV team is being transferred aboard the *Ohio* now. She'll be on station within eight hours."

"Roger that. I was worried we'd been forgotten when I heard about Pope."

"You're not forgotten, Master Chief. JSOC has assumed control of this operation at Pope's request.

"Roger that. Then you'll need to advise JSOC we have to finish off Kovalenko and his team before we exfil. Ivan and I don't need those bastards dogging us to Georgia when we least expect it—hold on a second." He turned toward Dragunov, who was talking on his own phone twenty feet away. "Hey, Ivan, what's the make of that piece of shit Kovalenko's guys are in—the red one?"

"LaForza," Dragunov said.

Gil told Midori, "I need to you find a red Italian La-Forza SUV. Somewhere in or around Palermo. Start with the outskirts on the east side."

"Master Chief, you've *got* to be kidding me. That's over sixty square miles."

"I'm not kidding you even a little bit," he assured her, turning again to Dragunov. "And that other piece of shit?"

"A Peugeot."

"The red SUV will probably be parked near a black Peugeot."

"A search like that could take days."

"I can give you a few hours," Gil said, "but that's all. We're running out of time down here. There's cops all over the place. Use the vehicle recognition software the Pentagon uses for spotting military vehicles. The computer will light up every LaForza on the grid within a few minutes. After that, all you gotta do is sort through the red ones."

"The shapes of military vehicles are a lot more defined than civilian models, Master Chief."

"Then enhance the resolution, Midori. I gotta swim over there and do your job for you?"

"Hey, all I'm saying is that I haven't used the software in that application before. I don't know what kind of results I'm going to get."

"Well, I'm telling you if you max out the res, you'll find the SUV."

"I'll get on it," she said. "Why is your hand bandaged?"

Gil looked at his hand and glanced up. "I got shot. I'm signing off now. I'll check back in an hour." He put away the phone and turned to see Dragunov grinning at him. "What's your problem?"

"Maybe we need a Russian satellite to do the search?"

"I don't think Sputnik's up to the task. You'll get your chance to impress me when we get to Georgia."

Dragunov laughed, gesturing at the girl. "Claudina wants to take her car and go."

Gil looked at her. "We still need your car, but you can—"

"Then I go with you." She crossed her arms in a fashion they were growing accustomed to.

He looked at her. "If the police catch up to us, there's going to be shooting, and people are going to die. Do you understand that?"

"The car is mine," she insisted.

Gil looked at Dragunov. "We gotta steal another set of wheels."

Dragunov shook his head. "Stealing another car is a big risk for us. This is a good place to hide until your people can find Kovalenko. Then we go and kill him, and we let her"—he pointed at Claudina—"take her chances."

25

ROME,
Italy

Fresh off the plane from Athens, agent Max Steiner showed up at the CIA safe house in Rome for a meeting with Chief of Station Ben Walton. They had served together in the Med with US Naval Intelligence during the latter part of the Cold War, and Steiner had been the CIA's go-to man in Greece for the past seven years.

"So what's going on?" Steiner asked. He was in his midforties, very tanned by the Grecian sun, and with thinning dark hair. "I got an operational immediate pulling me out of my province and sending me here. I don't even speak Italian."

Walton was a thick, barrel-chested man in his early fifties with a deep voice and close-cropped gray hair. "I sent the OI," he said. "A rogue element of the GRU hit the *Palinouros* and greased her entire crew—including Miller. The Italian navy is all over it."

"A *rogue element*?" Steiner's confusion was evident. "You're talking about Kovalenko's people—*our* people?"

"That's right."

"What the hell they do that for?"

"They're tying up loose ends," Walton said. "Yeshevsky's dead in Paris; so is Lerher. The entire op is blown."

Walton and Steiner had both helped to dupe Pope by falsely identifying Yeshevsky as the real Dokka Umarov during his voyage across the Mediterranean.

"Sounds like the nutty professor Pope went on the warpath."

"He did," Walton said. "And somebody just tried to kill his ass back in DC, but the hit went bad, and he survived. Now the president's naming him as director, and that can only mean one thing."

Steiner's tan complexion turned white. "Hell, they're on to us. It may even have been Pope's people who wiped out the *Palinouros*."

"Not likely." Walton turned to pour from a pot of coffee. "My GRU contacts here in the city tell me it was Kovalenko's men. I just got off the phone with the Maltese chief of station about ten minutes before you got here, and he said he was ordered by our people back home to hit Gil Shannon in Messina. And *that* operation fell flat on its face, too."

"Shannon got away *twice*?"

Walton nodded. "He's a slippery fucker."

Steiner took a chair, massaging his temples. "This isn't good, old buddy. If Shannon's operating in the Med, then he knows about us—he has to—and that means he knows who set him up in Paris. Does Pope know about the plot to sabotage the pipeline?"

"I think we have to assume so." Walton pushed a cup

of coffee across the table. "But if we're blown—or even just under suspicion—why haven't we been recalled to Mannheim for debrief?" Mannheim, Germany, was the location of the United States's military holding facility in Europe.

"Shit, that's obvious, old buddy. We've been disavowed."

Walton shook his head. "It's only forty-eight hours since the Paris op went bad. That's not time enough for all the facts to filter up. I'm thinking Peterson put the contract on Pope to prevent him consulting the president."

"But he fucked up," Steiner said. "It's only a matter of time before we're either recalled or disavowed." He got back to his feet, ignoring the steaming cup of coffee. "Look, it's obvious we backed the wrong horse. Senator Grieves's little intel coup isn't going to happen. The president pulled an end around and named Pope as director—which none of us saw coming. So the wishy-washy young Webb doesn't matter anymore. Pope's an entirely different animal. His nomination will absolutely be approved, and that bastard's gonna run the Langley guillotine day and night until he's cleaned out the entire agency."

Walton sipped calmly from his coffee, peering over the rim of the cup. "So what are you saying?"

Steiner smirked. "I'm saying it's time we sold our secrets to the Arab Emirates and got ourselves a change of venue, old buddy. A couple of million for what we know about the CIA is more than reasonable, and I don't know about you, but I can live just fine on a million bucks."

Walton sipped again. "You haven't touched your coffee."

Steiner picked up the cup, obligingly taking a sip. He retched instantly, dropping the cup and stumbling back against the counter, his face contorting horribly as he grabbed his throat, just managing to croak out "You fuck—!" before crashing to the floor, dead of cyanide poisoning.

Walton stepped over and stood looking down at the body, an ugly white drool oozing from the corner of Steiner's mouth. "Sorry, *old buddy*, but two million goes twice as far as one, and I've put in too much time to spend my retirement living beneath my means."

He went into the operations room and picked up a secure line, dialing a stateside telephone number from memory.

"Senator Steve Grieves's office," answered a young woman's voice.

"This is Ben Walton. Put the senator on the phone."

"Just a moment, sir."

The senator came on the line a minute later, saying, "I hope you're calling from a secure line."

"Secure as they come," Walton said. "Is it true what I heard about Pope? That he's going to be named director?"

Grieves replied, "I guess bad news does travel fast."

"Have you been in contact with Peterson?"

"Peterson knows better than to call me directly—as do you."

"I've called to tell you that I'm out," Walton said. "Don't bother looking for me. You won't find me. From here on, I think we should agree to keep each other's secrets and leave it at that. What do you say, Senator?"

There was a slight pause at Grieves's end. "I thought you'd want money."

"I'm covered for cash," Walton said. "Besides, this was never about money. It was about keeping the agency out of the hands of men like Webb and Pope. We tried, and we failed. That's just how it goes."

"What about Miller and Steiner?"

"Both dead. Miller was killed in the Med by the GRU, and I just found Steiner's body here in Rome. Looks like cyanide. It could've been anybody. That's why I'm getting out now—*today*—before it happens to me."

"What about Peterson?" Grieves asked. "Can I trust him?"

Walton chuckled. "You can trust Ken Peterson about as far as you can throw him, but I wouldn't worry too much. He's extremely good at keeping his ass covered, which means yours is probably covered too. Besides, people don't assassinate senators. It doesn't look good on CNN."

"Well, I guess this is good-bye and good luck then, Ben. You're right. We tried."

"One more thing before I go," Walton said. "If Peterson asks you for help with Gil Shannon, I seriously suggest you give him whatever he asks for."

26

NORTH OSSETIA,
Russia

Dokka Umarov sat around a smoky daytime campfire in a mountain forest, meeting with a group of commanders from the unrecognized Islamist Chechen Republic of Ichkeria. Even though the forty-nine-year-old Islamist militant enjoyed a certain amount of protection from "corporate" elements within the Russian government, he was careful never to remain in one place for very long. The Tenth Independent Spetsnaz Brigade of the Russian army wanted him dead, and it would stop at very little to take him out if it ever succeeded in nailing down his exact location long enough to coordinate an attack.

As the self-proclaimed emir of the unrecognized Caucasus Emirate, he was known to his Chechen supporters by his Arabized name: Dokka Abu Usman. To the Russian people, however, he was better known as "Russia's Bin Laden," owing to his many terrorist attacks against Russian civilians and Russian military targets. In 2014 he had even vowed to prevent the Sochi Olympic Games through acts of terror—an unrealized threat that was later regarded by many as a feeble attempt to draw additional Islamist militants to his cause.

Since then, he and his commanders had devised a more feasible strategy. They would blow up three separate pumping stations along the Georgian stretch of the Baku-Tbilisi-Ceyhan pipeline, a bold plan with three primary objectives:

Disabling the BTC would immediately disrupt Western economies by driving oil prices even higher than they already were. In addition, it would set the United States and Russian governments immediately at odds. For it was no secret that Russia was distressed by the fact that Western powers were enjoying unfettered access to oil fields beneath the Caspian Sea, and this was at least a partial reason for its 2008 invasion of Georgia via the Roki Tunnel, a three-thousand-yard underpass running beneath the North Caucasus Mountains. The third and most important objective of sabotaging the pipeline was to inspire an authentic insurgency, finally uniting Chechen Islamists under a single banner within the region.

Umarov had recently learned from his coconspirators inside the GRU—corporate men who desired renewed friction between Russia and the United States in order generate more military spending—that Spetsnaz operator Andrei Yeshevsky had been killed in Paris by the now-infamous Gil Shannon. Umarov knew of Shannon as the elite American sniper who had somehow managed to survive a coordinated Chechen–Al Qaeda attack on his Montana home the previous summer.

"What does this mean for us, Dokka?" asked Umarov's second in command, Anzor Basayev. "Will we have Spetsnaz support if Kovalenko and his men are dead as well?"

"Kovalenko is still alive." Umarov was Caucasian, light skinned with a long, deep beard. He always dressed in camouflage, much the way Bin Laden had chosen to dress, though Umarov was not an Arab and therefore never wore a turban.

"He'd better be," said one of the Ichkeria commanders. "We're going to need Spetsnaz operators. Our own men don't have the necessary training to infiltrate the pumping stations."

Unconcerned, Umarov drew patiently from a Russian cigarette, saying, "There are plenty of Zapad men available if we need them."

The Special Battalion Zapad of western Chechnya was the sister battalion to the vaunted Chechen Vostok Battalion of Eastern Chechnya, which had been sent to the Crimean Peninsula in the aftermath of the Ukrainian Revolution in February 2014. Both battalions were Spetsnaz, and both were composed of ethnic Chechens, but the Zapad Battalion had recently been disbanded, with many of its operators "released" from the Russian army due to concerns over their loyalty to the Russian Federation. A large number of these former Spetsnaz men had since become like Japanese *ronin*: disavowed mercenaries, guns for hire.

"I don't like the idea of using mercenaries," remarked another, lighting a cigarette of his own with a smoldering stick from the campfire. "They're expensive, and it's impossible to know where their loyalties lie. With Yeshevsky dead, Kovalenko's the only man left with personal knowledge of the pumping stations."

Umarov was accustomed to these common equivocations. Prevarication was the reason the Caucasus needed a single, undisputed leader, and a successful attack on the pipeline would bring him the requisite credibility and power. He almost had it now, but without an authentic insurgency, his troop numbers would remain too few. This was the most tragic aspect of the recent debacle in Paris. Umarov needed the Al Qaeda support that Yeshevsky had been sent there to negotiate for, and it would be months before another conference could be arranged.

In the meantime, the trick was to prevent his commanders from sensing his desperation. "I wouldn't worry too much about their loyalty," he said casually. "The Russian army has already turned them out. Who else are they going to fight for?"

"They should fight for Allah, not for money," said Umarov's nephew Lom. His name meant "lion." He was a hard-minded, spirited Muslim at the age of twenty-eight with dark hair and eyes, his beard closely trimmed. A solid unit leader and tactician, he possessed nearly ten years of combat experience against the Russian army.

Umarov drew from the cigarette, eyeing his half sister's youngest son, still in the process of determining the young man's value as a counselor. "Is Allah personally putting food on your table, nephew? If he is, then you are the only man I know to be blessed in this manner. A soldier of Allah needs to feed himself, to feed his family, to put a roof over their heads. Allah provides the means for this, but He does not choose the method. *War* is the means, and it is our duty to employ whatever method of making that war we can. Whether the Zapad men know it or not, they *will* fight for Allah. I remind you again that nothing happens which is not His doing."

Without rebuttal, Lom deferentially lowered his gaze to the fire, his calloused hands gripping the barrel of the AK-47 propped between his knees.

One by one, Umarov looked the rest of his commanders in the eye, allowing each man to feel the weight of his will. Then, sensing no significant disagreement, he smiled and remarked, "That being said, I sometimes wouldn't mind if Allah chose to move a little faster in our favor."

The men laughed dutifully, passing cigarettes to lighten the mood further. Then the sky began to shudder with the sudden roar of multiple turboshaft, rotary-winged aircraft.

"Crocodiles!" one of the security men shouted, and everyone sprang to their feet. The security detail grabbed up their PKM light machine guns and RPG-7s, scrambling to take up firing positions among the rocks and hardwoods.

Lom slung his AK-47, ducking into a nearby cave to reemerge with an Igla-S MANPADS (man-portable air-defense system). The Igla was a shoulder-fired, 72 mm antiaircraft missile with an effective range of twenty thousand feet, and it was the only one in camp.

"Do not miss!" shouted Umarov.

Lom gave his uncle a menacing grin and scrambled off up the craggy slope toward the summit, where there would be no trees to hinder his shot.

Three giant Russian Mi-24 "Hind" helicopter gunships roared over the camp in a tight V formation, their crocodile camouflage schemes and sky blue underbellies clearly visible through the bare tree limbs.

"One of them is a PN," Basayev observed as the helos flew on out of sight. He was referring to the latest and deadliest night-attack variant of the heavily armed aircraft. He looked at Umarov. "We're betrayed, Dokka. Your friends in the GRU have turned their backs on us."

"No." Umarov shook his head, tossing the cigarette into the fire. "The Tenth ISB has reconnaissance units operating in this region. We must have been observed over the past couple of days." He stalked off through the trees, where his forty fighters were rapidly digging in, calling out to them: "We're in for a fight! Spetsnaz will be hitting the ground to the west, but they won't attack until the crocodiles have returned to soften us up with rockets and cannon fire. Do not waste your RPGs on moving aircraft—but if one should be foolish enough to hover, hit it in the tail or high in the fuselage near the engine!"

Often referred to as a "flying tank" by Russian pilots, the Mi-24 was the most heavily armored helicopter in the world, its flight crew shielded within a titanium "bathtub" strong enough to protect them from 37 mm cannon shells. By design, the Hind—as it was referred to among NATO forces—could transport eight Spetsnaz troops in addition to its heavy load of ordinance, which included but was not limited to a 12.7 mm Yak-B minigun in a chin turret, up to four unguided free-fall bombs, and forty 80 mm rockets mounted on the helicopter's stub wings.

Four hundred meters to the west, the flight of three Hinds touched down in the tall grass near a shallow river just long enough to off-load twenty-four heavily armed Spetsnaz operators of the Tenth Independent Spetsnaz Brigade. The great birds of prey then lifted back into the air, resumed formation, and flew off again to begin their attack run on Umarov's camp.

Captain Smirnov, piloting the hi-tech Mi-24PN, was the flight leader at the point of the V. His aircraft carried a load-out of four five-hundred-pound iron bombs and a double-barreled 30 mm GSh-30k auto-cannon pod-mounted to the right of the cockpit. His job was to shock and devastate the enemy by dropping the five-hundred-pounders right in their midst. He would then provide support with the 30 mm auto-cannon while his wingmen, flying Mi-24Ds, hammered whatever remained of the encampment. Each 24D was loaded out with a Yak-B mini-gun and a pair of 80 mm rocket pods of twenty rockets each.

After the helos had expended the bulk of their ordnance, the Spetsnaz men would move in and mop up any survivors, their chief responsibility being the retrieval of Dokka Umarov's remains.

Smirnov spoke to his wingmen over the radio: "Keep it tight on approach. By now, they know we've off-loaded ground troops, so we'll make it look like we're leaving. No firing until after my bombs have hit. Then break right and left. We'll stand off at three different points and pound them to dust. Stay alert for RPGs and be ready to take evasive action."

LOM CROUCHED LOW on the rocky outcrop that overlooked the encampment below, watching the Hinds rise up from the valley floor to the west and come rumbling back in his direction. The bright sun glinted off their bubbled canopies, each deadly machine bristling with weaponry. His target was obvious: the shiny new Mi-24PN at the point of the formation, its load of four five-hundred-pound bombs evident even at four hundred meters. He would have to knock the machine from the sky before it could overfly the encampment; otherwise his compatriots below would be devastated.

Though the Hind was already within range, Lom knew it was equipped with improved countermeasures, so he decided to wait until the last possible second. He would be firing from a position about one hundred feet below the flight of helos as they approached from his right, and the missile would home in on the infrared heat signature of the Hind's twin turboshaft engines. The Mi-24PN had a cooler heat signature than the 24Ds, however, and Lom didn't want the missile locking onto either of the older aircraft.

He'd shot down an Mi-24D the year before, killing ten Russian soldiers, but he'd used an older MANPADS to do it—a Strela-3—so he could rely on previous experience only to a point. Living in the mountains and fighting with black-market weaponry made it difficult to stay in step with rapidly emerging technologies.

THROUGH HIS FLIR (forward-looking infrared) targeting system Smirnov could see the images of the Chechens hurriedly preparing their fighting positions among the trees and the rocks as he swept toward the target area. He chuckled over the net to his copilot, "Like shooting fish in a barrel. Five seconds . . ."

Then he heard the dreaded warning buzzer, and the instrument panel lit up with red lights flashing in the Cyrillic alphabet: РАКЕТЫ ВОЗДУХ=ЗЕМЛЯ. Surface-to-air missile.

He cut a startled glance out the left side of his canopy, just managing to glimpse the vapor trail of the missile streaking upward toward him at 1,300 miles per hour.

Detonating an instant before impact, the warhead's directed-energy fragmentation blast utterly devastated the engine compartment of the Hind, severing three of five control rods to throw the rotor completely out of balance, causing it to cant backward and slice off the aircraft's tail. The helo exploded midair, falling out of the sky along with its bomb load nearly a hundred yards shy of the enemy encampment, erupting against the forest floor in a giant secondary explosion that shook the earth for a quarter mile in every direction.

27

NORTH OSSETIA,
Russia

Major Nikita Yakunin heard and felt the explosion as he and his men were entering the forest. The Spetsnaz men immediately took cover, watching the sky as the two remaining Hinds broke north and south away from the target area just over three hundred meters ahead.

"Find out what the hell happened!" Yakunin ordered his RTO (radio telephone operator). Then he ordered three men forward to take up point across the line of advance, adding, "Keep your eyes open!"

The Hinds circled back around to engage the encampment from a safer distance.

"Where the hell are they?" demanded Yakunin, unable to see either helo. "It sounds like they're firing from Moscow!"

"They're standing off," reported the RTO. "Smirnov was shot down with a missile."

Yakunin's intel reports had said nothing about Umarov's men possessing MANPADS.

"A missile or an RPG?"

"A missile! The pilots are afraid to get any closer, and their rockets are impacting in the trees. They don't have a clear shot on the camp."

"Tell them to fly higher!" Yakunin ordered.

The RTO relayed the order. "They say they'll be vulnerable to missile attack if the enemy has line of sight. Their orders are not to directly engage in the presence of a missile threat."

"What fucking use is an attack helicopter if can't be used to attack?"

The RTO shrugged. "Do you want me to ask them that?"

Yakunin glared at him and then ordered his men to form up in three columns of eight.

"You tell those cowards in the sky to keep the enemy pinned down as we advance!"

The RTO immediately relayed the command.

UMAROV TOLD BASAYEV to get on the radio to their friends camped to the east. "Tell them we need reinforcements," he said calmly, with Russian rockets exploding in the treetops. Debris showered down on the encampment, but so far no one was hit.

Basayev ducked into the cave to grab the radio, and Umarov rallied five men.

"See that crocodile?" He pointed south through the treetops at the Hind, where the land sloped gradually away from the encampment. "He's holding his position— firing sporadically to keep our heads down. That means the Spetsnaz are advancing! The five of you take RPGs and run through the forest to get beneath him. You will fire at the same time: to his left, right, rear, and front!" He pointed his finger, singling out one of the men. "*You* will fire straight up the middle! He'll be completely bracketed, with nowhere to maneuver. Now run! Bring him down!"

The Chechen fighters slung their AK-47s and took off through the trees to the south, each with an RPG-7 over his shoulder.

Lom appeared at Umarov's side. "Where do you want me, Uncle?"

Umarov put a hand on his shoulder and grinned. "Great shot! You saved us."

Lom shrugged, knowing the value of humility in combat. "He practically flew right into it. Where do you want me?"

"I want you to run east as fast as you can," Umarov said. "Take the old *koza* trail. Find Prina's people and lead them back here."

"Why don't we all escape that way?"

Umarov shook his head. "We can't fight a running battle against Spetsnaz and crocodiles. We'll be destroyed. This is a good position. We'll make our stand here and let them batter themselves bloody. Now, run. Run as fast as you can."

Lom darted off through the trees, adrenaline coursing through his veins.

Umarov called for three more men with RPGs.

The first five grenadiers scrambled through the trees with their RPGs, the *ripping* sound of the helo's Yak minigun cutting through the air, and its red tracers snapping the limbs of the hardwoods high above them as it fired on the camp from an oblique angle. They were arriving at their optimal firing position when the pilot spotted them and canted the aircraft in their direction, letting loose a torrent of machine-gun fire and rockets.

One of the grenadiers was hit in the torso with a burst of 12.7 mm fire and virtually exploded in a splash of blood and guts. Without missing a step, the grenadier behind him snatched the fallen RPG from the ground and continued on. An 80 mm rocket detonated against the ground directly in front of him and blew off his legs.

The remaining men stopped abruptly to take up firing positions. The leader called out three separate firing points, and they fired simultaneously, bracketing the Hind as best they could from the left, right, and dead-on.

The pilot saw the rockets streaking toward his aircraft and knew his best chance was to yank back on the stick and show his titanium underbelly. All three rockets missed, and he canted the nose forward again to let loose another hellish torrent of machine-gun fire. With the crew's attention focused on killing the remaining Chechens, neither man spotted the second team of grenadiers that Umarov had sent southeast to flank the helo once it had engaged the sacrificial first team.

The three men fired in unison, and all three RPGs detonated against the starboard side of the aircraft, which broke apart in the air, exploding in an orange-black fireball and crashing in pieces to the forest floor.

YAKUNIN HEARD THE second explosion and swore a blue streak, realizing there would be very little to keep the enemy from escaping eastward once the last remaining Hind ran out of ammo. "That bastard Umarov has more luck than anyone I've ever heard of!"

He ordered his men to double-time it the last two hundred meters, fearing his prey might already be fleeing.

When they arrived at the perimeter of the Chechen encampment, they were met with a hail of machine-gun fire. The RTO was hit in the face and went down, his mandible and teeth shot completely away, leaving his tongue dangling from the open neck. The wound was survivable, but the man would never speak, eat, or look like a human being again.

Yakunin shot him through the head with his AK-105 carbine and ordered one of the others to take over the radio.

Without being told, the Spetsnaz broke into groups of three, leapfrogging aggressively through rocks and trees with AN-94 assault rifles in 5.45 mm. They took hits, and one man went down, but they were heavily armored and determined to kill Umarov before he escaped again. Half the AN-94s were fitted with GP-34 40 mm grenade launchers (similar to the American M203) mounted below the barrel. They fired a veritable hail of 40 mm grenades into the Chechen encampment.

Dirt and rock and splintered trees flew in every direction as Umarov's men were forced flat to the ground under the heavy barrage. The Chechens had used their entire supply of RPGs bringing down the second Hind, and seven more men were killed quickly. The remaining helo began to engage from the rear. Rockets exploded near the encampment, and the Yak minigun began finding targets.

The Russians had the Chechens blocked east and west, and the rocky slope mitigated any hope of fleeing to the north. The only avenue of escape was to the south toward the open country. But there they would surely be caught out and killed by the Hind, even if they managed to outrun the Spetsnaz, which was unlikely.

Basayev appeared at Umarov's side with the radio telephone unit. "They're coming!" he shouted over the din. "Prina's men are close enough to hear the shooting. Can we hold for ten more minutes?"

Umarov peered up through the trees, looking for the Hind. He could still hear the machine, but it seemed to have circled south, probably attempting to cover both escape routes.

"Fall back!" he shouted to his men, hating the order but knowing there was no other hope except to link up with Prina's men, who would have the RPGs needed to even the odds against the Spetsnaz and keep the aircraft at bay.

Four men volunteered to stay behind and cover the retreat, knowing it meant their deaths.

Umarov smiled at them. "Allah be with you!" He then fell back through the forest with the remainder of his force: fifteen men out of the original forty-five.

THE SECOND THE return fire began to trail off, Yakunin knew that the Chechens were retreating. "Move forward! They've broken!"

The Spetsnaz maneuvered directly into the Chechen encampment, maintaining fire superiority and moving from cover to cover. A light machine gun cut loose from between two boulders, its 7.62 mm fire cutting apart two men from less than fifty feet away. The position was reduced immediately by a barrage of 40 mm grenades, and the Spetsnaz swept past.

"It's a defense in depth!" Yakunin called out. "Take care!" He slowed their advance, knowing that a running fight could be twice as dangerous.

"Grenades!" Everyone hit the dirt as four black orbs landed in their midst.

The grenades exploded at the same time, each RGD-5 packed with four ounces of TNT. Bodies were lifted into the air, and Yakunin felt hot shrapnel bite into one of his legs.

Two more grenades rained down from an unseen position, exploding among the Spetsnaz, and Yakunin ordered his people to fall back. "Find that filthy son of a whore!" he screamed.

As if to oblige, the Chechen jumped from behind a tree eighty feet away with an AK-47, firing and hitting the major on the breastplate of his body armor.

Yakunin was knocked back by the force of the bullets, which failed to penetrate, though one did tear off most of his left ear.

The Chechen was gunned down an instant later.

"Find Umarov's body!" Yakunin swiped at the side of his head with a gloved hand to see the glove covered in blood.

The medic arrived at his side. "The ear's gone, Major. I'll dress the wound."

"Later!" Yakunin shouldered past. "Find Umarov!"

The Spetsnaz fanned out to examine the bodies, all of them well acquainted with Umarov's face. Each body was knifed in the throat to make sure it was dead.

One of bodies leapt to its feet as a Spetsnaz corporal reached to turn it over. The Chechen shot the corporal in the groin with a pistol, and the corporal dropped to his knees, pressing the trigger mechanism on a spring-loaded ballistic knife. The steel blade struck the Chechen in the chest, partially severing the aorta. Both men were on the ground bleeding out when a sergeant bound forward and shot them both.

"Major!" the sergeant called. "Dokka Umarov is not here!"

"After him!" The sudden *ripping* sound of the Yak minigun to the east told them the Hind had reacquired the retreating Chechens. "Now we've got his ass!"

28

SICILY

Gil lay prone in the brush on a bluff overlooking the goat farm three hundred yards below. Peering through the scope of the G28 sniper rifle, he could clearly make out the red LaForza and the black Peugeot, both parked behind the house with Kovalenko's car, where they could not be seen from the country road.

"It's them, all right," Gil said, moving aside for Dragunov to have a look. "Midori got it on the first try."

Dragunov watched as one of Kovalenko's men stepped out the backdoor of the house, smoking a cigarette. "Demetri," he muttered, recognizing the Chechen Spetsnaz man. "*Mudak!*" Jacket!

Gil saw him fingering the trigger. "Ease off, Ivan. We only got twenty rounds. I don't want you wasting my ammo."

Dragunov moved aside with a smirk. "I can shoot as well as you."

"I know," Gil said, getting back behind the rifle and pulling the stock into his shoulder. "You can probably fuck as good as me too, but this ain't fantasyland."

Dragunov chuckled. "Do you think Claudina will still be there with the car when we get back?"

They had left Claudina with her car a half mile up the road, and she had promised to wait, but Gil didn't expect to see her ever again. "Not even thinkin' about it," he said, dialing in the scope. "Why? You in love?"

Dragunov chuckled again. "Fuck you, American. I just don't feel like walking all the way to San Vito to meet your pussy SEAL team friends."

Gil smiled, placing the reticle on the head of the man Dragunov had referred to as Demetri. "We'll take Kovalenko's wheels. How's that sound?" He squeezed the trigger and blew off most of Demetri's head from the nose up. The body dropped beside the stone house, and Gil saw a puff of dust as the .308 ricocheted off the wall. "And down went McGinty."

Dragunov hunkered in. "Who's McGinty?"

"A drowned Irishman. Look sharp now. Those other pricks may have heard the round hit the house."

They waited more than five minutes before another Chechen came out. He spotted the body near the far end of the house and turned to duck back inside, but Gil squeezed the trigger again, scoring a second head-shot that blew the Chechen's brains into the house through the window of the backdoor. The body crashed to the floor half in and half out of the house.

"That'll kindly spoil a man's dinner plans."

"You should have let me identify him," Dragunov said. "If it was Kovalenko, we could have gotten the hell out of here."

"It was that bald prick who shot me in the fuckin' hand back in Messina."

"Anton," Dragunov growled. "Another *sukin syn*."

"Well, he's a dead *sukin syn* now." Gil pulled back a little farther into the brush. "We gotta be real careful from here on. If Kovalenko knows his shit, he'll roost in that upstairs window."

"Can you see inside?"

"Not as well as I'd like," Gil admitted.

"Then he won't roost there—not if there's any chance you can see in. He'll move out the front to hunt us on the ground."

"Then you'd better get Midori back on the phone. Tell her to watch if anyone comes out."

Dragunov had Midori on the satellite phone a minute later, explaining the situation.

The bluff was high enough for Gil to see beyond the house but still low enough that the leeward defilade stretched for a hundred feet or more. The best thing Gil and Dragunov had going for them was that there was no way for Kovalenko or his men to reach any of the vehicles without falling under the gun.

"He may wait until night," Dragunov remarked.

"Only if he's a damn fool. For all he knows, we've called for backup."

"He's as patient as a snake."

"Yeah, well, so am I," Gil said. "And we've got the fucker boxed in. I can send you for pizza and beer if comes to that. Meanwhile, they're stuck in there."

"A beer sounds good," Dragunov said. "I'll be back to check on you later."

"Just don't come back drunk," Gil said with a grin.

"Last thing I need is a drunk Russian stumblin' around in the weeds to give away my position."

"Fuck it, then," Dragunov said. "We'll drink after."

"You're buyin'."

KOVALENKO HAD THE AWS rifle set up across the kitchen table on its bipod, scanning the terrain beyond the farm, but the glare of the sun on the kitchen window made it difficult to see with much detail.

"They have to be up there on the bluff," he muttered.

"How in hell did they find us?" Vitsin wondered aloud. "There's no way they could have followed us—none."

"Satellite." Kovalenko's eye was still to the scope. "You came in a red car, remember?"

Vitsin suddenly felt very stupid for not having told Tapa—the team's car thief—to steal something else. "Do you think that's how?"

"That's the American out there," Kovalenko said, half to himself. "The damn Americans have everything. He probably had satellite surveillance in Paris too. Those fools we relied upon in the CIA are worthless. If we hadn't needed their help planning the pipeline operation . . ."

He shook his head. "They fucked us somehow, but it doesn't matter now. Lie down with a whore, you get what you pay for."

"Maybe we could run for the cars," Vitsin suggested. "Could he get all five of us?"

"We'd be dead before anyone could even turn a key." Kovalenko wiped a bead of sweat from his brow, glancing down at Anton, who still lay half in, half out of the house, his head blown apart like a ripe watermelon. "The American has a rifle, which means his people are supplying him. And that means we don't have all day and night."

"For all we know," said one of the others, a veteran named Zargan, "there could be an entire Spetsnaz team out there waiting to hit us when it gets dark. We should barricade the house."

"Make the necessary preparations," Kovalenko ordered. "And someone drag Robert inside so we can close the door." Then an idea occurred to him. "Tapa, go upstairs to the bedroom and get the blanket from the bed to wrap the body."

Tapa went up the stairs, and Kovalenko put his eye back to the scope.

Zargan used the poker from the fireplace to hook Anton's belt and drag him the rest of the way inside. Vitsin kicked the door closed.

Tapa stepped into the bedroom, grabbing the wool blanket from the bed. A window pane shattered, and he was thrown against the wall with the force of mule kick, the ball of his shoulder joint shot completely away.

Kovalenko spotted the small dust cloud kicked up by Gil's shot, shifted his aim a fraction of a degree and fired.

When Gil saw Tapa's dim figure in the upstairs window, he squeezed the trigger and rolled immediately to his left, knowing that Kovalenko or someone else might be scanning the bluff. An instant later, a round cut through the air exactly where Gil's head had been, close enough for him to feel the energy of the bullet as it passed. Both he and Dragunov pulled quickly back out of sight.

"That fucker's fast!"

"I told you," Dragunov said. "He's been shooting since he was a child."

"That was *too* fast! He sacrificed that guy to draw me out."

Dragunov's face was grim. "That's why he's called the Wolf. Kovalenko is willing to do whatever it takes to win."

Gil sat back on his haunches, holding the sat phone in the crook of his neck and lighting a cigarette as he spoke with Midori. "Keep an eye on things," he told her. "We're eyes off target for the moment."

"Nothing's happening," she said. "Are you hit again?"

"No." He drew from the cigarette to settle his nerves. "But that bastard's almost killed me three times now. I'd like to get just one shot at him."

Dragunov reached for Gil's smokes. "Maybe if you had waited," he said under his breath.

"Hey, smoke your own," Gil told him.

Dragunov gave him the finger and shook a cigarette from the pack, lighting it with a wooden match and lying back in the dry grass to stare up at the sky. "We're going to have to fight them in the dark again. I hate fighting in the fucking dark."

29

WASHINGTON, DC

General Couture was in the White House kitchen drinking coffee and chatting with the French chef, who was making him an early breakfast, when the White House chief of staff came looking for him.

"I heard I might find you in here," Brooks said with a smile.

Couture shook his hand. "I learned as a second lieutenant to make friends in the kitchen." He gave the chef a wink. "Whattaya got?"

Brooks hesitated, glancing at the chef, who stood over the stove sautéing a pan of mushrooms.

"Don't worry about old Jacques," Couture said, patting the chef on the shoulder. "He's on our side. What's up?"

"The SDV team's been transferred aboard the *Ohio*," Brooks said. "She'll be on station off the point of San Vito Lo Capo within the hour, ready to bring Shannon and Dragunov aboard."

"Comms?"

"They have a sat phone. It's less than ideal, but it's going to have to do. As we speak, they've got Kovalenko cornered in a house outside of Palermo. Pope's technician says it's still touch and go."

"Sicilian authorities?"

"Still searching for them to the south in Corleone." Brooks shrugged. "Don't ask me why."

Couture answered with a shrug of his own. "Small mercies." He took a drink from his coffee. "Latest intel out of Georgia says the Spetsnaz are moving against Umarov, so with any luck, Shannon won't have to go to Georgia."

"Speaking of Georgia, the president is wondering whether to call a meeting with British Petroleum. He thinks maybe we should brief them on the pipeline plot. Thoughts?"

Couture shook his head, leading Brooks away from the stove and out of earshot from the chef. "Fuck BP. It's not even an American corporation. We're not letting that camel's nose back under our tent. If the pipeline gets hit, they can learn about it in the news like everybody else. All they have to hear is a whisper about trouble along that pipeline, and they'll have their Obsidian mercenaries tear-assing all over southern Georgia—doing God *knows* what—and the last thing we need is a bunch of corporate warriors getting in the way if Shannon ends up in-country."

"Okay. So how should I put that to the president?"

"Just like that," Couture said evenly. "You don't have to sugarcoat shit with him anymore. He gets it now. That fucking idiot Hagen is out, and you're in. No more dog and pony show."

"About Hagen . . ." Brooks lowered his voice even more. "I've just been given reason to believe that Pope may have something *clandestine* in mind for him."

Couture took another drink of coffee, locking eyes. "Glen, do you know how many men I've lost under my direct command during my long and storied career?"

Brooks shook his head.

"Six hundred forty-three men and women," Couture said. "That's not counting the suicides among those who made it home. Tim Hagen's no better than any of them, and if Pope's got something *clandestine* in mind for him, then I'm guessing he's earned it—in spades."

"Okay. Suppose I had direct information—proof?"

"Do you?"

Brooks thought it over and then let out a sigh. "I don't know. Not for sure."

"Then look at this way," Couture said. "If not for Pope, we'd have lost two supercarriers and a huge chunk of the Pacific Fleet to that nuke last summer—not to mention half a million lives or more. Now, I know you've never met Hagen personally, but I know the little prick as well as anybody, and I wouldn't piss in his mouth if his teeth were on fire."

Brooks grinned. "Senator Grieves speaks rather highly of him."

Couture's scarred face turned to stone. "Senator Grieves would. Leave Hagen to Pope—that's my recommendation."

30

NORTH OSSETIA,
Russia

Yakunin and his Spetsnaz were in hot pursuit of Dokka Umarov and his men, charging through the forest in a running battle against a stubborn Chechen rearguard action designed to buy time for Umarov's escape. The staccato of automatic-weapons fire was constant, interspersed with exploding 40 mm grenades and the occasional burst of fire from the supporting Hind helicopter, which by now was running low on ammo.

Yakunin drove his men hard, determined to see the end of Dokka Umarov. He estimated that they had burned through half their ammunition, but he was confident they would soon finish off the middling force of Chechens.

All of his instincts were proven dead wrong, however, the second he and his men ran head-on into the defensive line set up by Prina Basayev and his Chechen force from the east.

A barrage of RPG-7s streaked across the forest, detonating among Yakunin and his Spetsnaz. Bodies flew into the air, were hurled into trees, blew apart. Fifteen men were obliterated in the blink of an eye, and the remaining few were quickly picked off.

Yakunin landed on his belly, bleeding from multiple wounds. He felt broken inside, reaching for his carbine only to find that his right arm was missing from the elbow down. The firing died off, and he blacked out.

He came too with someone kneeling on his back, rifling his trouser pockets. The Chechen flipped him over and began rifling his harness, jamming the spare magazines and grenades onto a battered rucksack.

"My men?" Yakunin croaked.

"All gone," the Chechen said, not even bothering to look him in the eye as he flipped open Yakunin's wallet.

"The photo." Yakunin reached out with what was left of a bloody left hand.

The Chechen looked at him, took the photo of the major's wife from the wallet and stuck it between Yakunin's only two remaining fingers.

Yakunin stared at the photo as the Chechen stripped him of his gear and body armor.

Dokka Umarov appeared, waving the fighter away. "You are the commander?"

"Da," Yakunin croaked, still staring at the photo.

"Who betrayed my location?"

Yakunin glanced up, knowing he didn't have long to live. "You were observed by a reconnaissance team. We almost had you this time, *ublyudok!*" Bastard!

Umarov nodded sullenly, holding Yakunin's carbine. "Yes, I admit I got lucky. But luck is the only quality in a commander that really counts."

"True enough," Yakunin admitted, choking on the blood rising up the back of his throat.

Umarov knelt beside him to poke a cigarette into the corner of his mouth, lighting it for him with a match. Then he gestured with the carbine. "You want to go quick? Or to wait?"

"I'll wait," Yakunin whispered. "It won't be long."

Umarov stood up and slung the carbine, giving orders to his men. "Leave nothing of value!" They could hear the Hind, long out of ammo, flying away to the northwest. "They may send more crocodiles, so we'll travel southeast until nightfall, then bear west over the mountain to link up with Mukhammad."

Umarov was joined by Lom on the march out. "It was close," the younger man said.

"Yes," Umarov agreed. "They should have killed us to a man. They had every advantage, but war is like that sometimes. The superior force does not always win."

"It was the will of Allah. He was with us."

"He is with us always, but you would do well not to place too much credit or too much blame where He is concerned. There will be days when He expects you to take care of yourself, and you will never know which days those are. Today may have been such a day."

Lom thought about his uncle's words as they marched along through the afternoon, attempting to reconcile them with those in the sixth *surah* of the Qur'an, verse seventeen: "And if Allah should touch you with adversity, there is no remover of it except Him. And if He touches you with good—then He is over all things competent."

By sundown, Lom concluded that his uncle either possessed a deeper understanding of the Qur'an than he did, or he had allowed himself to become jaded after so many years of war.

He looked toward the head of the column, where Umarov marched alongside the Basayev brothers—Anzor and Prina. "He is Allah in the heavens and in the earth," he whispered to himself. "He knows your secret thoughts, and your open words . . . and He knows what you earn."

31

SICILY

"There goes the sun," muttered Ivan Dragunov.

Gil glanced toward the horizon, the stock of the G28 still pulled into his shoulder. "I've been thinkin'. Suppose Kovalenko's men brought night vision. We could be in for a shift in the initiative here."

Dragunov considered the possibility. "If Kovalenko had infrared, we'd already be dead. It's not likely the men brought night vision with them."

Gil adjusted the sat phone's earpiece. "Midori, you still reading us?"

"Roger. I copy direct." Midori was now monitoring both of their phones on separate channels back in Langley, and they could both hear her, but they could not hear each other.

"You still got visual on us?"

"Roger that as well."

"Okay." Gil took the 1911 pistol from the small of his back and gave it to Dragunov. "As soon as the light fades, you can work your way down close to the house on the blind side to the east. Stay away from the barn and the goat pens, though. If those fuckers start bleating, Kovalenko's gonna know what we're up to."

Gripping the Italian cop's Beretta, Dragunov tucked the 1911 into his belly.

"You know how to work a 1911?"

"Of course," Dragunov said. "It was the preferred weapon of my enemy for a long time."

Gil chuckled. "It's still my preferred weapon."

"I suppose you're staying up here where it's safe?"

"Well, this ain't exactly a close-quarter weapon, Ivan. We have to play to our strengths."

"I'll man the rifle," Dragunov said, taking the 1911 back out of his pants.

Gil moved away from the G28, almost preferring to take the fight to the enemy, and put out his hand for the pistol. "Okay, chief."

His bluff called, Dragunov put away the pistol again. "Don't miss, Vassili—and don't shoot me by mistake."

Gil repositioned himself behind the rifle. "Midori will make sure I know where you are at all times. Right, Midori?"

"Roger that."

When the light faded, Dragunov moved out to the east, skirting the farm until he reached the edge of the road. Visibility was less than fifty feet in the darkness. "No movement outside the house?" he asked Midori.

"None," she answered. "You're exactly in line with the blind side of the house now. You should be able to advance without being detected. I'll vector you in."

Over the next couple of minutes, she fed him directions for the most expedient approach to the house, helping him to skirt copses of trees and brush without getting disoriented in the dark. He arrived at the eastern side and lowered himself into a crouch with his back to the wall, trading the Beretta for the 1911. "Make sure Gil knows I'm in position," he said in a low voice, knowing that whispers carried in the dark.

"Roger."

Back up the bluff, Gil scanned the silhouetted terrain below. There was no light inside the house; not so much as a candle burning. "I can't see much of anything from here," he said. "It's just too dark. Advise Ivan I'm moving in closer."

He began to slither forward down the slope, knowing that if Kovalenko possessed even a chintzy nightscope, he was a dead man.

"Stop!" Midori said. "A man with a rifle just climbed out the opposite side of the house from Ivan."

Gil backed into his hide among the brush. "What's he doing?"

"Nothing. Just waiting."

"Do I have line of sight from my position?"

"Negative," she said. "He's still around the corner. Ivan's asking what he should do."

"Tell him to hold position." Gil knew that Dragunov would willingly defer to his judgment because he held the high ground. "We'll give the situation time to develop."

Inside the house, Kovalenko decided that his enemies did not have night vision capabilities. The badly wounded Tapa had voluntarily crept past the kitchen window three different times without taking a bullet. So Kovalenko sent Zargan out the side window with orders to stalk the American sniper. He understood they might be under infrared satellite surveillance, but there was simply no other choice.

"We have to put an end to this," he said to Vitsin and two other Spetsnaz men. With Zargan outside now, there were only four of them left in the house, and though Tapa was bearing up well under incredible pain, he was fast losing what little remained of his combat effectiveness. "Either we fight our way out, or we die here on this fucking goat farm."

"I'll stay behind to cover your withdrawal," Tapa said, holding a Kashtan submachine pistol against his leg, his right arm now bound tightly across his chest with a torn bedsheet.

Kovalenko patted him on the good shoulder, regretting having sacrificed him for a shot at Gil. He knew in his gut that the American was still out there and still very much alive, because the goats were still bleating in their pens, when they should have been bedded down for the night. "We'll take you with us if we can. First, we have to find out whether we have an open avenue of escape."

"Is it just me," asked Anatoly, a Chechen born in Moscow, "or are the goats carrying on more these past couple of minutes?"

"It's not you," Kovalenko said. "They picked up just before Zargan went out the window. The enemy is near—probably around the blind side of the house. Get ready now. You're next out."

32

CIA HEADQUARTERS,
Langley, Virginia

Midori's dark eyes watched the giant plasma screen in front of her as Anatoly climbed out on the west side of the house, her shoulder-length black hair falling forward as she leaned in slightly. "A second man just climbed out the same window."

"Roger," Gil replied in her left ear.

In her right ear, she heard Dragunov rub his thumb over the mike in acknowledgment, realizing he wanted to remain completely silent now that two of the Spetsnaz were outside the house with him.

"Make sure you're giving Ivan second-by-second updates," Gil reminded her.

"Neither Chechen is moving," she answered, her eyes fixed on the infrared heat signatures. "They're facing north and south—both holding at the corners."

The first man stepped cautiously past the corner of the house and held his position, scanning the terrain over the open sights of an AS Val, a Russian-made silenced automatic rifle in 9 mm.

"Gil, you've got line of sight on the first target. Can you see him?"

"Negative," he said. "It's all ink down there. You don't have a giant spotlight on that satellite, do you?"

She smiled, running her fingers over the keyboard. "I'm going to see if I can help you another way. Adjust your aim as best you can, then hold position."

"Roger."

She watched as he adjusted the aim of the rifle barrel toward the corner of the house.

"That's what feels best to me," he said, "but I can't really see the house."

"Copy that," she said. "You're a few degrees off. Stand by."

"Roger that."

She heard the doubt in his tone, but that only made her all the more determined, quickly bringing up a trajectory overlay normally used for aiming artillery rounds and placing it over the video feed. She then right-clicked on the Spetsnaz man and—zooming in for the best resolution—drew a straight line to the bolt on Gil's rifle.

"Gil, adjust three degrees left."

She watched as he overadjusted slightly, keeping an eye on a separate screen to make sure the target hadn't moved. "Now half a degree back to the right."

Gil adjusted a fraction of a degree, and the barrel came perfectly in line with the line she had drawn across the screen. "Your horizontal aim is perfect," she said. "How do you think you are on the vertical?"

"Feels good. I've been holding this angle all day."

"In that case, you should be clear to fire."

Gil didn't hesitate. She saw the rifle buck against his shoulder and the heat signature of the gasses expelled from the end of the suppressor. In the other screen, the Spetsnaz man flew backward off his feet, writhing on the ground for a moment and then falling still.

"Target down!" she said as the second Spetsnaz man turned and moved toward his downed compatriot. "Ivan! If you move fast around the north side, you can take the second man from behind!"

Dragunov didn't hesitate, either. She watched him take off around the front of the house, rounding the far corner as Anatoly was pulling Zargan into the lee of the building. He fired twice, with both hands gripping the 1911 before him. Anatoly sprawled forward onto his face, and Dragunov danced away again, sprinting back around the front of the house to return to the safety of the blind side.

"Better than a video game!" his gravelly voice growled excitedly in her right ear.

Midori grinned. "Nice shooting, boys. Two tangos down. Gil, Ivan is back in position."

"You're a natural, Midori. If I didn't know better, I'd think Pope was there watching over your shoulder."

She glanced over her left shoulder to see Pope smiling at her from the corner, propped up in a hospital chair, flanked on either side by General Couture and White House Chief of Staff Brooks. A pair of navy male nurses sat nearby, monitoring Pope's vital signs. They had arrived ten minutes before the sun set on Sicily.

"Look there," Pope said quietly, pointing up at a second bank of monitors.

She looked up at a wider angle of the surrounding countryside. A car with a light bar on the roof was coming quickly up the road. "Master Chief, there's a patrol car approaching fast a quarter mile from the east. I'm guessing they must have heard Ivan's pistol shots."

"Marvelous," Gil replied.

33

SICILY

"What the hell is going on out there?" Kovalenko snarled.

Vitsin threw himself against the wall to the right of the window, stealing a quick glance outside to see Anatoly's body sprawled over Zargan's. "They're both dead!"

Without warning, Tapa burst out the back door, headed for the blindside of the house with the submachine pistol thrust before him. Without morphine, his pain had begun to increase exponentially over the past few minutes, and he knew that within the hour, he would be completely useless. It was better to die in combat than to have to be killed by his comrades.

He stalked around the corner of the house to see red and blue strobe lights flashing a hundred feet away by the road, a pair of weapon-mounted flashlights coming toward him through the trees. Hearing the crackle of police radios, he turned back to warn the others and was slugged in the face with a 1911 pistol, falling to the ground unconscious.

Dragunov grabbed Tapa around the head and twisted viciously, breaking his neck and dragging the body into the brush before running off up the hill toward Gil's position.

A second patrol car skidded to a stop near the first, and two more policemen jumped out, running toward the house with MP5 submachine guns.

Kovalenko saw the police through the front window of the house and ordered Vitsin out the back. "Police!"

They went out the back door, and Vitsin was cut down by a burst of fire from an MP5.

Kovalenko whipped around and fired the AWS rifle. The 7.62 mm round cut through both the cop who had killed Vitsin and the cop right behind him, dropping them both dead in their tracks. He slung the sniper rifle and grabbed up one of the MP5s, taking off cross-country on foot to the west.

The other two cops were storming the front of the house as he disappeared into the night.

ATOP THE HILL, Gil and Kovalenko pulled back out of sight, preparing to withdraw cross-country to the south.

"The police are in the house," Midori said. "One of the Chechens is escaping east on foot. Looks like he's gonna get away."

"What do you think?" Gil asked Dragunov. "Wanna run his ass down?"

Dragunov adjusted the Beretta tucked in the flat of his belly. "I think we keep moving. There's no way to know if it's Kovalenko, and this entire area will be crawling with police very soon."

That was good enough for Gil. They took off overland to the south.

"I have some good news for you," Midori announced.

"Gimme," Gil said, chugging along.

"One of our in-country operatives has just stashed a car for you two miles southeast of your position. It's parked behind a pizza restaurant. I'll vector you to it."

"Where was this guy earlier? We could have used him."

"It's taken time to marshal our resources," Midori replied. "And technically, he's not really an operative. He's a pilot from our naval air station there on the island. He was ordered to stash the car for you guys and catch a cab back to the base. We're playing this off the cuff, Master Chief."

"Thank God for the navy," Gil muttered. He hurled the G28 into the brush, knowing it would only slow him down; his right foot was already beginning to give him trouble again. "Gimme my gun back, Ivan."

Dragunov handed him the 1911, and they made toward a road at the bottom of the hill.

Kovalenko ran without stopping for the next thirty-five minutes, the bullet wound to the back of his thigh throbbing like hell. He finally stopped at a small house in a quiet neighborhood and sneaked in through an open window. He found the owners sleeping in their bed and murdered them with the last two bullets in his suppressed pistol. Then he pulled all the drapes and got on his satellite phone to Rome CIA Chief of Station Ben Walton.

"What kind of fucking game are you playing?" he demanded.

"No game at all," Walton replied calmly. "The operation is scrubbed, and I've gone off the grid. As a matter of fact, I was about to drop this phone in the sewer when you called."

"The operation is not scrubbed!" Kovalenko shouted. "I'm running for my life over here on this fucking island! My entire team is dead—just like you're going to be if you don't find a way to get me out of here! I know where you're running to, and I have friends there as well!"

"Calm down," Walton said.

"Don't tell me to calm down!" Kovalenko screamed. "I will find you and carve out your liver, you fucking American pig! Are you listening? Are you listening to me?"

"I'm listening," Walton said. "Tell me what happened."

Forcing himself to talk in a normal voice with no little effort, Kovalenko gave him the thumbnail version of the past twelve hours.

"Okay, well, you're in luck," Walton said. "Shannon and Dragunov are going to be extracted off the point of San Vito Lo Capo via a SEAL delivery vehicle. If you can get there ahead of them, you might manage to pick them off on the beach."

"How do you know that?" Kovalenko challenged. "How do I know that isn't more CIA shit?"

"I know because there are loose lips in the White House," Walton said. "Hell, there are loose lips all over DC these days. But hey, you know what? You can either take my word for it or go fuck yourself, Sasha. We're both up to our asses in this mess. I'm sorry I can't get you off the island, but I just gave you Gil Shannon—if you want him."

"I want him," Kovalenko grumbled. "You *bet* I want him!"

"Well, then, you'd better get a move on, because I doubt very seriously he'll be hoofing it all the way to San Vito. The US Navy has a lot of resources on that island, and they can't afford to have their most recent Medal of Honor winner captured and prosecuted by the goddamn Sicilians."

With much of his anger suddenly abated, Kovalenko began to feel like Walton was one of the few friends he had left in the world. "So you're a man without a country now, eh?"

"I'm afraid so," Walton said. "I gambled and lost. Stupid, but that's how it goes sometimes. I'll make out all right. So will you. You'll think your way off that island, and once you get yourself back to the mainland, you're back in business. Umarov needs men like you—especially if he still plans on hitting the BTC."

"He'll never give up on the pipeline," Kovalenko said.

"You might want to forget Shannon," Walton advised. "Lay low. Sicily's a big island. Your friends in the GRU can find you a place to hide until the heat is off."

"You're right," Kovalenko said, realizing there was an off chance someone might be listening. "Forget Shannon. The *podlets* isn't worth the risk."

34

WASHINGTON, DC

Head Chef Jacques Bonfils was in the dry goods storage room at the back of the White House kitchen, sorting through a case of caviar, when he heard the door open and close. He stood up and turned around to see a very angry looking General William J. Couture standing there in his chief of staff uniform, his scarred face menacing and cruel.

"Mon général," Bonfils said in French, a confused smile on his face. "What seems to be the matter?"

Couture stalked across the room and slugged the chef in the stomach so hard that Bonfils nearly coughed up a kidney on his way to the deck. A jar of caviar fell from the chef's hand and broke against the tile. "You've got one chance to tell me who you've been talking to!"

Bonfils was on his knees and holding his belly, unable even to breathe, much less talk.

"NSA just overheard an interesting conversation," Couture went on. "Seems there's a leak here in the White

House." He kicked Bonfils over onto his side and reached down to grab his wrist, twisting it until Bonfils cried out in pain. "Talk!"

"Grieves!"

Couture reduced some of the tension on the wrist. "Who Grieves?"

"Senator Grieves," Bonfils groaned.

"Bullshit, Jacques. Grieves isn't stupid enough to talk to you."

"His aide. I talk to his aide."

Couture released Bonfils's arm and let it drop, kneeling down beside him. "Okay. Here's how this is going to go, you Frog traitor. You're going to tell the Secret Service everything you know. Otherwise I'm personally going to have you rubbed out! Got it?"

Bonfils retched, still holding his belly in pain. "*Oui, mon général.*" Tears rolled from his eyes.

Couture stood up and jerked Bonfils to his feet, shoving him toward the door.

Bonfils opened the door and was immediately taken into custody by four Secret Service agents.

"He slipped on some caviar." Couture then made eye contact with the assistant chef standing across the kitchen, saying, "Better get somebody in there with a mop. There's caviar and puke on the floor. Though how anybody can tell the damn difference . . ."

COUTURE STOOD BEFORE the president's desk a short time later. "It's my fault, Mr. President. I mentioned Operation Falcon in front of Bonfils. Glen is a witness. I'm prepared to offer my resignation forthwith."

"Have a seat, General." The president turned to Brooks, who was already seated. "Is that true? You were present?"

Brooks nodded. "I'm prepared to offer my resignation as well, Mr. President. Strictly speaking, I should have reported the general myself."

Couture looked at Brooks. "Glen, that wasn't my point."

"I know it wasn't, Bill, but that doesn't change the facts."

The president held up his hand. "Stop. Before the two of you rush to fall on your swords before the emperor . . . you should know that I'm equally guilty." He pushed back from the desk, allowing his gaze to drift around the room for a moment. "Hell, we've grown decadent from the top down, haven't we?"

Couture exchanged uncomfortable glances with Brooks.

"The other day . . ." the president said. "Out there in the hall . . . I told Maddy about my upcoming meeting with Pope. I said to make sure it didn't appear on my official schedule. I was distracted, and I wasn't paying attention to who was around. Bonfils was standing just a few feet away, waiting to ask me what I wanted for dinner. The first lady usually handles that, but as you know, she's in Missouri visiting her family." He got up from the chair and turned to look out the window overlooking the lawn below.

"So, gentlemen, in all likelihood, I'm the leak that nearly got Pope assassinated." He turned around. "Regardless, the people who work in this building *all* have top secret clearances, and every goddamn one of them knows they're not to repeat what they hear within these walls. Christ Almighty! If it's not safe to talk in the White House, where the hell *is* it safe?"

He sat back down, drumming his fingers on the desk. "Is Falcon going forward?"

"As we speak, sir," Brook replied. "The *Ohio* is in contact with Shannon, and the SDV team is preparing to launch."

"What about this maniac Kovalenko? Where's he?"

"We've lost him," Couture said. "The satellite couldn't track him and Shannon both."

"So the possibility remains that he *will* attempt to interfere with Shannon's extraction—despite what he said to Walton?"

"Affirmative," Brooks said.

"Should we postpone Falcon? Change the extraction point?"

"At this point, sir, the dangers of having Shannon and Dragunov on that island far outweigh any threat posed by Kovalenko. Sicilian and Italian authorities realize that elements of the CIA and the GRU have both violated their sovereignty, and they're extremely determined to obtain proof to that effect. At least four Sicilian police officers are dead, and a number of civilians as well."

"How many of those killings are Shannon's doing?"

"According to Shannon, none."

The president looked at Couture. "Do you buy that?"

Couture nodded. "I do, sir."

The president drew a breath and sighed. "Okay. So what about the mysterious Agent Walton? Is he really off the grid?"

"It appears so," Brooks answered. "But I've spoken with Pope about him, and I'm confident that situation will work itself out."

An ironic grin spread across the president's face. "*Work itself out*, Glen?"

"Those are Pope's words, Mr. President. I asked him what he thought we should do about Walton's betrayal, and he said to me, 'Glen, I wouldn't worry too much about Ben Walton. These things have a way of working themselves out.'"

Maybe it was the tension, but Couture couldn't help but laugh. "I'm sorry, Mr. President. Forgive my levity. It's just that Pope—oh, hell, I don't know."

The president sat nodding. "I think I understand, Bill. No one has any business being so valuable and so dangerous all at the same damn time."

35

CAPO SAN VITO,
Sicily

The Cape of San Vito was on the northwestern point of the island, two miles wide and five long with particularly rocky terrain running the length of the western shoreline. Gil and Dragunov were now well ensconced among the rocks, having ditched their car in the village of San Vito Lo Capo a click and a half to the east. Nothing but a lonely stretch of dirt road lay between them and the open waters of the Mediterranean a hundred yards away.

Gil scanned the water through a pair of infrared binoculars that had been stashed beneath the driver's seat of the car, watching for the telltale flash of an infrared strobe that would be invisible to the naked eye.

"Typhoon actual, this is Typhoon main. Do you copy? Over."

Gil picked up the sat phone, answering the USS *Ohio's* transmission: "Roger that, main. I copy. Over."

"Actual, be advised your driver is parking the car. Over."

"Parking the car" meant that the SEAL team from the *Ohio* had arrived at its insertion point and was now in the process of "parking" the SDV on the ocean floor in 5 fathoms, or 32 feet, of water. The divers would be using rebreathers for stealth, recycling their unused oxygen to eliminate the large bubbles released by standard scuba tanks. The *Ohio* waited silently three miles out in international waters, 160 feet below the surface.

"Roger that, main."

Gil looked at Dragunov. "Ready to get wet again, partner?"

Dragunov rubbed a hand over his face in the darkness. "This is always when I am most nervous—waiting for extraction."

"Me too. Glad to hear it's the same for Russians."

"It was the same for the British at Dunkirk," Dragunov said grimly. "The same for the Greeks when Themistocles ordered the evacuation of Athens. It's always the same when the enemy is on your heels, and you're about to show him your ass."

The captain of the *Ohio* had already advised them that the extraction point was compromised, and they had agreed to proceed with the exfiltration; given their collective physical condition, another twenty-four hours on the island without food and water would be too dicey. Both men suffered from dehydration and suppurating wounds, and Gil had begun to run a low-grade fever, signaling the onset of infection. Without proper hydration, such a fever could quickly turn severe, particularly under the stress of combat conditions.

"How much longer?" Dragunov asked.

"They'll park the SDV two hundred meters out then swim in beneath the surface. They're lugging our dive gear, so that'll slow 'em down a bit, but we should see the strobe in ten minutes or so. Only thing that concerns me is the delay in comms." The *Ohio* had to relay its sat phone communications to the SDV team by radio, and this made it impossible to communicate with the divers in real time.

Dragunov grunted. "Kovalenko's here. I can feel him."

"Sorry to hear it. That fucker's too good with a rifle." Gil scanned up and down the coast through the binoculars, seeing nothing but jagged rocks on their side of the road in both directions. "At least it's inside-a-black-cat dark out here."

"Maybe you shouldn't have thrown away our rifle."

"Woulda, coulda, shoulda," Gil muttered. "You can stay here on the island if you want. I'm not sure we need a Spetsnaz major aboard one of our subs anyhow."

"Why? Do you think I have a microcamera hidden up my prick?"

Gil snorted, secretly aware that Dragunov would be sequestered immediately aboard the *Ohio*, kept in the wardroom. There he would be well treated and well fed but unable to mingle with the crew or see anything of any intelligence value whatsoever.

"What are the chances they'll let me see the con?" Dragunov asked, smiling from the side of his face.

"Ivan, you got a better chance at seein' a Swiss combat medal than you do the con of that submarine."

A little over a hundred meters to the south, also well hidden among the rocks, Kovalenko lay in wait with the AWS, still cursing the GRU operative who had failed to supply a nightscope for the rifle.

"Hey, what the hell do you want from me?" the smart-ass had said to him. "You're lucky I came up with anything on such short notice."

"Tvayu mat'," Kovalenko murmured, biting off a chunk of chocolate and chasing it down with a long drink of French mineral water taken from the house where he had killed the Sicilian couple in their sleep.

There was no rolling surf along the shoreline, and that was good because it meant there was less noise, and any wake kicked up by a boat would be more likely to stand out. He knew how much the American SEAL teams liked their high-speed Zodiac boats, and he was looking forward to shooting one of them up.

There had been no sign of the Italian navy since his arrival the hour before, and he assumed this was because the Americans had probably *suggested* that the Italians steer clear of the cape for the night, but there was never any telling how much cooperation took place between the two governments. The Italians and the Americans were forever pretending to be at odds while secretly jerking each other off under the table.

"Kozly." Jackasses.

Kovalenko pulled the rifle into his shoulder and scanned the shoreline for movement, looking for lights or reflections out on the water. Unable to see much of anything, he settled in to wait, certain that Dragunov was hiding somewhere along the shore and that the American sniper was with him.

Watching through the binoculars, Gil spotted the infrared strobe beneath the surface of the water and grabbed the sat phone.

"Typhoon main, I have visual on the strobe. Team is clear to surface. Over."

"Roger that, actual. Relaying now."

A couple of moments later, the heads of two SEALs from SEAL Team IV appeared above the surface.

"Let's go, Ivan! We're on."

They moved out of the rocks, taking it slow as they covered the fifty yards to the dirt road. Once across, they doubletimed it to the waterline, slowing again as they moved into the water to avoid making noise or kicking up a froth.

The waiting SEALs crouched low in the waist-deep water fifty yards from the water's edge, having switched out their full-face diving masks for night vision goggles. They watched for danger as the Spetsnaz man and their fellow SEAL waded out to meet them. Then they rose up to their full height, each of them holding a second set of dive gear. They were armed only with suppressed M11s (SIG-Sauer P228s).

No one said a word as the SEALs began helping them into their dive gear. They were almost home, and no one wanted to risk ghosting the mission.

KOVALENKO WAS STILL studying the shoreline when a car came around the curve to the north, stopping abruptly with its headlights shining on four divers standing out in the water 150 meters from his position.

"Blyat'!"

He swept right and fired without even bringing the rifle to a stop, picking off one of the divers. The other three dropped below the surface as Kovalenko steadied the rifle and fired into the water. The water began to bubble, and one of the divers resurfaced with air hissing from his rebreather, which he immediately threw off.

Kovalenko fired again, and another diver resurfaced holding his chest.

Dragunov hurled the hissing rebreather into the water, jerking the Beretta from his pants and firing at the car. The car immediately backed away through the curve, and darkness swallowed them again.

Gil barked into the radio-equipped face mask of the wounded SEAL cradled in his arms: "Typhoon main, be advised we are taking fire! Repeat. Taking fire. One KIA. One severely wounded. Request immediate surface evac— over!"

Dragunov waded over to him. "I can use the dead man's gear. Let's go!"

"We can't," Gil said, pushing the wounded SEAL into Dragunov's arms. "He's hit through the lung. The dive would kill him."

The *Ohio* answered his transmission: "Typhoon actual, stand by for immediate surface evac. Over."

"Roger that, main—expedite! We're standing by in the shallows." Gil dropped the mask and pulled on the SEAL's night vision goggles. Then he took the M11 pistol from the holster on his leg. "Keep him alive, Ivan. I'm going after Kovalenko."

"What the fuck are you talking about?" Dragunov hissed. "Stay here in the goddamn water! Your people are coming for us."

"They're three miles out, coming in rubber boats that make a lot of noise. Right now Kovalenko is displacing for a closer shot, and if I don't take him out before the surface team gets here, he'll kill every damn one of us."

"Shit!" Dragunov swore, holding the wounded SEAL so that his head and chest were out of the water. "Don't get killed!"

36

ABOARD THE USS *OHIO*,
Mediterranean Sea

"Chief of the Watch, emergency blow!" said Captain Daniel Knight, ordering the boat to the surface. "All lookouts to the bridge."

"Aye, sir!"

Knight crossed the con to the SEAL team leader, Senior Chief Dexter "Dex" Childress, who had just heard over the radio that one of his SEALs was dead and another wounded so badly that he couldn't return to the *Ohio* via the SDV.

"You'll be going ashore hot, Chief, so take whatever you think you'll need."

Childress, thirty-five, was of medium build, with a perpetual five o'clock shadow. "Aye, sir. Any idea who's doing the shooting?"

"You know what I know, Chief. Let's just hope it's not the Italian navy, or we'll all be standing tall before the man when this is over."

"Roger that, Captain."

Minutes later, Childress stood on the deck of the surfaced submarine with his NVGs on, watching as six other SEALs finished inflating a pair of black CRRCs—Combat Rubber Raiding Crafts.

"I guess so much for a low-impact exfil, eh, Senior Chief?"

Childress looked at his number two, Petty Officer Winslow. "I warned the head shed to send more men, Winny. What the fuck else could I do?" He felt sick to his stomach, never having lost a teammate before. "Fucking half measures."

"We'll get it sorted," Winslow said, bumping him on the shoulder. "We'll get it sorted."

The boats were ready and in the water a minute later. The SEALs loaded up four men to a craft.

Knight stood in the conning tower, watching them through a pair of night vision binoculars as they sped away.

"What do you think, Captain?" asked the chief of the boat.

Knight glanced at him. "I think we're probably about fifteen minutes away from an international incident, Chief—but we'll see."

"How long before we contact Fleet Command, sir?"

"Let's get below and do that now. The admiral's going to have a cat. All lookouts below, and prepare to submerge the boat to one-six-zero feet."

"Aye, aye, sir."

Childress sat in the team leader's position on the forward port side of the boat, watching out over the gray-white surface of the water through infrared, the cold sea spray on his face. He and his men were headed into allied waters—armed to the teeth—without the Italian government's permission.

Winslow spoke to him over the radio headset as they raced along the surface. "What are the rules of engagement, Senior?"

Childress glanced over at the other boat, seeing Winslow looking back at him. "Whatever's necessary to make sure no more of our people get killed." He took an instant to make sure of his feelings and then added: "I'll accept full responsibility."

"Roger that," Winslow said. "I've got your back."

Within ten minutes, they were in sight of the extraction point, and Childress spotted a man on the beach, kneeling over another man. As they drew closer, he realized the kneeling man was performing CPR—and that another, much cooler body lay not far off, with its legs still in the water. He signaled the coxswain to head directly for them, and the coxswain gave him a thumbs-up.

"Come on, you stupid American," Dragunov growled. "Breathe!" He gave the dying SEAL a precordial thump to the sternum in an attempt to get his heart going again. He could hear the encroaching boat motors behind him as he lifted the SEAL's chin and breathed into his mouth. He then resumed CPR: fifteen chest compressions for every two breaths.

The boats came ashore on either side of him, and two SEALs rushed to take over CPR as four others spread out in a defensive arc.

"Sir!" Childress said. "Are you Major Ivan Dragunov?"

"Yes," Dragunov said, sitting back in the water to rest against his arms, his chest heaving. "I'm sorry I couldn't save him. I did my best."

"I appreciate you—"

"He's got a pulse!" Winslow said, his tone desperate. "Permission to haul ass, Senior Chief?"

"Go!"

Both the dead man and the dying SEAL were loaded immediately into the CRRC, and the secondary team raced back out to sea in the dark.

"Major, where is Chief Shannon?"

Dragunov got to his feet and pointed inland. "He went after Kovalenko to keep him from killing you as you came ashore. He could be dead, for all I know. But I think probably he is still alive because Kovalenko hasn't shot at us. Give me a weapon, and I'll go look for him."

"Negative," Childress said, scanning the shoreline but seeing no heat signatures. "We have to go, sir."

"That's your man out there," Dragunov said. "You're going to leave him?"

"I'm sorry. We don't have a choice. You'd better get in the boat now, sir."

To Dragunov's own surprise, this angered him. "Shannon told me SEALs don't leave their people behind."

Childress felt like shit. "We don't leave our people behind, sir, but this is different. We have to go."

"*You* go!" Dragunov said, waving them off. "I'm going after Shannon. You won't give me a weapon? Okay, give me your night vision!"

Childress signaled for the other three SEALs to surround the Russian officer. "Major, the second that boat slid ashore, you became my responsibility. My orders are to see you safely aboard the *Ohio*, and that's exactly what I intend to do—with or without your cooperation, sir."

Dragunov stood glaring, glancing over his shoulder at his competition and finding it formidable.

Childress could see him swaying on his feet. "Major, you're dog-ass tired, sir. Why don't you get in the boat? We're running out of time here."

"*Chort!*" Dragunov snarled, walking into the water and getting into the CRRC.

The SEALs shoved the boat into deeper water, and Childress climbed in beside Dragunov, putting a hand on his shoulder. "Don't worry about Chief Shannon, Major. He's survived a hell of a lot worse."

"I know," Dragunov grumbled as the motor was started. "I was watching on satellite when they tried to kill him in the Panjshir Valley."

"Say again?" Childress said over the drone of the motor.

Dragunov shook his head, feeling very tired suddenly. "Nothing . . . nothing."

37

SICILY

Gil could feel the Wolf among the rocks now, and he some-how knew that Kovalenko could feel him as well, a strange electricity pervading the air. He realized the folly of hunt-ing a Spetsnaz sniper over unknown terrain with nothing more than a pistol, but there was an arrogance within him that was tired of being beaten to the trigger, tired of run-ning away. He and the Chechen had drawn each other's blood, and there was no avoiding the now-personal nature of their enmity. So far each had survived what the other had thrown at him, but each was painfully aware that the contest would remain unfinished until one or the other had proven himself the better man.

Gil had lost the sat phone in the water, so there was no calling on Midori or the *Ohio* for support. He was com-pletely on his own, and it was only a matter of time before the driver of the car called the police. Soon the entire cape was likely to be crawling with carabinieri—and dogs.

He moved south for a hundred meters, stopping when his instincts told him the enemy was near. Poking his head around a boulder, he saw in the greenish-black field of his NVGs the figure of a man positioned in the rocks seventy-five yards to the south. The enemy sniper was aiming a rifle over the top of a jagged outcrop, obviously focused on the dirt road, leaving his rear entirely exposed. This made little sense to Gil until he moved east and saw that the grassland opposite the escarpment was sectioned off by the chest-high rock walls of what appeared to be ancient Sicilian farmlets. Any maneuvering through those farmlets would be slow and tedious, leaving him vulnerable every time he climbed over one of the walls.

The only viable route of advance was over the rocky escarpment, which would mean taking his eyes off of Kovalenko for lengthy periods, maybe even losing his line of sight completely until he drew within just a few feet. He searched for a landmark parallel to Kovalenko's position that he could use as a geological reference point to keep track of his progress. The last thing he needed was to step blindly around a rock and suddenly find himself face-to-face with the enemy.

Gil was unable to find a definite geological reference, so he settled for what looked like a soda can alongside the road roughly even with Kovalenko's position. He moved out, keeping tabs on the Chechen as best he could until a sheer rock face forced him up and over the top of the jagged escarpment, completely out of view of his target. The going was unsteady over the jagged rock, but within thirty feet, he came to a wide crevasse ten or twelve feet deep. He marked the location of the can and lowered himself down carefully, creeping forward toward the opening of the crevasse, expecting to emerge with a clear shot at Kovalenko from less than twenty feet.

He felt a slight pressure against his right shin and froze in place, but it was already too late. An empty mineral water bottle, stuck upside-down on a stick, tumbled from the shadows overhead and shattered against rocks, making a noise loud enough to wake the dead.

"Stupid motherfucker!" he swore silently, crouching to touch the black bootlace that had been stretched across the crevasse as a trigger for the ad hoc booby trap.

"Throw out your weapons!" called a voice with a Chechen accent. "You're cornered. There's no escape."

Gil took a quick glance around, seeing no immediate line of retreat.

"Come and get me!"

"It was you in Paris, yes?"

Gil made a closer examination of the walls. They were too smooth to climb and too far apart to brace himself between them and shinny out.

"You can forget climbing out!" Kovalenko called to him. "That *was* you in Paris, wasn't it?"

"Yeah. So the fuck what?"

"Who told you to look for us there?"

"Fuck you care?"

Kovalenko chuckled. "I lost a good friend that night. I want to know who else to kill."

Gil thought that over, deciding, "What the fuck? I just might die in this fucking rat trap."

"His name's Tim Hagen. Cocksucker wants me dead—don't ask me why."

"I will remember his name," Kovalenko replied. "Now throw out your weapons."

"Eat me."

"I promise to let you live."

Gil didn't even dignify that with a response.

"Listen, I don't need to kill you to keep you from following me."

"Fuck is *that* supposed to mean?"

"It means I give you my word as a soldier to only shoot you in the knee. That's a healthy compromise, no?"

Gil laughed.

"Listen to me!" Kovalenko insisted. "I no longer *want* to kill you. You've proven a worthy adversary—and I've proven myself the better man. Let us settle this like those who came before us. Yield to me, and you will live. I swear it."

Gil shook his head, believing the Chechen actually meant what he said. "I'm not volunteering to be shot in the fucking knee."

"In the elbow, then. I give you the choice."

"You're a generous *sukin syn*, I'll give you that."

It was the Chechen's turn to laugh. "I like you, but soon my people will arrive. They will have grenades. Do you want that?"

"Bullshit," Gil said. "We both know ain't nobody comin' except the police. I'll take my chances with them."

There was a long pause, and Gil moved to the back of the niche, watching for Kovalenko to appear above him.

Almost an entire minute passed before the Chechen spoke again. "You have night vision, yes?" There was a perceptible urgency in his tone that hadn't been there before, and his voice was coming from a lower angle among the rocks.

"Why you wanna know?" Gil inched forward with the pistol ready to fire over the lip of the opening.

"Throw it out to me, and I'll leave."

"No. Get your own."

This time there was no reply, and after five minutes of waiting Gil began to feel as though he were alone. "What the fuck's goin' on?" he muttered.

An animal growled above him, and he looked up to see a Doberman pincer. It snarled and showed its teeth. Then a second Doberman appeared, and both dogs started barking crazily, letting their handlers know exactly where they were.

"Sorry about this, guys." Gil aimed the suppressed M11 upward and shot both dogs through the bottom of the jaw, killing them instantly.

He moved to the opening of the crevasse and stole a look around the corner, seeing Kovalenko running away down the dirt road to the south, already well out of pistol range.

A police car came jouncing through the curve to the north, its red and blue lights dancing off the rocks, and Gil watched on as Kovalenko turned around, dropped calmly to a prone position, and pulled the rifle into his shoulder.

The Chechen fired two shots in quick succession. The police car swerved off the road, and Kovalenko was back up and running a second later.

There was a lot of shouting now coming from above and behind Gil's position, the handlers calling excitedly to their dogs.

Gil stepped out of the crevasse and slid down the face of a boulder.

"Halt!" a voice shouted from above as he scrambled toward the road.

Pistol shots rang out, and bullets ricocheted off the rocks at his feet as he darted across. A bullet zipped past his left ear, and he disappeared into the darkness.

Three more police cars came through the curve with

searchlights cutting back and forth. One of the lights locked onto Gil, and he sprinted for the sea. The cars slid to a stop as he was running into the water, and a burst of submachine-gun fire stitched the surface. A bullet pierced his right calf, and he dove into barely thigh-deep water, bashing his face against the rocky bottom and stroking wildly for the safety of the deep.

He swam until he thought his lungs would burst, daring to surface only at the last possible second, still only fifty yards from shore. Gil was marked almost instantly by the beam of a flashlight and driven back under by more machine-gun fire. He swam harder than he'd ever swum in his life until at last the bottom fell away, enabling him to dive deep enough to strip his shoes and clothing, racing to the surface for another precious gulp of air.

He swam northward, managing to leave the searchlights behind, stroking smoothly beneath the surface. Entirely in his element now, Gil made his way back to the SEAL team extraction point, where the two frogmen had been shot. It took five minutes of cautious searching, but he found the dead SEAL's dive gear and slipped beneath the surface to put it on. Then he poked his head out of the water one last time, pulling on the full-face mask equipped with through-water communications and disappeared for good beneath the surface.

"Typhoon actual to Typhoon main. Do you copy my traffic? Over?"

Ten seconds later, he was answered by the *Ohio*: "Go ahead, actual. We copy."

Now that he had swim fins, Gil was quickly leaving the shore behind him. "Main, be advised the target has escaped due to intervention of local law enforcement. I am now in the water and safely away. Break."

"Go ahead, actual."

"Can you lock out a second SDV team to help me locate the first vehicle? I was unable to retrieve the transponder unit, so I'm swimming blind. Over."

"Roger that, actual. The team is gearing up. ETA at outer marker twenty-five minutes. Over."

"Copy, main. I'll be standing by out at the outer marker."

38

BETHESDA NAVAL HOSPITAL,
Bethesda, Maryland

Pope sat in his hospital bed talking on the phone with Vladimir Federov of the GRU.

"Dragunov is now safely aboard the submarine?" Federov asked.

"That's right," Pope said. "He lost a finger on Sicily, but other than that, he's in pretty good shape. Our man is a bit more banged up. But they've both been tended to by the surgeon aboard the *Ohio*, and after thirty-six hours' rest, we can put them ashore in Europe. All we need is for you to arrange the when and where."

"What about Kovalenko?"

"That fish got away," Pope said. "I understand your people attempted to take out Dokka Umarov yesterday? How did it go?"

Federov didn't respond immediately.

"We overheard some radio traffic," Pope volunteered.

"Well," Federov said, "then you must already know how it went. Umarov wiped out an entire Spetsnaz team. Neither of us is doing very well, Robert."

"These are still the early innings. Is Moscow giving you trouble?"

"My superiors are not patient men," Federov said. "The French government has identified Yeshevsky and the other men that Shannon killed in Paris. Their Ministry of Foreign Affairs is giving our ambassador a difficult time."

"I take it you're no longer in Paris?"

"I'm in Bern now," Federov said. "The DPSD wanted to question me. I thought it better to avoid that." The DPSD was the French military's Direction de la Protection et de la Sécurité de la Défense, charged with counterespionage.

Pope chuckled. "I can imagine you did. They've made a couple of subtle inquiries at our embassy, but our ambassador there doesn't know anything."

"My superiors are worried your State Department will leave us holding the bag on this if it goes public."

"I can understand that," Pope said. "And while I can't promise that won't happen, I do know that my president and his closest advisers are pleased by the level of cooperation we've enjoyed thus far. We both have mud on our faces, and if it went public today, I'm confident my president would be willing to accept an equal amount of responsibility—as long as your superiors would be willing to admit this has been a joint operation."

Federov chortled. "That would certainly cause a certain amount of gossip within the NATO community."

"I'm not sure *gossip* is the right word," Pope replied, "but I take your point. Anyhow, it's a new world. The Islamists are about to join the nuclear weapons community, so Russia and the United States are going to have to learn to work together. NATO may even one day become irrelevant. Regardless, it's our job to make sure this little mess we've created *doesn't* go public. In fact, the future of the CIA probably depends on it."

"Senator Grieves is still pushing to dissolve the agency?"

"Yes, and he's gaining influence within the Senate. Not nearly enough yet, but a scandal like this wouldn't help our cause." Pope did not go on to share that Grieves was now the subject of an FBI investigation into possible treasonous activities.

"Have Western oil companies been advised on the plot to disrupt the pipeline?" Federov asked.

"No," Pope answered. "We've decided to leave them in the dark. There was some trouble six months back with an oil platform off the coast of Nigeria, and their mercenaries made our job ten times harder than it needed to be, so we're leaving them out of it this time."

"Fine. How soon will the *Ohio* be able to put our men back ashore?"

"That depends on where you make the arrangements."

"How about Turkey?" Federov suggested. "I have a number of resources there."

"Good," Pope said. "I'll run it through the proper channels and get back to you in twenty-four hours."

"That will give me the time I need," Federov said. "Now, tell me: How are you feeling? I was more than slightly relieved to hear you had survived the attempt on your life."

"The doctors tell me I'm mending well. Thank you for asking."

"And the filthy traitors who ordered the attempt?"

Pope was quiet for a moment. "Well, you know the old saying, Vladimir: it's stupid to fail."

39

ISTANBUL,
Turkey

Istanbul was Turkey's largest city, with a predominantly Sunni Muslim population of fourteen million. It covered two thousand square miles and was the focal point of Turkish cultural, economic, and historical interests.

Gil and Dragunov were put ashore in the dead of night at Aytekin Kotil Park, where they waited among the Cretan palms for a half hour until Dragunov received a text message from their GRU contact telling them to rendezvous with him at the main entrance.

The contact was a big, dirty-looking Russian with an unshaven face, and at three paces he smelled as though he hadn't bathed in weeks. His name was Vlad, and it was obvious that he hated Gil on sight.

"You brought an American," he said to Dragunov in Russian. "Why wasn't I told?"

"You were told there were two of us," Dragunov replied in the same language. "That was all you needed to know. Now, let's move. I don't like standing around in the open."

They got into a small car with Gil sitting in the back, and Vlad drove out of the park onto Kennedy Avenue, a coastal road named for the US president John F. Kennedy. Gil saw the street sign that read "Kennedy Caddesi" and smiled. He was a long, long way from home, and seeing the Americanism was a comfort.

"Where are we going?" Dragunov kept a hand in the pocket of his US Navy peacoat, where he gripped a concealed 9 mm Beretta M9 pistol.

"Whorehouse," Vlad answered, eyeing Gil coldly in the mirror. "We won't be bothered. Prostitution is legal here, and we're protected by the police."

Unable to understand a word of what was being said, Gil pretended not to notice Vlad's disdain, keeping his facial expression neutral and avoiding all eye contact. The last thing he wanted was to get into a pissing contest with the GRU in a Muslim country. Still, like Dragunov, he too had his hand in his peacoat gripping a navy-issue M9. Gil also had two spare magazines in his left hip pocket.

They drove through the lighted streets of the city until Vlad turned down a dark alley and pulled up to an unassuming-looking concrete building with two men standing outside in a dimly lit parking lot. A heavy fog was setting in, and the air was cold. There were six cars parked in the lot.

Vlad killed the motor, and they got out. A fat man with a bald head took Vlad aside and spoke with him in a low voice as Vlad lit a cigarette. When they finished talking, Vlad waved for Dragunov to follow him inside.

Gil nodded at the two men standing watch as he

brought up the rear, keeping a wary eye out as they crossed the threshold into the building. The pervading scent was unmistakable: heavy perfume and marijuana. At a table inside the door, two more men sat watching television, and nine scantily clad young women lounged around on sofas and chairs in the shadowy foyer. A couple of the girls met Gil's gaze, one managing a halfhearted smile, but most averted their eyes.

Gil felt his gut start to churn. "What the fuck is this place?" he muttered to Dragunov as Vlad stood talking with the men at the table.

Dragunov glanced around at the women. "What does it look like?"

"I thought we were going to a GRU safe house."

"This is it," Dragunov said. "What were you expecting? Something from a Jason Bourne movie?"

"Back here." Vlad led them through a red-beaded curtain and down a long corridor of closed doors to a well-lighted kitchen area. Two more young women sat slurping soup at a card table, and he barked at them in Russian, causing them to get immediately up and flee the room.

"All they do around here is eat," he griped to Dragunov. "If they're not eating, they're bitching about something. Ungrateful cunts."

Dragunov nodded. "Coffee?"

"Over there."

"Want some?" Dragunov asked Gil.

"Sure." Gil took his cigarettes from the other coat pocket and lit one as Vlad walked out of the room through a blue-beaded curtain down a second corridor, growling orders at someone unseen. "He speak English?"

Dragunov shrugged. "Probably not, but watch what you say around him."

"These girls are sex slaves. You know that, right?"

Turkey was one of the world's most popular destinations in human trafficking. It was estimated that as many as eight thousand women may have been enslaved there, and the Russian mafia controlled a big part of the industry. They imported their women primarily from Russia, Poland, and Ukraine, but other crime organizations imported them from Armenia, Azerbaijan, Belarus, Bulgaria, Georgia, Greece, Indonesia, Kazakhstan, Kyrgyzstan, Moldova, Romania, Turkmenistan, and Uzbekistan. This overt abuse of Turkey's liberal prostitution policies had caused many Turkish municipalities to stop issuing licenses for new brothels and to refuse the renewal of licenses for existing brothels. This did little, however, to stem the flow of human traffic. The syndicates were too well established, and police officials were too easily bribed into compliance.

Dragunov took a seat at the card table with his cup of coffee. "It's not our responsibility," he said.

"What's the GRU doing working with the Russian mob?"

A shadow crossed Dragunov's brow as he sat looking up at Gil. "You're saying the CIA never works with criminals? That no one ever gets fucked?"

Gil sat down across from him. "One of those girls out front can't be a day over sixteen."

Dragunov gazed at him. "What do you want me to do about it?"

Gil leaned back in the folding chair, exhaling with a sigh. "Nothin'."

"Good," the Spetsnaz man said. "Because there's nothing that can be done. This is Turkey, and even if it was Ukraine or Belarus, what are we going to do, eh? Start a war with the Russian mafia?"

"Doesn't sound like the worst idea I ever heard."

One of the older women, perhaps twenty-six or so, came into the kitchen, her black hair flowing around her shoulders, and went to the coffee pot. It was empty, so she took a coffee can down from the cupboard. Her black nightgown was transparent and left nothing whatsoever to the imagination, her upturned nipples and dark patch of pubic hair clearly visible.

Gil couldn't help being stirred, so he turned away.

Vlad came into the kitchen, grinned when he saw the woman making coffee, and said something to Dragunov.

Dragunov looked at Gil. "I guess she speaks English, if you'd like to fuck her."

Gil glanced at Vlad and shook his head. "Tell 'im no thanks."

"He says no charge—professional courtesy."

Gil looked at the girl, who immediately lowered her eyes. "No thanks," he muttered.

Vlad chortled, speaking at length with Dragunov before leaving the room again.

"What was all that about?"

"He says we'll leave in the morning and drive to Georgia. We'll cross the border with one of their shipments. It's all set up with the border guards. There won't be any trouble."

"Shipments of what?"

An ironic grin crossed Dragunov's face. "What do you think?"

A short time later, they were busy discussing their plan to eliminate Dokka Umarov, when Vlad marched one of the teenage girls into the room, gripping a handful of her blond hair. He took a half-inch dowel rod from behind the refrigerator and began to beat the girl across her backside, snarling at her in filthy-sounding Russian as she squealed in pain.

Gil stood up from the chair. "That's enough, god-damnit!"

Dragunov was on his feet an instant behind him. "Gil, this isn't our business."

"I don't give a good goddamn!" Gil was on the verge of drawing the M9.

"What's he saying?" Vlad demanded.

Two more big men appeared through the blue-beaded curtain, one with a submachine pistol slung under his arm.

Dragunov ignored Vlad, his eyes cutting into Gil. "Do you want to get us both killed? The girl too? Because this foul-smelling bastard will cut her throat just to spite you."

"What did he say?" Vlad demanded again. "Tell me what he said!"

Dragunov turned around. "He's not used to this. You know how soft the fucking Americans are. Maybe you could beat the bitch in the other room."

Vlad glanced at Gil and laughed. "You're serious? Is he queer or what?"

Dragunov shook his head, realizing it was going to be long twelve hours with this gang. "He just doesn't want to see you beating the girl, that's all."

Vlad let go of her hair and tossed the dowel rod onto the table. "Then he can do it. She refused to suck the cus-tomer's dick, so she gets thirty lashes with the stick. That's the rule."

Dragunov knew he had to defuse the situation. "That's not his job. All I'm asking is for you to do it in the other room. I'm asking you one Russian to another."

Vlad shook his head. "This has nothing to do with you and me." He pointed at Gil. "It has to do with him and that fucking look in his eyes. You tell him he can give the girl her thirty lashes, or I'll give her sixty—right here in front of him."

"This isn't professional," Dragunov said, his tone suddenly peremptory. "He's just a sheltered American."

Vlad shook his head, staring at Gil who stared right back at him. "No, he's not sheltered. Not this one. This one is a killer—I can see it. He's already killed me fifty times in his mind. You tell him what I said, or I'll beat this fucking whore to death. Tell him!"

Dragunov looked at Gil. "He wants you to beat the girl—or he'll kill her."

Gil smiled, his gaze still locked with Vlad's, silently consigning himself to death. "Let him kill her."

"What?"

"I said, let him kill her. He'll be dead before her body hits the floor."

To give himself and everyone else a moment to decompress, Dragunov took Gil's cigarettes from the table and shook one loose from the pack, taking time to light it before finally saying to Gil, "I'm not going to tell him that."

"Then I guess we got a problem," Gil said, still locked in a stare-down with Vlad.

"What's he saying?" Vlad asked, glad for the excuse to break eye contact with the American who obviously wasn't afraid to die.

Dragunov drew from the cigarette. "He said he doesn't beat women, but you should be his guest to beat her as many times as you want."

"Good!" Vlad grabbed the stick from the table and seized the girl by the hair again, giving her a thrashing the likes of which no one in the room had ever seen. She screamed the entire time, trying to block the blows with her hands, and receiving a couple of broken fingers for her troubles. The stick finally snapped after sixty-five lashes, and Vlad threw her on the floor at Gil's feet, where she lay sobbing in agony.

"Fuck you!" Vlad said with a sneer in passable English. "This is my house!" he added in Russian. "These whores belong to me!"

Gil was as calm as the sea on a windless day, having decided his course of action after the first couple of blows, tuning out the girl's agonized cries.

"That was your doing," Dragunov told him quietly. "Has he made his point now?"

Gil nodded. "He's made his point."

Vlad shouted for the other women to take the girl to her room, to get her cleaned up and back to work.

The girl was taken away, and Gil crushed out his cigarette in the ashtray on the table, exhaling from the corner of his mouth. "You might wanna finish that smoke, partner."

Dragunov looked at him, his adrenaline surging. "Why?"

"'Cuz there's gonna be a gunfight, and I don't think you wanna be standin' there with your dick in your hand."

"Don't." Dragunov's face was composed, but he was readying himself for violence. "Don't make me shoot you."

"Before this shit kicks off," Gil said, casually tucking the pack of cigarettes away in his pocket, "I wanna thank you again for saving that SEAL's life on the beach. You taught me something about Russians I never knew."

Dragunov leaned forward to crush out the cigarette, knowing there was no way to stop what was to come. "What was that?"

"That you're no worse than the rest of us." Gil jerked

the M9 from his pocket and shot Vlad right between the eyes. Vlad's head snapped back, and his body dropped to the floor like a sack of cement.

Dragunov was only barely behind on the draw, whipping around and shooting the two men behind him as they grabbed for their guns.

Women screamed, and men began shouting from what seemed like all over the building. Chaos reigned during the next ten or fifteen seconds, as panicked customers stumbled into the corridor, hopping clumsily into their pants as they made for the exit.

"Grab the Uzi!" Gil ducked clear of the doorway as both Russians from the front of the house came barreling up the hall, slugging the customers aside with their pistols in their haste to reach the kitchen.

Gil shot one dead the second he appeared, and the other pulled back, throwing himself into one of the bedrooms.

Dragunov made sure the Uzi pistol was ready to fire, and stole a look through the blue-beaded curtain. "There are more men in back."

"Any idea how many?"

"Enough that I should shoot you and offer them your fucking head," Dragunov growled in his gravelly voice.

Gil changed out the partial magazine for a full one. "Think it would do any good?"

"It's worth a fucking try!"

Gil stole a look down the corridor leading to the exit. The woman with long black hair stared back at him from two doors down. "Come here!" he said, beckoning with his hand.

She stole a glance toward the exit and came scurrying into the kitchen. He grabbed her arm and swung her around him into the corner. "Where do they keep your passports?"

"A safe in the office." Her Russian accent was strong, but she was easily understood.

"What fucking passports?" Dragunov snarled from across the room. "What are you talking about?"

"Extraction! You think I'd let him beat that girl if I wasn't getting her out of here?"

"That's not our mission!"

Gil chuckled. "Yeah, well mission parameters change, Ivan." He looked at the woman. "What's your name?"

"Katarina."

"Who can open the safe besides that asshole over there?"

She glanced at Vlad's body. "His brother Lucian. The bald one out front with the big belly."

"Hear that, Ivan? Don't shoot the fat bald fucker. You clear the back while I clear us a way out."

Dragunov didn't like the idea of splitting up, but they were fighting a battle on two fronts. He slid one of the dead men's pistols across the kitchen floor to Gil. "Don't get killed, you fool."

"I won't if you won't."

Gil wrapped around the corner with a pistol in each hand, stalking boldly into the first bedroom, where the Russian had taken cover. He caught him completely un-prepared and shot him twice in the head. A teenage girl cowered on the bed in the corner, and he waved her into the corridor, signaling for her to gather the others from their rooms and take them to the kitchen. There was a burst of fire from Dragunov's Uzi down the back hall, and she grabbed onto Gil, but he pushed her away, hazing her toward the kitchen.

"Katarina, call them to the kitchen!"

Katarina poked her head around, calling the others out of hiding, and five more girls emerged from their rooms.

"Lucian!" Gil shouted through the red-beaded curtain.

Someone answered in Russian from around the corner to the right.

"Dumb fuck," Gil thought to himself, now knowing his target's location and that the hall entrance was bracketed to the left and right.

There was a wild exchange of gunfire in the back of the building, Dragunov's Uzi followed by a few lengthy blasts from an AK-47. Seconds later, men were screaming in hand-to-hand combat. Gil jammed one pistol down his belt and stepped to the right side of the hall, peering through the beaded curtain to his left, visually cutting the lobby into sections as if it were a pie, each minute step forward revealing another thin slice of the room. He glimpsed a man's shoulder and fired through the beads.

The Russian twisted into the wound, grabbing it with his right hand, and Gil shot him in the spine between the shoulder blades. The women in the foyer cried out, and he shifted to the left side of the hall, cutting the pie to the right in search of Lucian.

A fusillade of shots rang out, and several severed strands of beads showered to the floor. Gil summersaulted through the curtain over his right shoulder, twisting to his left and shooting Lucian three times in the brachial nerve bundle of his shoulder, instantly paralyzing his gun arm and knocking him over backward.

The women in the room jumped to their feet and fled through the curtain to the kitchen. Gil checked Lucian for additional weapons and hauled him to his feet. "Game over, fuck stick!"

Dragunov appeared through the curtain with dark red blood covering his face from the nose down. "All clear in the back."

Gil saw the blood. "How bad are you?"

Dragunov swiped at his face, spitting blood and viscera onto the floor. "It's not mine. I had to bite the big bastard's throat."

A minute later, they were in the back office with Lucian on his knees in front of the safe.

"Open it!" Dragunov thumped him in the head with the muzzle of his M9.

"Fuck you!" Lucian sneered in Russian.

Gil looked at Dragunov. "We don't have all night here."

"Tie his hands," Dragunov said. "I'll be back."

Gil kicked Lucian onto his face and ripped the phone cord from the wall, using it to bind the Russian's hands as tightly as he could. The man groaned in pain.

Gil then rolled him onto his back as Dragunov returned with four women in their midtwenties. "What's goin' on?"

"They'll make the man talk."

That's when Gil realized each of the women held a serrated steak knife from the kitchen. They swarmed over Lucian, ripping and sawing through his clothes. He tried to reason with them in panic, but they swore at him and spit in his face. One of them grabbed his ear and began to saw it off. He screamed, and they slashed at his exposed groin. He kicked at them, but one of the girls jumped on his legs to hold him down, and he howled like a man put to the rack.

Dragunov allowed the mutilation to continue for a few seconds before calling them off. Then he stood glowering over the hyperventilating Russian. "Are you going to open the box or let them feed you your balls?"

"I'll open it!" Lucian gasped, an ear and part of his nose already carved off, his genitalia slashed and bleeding. "Let me up!"

Gil cut his hands free, and Lucian flexed his fingers, quickly working the combination, his clothes half torn from his body.

"He'll have a gun in there," Gil warned.

Dragunov gave him a wink. "Probably the reason he's agreed to open it."

The second Lucian turned the handle, Dragunov shot him in the back of the head and kicked the body aside. Inside the safe was a Tokarev pistol, along with multiple bundles of Turkish lira and a stack of eighteen red passports bound with a thick rubber band.

Gil stuffed the passports into his pocket, and the women began to protest immediately. He saw Katarina standing in the doorway. "Kat, explain to them I don't want them losing their passports before we get to the airport. There's gonna be a lot of confusion between here and there."

Katarina told the others what he'd said, and that seemed to settle them for the moment.

"Get them dressed and ready to go," Dragunov said to Katarina solemnly in Russian. Then he looked at Gil. "You're going to make a lot of trouble for the Kremlin with this."

Gil knelt in front of the safe, stacking the bundles of cash on top of it. "Not if you guys know a damn thing about PR."

"Putin is not exactly a PR specialist."

"Fuck Putin," Gil said, getting to his feet. "I don't work for his ass."

"I *do*."

"Then I'll take them back to Moscow by myself, and you can blame it all on me—however you want it. But I'm blown here, so I gotta get the fuck out of Turkey before word of this gets around."

"What are you talking about? You can't go to Moscow. You don't have—"

Gil held up his Russian passport. "I'm flying home to Mother Russia, and not even Putin can stop me."

40

THE WHITE HOUSE

Chairman of the Joint Chiefs General Couture hung up the phone and looked across the room at White House Chief of Staff Glen Brooks. "You'd better get the old man, Glen. The shit is about to hit the fan in Eastern Europe."

Brooks put down the report he was reading. "They hit the pipeline?"

Couture shook his head. "That was Pope. Shannon just knocked over a Russian whorehouse in Istanbul. Now he's getting ready to fly eighteen female abductees home to Moscow."

Brooks gaped at him. "He can't do that."

"Wanna bet? He's a got a Russian passport and three hundred thousand dollars' worth of Turkish lira. He can do just about anything he wants at this point."

"No, I mean he can't do that," Brooks said, getting up. "He's on a mission. He's got orders."

Couture stared across the room with his hands on

his hips. "Where the hell have *you* been the past eighteen months?"

"But—"

"But *hell*," Couture said, stepping forward. "Didn't you read the file I sent over on Operation Tiger Claw?"

"I skimmed it."

"Did you skim the part where Shannon brought a pregnant Iranian back from Iran—a pregnant Iranian he'd been ordered to kill by that idiot Lerher?"

"I didn't catch that part, no."

Couture dry-wiped his mouth. "If we don't play this right, it's going to rain dung. President Putin is one suspicious son of a bitch, and it's all too possible he'll think we staged this as a stunt to make him look like a fool. Not to mention that Shannon's head is packed with intel we don't really need the Russians to have."

Brooks stepped around the table. "I'll get the president."

"Hold on a second. Let's make sure we're on the same page."

"Meaning?"

"Meaning, what are we going to advise?"

Brooks looked at his watch. "How soon does Shannon land?"

"Pope doesn't know, but they're not even in the air yet, so we've got time. Shannon still has to get them to the airport and buy the tickets. He called Pope so State would have time to contact Moscow before their arrival."

"Why the hell is he flying with them? Why doesn't he just put them on the plane?"

"Because the Russian mob is going to be hot on his ass."

"And his solution to that is flying to Russia, for Christ's sake?"

"All he's got is a Russian passport."

Brooks let out a sigh, and they each grabbed a chair.

"Okay," Brooks said. "So we check the scheduled flights out of Istanbul. That will give us some idea of the time frame we're working with. From there we can judge how soon to contact Moscow."

Couture nodded and picked up the phone, directing his aide to print off a list of flights leaving Istanbul for Moscow over the next twenty-four hours.

"What about the Spetsnaz guy?" Brooks said. "Is Dragunov dead, or what?"

"Pope didn't mention him. What we need to figure out right now is how to advise the president before he gets on the horn to Putin."

Brooks sat thinking. "What about grounding the flight? We have people in Istanbul who can make that happen, right?"

"You mean maroon them there?"

"Sure," Brooks said. "Why not? Look, Shannon exceeded mission parameters—something he's apparently done before—so he'll have only himself to blame. Once he realizes we're not letting him out of Turkey with those women, he'll have to abandon them and get his ass back on track with the mission he was sent in there to carry out. He's a resourceful man. I'm sure he'll find his way to Georgia without the Russian mob catching up to him."

"And the women?"

Brooks shrugged. "They're prostitutes."

"I told you they were abducted," Couture said. "They're victims of the slave trade."

"Not our responsibility, Bill. Hell, their own government doesn't even care about them. Why should we risk straining our relations with Moscow over a few Russian runaways? We're already in enough of a tussle with Putin over the mess in Ukraine."

Brooks saw the strained look on Couture's face. "Look, it's heartless. I know that. But what we're talking about here is an American CIA agent flying into *Moscow* on a *Russian* passport with eighteen Russian prostitutes. Come on, Bill! We can't allow that to happen if it's within our means to stop it. We just can't. What you said about Putin is exactly right. He'll think we did it to make him look stupid. Hell, he'd be stupid *not* to think so."

Couture was silent for a long moment. "Is that how you're going to advise the president?"

Brooks nodded. "That's where I come out, yeah. What about you?"

The general got up from his chair. "I respect you sticking to your guns, Glen, but I'm going to advise we allow the State Department to do their job."

"Fair enough," Brooks said, getting to his feet. "Now, let me go and pull him away from the first lady."

Couture chuckled. "You deserve hazard pay for that."

"So far she and I get along pretty well."

When the door closed, Couture reached for the phone again. "Bob, it's Bill. Listen, you'd better advise Typhoon he might have to find alternate transport for himself and his cargo. I don't know for sure yet, but the president may elect to ground the flight."

41

MEXICO CITY,
Mexico

The phone rang on the nightstand beside the bed, and Tim Hagen stepped into the bedroom to answer it. "Hello?"

"Are you alone?" asked Ken Peterson.

Hagen glanced across the hotel suite at his two Mexican bodyguards, who sat watching a soccer game on television. "Hold on a second." He went to close the door and then returned to the phone. "Okay, what is it?"

"The FBI busted Grieves's informant inside the White House—we're all burned. To make matters worse, Shannon got out of Sicily, and Pope's been given Secret Service protection. I'm calling to warn you because we go back a long time, but I'm striking camp and bugging out."

Hagen sat down on the bed, weak in the legs. "Bugging out to where?"

"Never mind that. You need to think about where *you're* going."

"But there's no proof we've done anything."

"There will be," Peterson said. "The Frenchman is talking, so it's only a matter of time before the good senator from New York is forced to give us up for accessing the CIA mainframe."

"What mainframe?" Hagen knew Peterson was shrewd enough to have already turned state's evidence and that the FBI might be listening in on the call.

Peterson chuckled sardonically. "Tim, don't get paranoid. Nobody's listening. I haven't gone to the Feds. The writing's been on the wall for a long time now, so believe me, I've prepared for this eventuality. With men like Pope and Webb running the CIA, the US is screwed. How long do you think it'll be before those two clowns let another nuke into the country? I did what I did to try and save the agency, but I failed. So it's time to fall on my sword or run like hell, and I'm not the type to fall on my sword."

Hagen sat with his head in his hand, having hardly heard a word. "It should've been the simplest thing," he muttered to himself, unable to believe that Shannon was still alive, with so many others dead. "He's only one man, for God's sake. There has to be a way to stop him!"

"Tim, did you hear what I just told you? Killing Shannon doesn't solve our problems anymore. There's going to be a federal investigation. We're burned!"

"Stop saying that!" Hagen flared. "We can handle a goddamn investigation. The evidence against us is practically nonexistent. All we have to do is keep Grieves from opening his fat mouth!"

Peterson sighed at other the end of the line. "And how do you propose we accomplish that? You got photos of him shagging a hooker too?"

"As a matter of fact, I'm talking about something a hell

of a lot more certain than blackmail. And with Grieves out of the way, the only one left to worry about is Shannon."

"Christ Almighty. What is your obsession with that guy?"

Hagen stood up from the bed, his rage finally boiling over. "He's Pope's right-hand man, you pompous ass! And Pope destroyed everything I worked ten years to achieve! I was run out of the White House in disgrace because of him! *That's* my fucking obsession, Ken!"

Peterson was incredulous. "So that's what this was all about? You blew our entire operation over a personal vendetta? You stupid, stupid son of a bitch. No. *I'm* the stupid son of a bitch. I should've known you didn't give a shit about protecting the country. You've never given a shit about anyone but yourself."

Hagen smirked. "Like the country ever gave a shit about you? Wake up, Ken. It's a zero-sum game. Whoever's got the most at the end wins, and I don't plan on walking away from the table anytime soon."

"At the end of what, Tim?"

"Life!" Hagen slammed the phone down in the cradle. He had one card left up his sleeve, and it was time to play it.

42

ISTANBUL,
Turkey

Gil stood in the street in front of the brothel, watching the end of the alley. The fog had settled in. There were two cars and an unknown number of men blocking the alley at fifty yards.

"We didn't clear out fast enough."

The women were crammed into a small van in the parking lot, all of them more than a little anxious to leave.

Dragunov grunted. "You thought this would be easy?"

"The only easy day was yesterday. Any suggestions?"

Dragunov looked at the rooftops, scanning to the end of the alley. The buildings were built wall to wall. "There's a Kalashnikov inside. I can go over the rooftops and hit them from above."

"How many rounds for the rifle?"

"One magazine."

"Thirty rounds goes fast once you start taking return

fire." Gil glanced around for another option, but there wasn't one. "How fast will the police respond, do you think?"

Dragunov shrugged. "That depends on their relationship with these people. Vlad said they were protected, so if they *do* come, it won't be to help us."

Gil got on his sat phone to Langley, giving Midori their location and asking for satellite surveillance. "What I need is an exact head count on how many men are blocking our escape."

"I'm sorry, Gil, but I don't have a satellite over your location. The satellite we used for the Sicily op has already been retasked."

"Can't you free it up?"

"Not in time to help you with your situation. Also, I just got off the line with Pope. He said you may have to find another way out of Turkey. The president is considering using assets to delay any flight you board with those girls—citing engine trouble. They're worried a rescue of this nature could cause political trouble with Putin."

"Shit," Gil swore. "Again with Putin."

"So far, grounding the flight is still just an option," Midori clarified. "Apparently Couture supports letting you proceed. He's the one who warned Pope."

"Well, I'll have to count on Couture, because there ain't no other way outta here with these girls. Make sure Pope understands that."

"He does."

"Okay. Typhoon out." Gil tucked away the phone. "We're on our own, Ivan, so be fast up there."

"What did she say about Putin?"

"The White House is afraid of pissing off the Kremlin."

"This is a stupid idea," Dragunov said with a sigh. "I should have shot you."

"There's still time to do that," Gil said with a grin.

Dragunov glanced at the desperate female faces peering back at him through the van's fogged-up windows. "Get ready to fight."

"Roger that. I'll move the second you open up."

Dragunov went back inside the brothel, and a couple of minutes later, he signaled Gil from the roof. He made his way over four rooftops with the AK-47 until he reached the street, peering over the edge of the roof to see six men waiting below in the fog. The streetlights along the block were burnt out, and visibility was dim. He listened to them talking and realized they were confused about what exactly had taken place in the brothel. One of Vlad's men had apparently gotten a call off, but he hadn't lived long enough to give much in the way of details. They were concerned about walking into an ambush, and one of them kept calling someone on the phone but got no answer. Dragunov guessed he was calling Vlad, who was already dead with a bullet between the eyes. One of the men had a machine gun slung over his shoulder, but the others seemed to be carrying nothing more than pistols beneath their jackets. Dragunov switched the select-fire lever to single shot and sighted on the chest of the man with the MP5.

The report of the rifle was like a cannon blast, shattering the foggy silence. The man with the machine gun was thrown to the ground with his heart exploded in his chest, and Dragunov dropped two more men within a couple of seconds as the other three pulled their pistols and began firing at the rooftop.

With Dragunov's first shot, Gil had bolted up the alley. He covered half the distance and ducked into a doorway, opening up with the M9 and dropping one man who had taken cover on his side of the roadblock.

The last two Russians poured fire in Gil's direction, driving him behind the cover of the doorway, but Dragunov shot them both down from above.

"Clear!" he shouted.

Gil dashed toward the roadblock to drag the bodies into the shadows as Dragunov ran back to the brothel. Within three minutes, Gil had both cars moved out of the way, and Dragunov pulled up with the van.

On the way to the airport, Gil threw his pistol out the window into a vacant lot. With only a few rounds left in the magazine, there was no point to risk getting caught with it. He took the passports from his pocket and began passing them out, telling Katarina to make sure they didn't lose them.

Many of the young women kissed their passports, clutching them to their breasts with tears streaming down their faces.

"In your coat pockets!" Gil said, pantomiming, and they quickly tucked them away.

They arrived at the airport without incident, parking in the parking deck. Dragunov killed the motor and turned around in the seat, admonishing the girls in Russian to remain calm and to act natural no matter what happened inside the airport.

"Our passports haven't been stamped at the port of entry, so there are going to be questions," he explained. "If we can't bribe our way onto the plane, we'll have to involve the Russian Embassy, and that will mean a very long night. So let me do the talking. Understood?"

The women nodded in earnest, and Dragunov looked at Gil. "We could take them to the embassy and drop them off. I can call Federov and arrange for another—"

Katarina began to protest, and he whipped his head around. "What did I tell you?"

"Look, the longer they're in Turkey," Gil said, "the longer they're at risk. Too damn much can go wrong. Let's see if we can get on a plane."

The airport was busy even at that late hour, but the moment the twenty of them entered the airport, they drew the immediate attention of security personnel. The armed men watched closely, talking furtively into their radios. The group was stopped before making it anywhere close to the Aeroflot ticket counter, and two stern-looking Turkish officials appeared from behind a wall, giving instructions to the chief of security.

"This means trouble," Dragunov muttered. "They were expecting us."

"Roger that," Gil said. "I told you we shoulda gone to the embassy."

Dragunov turned and gaped at him.

43

THE WHITE HOUSE

The door to the Oval Office opened, and Secretary of State John Sapp entered the room.

The president stood up from behind his desk. "Thank you for coming on such short notice, John."

"I came as quickly as I could, Mr. President." Sapp crossed the office and shook hands with the commander in chief, turning to shake hands with Couture and Brooks before sitting down.

"Gentlemen," the president said, "I've asked John to weigh in on the stalemate between the two of you. He probably has a better understanding of the Russian mind than any of us."

The sixty-year-old secretary of state had spent ten years as the US ambassador to the Soviet Union during the Cold War. He was a tall, slender man with gray hair and discerning gray eyes.

"Glen," the president said to the White House chief of staff, "give John your thoughts on grounding the plane in Istanbul."

Brooks sat forward in the chair and explained to Sapp why he thought Gil Shannon should be prevented from flying what he referred to as "a planeload of prostitutes" into Moscow.

Sapp listened thoughtfully, nodding after Brooks had finished. "It's absolutely a possibility that Putin will take offense at this. He doesn't trust us. He doesn't trust anyone with altruistic motives. But, then again, sociopaths aren't capable of altruistic emotion. He sees everyone as the enemy, even those within his own government. He's much like Stalin in that regard."

Brooks, feeling vindicated, sat back in his chair. "That's my exact point."

"But I don't recommend grounding the flight," Sapp went on to say, "and I'll tell you why."

Brooks stiffened.

Sapp crossed his legs, calmly resting his hand on his knee. "Consider this emergence in the broader scope: Russia knows they're indirectly responsible for last year's nuclear attacks on American soil. It's a significant embarrassment for them, and they've been trying to wriggle out of it, but they're going to have to acknowledge their culpability very soon now, and they know it. China's finally ready to confirm the isotope test results, and that's going leave Russia as the odd man out on the UN Security Council. Everyone—the Russians included—are going to have to face up to the fact that the uranium was enriched at the Ural facility.

"And make no mistake: Putin is as aware of the paradigm shift as we are. It's not Russia versus the United

States anymore. It's Russia and the US versus Islamic extremism. Imagine the results of a man like Dokka Umarov getting his hands on a stolen nuke. He'd incinerate Moscow. Putin's willingness to work with us on this pipeline plot has nothing to do with protecting the pipeline. He's afraid of Umarov and his network, and anything he can do to weaken Umarov is good policy. What Russia is attempting to do, however, is manipulate us into helping them on their terms. They want to be in a position to dictate policy well into the future.

"What Master Chief Shannon has inadvertently given us here is an opportunity to level the playing field; a chance for *us* to do the manipulating. My recommendation is to let the plane take off. I can talk with Prime Minister Medvedev over the phone once it's in the air. He and I have a rapport, and contrary to popular belief, Putin does listen to him—more than anyone has any real idea. I can *suggest* that Russia use this little rescue as an opportunity to improve their public image in the wake of their failure with the suitcase nukes. Taking a public stand against human trafficking will play well for them, and if they're worried about creating unnecessary friction with the Russian mafia, they can always say these unfortunate young women were being held by Islamic terrorists. Who's going to be the wiser, except for the victims?"

"What about the Turks?" Brooks interjected. "They're holding Shannon and the others for us at the airport, and they're not at all happy about this 'little rescue.'"

Sapp shrugged. "The Turks have to play this however we ask them to."

"Oh?" Brooks smiled. "And why is that?"

"Because of the earthquake last month," Sapp replied easily. "We've pledged more than a billion dollars in relief—only half of which has been paid so far—and that doesn't include our recent increase in military aid. So the Turks are not going to be a problem. The only problem is Putin, and I'm confident I can get Medvedev to make him see the opportunity in this."

The president looked at Couture. "How soon do we have to make a decision?"

"Next flight leaves in ninety minutes."

"John, do you see any possible downside?"

"Nothing long lasting," Sapp answered. "The only real risk is to Master Chief Shannon. Once he arrives in Moscow on a Russian passport, he could become a pawn, but I don't think they'll hurt him. They may hold on to him for a while, long enough to make their point, but Major Dragunov was well treated aboard the *Ohio*, so I think they'll return the courtesy. As I've said already, they're going to need us in the future, and they're smart enough to see this opportunity for what it is—provided it's put to them in the correct tone. Tone is always very important with the Russians, especially with Stalinists like Putin."

"General," the president said, "make sure Shannon and his people are aboard that plane when it takes off."

"Yes, sir." Couture got up from his chair and left the room.

The president's phone chimed on the desk, announcing an incoming text message. He picked up the phone expecting to see a text from his wife, but to his surprise, the message was from Tim Hagen. "What the hell could this possibly be about?" he muttered, warily opening the message to see a frozen video image himself and a young Asian woman. The shock effect was instantaneous. His heart began to race, and he began to sweat immediately.

Brooks exchanged glances with Sapp, both of them

seeing the color drain from the president's face. "Sir, are you okay?"

"Get my car ready, Glen. I'm going over to talk with Pope."

"At this hour, sir?"

The president stood up from his chair. "I asked you to get the car ready, Glen. Get it ready now."

44

ISTANBUL,
Turkey

Gil and the others sat cooling their heels in a large briefing room usually reserved for airport security personnel. Most of the women were crying because the mob money and their passports had been confiscated.

Dragunov sat in the corner looking pissed, with his arms folded over his chest. "Do you have any more good ideas?"

Gil shook his head. "Fresh out."

"Maybe next time you'll listen to me."

"Maybe," Gil muttered, taking the pack of cigarettes from his peacoat.

One of two armed security men near the door stepped forward, wagging his index finger. "No smoking!"

"Roger that." Gil put the smokes back into his pocket.

Dragunov smirked. "There will be plenty of smoking in prison."

Gil looked at him. "That meant to be a double en-tendre?"

"What the hell is that?"

The door opened, and one of the Turkish airport of-ficials stepped into the room, their passports in his hand. Everyone gawked in silence as he walked through the room handing them out. Gil's was the last to be returned.

"Let's go," the official said in accented English. "The plane is now boarding."

Katarina translated what he said, and the women all popped out of their chairs, making for the door.

Gil tucked the passport away with the cigarettes, ex-changing suspicious glances with Dragunov. "The plane to where?" he asked the official.

"Moscow! Where else? Now, follow me."

Dragunov shouldered past Gil on his way to the front of the line. "Bring up the rear and keep your eyes open," he said in a low voice. "It's possible they're giving us back to the mafia."

The official led them down a long white corridor. They emerged from a doorway just beyond the security check-point where late-night travelers were busy taking off their shoes and stepping through metal detectors.

"Wait here," the official told Dragunov. "I have to get your boarding passes."

The women huddled together, talking guardedly among themselves.

"What do you think?" Gil said.

Dragunov grunted, putting a hand on his shoulder and pointing beyond the bank of metal detectors. "It looks like our friends have come to see us off."

Gil looked over to see a pair of angry-looking Rus-sians in black leather jackets staring back at them. He gave them the finger and formed the words *Fuck you* with his lips.

The Russians stared a few moments more. Then they turned and left.

"Adios, assholes."

"You think we've won," Dragunov said. "But we've made very dangerous enemies tonight. They will hunt us forever."

"Well, I don't speak Russian," Gil said. "So when you get the chance, do me a favor and tell 'em to get in line behind Al Qaeda, the RSMB, the ACLU, and every other motherfucker who wants a piece of me."

The Spetsnaz man chuckled. "I'm going to catch hell for not shooting you. Because of this, the GRU will never be able to work with them in Turkey again."

"Too bad." Gil pointed to where the women were joyfully receiving their boarding passes from the airport official. "Don't tell me that doesn't make you feel good."

Dragunov nodded. "Yes, but it wasn't our mission—and you know that."

They boarded the plane a short time later, and the captain of the plane joined them in the back. "Are you Major Ivan Dragunov?" he asked in Russian.

"Yes."

The captain gestured at Gil. "And this is the American?"

"Yes. Ugly, isn't he?"

The captain grinned. "Major, I need for you to collect the passports from these women and send them forward to the cockpit. Moscow wants a complete list of names so they can begin to notify the families."

The women immediately began to object.

Gil reached across the aisle, putting his hand on Katarina's arm. "What's going on now?" She told him what the captain had said, and he shook his head. "Tell them not to give up their passports again until we arrive at Moscow customs."

Katarina quickly told the others, and they all defiantly jammed their hands into their coat pockets.

Dragunov elbowed him in the ribs. "What the hell are you doing?"

"They can write their names down on a sheet of paper. These girls are traumatized as hell, and you wanna take their fuckin' passports again?"

The captain stared at Gil. "Mr. Shannon, no one is going to steal their passports aboard my aircraft."

"You can call me Master Chief Shannon, Captain."

The captain smiled dryly. "Very well, *Master Chief*. If you would ask these young ladies to write their names down for me and pass the list to the cockpit? Then perhaps my government can get on with its work."

"Hear that?" Gil asked Katarina.

She nodded, saying "Thank you" to the captain in English.

The captain nodded. "I'll have the attendant bring paper and something to write with." He then returned to the cockpit and closed the door.

Dragunov looked at Gil and smirked.

"You're doin' a lotta smirkin' tonight, Major."

"You seem to have no idea where you're going," Dragunov said, putting his seat back and making himself comfortable. "You will, though, soon enough."

"Don't get *too* comfy over there. You're gonna have to return that seat to its upright position before we take off."

Dragunov closed his eyes. "Leave me alone, Master Chief. A crazy American has been trying to get me killed for days, and I'm very tired."

45

BETHESDA NAVAL HOSPITAL,
Bethesda, Maryland

Robert Pope opened his eyes to see the president standing at the foot of his bed in the subdued lighting of his hospital room. His first thought was that something had gone terribly wrong in Turkey. "Has something happened to Gil, Mr. President?"

The president shook his head. "No, Gil's fine. He and the others left Istanbul for Moscow half an hour ago. I'm here at this untimely hour because I need your counsel on a very personal matter."

Pope adjusted himself in the bed, wiping his face with his hands to wake himself up. "You look worried, sir. What can I do for you?"

The president took the phone from his pocket and stepped around the side of the bed. "I received this . . . *message* . . . from Tim Hagen two hours ago." He put the phone into Pope's hand and touched the screen to start the video clip.

In the video, the president was sitting beside a young Korean woman in the back of a limousine. He was clearly drunk and quite taken with the young woman. He was kissing the side of her face, running his hand in and out of her blouse and up and down the inside of her thigh, beneath her skirt. She was laughing and rubbing the bulge in his trousers. The voice of Tim Hagen could be heard very close to the phone, talking and chortling as if he were having a conversation with someone on the other end. After twenty seconds, the video cut to the president performing cunnilingus on the woman. Twenty seconds later, it cut again to her straddling him, and the president moaning that he was about to climax. After a full minute, the video stopped.

Pope gave the phone back to the president. "That's obviously an edited version?"

"Yes," the president said quietly, slipping the phone into his jacket. "I expect it probably is."

"And you had no idea he was filming you?"

"None. We'd just won the Iowa caucuses, and I was drunker than the Lords of London. I thought he was bragging to someone about the victory." The president massaged the bridge of his nose with his fingers. "I trusted that man with my life, and he put me in the White House. I had no idea I'd made a deal with the devil."

Pope blessed his luck. "Why have you shared this with me, sir?"

"Hagen's letting me know that if he goes down, he's taking me with him. My wife is nothing like Hillary Clinton. She would divorce me immediately—and publicly."

Pope nodded his understanding. "With respect, Mr. President, that doesn't really answer my question."

The president spoke to him gravely. "Can you stop this video before it goes viral?"

"Is this a frank and open conversation, sir?"

"It is."

"In that case, I can stop it with a ninety percent certainty," Pope replied. "But I'll have to remove Hagen from the game board to do it. There's a slight chance he's arranged for the video to go viral in the event of his death, but under the circumstances, I believe that to be unlikely."

"Under what circumstances?"

"I'm extremely close to Hagen, Mr. President. I have been since shortly after I ended up here. For all intents and purposes, I might as well be in the room with him at this very moment. If he's arranged for that video go viral automatically, he did so a long time ago—which isn't likely, in my opinion."

The president let out a heavy sigh and stood away from the bed, resting his weight on the back of a chair near the window. "I can't give you an order like that to protect my own hide."

"You don't have to order anything," Pope said. "All you have to do is agree not to ask any questions about him after tonight. Hagen's a traitor, Mr. President. Innocent people are dead because of him and his coconspirators."

"But can you prove that?"

"In a court of law? No. But one of the CIA mainframes was accessed by an old series of codes that Hagen would have had access to during his time as chief of staff. Normally that series of codes would have been canceled after Hagen's resignation, but the agency's a mess, and a number of department heads have been slacking off. The day I get out of here, I plan to fire more than fifty people."

The president felt sick to his stomach. "I know I'm a pathetic coward for asking you this, Robert, but what are the chances of it coming back to bite us if he's removed?"

"Zero," Pope answered. "He'll simply vanish. The FBI will be left to assume that he's gone on the run. He has plenty of money offshore, so it's more than believable. He should have run already, but he's a very foolish man."

"Foolish how?"

"Foolish in that he's too stubborn to admit that he's lost. He lost the day you asked for his resignation. He's the one who burned Gil in Paris, Mr. President. He did it to get revenge against me—and Gil—for reasons probably only he would truly understand."

The president stared. "You said you're in the room with him right now. That means you'd already planned on his *disappearance*, doesn't it?"

Pope smiled. "Maybe not quite this soon . . ."

"So I've unnecessarily shown you my ass this evening."

"I wouldn't say so, sir. A man like Hagen could do a lot of damage with that video in a very short period of time. The sooner he takes a little vacation, the better."

"A vacation . . ." The president thought it over at length, at last deciding that Hagen had asked for whatever Pope had in mind for him. "Okay. I won't ask about him again. Now, what about the CIA? Can you save it, or will I have to dissolve it?"

"If I'm given a free hand, sir, you won't even recognize the CIA nine months from now."

The president touched Pope on the shoulder. "Heal up, Robert. I'll look forward to seeing you at the White House for dinner the day you're released. We have a lot to talk about."

"I appreciate the invitation. Thank you."

The president went to the door and was about to step into the hall when he turned on his heel. "Will Putin let Shannon out of Russia, or will he hold on to him?"

Pope grinned. "Do not fear, sir. Everything is going according to plan."

The president shook his head as he slipped out of the room.

46

MOSCOW,
Russia

More than half of the young Russian women rescued from the brothel in Istanbul had family waiting for them at the Domodedovo Airport southeast of Moscow when the plane landed shortly after sunrise. The women cheered the moment the wheels touched down and smothered both Gil and Dragunov with kisses upon deplaning.

The rescuers were not afforded the opportunity to see the women reunited with their loved ones, however. The Russian media had been invited to film the tearful reunions for propaganda purposes, and the Kremlin had given express orders for Gil and Dragunov to be kept away from the cameras. They were ushered immediately from the plane to a waiting blue and white Mi-8 helicopter, which lifted off the moment the door was closed.

The Mi-8 was a large military model, but there was nothing military about the luxurious interior. Gil sat across a table from Dragunov, facing forward as they were served coffee and orange juice. "Something tells me this isn't standard treatment," he said dryly.

Dragunov sat looking pensively out the window. "This is Putin's personal helicopter."

Gil glanced around. "You're kidding me."

The Russian looked at him. "I would never joke about Putin."

"Well, you don't have much of a sense of humor, anyhow. Where are we going?"

Dragunov asked the Russian sergeant who had served their coffee. "We're going to the Kremlin."

"What do you think that means?"

"I don't know, but what it does *not* mean is that they intend to pin medals to our chests, I can assure you of that. Your people must have contacted Moscow before we boarded the plane in Istanbul. They were too well prepared for us at the airport."

Gil grinned. "Washington likes to keep things tidy with you guys. You're too touchy."

Dragunov was agitated by Gil's lightheartedness. "You still don't understand, do you? This is Russia."

"I understand that, Ivan, but what do you want me to do about it? Sit over here pissing myself? What's gonna happen is gonna happen."

"That's an easy attitude for you to take," Dragunov said irritably, looking out the window again.

Gil realized for the first time that Dragunov was legitimately spooked. "What are you so worried about? You weren't this rattled when we had people shooting at us."

Dragunov turned toward him again. "Do you think Putin would send his personal helicopter for a lowly major returning from a failed mission?" He shook his head. "This helicopter is for you. It has nothing to do with me. You're probably going to be treated like a celebrity. I'm going to be demoted and tossed into an infantry brigade. I'll probably be in Ukraine before tomorrow night. My career is ruined because of this!" He swore foully in Russian and asked the sergeant if there was any vodka aboard.

The sergeant produced a bottle of Russian Standard vodka from a small refrigerator and poured the major a drink.

A short time later, Gil saw looming in the distance the five gold onion domes of the Dormition Cathedral located within the walls of the Kremlin. "It's an awesome sight, Ivan."

For a moment, Dragunov seemed to forget his concerns, moving around to Gil's side of the table and pointing out the window to the northwest. "There near the horizon is the town of Khimki, where we stopped the Nazis in December of '41—barely eight kilometers outside of Moscow."

Gil converted the distance in his head to just shy of five miles.

Within a minute, they buzzed past the multicolored onion domes of St. Basil's Cathedral located just outside of the Kremlin near Red Square. Seconds later, they were over the landing threshold of the Kremlin helipad, constructed two years earlier in the southeast corner of the Kremlin compound. Russian presidential motorcades were infamous for causing traffic jams, and President Putin had ditched his Mercedes limousine in 2013 in favor of faster, less obtrusive transportation.

The Kremlin—meaning "fortress"—had been constructed over a period of thirteen years from 1482 to 1495 and covered almost twenty-eight acres in the heart of the city. It was surrounded by a defensive brick wall more than a mile in circumference, ranging in height from sixteen to sixty-two feet, and in thickness from eleven to twenty-one feet.

The sergeant opened the helo door, and they stepped down the short staircase to the pad, where they were received by a large contingent of Russian military personnel. Winter had not yet relinquished its grip on the city, and though there was no snow on the ground, it was still cold enough to see everyone's breath.

"Major Dragunov," said a stern-looking Spetsnaz colonel, "you will come with me."

Dragunov saluted, responding, "Yes, sir!" He turned to offer Gil his hand. "In case we never see each other again."

Gil matched his grip. "It's been a privilege, Major. I'm sorry we missed our man."

Dragunov smiled a melancholy smile. "Perhaps next time, eh?"

Gil watched as he was led away toward the western part of the fortress, accompanied by eight armed Spetsnaz soldiers.

"Master Chief Shannon?" said another Russian colonel in nearly perfect-sounding English. "I am Colonel Savcenko. I will be your interpreter during your stay here at the Kremlin."

Gil saluted the colonel at once. "I am at your orders, sir."

The colonel returned the salute. "If you will follow me, please?"

"Of course, sir."

They were escorted northward by no fewer than a dozen armed soldiers toward a large building referred to as the State Kremlin Palace.

"How was your flight from Istanbul, Master Chief?"

"A little tense at times," Gil replied, his hands in his pockets against the cold. "The girls have all been severely traumatized. I don't think they believed they were really coming home until the wheels were on the ground."

"They'll be well taken care of," the colonel said. "May I ask you for the passport you were issued in Paris?"

"Yes, sir." Gil took the passport from his coat pocket and gave it to the colonel, who passed it off to a major, who tucked it away inside his own coat. "Is my government aware of my arrival, sir?"

"I believe so," the colonel said. "I'm told someone from your embassy will call on you this evening. Before that, the president would like a private word with you over an early lunch—if you're feeling up to it."

Gil cleared his throat. "President Putin, sir?"

The colonel met his gaze. "Will that be all right with you, Master Chief?"

"Absolutely, sir. I'm just a little shocked the president of Russia would bother meeting with a virtual nobody such as myself."

The colonel smiled and continued walking. "You give yourself too little credit, Master Chief. You're a very accomplished soldier. We have been following your career rather closely here in Moscow over the past eighteen months—ever since your mission into Iran last year."

Gil went on alert. "I've never been to Iran, Colonel. I'm afraid you have me confused with someone else."

The colonel laughed. "Perhaps we do."

They walked along in silence the final few yards to the Kremlin Palace, where Gil was led inside and shown to a small suite. The room was much like a hotel room, but instead of a bed, there was a black leather sofa.

"I assume you would like an opportunity to shower

and change your clothes before your meeting with the president."

"Very much so," Gil said. "Thank you, Colonel."

"There is a change of clothes in the closet. I'll return for you in half an hour."

Savcenko stepped out, pulling the door to, and Gil dropped down on the sofa, stretching his arms across the back of it and extending his legs. "Holy shit," he muttered. "Six hours ago, I was in a Turkish whorehouse, and now here I sit in the fucking Kremlin getting ready to break bread with Stalin Junior. My wife would never believe this."

47

MEXICO CITY,
Mexico

Tim Hagen sat on his hotel bed dressed in his pajamas,
drinking Dos Equis beer and wondering how the president
of the United States had responded to the video clip. He
laughed drunkenly, thinking of how shocked the big, bad
commander in chief must have been the moment he realized that his tryst with the Korean girl had been recorded
for posterity. Hagen knew the CIA might soon move to
take him out, but that wasn't going to do the president any
good. In the morning, he would set up a delayed upload
that would require him to enter a password every twelve
hours. After one missed entry, the video would upload automatically to YouTube, Vimeo, Facebook, Ustream, and a
half dozen other websites. Within twenty-four hours, the
video would go viral, and the president would go down in
flames as the most humiliated world leader in history.

Hagen went into the bathroom to take a leak, and when

he came back out, he found both of his Mexican bodyguards standing in the bedroom doorway waiting for him.

"What's wrong?" he asked, fear surging through him.

"Nothing," said the head bodyguard, taking a silenced .380 Walther pistol from beneath his shirt. "Sit down on the bed."

"What? What the fuck is going on?" Hagen asked in dismay.

The other bodyguard stepped forward and took him by the arm. "Have a seat, señor."

"You guys can't do this," Hagen said, beginning to cry as he sat down on the edge of the bed. "You work for me. Whatever they're paying, I'll quadruple it! We can go to the bank in—"

"Be quiet." The head bodyguard called into the other room in Spanish, and two beautiful, young Mexican women with long, raven hair came in wearing nurses' uniforms. One of them was pushing a wheelchair.

"What the hell is going on?" Hagen demanded, swallowing hard. "You guys are supposed to protect me!"

"The señoritas are going to get you ready to leave," the bodyguard told him. "Don't give them any trouble, and we won't give you any trouble. Okay?"

One of the women rolled up the sleeve of Hagen's pajamas and tied off the arm with a rubber hose while the other prepared a hypodermic needle.

"Don't do this," Hagen said, tears welling in his eyes. "Please, don't do this."

The young woman smiled at him as she sat down beside him and poked the syringe into his vein, injecting him with 10 cc of Thorazine. Hagen's eyes rolled back in his head a few seconds later, and he flopped over on the sheet mumbling.

Next they took a pair of clippers from their medical bag and buzzed off all of his hair, sweeping it carefully from the sheet and flushing it down the toilet. The bodyguards then lifted Hagen into the wheelchair, and the women lathered his head with shaving cream, giving him a skillful straight-razor shave that left him completely bald and without a single nick. Then they shaved off his eyebrows and plucked out his eyelashes. After applying a little bit of movie makeup to give him a pallid complexion, he looked exactly like a cancer patient undergoing chemotherapy.

Hagen was vaguely aware of what was happening to him, but it was difficult to move his arms and legs, and he could hardly keep the saliva in his mouth, much less form any words.

His "nurses" gently put his slippers on his feet, folded a blanket neatly over his legs, and hooked him up to an IV tube. Then they twisted their hair up beneath their nurses' caps and wheeled him down the hall to the elevator.

There weren't many people in the hotel still awake at that hour, but those who were saw only a rich American dying of cancer as he was rolled through the lobby to the main exit. One tourist paused on his way in to hold the door as the women wheeled Hagen out to a waiting handicapped van.

Hagen had no idea how much time had passed by the time he began to come around, but when his vision finally began to clear, he found himself strapped to the wheelchair facing a bright blue swimming pool beneath the hot Mexican sun.

"How are you feeling, Señor Hagen?" asked a Mexican man with bulging dark eyes. "The girls gave you a shot of adrenaline to help bring you around."

Hagen recognized the man as Antonio Castañeda. "What are you going to do me?"

"Nothing," Castañeda said, sipping from a glass of tequila. "It was only my job to get you here. My associate Mariana is going to come over and ask you some questions now. I expect they'll be rather pointed questions, and I expect you to answer them to the very best of your ability. Is that understood, señor?"

Hagen nodded, remembering from somewhere in his foggy memory banks that Castañeda was known for toying with his victims before he killed them. "I understand."

"Good." Castañeda looked across the patio and made a come-here gesture with his hand.

Agent Mariana Mederos appeared, and Castañeda got up to give her his chair. "The gentleman is all yours, *hermosa*."

"Thank you," Mariana said dryly.

Hagen looked at her. "Who are you?"

"I'm with the CIA," she said. "That's really all that matters. I have some questions for you to answer."

"And then what?" Hagen said. "I get a bullet in the head?"

"Mr. Hagen, I wasn't sent here to kill you. I'm not an assassin. It's my guess you'll eventually end up back in the US, where you'll be prosecuted for treason."

"You can't use this interrogation as evidence against—" He chuckled sardonically. "It doesn't matter. Pope sent you."

Mariana took her sunglasses from the top of her head and put them on. "I need the names of everyone involved in the attempt to take over the CIA, as well as those who had any hand in exposing the Paris operation."

Hagen cast a glance across the patio, where Castañeda sat talking with an American man he recognized vaguely.

His two former nurses were sunbathing naked on the far side of the pool.

"And if I refuse to give you the names?"

Mariana frowned. "I thought Señor Castañeda already covered that with you."

Hagen looked down at the water. "He didn't go into specifics . . . but that doesn't matter, either. The names you want are Ken Peterson, Senator Steve Grieves, Ben Walton, Max Steiner, and Paul Miller. Steiner and Miller are already dead, but Pope knows that." He looked at her inquisitively. "Do you even know why the Green Beret is here with you?"

She ignored the question, thinking the Thorazine must still be tweaking his thoughts.

"Who sent Jason Ryder to kill Pope?"

"Ryder worked for Peterson."

"How much of the plot does Grieves have personal knowledge of?"

"You'd have to ask Peterson about that. Grieves and I never spoke of it. There was no need. Our personal business was strictly political."

Mariana questioned him for a couple more minutes. Then she stood up and walked back across the patio.

Daniel Crosswhite stood up from where he'd been talking with Castañeda. "Got everything you need?"

"Yeah. He's confirmed our intel." Crosswhite walked off, and she turned to Castañeda. "Your help in this matter has been valuable. Thank you. I expect someone to be in touch soon with instructions on where to deliver him."

Castañeda smiled at her. "Can I get you something to drink, Mariana?"

"No, thank you," she said, glancing across the patio, where Crosswhite was crouched in front of Hagen's wheelchair. "What's he doing?"

"I believe he's carrying out the rest of Señor Pope's instructions."

"What? He doesn't have any instructions from—"

Crosswhite looked into Hagen's eyes. "You tried to kill my best friend, you fuckin' cocksucker."

Hagen stared back at him, smirking. "There's no need to make this personal, is there, Danny?"

"The fuck there isn't," Crosswhite said. "If you had time, I'd tell you a story about a young girl who got her throat cut."

Hagen shrugged. "I don't know anything about that."

"Who hired Ryder?"

"I already told Pope's bitch." Hagen saw Mariana coming back in their direction. "Why don't you just get it over with?"

Crosswhite reached out to flip the break levers on the wheelchair. "Adios, *puto*."

"Don't!" Mariana shouted.

Crosswhite stepped behind the wheelchair and pushed it over the edge at the deep end of the pool. There was a mild splash, and Hagen went straight to the bottom.

Mariana froze in place, utterly aghast. "What the *fuck* do you call that?"

"Swimming lesson." Crosswhite looked into the water at Hagen's shimmering image twelve feet down. "Doesn't look like he's doin' too good, does it?"

48

THE MOSCOW KREMLIN

Gil was now dressed in a suit and tie with a black leather overcoat that fit him perfectly. He had spent the past couple hours on a private tour of the Kremlin with Colonel Savcenko, and they now stood outside admiring the giant bronze Tsar Cannon on display near the Dormition Cathedral. Cast in 1586 as a defensive weapon for the Kremlin, "Russia's Shotgun" was an 890 mm bombard that weighed thirty-nine tons—nine tons more than a Sherman tank.

"Hell of gun," Gil said. "Has it ever been fired?"

"Not in battle. Though there is evidence inside the bore that it has been fired at least once."

A contingent of five men rounded the corner of the cathedral and began walking in their direction. Gil recognized President Putin immediately.

"The president does speak English," Savcenko said, "so you can speak directly to him, but he will probably choose to speak to you through me."

"I understand." Gil girded himself for what he expected to be a weighty interview.

President Putin approached appearing quite serious, though not entirely unfriendly. His pale blue eyes were almost lifeless, but his face conveyed a certain calm, and Gil sensed no immediate danger.

"Master Chief Shannon," Putin said in his gentle voice, offering his hand with a kind, though not overly cheerful, smile. "It is a pleasure to meet you."

"It's an honor to meet you, Mr. President." Gil matched his grip, which was firm and confident but in no way aggressive or challenging. "Colonel Savcenko has been giving me a tour. This is a fascinating place, sir."

Putin nodded, holding Gil's gaze. "The Kremlin has a rich history."

"I've begun to see that for myself, sir."

"Are you hungry?"

Gil could sense Savcenko's mild discomfiture at being left out of the loop, and he realized that Putin must be breaking with the norm by speaking in English. He took that as a favorable wind. "Yes, I am, sir."

"This way," Putin said with a wave of his hand. He said something to Savcenko in Russian, and the colonel began interpreting for Gil as they walked along. "You and Major Dragunov have been on an adventure."

"We have, sir. Major Dragunov is a brave man, a fine soldier. I'm proud to have worked with him. Unfortunately, Sasha Kovalenko is a brave man as well, and he got away."

"What will your superiors say when you return?" Putin asked pointedly. "About deviating from the mission?"

Gil decided to gamble on the favorable wind. "I'll probably get my ass chewed, Mr. President."

Upon hearing the translation, Putin paused midstride to look at Gil, almost cracking a smile, though not quite.

Gil kept a military bearing. "I'm not exactly sure how that translates into Russian, sir."

Putin chuckled, in spite of himself, and Gil saw they were going to get along.

A short time later, they were served in an ornate dining room in the Kremlin Palace, just the two of them, with the translator off to the side and Putin's security men standing at parade rest at four points around the room.

"I have never eaten in here," Putin remarked, placing a linen napkin into his lap.

Gil did the same with his own napkin, noting a portrait of Joseph Stalin on the far wall and feeling the infamous dictator's eyes boring into him.

"It seems to be a day of firsts, sir."

"It does," Putin said. "Vodka?"

Gil hated vodka. "Please. Thank you, sir."

Putin signaled for the male waitron to pour Gil a drink and dipped his spoon into a bowl of borscht.

Gil did the same.

Putin looked up from his bowl and spoke directly to Gil in English: "Have you ever eaten borscht?" The soup was made from beets, potatoes, and cabbage.

"No, sir," Gil said, wiping his chin with the napkin. "But it's very good."

They continued with small talk throughout the first course and most of the second, which consisted of meat and potatoes. Not until the third course—tea and cake—did Putin come around to the events of the past forty-eight hours.

Savcenko turned to Gil with a stern look and translated, "You are aware of the awkward position this rescue has put me in?"

Gil set down his cup of tea. "I am, sir."

"Why do you think your superiors allowed you to leave Turkey with those women?" Putin's eyes were once again cold and lifeless.

"May I speak freely, Mr. President?"

"Of course."

"I think they let us take off because they knew I'd burn down half of Istanbul if that's what it took to get those girls out." Gil sipped his tea. "Now, that's an exaggeration, of course, but Colonel Savcenko tells me the GRU has been following my career for the last year and a half. And if that's true, sir, then they must have told you by now that I can be very determined when I want to be."

Putin smiled. "It has been mentioned."

"Well, with that being said, Mr. President, I'm guessing my superiors decided it was probably easier to let me have my way than to risk me making things worse."

Putin sat back, attempting to read Gil's demeanor. "You don't think they allowed it in order to put me into an awkward position?"

Gil shrugged. "It's possible, sir. Your government and mine have been at odds over Ukraine for some time now. But that's politics, Mr. President. I don't know much about it, and I'm very careful not to involve myself in it. I'm a Navy SEAL, sir. I go where I'm told and do what I'm told." But even Gil was hard-pressed not to laugh. "Well, sir, that last part's not entirely true, but I think you understand my point."

Putin sat nodding, unable to entirely suppress his own smile, speaking directly in English once more. "Here in Russia, things would be very different for you."

"I am entirely aware of that, Mr. President, and if my actions have put you in an awkward position, I hope you will accept my sincere apologies. I cannot, however, apologize for bringing those girls home. It was the right thing to do, sir, and I do not regret having done it."

Putin raised his hand to the translator to silence him. He looked at Gil for a long a moment. "You are a man of principles."

"I'm not sure if that's it or not, sir. My father was a Green Beret during the Vietnam War. Toward the end of the war, he was sent on a mission north of the DMZ. He was forced to kill innocent women and children on that mission, and he never forgave himself for it. After the war, I watched him drink himself to death. I'm not a psychologist, sir, and I don't spend too much time thinking about it, but I suppose it's possible that I feel some inner need to make up for the people he killed."

Putin added a shot of vodka to his tea and sat back in the chair. "Tell me about the pregnant woman you brought back from Iran."

Gil stared at the table for a moment and then looked Putin in the eye. "Mr. President, I've come to respect you very much during our short time together, but you know that I can't talk about Iran."

"I suppose not," Putin said with a sly smile. He fell silent, but after a pause, he spoke again in Russian. Savcenko translated for Gil. "You also rescued Warrant Officer Sandra Brux against orders, correct?"

Gil realized that Putin had been thoroughly briefed, and he understood there was no point to denying his actions in the Panjshir Valley. "I did, sir. Yes."

Putin drank from his tea as Savcenko turned to Gil. "I'm curious how many more times you will need to disobey orders to pay for the sins of your father."

Gil thought about that. "It's a good question, sir. I don't know the answer myself."

"Would it surprise you to hear that Major Dragunov has accepted responsibility for bringing the girls home?"

"Not at all, sir."

"Why not?"

"Because we've fought together, sir. He's saved my life, and I've saved his. Combat forms a bond, Mr. President, and warriors like us—well, sir, we tend to take all that gung-ho shit seriously."

Putin laughed, his eyes suddenly much less lifeless than they had been, but the moment of levity was short lived. "I wanted to talk with you to learn the mind of an American Special Forces operative. This is a rare opportunity for me."

Gil smiled. "I understand, sir. May I ask a question of my own, sir?"

"You may, yes."

"Will Major Dragunov be punished, sir?"

Putin didn't answer for a long time. Finally, he said, "Sasha Kovalenko has been spotted in Belarus. By now, he's making his way back to South Ossetia. Would you be interested in another opportunity to face him?"

Gil felt his blood begin to pump. "Very much so, Mr. President."

"Major Dragunov will be pleased." Putin took another drink of tea. "He would very much like the opportunity to redeem himself. But I will need for you to give me your word that you will not deviate from the mission this time."

Gil held Putin's gaze for a long moment, hoping that Pope would never get such a bright idea. "You have my word, Mr. President."

"Very well," Putin said. "Major Dragunov is preparing your weapons and equipment. Your plane leaves in an hour."

"Excuse me, sir, but I was told that I'd be meeting with someone from my embassy this evening."

"Well, you can if you like," Putin replied, "but that will mean missing your chance to accompany Major Dragunov."

Gil chuckled. "In that case, sir, will you give the American ambassador my regards?"

"I will do that," Putin said with smile. He then addressed Gil in English: "Shall we drink to your mission, Master Chief?"

"Absolutely, Mr. President."

They toasted the mission, and it was all Gil could do not to gag on the pint-size shot of vodka.

49

IN THE SKY OVER THE CAUCASUS MOUNTAINS

The Russian An-72 transport jet cruised along at three hundred miles per hour, not much more than three thousand feet off the deck.

Gil sat across from Dragunov dressed in Russian combat gear. "This is fucking insane."

Dragunov smiled, drawing calmly from a cigarette. "Not as crazy as jumping out the back of a 727 over Iran."

Gil smirked, shaking his head. "I don't know where you people get your information." He knew that Dragunov was referring to Operation Tiger Claw, the mission in which he had infiltrated Iranian airspace via a Turkish Airlines flight almost two years earlier.

"From a reliable source," Dragunov assured him.

"Yeah? Maybe you'll introduce me to that source sometime."

"Maybe." Dragunov's gaze was confident, much more

so than when they'd gotten off the helo back at the Krem-lin. "Tell me about your meeting with Putin."

Gil shrugged. "There's not much to tell. First he com-plained about what a huge pussy you are, and he then asked if I'd go along to look after you."

The Spetsnaz man laughed.

"I felt bad for the guy," Gil went on. "I couldn't tell him no."

Dragunov sat smiling. "You used an SVD for the Iran assassination, correct?" An SVD was the Dragunov SVD sniper rifle in 7.62 × 54mmR (rimmed), invented by Ivan's grandfather.

Gil's eyes narrowed. "I was never in Iran . . . Ivan."

"It doesn't matter," Dragunov said. "The rifle you have now is even better than the one you carried in Iran. It's a match weapon taken from the Kremlin Armory."

The SVD in Gil's load-out was essentially brand new, with a black polymer stock, and equipped with the standard-issue PSO-1 scope, suppressed. The SVD held a ten-round box magazine, and Gil carried eleven mags. His main combat weapon would be a 5.45 x 39 mm AN-94 assault rifle with a GP-34 40 mm grenade launcher. His sidearm was a 9 mm Strike One Strizh. The rest of his load-out consisted of an NR-40 Russian combat knife, a dozen 40 mm grenades for the GP-34, six RGN hand gre-nades, medical bag, Russian third-generation night vision, radio headset, high-energy food bars, a water bladder simi-lar to a CamelBak, and various incidentals.

"What speed are we jumping at?" Gil asked. "A couple thousand?"

"No," Dragunov chortled. "One hundred miles an hour from five hundred feet. How fast was the 727 flying when you jumped into Iran?"

Gil ignored the question. "We should be HALO-ing in. This is fucking nuts."

Dragunov crushed out the cigarette against the sole of his boot. "This way we'll hit the ground exactly where we want to be."

"With a pair of broken legs. Nobody uses drag chutes anymore, Ivan."

The Russian double-checked his equipment, which was essentially identical to Gil's. "The moon is waxing," he said. "Umarov's people watch the sky, and they have early warning patrols all over the mountains."

"Well, with this noisy pig buzzing the treetops, I'm sure they won't expect a fucking thing."

"That's right," Dragunov said. "Only a fool would jump out of a jet plane at five hundred feet in the middle of the night."

Gil pulled on his helmet and gathered the drag chute into his arms. "Fuckin' nuts," he muttered.

The red jump light came on a few moments later, and both men got to their feet, standing side by side as they waited for the ramp to drop.

"How much trouble are you in back in Moscow?"

"Enough," Dragunov said. "But if I bring back Kova-lenko's head, all will be forgiven."

"What if we bag Umarov, too?"

"If we can kill Dokka Umarov, I'll be made a Hero of the Russian Federation." This was Russia's version of the American Medal of Honor.

"And what about me?"

"You?" Dragunov bashed him on the shoulder and laughed. "You, my friend, you'll be given a cheap bottle of vodka and a free plane ride home."

Gil laughed.

The ramp went down, and the light turned green sixty seconds later. They walked down either side of the ramp and tossed their drag chutes into the wind. The drag chutes were caught by the slipstream, and their main chutes deployed instantly, jerking them both from the ramp and out into the night sky. The engines of an An-72 are mounted on the tops of the wings, near the fuselage, rather than beneath the wings like most jet aircraft, so there was little jet wash to contend with. Still, when the chute deployed, the harness jerked into Gil's groin so hard that he thought his testicles might have ended up in his throat.

There was barely enough time to stabilize their descent and get their bearings before they were dropping through the treetops three hundred feet apart.

Gil landed with both feet together in the crotch of a hardwood ten feet off the ground. He got loose from the harness and attached the night vision goggles to his helmet, scanning the terrain below for signs of movement. Seeing nothing, he shinned down the tree and unslung the AN-94.

"Typhoon to Carnivore," he said quietly into the headset. "Do you read? Over." He waited ten seconds and tried again. "Carnivore, this is Typhoon. Do you read?"

He began to move slowly in the direction of where he had seen Dragunov drop into the forest. A stick snapped, and he froze, lowering himself into a combat crouch near the base of a tree, scanning the gray-black woods through the digital night vision goggles.

"Typhoon to Carnivore," he said in as low a voice as possible. "Do you copy my traffic? Over."

Nothing.

He switched the channel. "Typhoon to Archangel. Do you copy?"

"This is Archangel," answered a voice in Russian-accented English. "What is your status? Over."

"Archangel, be advised I am on the ground but unable to establish radio contact with Carnivore. Over."

"Copy, Typhoon. We will attempt to establish contact. Stand by."

Gil waited a full a minute.

"Typhoon, Carnivore does not answer."

"Roger that, Archangel. Will attempt to locate on foot."

He moved out again, covering some two hundred feet before the sounds of voices drove him to cover behind a group of boulders. The voices were low, but the tone of conversation sounded confused.

Letting the AN-94 hang from its three-point sling, Gil drew his pistol and screwed the silencer to the end of the barrel. Then he moved forward through a gap in the rocks, spotting five bearded Chechen soldiers standing in a loose huddle. They gestured at the surrounding forest, shrugging as if they'd been unable to find something. Gil noted they had no night vision, but a small amount of light from the sliver of moon shone down through the bare limbs of the trees.

He was maneuvering through the rocks when he spotted Dragunov dangling from a tree twenty-five feet off the ground directly above the Chechens. He was swaying slightly with his arms dangling at his sides, his chin resting on his chest as though he were unconscious.

Gil hunkered down, balling a green and black *shemagh* over his mouth so that his whispering wouldn't carry. "Carnivore, this is Typhoon. I have a visual on you from your left at ten o'clock. If you can hear me, open and close your hands."

He watched as Dragunov opened and closed his hands three times.

"Okay. Give me some time to figure this out. Don't go anywhere." He backed away around the boulder, detaching from both rifles and making sure the sheath strapped to his right thigh was unsnapped.

50

THE WHITE HOUSE

Chief of Staff Brooks hung up the phone and turned to where the president and General Couture sat eating a dinner of prime rib and red wine. "That was Jay Tierney." The US ambassador to Russia. "Shannon just made his shit list."

The president looked at Couture as he poured himself a third glass of wine. "He's been known to have that effect on people. Where is he now?"

Brooks retook his seat at the table. "Apparently he and Dragunov parachuted into the Caucasus about fifteen minutes ago. They're going after Kovalenko and Umarov."

The president lifted his glass. "What business does Tierney have being pissed about that?"

"None, sir." Brooks reached for his glass of ice water. "He's pissed because Shannon had lunch with Putin this afternoon and then took off without bothering to call Tierney to tell him what was discussed."

Couture kept quiet, waiting to hear what the president would say.

The president sat back and sipped calmly from his glass of Merlot. Neither Couture nor Brooks was aware of it, but Pope had phoned two hours earlier to let him know about Gil's meeting with Putin and that Gil was en route to the Caucasus. Pope had also mentioned to the president that he no longer had anything to worry about concerning his celebrations after the Iowa caucuses.

He smiled at Brooks. "Get Tierney back on the phone."

Brooks wasn't sure he'd heard correctly. "Sir?"

"Yeah, get him back on the phone." The president gave a wink to Couture. "Tell him now he knows what it's like to have Shannon treating you like you don't fucking count."

Couture chortled, and Brooks realized the president was kidding about the callback. "You don't seem surprised that—"

"I'm not," the president said. "It's been Pope's plan all along to send Gil after Umarov. The pipeline is still under threat, and Putin has saved us valuable time." Then he chuckled, unable to deny feeling the wine. "I sure wish I could be there to see Putin's face when Shannon finds a way to fuck him."

Couture was caught completely off guard and laughed out loud.

"Hey, you really wanna laugh?" the president asked. "This is true: Pope told me Putin made Shannon give his word that he wouldn't deviate from the mission." He threw back his head with a raucous guffaw, slamming his free hand down on the table. "Goddamnit, how come *we* never thought of that?"

Couture choked on his wine, putting the glass down as he laughed.

Brooks, who hadn't had a drop to drink all evening, sat gaping at them both.

"Oh, for Christ's sake," chortled the commander in chief. "Lighten the fuck up, Glen. After all, you helped train the disobedient son of a bitch."

In truth, Brooks had had nothing at all to do with Gil Shannon's training, but he knew there wouldn't be any use in trying to make that point, so he smiled and reached for the bottle of wine.

"Drink up," the president said. "We leave for the Pentagon in five minutes. We don't want to miss the show."

51

THE CAUCASUS MOUNTAINS

Gil knew the Chechens might spot Dragunov dangling above them at any second. He picked up a fallen branch the size of a ball bat and hurled it through a gap in the trees behind his own position. The branch landed with a heavy thud, and the Chechens fell silent, bringing their AK-47s to bear. He watched as the leader gave orders to fan out left and right, and considered how best to deal with them; even a single rifle shot might be enough to bring the entire forest down on his head.

Two men flanked right around the boulders, and two flanked left, cutting into the forest at an oblique angle. The leader came directly toward Gil's position. Gil drew his knife. The Strike One was loaded with subsonic ammo, but even with the suppressor, it would make too much noise given the close proximity. The Chechen leader came on, and he was almost within striking distance when one of the limbs supporting Dragunov's weight snapped with a sharp crack. The parachute ripped, and Dragunov plummeted toward the forest floor, jerking to a stop with his heels twelve inches off the ground.

The Chechens scrambled back in that direction, calling out as they moved.

Gil pounced on the leader from behind, ramming the knife into the side of his neck to sever the trachea and ripping it out the front. He tossed the body aside and joined in the wild dash toward Dragunov's position, taking advantage of the enemy's confusion to sweep in among them as they converged on the helpless Russian dangling in the harness and struggling to draw his pistol.

One of the Chechens punched Dragunov in the face, and another slugged him in the ribs with the stock of an AK-47.

Gil buried the knife in the back of the slugger's head, whipping around to open fire on the others at point-blank range. His assault was so swift and sudden, they scarcely had time to realize what was happening. He shot all three in under a second and holstered the pistol, retrieving the knife from the dead man's skull. Then he cut Dragunov loose from the harness and helped him to rest against a log.

"You okay?"

"The *ublyudok* cracked one of my ribs," Dragunov growled.

Gil wasted no time getting him ready to fight, attaching the night vision goggles to his helmet and unslinging his AN-94. "Rest here and catch your breath." He shoved the rifle into the major's hands. "I gotta grab the rest of my shit."

When he returned, Dragunov was on his feet and shrugging out of his combat harness.

"What's wrong?"

"You have to wrap my ribs. I can't shoulder a rifle with this kind of pain."

They stripped his gear, and Gil bound his torso tight with an elastic bandage. Dragunov was suited back up and ready to move within a couple of minutes.

He bumped Gil affectionately on the shoulder. "If that branch had broken before you drew them off, they'd have torn me apart."

"There's no accounting for luck in combat, partner—we got lucky." Gil took out his GPS unit to double-check their bearings, and Dragunov got on the radio to Archangel with a situation report.

"Ready to go?" Dragunov asked, holding the cracked rib on his left side.

"Yeah, let's get the fuck outta here before another patrol comes along. We got a lotta real estate to cover, and I wanna be in position to take that fucker out before first light."

Kovalenko had been spotted in a truck near the South Ossetian–Russian border the day before, and they were headed for his projected insertion point: a one-lane bridge at the bottom of a river valley north of the remote Sba Mountain Pass. Dokka Umarov was known to have teams of insurgents operating in that region, and according to GRU intelligence, it was the most expedient location for Kovalenko to link up with Umarov's people. The fact that Gil and Dragunov had already run afoul of a Chechen patrol seemed to confirm the intel.

They moved out with Gil on point, and he set a brisk pace, relying on their night vision to give them an edge.

An hour after Gil and Dragunov cleared the DZ, a hooded figure cloaked in a ghillie suit crept into the kill zone, gripping a suppressed AK-105 assault rifle in 5.45

mm. He carried a Russian-manufactured ORSIS T-5000 precision sniper rifle in .338 Lapua Magnum with folding stock slung over his back. Crouching low in the darkness among the bodies of Umarov's men, he removed his night vision goggles and used a thermal monocular to scan the terrain for any lingering footprint-shaped heat signatures. When he was sure that he was alone, he examined the bodies and weapons, drawing back the bolt of each AK-47 to sniff the breach. The bodies were cool to the touch, and the breaches of the rifles smelled like clean gun oil.

Sasha Kovalenko then threw back the hood on the ghillie suit and rose up, studying the grisly scene of battle with prurient interest. Whoever had killed the four men at his feet had done so at point-blank range, and with such speed that not one of them had gotten off a single shot. Looking up into the tree, he saw the camouflaged canopy hanging torn from a broken limb.

Sixty feet away, he found the patrol leader's body and knelt beside it, taking note of the grisly manner in which he'd been slain—stabbed through the side of neck, instantly severing the larynx for a guaranteed silent kill. Instinct told Kovalenko this was the work of the American. He must have taken the leader from behind before engaging the rest of the patrol where they had found Dragunov hanging from the tree. Had Dragunov been unconscious? Was he injured? And how had the American gotten so bloody close to them without drawing fire? It was all open to surmise, but one thing was certain: the prey had taken the bait, and this time Kovalenko held every advantage.

Within three minutes, he picked up their trail and moved out at a comfortable pace. There was no need to hurry. His job wasn't so much to kill them as to prevent their escape.

52

HAVANA,
Cuba

It was growing dark when Daniel Crosswhite landed at José Martí International Airport in Cuba.

The customs officer held the rubber stamp poised over his passport. *"Quieres el sello, señor?"* He was asking if Crosswhite wanted his passport stamped. Cuban customs officers were aware that Americans could get into trouble with the US government for traveling to Cuba—more specifically, for spending American money in Cuba—and they rarely stamped American passports because of it.

Crosswhite shook his head and smiled. *"No, gracias."*

The official returned his smile and gave him the passport, welcoming him to Cuba. *"Bienvenido, señor."*

"Gracias."

Crosswhite bought a cheap cellular phone from a kiosk and then caught a cab in front of the airport. "Mercure Sevilla Hotel, *por favor.*"

Built in 1908, the Mercure Sevilla Hotel was famous for its Moorish architecture and ornate rooms, but Crosswhite barely paid the decor any attention, dumping his bag in the closet and heading back downstairs to the lobby. He found the doorman outside and slipped him a fifty-dollar bill. Most tourists used US currency in Cuba, though the euro was widely accepted as well. *"Dónde puedo encontrar una muchacha, amigo—una muchacha buena?"* Where can I find a woman—a fine woman?

The doorman was dark complexioned, in his early thirties. He smiled, answering in good English, "You can't bring a girl here to the hotel, señor."

A shadow fell over Crosswhite's face. "What the fuck are you talking about?"

The doorman took him aside out of earshot. "This is the tourist section," he explained. "Local woman aren't permitted inside the hotels, so they take you to their homes."

Crosswhite's eyebrows soared. "You're shitting me." He began to dig around in his pocket. "What's your name, amigo?"

"Ernesto, señor."

"Ernie, I'm Dan." They shook hands. "I'm gonna be here a few days on business. You gonna be around if I need you?"

Ernesto smiled. *"Estoy a sus órdenes, señor."* I am at your orders, sir.

"Excellent," Crosswhite said, slipping him another fifty. "Now, listen. I need to know if any other Yankees show up here at the hotel—military-lookin' assholes like me. *Comprendes?*"

Ernesto continued to smile, enjoying the sudden intrigue. "I'll keep my eyes open, señor. Rely on me."

"I will," Crosswhite said, giving him a slip of paper

with the number to the cellular he'd purchased at the airport. "If you see anything unusual around here—any fucking thing at all—you call me. *Comprendes?*"

"I understand exactly what you need, señor. Do not worry."

"One other thing: the last digit isn't really a four—it's a *five*. Can you remember that?"

"*Sí, señor.*"

"*Bueno*," Crosswhite said. "Now, about the girl? I want her thin . . . early twenties . . . long, dark hair. You got one in mind?"

Ernesto grinned. "Paolina will be perfect for you, señor."

"Paolina!" Crosswhite reached into his jacket for his smokes. "You and me are gonna get along, I think." He shook loose a pair of cigarettes and gave one to his new friend.

"Paolina is a good girl," Ernesto said, lighting the cigarette as Crosswhite held the lighter. "You have to be a gentleman. Her parents are very proper."

Crosswhite's mouth fell open. "Her fucking parents? Dude, what the fuck are you talkin' about?"

Ernesto laughed. "This is your first time in Havana?"

Crosswhite took a drag. "I'm guessing you can tell."

"I will take care of everything, señor. She will arrive here by taxi in twenty minutes. Then you can ride with her to her home. Her mother will cook you a nice meal."

"Ernie, I don't wanna meet her goddamn parents."

"Relax," Ernesto said. "You hired me, no? Allow me to do my job."

Crosswhite pointed at him, a half grin on his face. "If this gets fucked up, Ernie, I'll jerk a knot in your dick. I mean it."

Ernesto smiled, exhaling a cloud of smoke. "You are going to love her. I swear it. You won't want to ever leave Cuba after tonight."

Paolina's cab pulled up in front of the hotel a half hour later, and Ernesto opened the door for Crosswhite to get in with her.

The moment their eyes met, his heart melted, and he almost got back out of the cab. She couldn't have been a day over twenty-one, and she was the very picture of innocence, with soft, dark eyes, brown skin and long, kinky black hair.

"Soy Paolina," she said in a soft voice. *"Mucho gusto."* It's nice to meet you.

"Soy Dan. Mucho gusto."

They arrived at her house in a poor neighborhood about fifteen minutes later. Paolina led him inside by the hand and introduced him to her parents—Duardo and Olivia Garcia—who stood waiting for them in the kitchen beside a table set for four. A television played cartoons in another room where a pair of small children could be heard romping around.

Crosswhite had never been more uncomfortable in his entire life, and he regretted having come, but he smiled at her father, who looked the same age as him, and offered his hand. *"Mucho gusto, señor."*

Duardo's grip was firm, and his gaze was steady. *"Mucho gusto. Bienvenido."* He motioned Crosswhite into a chair and sat down across from him with a friendly smile as Paolina set about helping her mother to serve the meal. When the table was ready, she took the chair beside him.

No one in the family spoke English, so dinner conversation was entirely in Spanish. Early in the meal, Paolina's mother excused herself from the table and went into the other room to settle a dispute between the children. Cross-white had assumed the children to be Paolina's siblings, but when one of them used the word *abuela*, meaning "*grand-mother*," he realized that at least one of them was probably Paolina's. He had already made up his mind there was no way he was going to bed her with her parents right in the other room, so he didn't see any reason not to ask a few personal questions.

Paolina admitted one of the girls was her three-year-old daughter and that the other was her four-year-old sister. Paolina's father chuckled proudly, boasting that both little girls were beautiful and hot tempered like their mothers.

Crosswhite glanced at Paolina, trying to imagine such a meek girl being hot tempered. He smiled at Duardo, lik-ing him, and asked what he did for a living.

Duardo said he worked as a gardener in a gated neigh-borhood, and the second he learned that Crosswhite had been a soldier in Afghanistan, the conversation turned to guns. It wasn't long afterward that Duardo asked his wife to get out a bottle of seven-year-old Havana Club rum. The bottle had never been opened, and Crosswhite began to protest, but Duardo insisted, and soon both men were laughing like old friends. It grew late, and Paolina's mother excused herself once again, saying that she needed to put the children to bed. As she left the kitchen, it was obvi-ous she would not return, and Duardo got to his feet. He offered Crosswhite his hand and told him that he had enjoyed meeting him and followed after his wife, bidding Crosswhite good night.

Crosswhite stared after him for a moment and then turned to Paolina, saying that he should probably be get-ting back to the hotel. The atmosphere became immedi-ately awkward, and he came clean with her, explaining that he had never been to Cuba before and that he had not expected to be received so kindly by her family or to end up making friends with her father.

She stared at him, and for a second he thought she was going to cry.

"No, don't cry," he said in Spanish. "I'm still going to pay you for your time and everything."

Tears spilled from her eyes, and he realized he'd given offense where he hadn't meant to.

"I'll call the cab," she said, getting up from the table. "I don't want you to pay me. There's no reason."

He caught her gently by the hand, and she sat back down.

"Look, I'm not accustomed to girls like you," he said softly. "You're too . . . you're too precious and sweet. I'm accustomed to women who are wild and reckless. Do you understand?"

She touched his face. *"Tal vez es por eso que estás tan solo en el mundo."* Perhaps that's why you're so alone in the world.

53

THE CAUCASUS MOUNTAINS

Gil was still on point, moving cautiously along a rough mountain trail through the forest when Dragunov's iron grip clamped onto his left shoulder. He froze in place, and the Russian moved up against his back, sliding his arm forward over Gil's shoulder with his index finger pointing straight ahead. At first Gil couldn't figure out what the hell he was pointing at. All he saw in the gray-black field of the night vision goggles were more trees and the trail leading up the grade, bearing gradually off to the left.

Dragunov wagged his finger up and down, and that's when Gil saw it: the faint glint of moonlight reflecting off of a monofilament line at the very tip of Dragunov's finger.

Gil began to back away, but Dragunov stood firm as an oak, trailing the tip of his finger a few inches up and to the left. Gil searched beyond the finger, studying the terrain itself, and his bladder filled with ice water. There were at least ten men stretched across their approach at fifty feet, all of them expertly ensconced among the rocks and dead-falls, absolutely motionless and appearing very much a part of the forest. Dragunov twisted at the waist to turn Gil to his right, pointing off the trail where at least ten more men were equally well disguised as natural features of the landscape.

They had walked into a textbook L-shaped ambush.

Gil knew that most, if not all, of the enemy had to be aware of their presence, the sliver of moon providing enough light for experienced warriors to easily detect movement at fifty feet. The only reason they had not yet opened fire was that they'd been ordered to wait for the trip flares that were almost undoubtedly spread across the line of advance. Tripping one monofilament line would likely send up an entire series of star clusters that would bathe the entire scene in virtual daylight, leaving Gil and Dragunov to die in a murderous cross fire.

Gil nodded and shrugged his shoulders, unsure of how else to ask Dragunov what they should do. They sure as hell couldn't discuss it verbally, with the enemy close enough to piss on them.

Dragunov pushed down on Gil's shoulder. The two of them lowered themselves into crouched positions and began backing away slowly. After they'd withdrawn per-haps ten feet, the forest exploded around them. They threw themselves against the ground as rifle fire and tracers from PKM machine guns streaked over their heads—close enough that Gil could feel their heat raising the hairs on the back of his neck. They shoved themselves along back-ward on their bellies, bullets grazing their helmets, nicking their body armor, and shattering the radio units attached to the backs of their harnesses.

Dragunov rolled from the trail into a shallow defilade and pulled Gil in after him, giving them a moment of respite.

"They were here waiting for us!" Gil shouted over the din.

"I know—we're betrayed!"

The flares went up, and it was suddenly as bright as Wrigley Field on game night.

Gil rose up just long enough to fire a 40 mm grenade into a PKM machine-gun nest. The grenade detonated on impact, and men screamed.

Dragunov fired a grenade across the trail where the enemy was displacing to outflank them, killing three.

An RPG streaked out of nowhere, detonating against a nearby tree. Dragunov sprang up, using the pall of smoke for cover as he grabbed Gil's harness. "We're leaving!"

They pulled back under the cover of the smoke and hightailed it into the darkness. The firing kept up for another twenty seconds, but it was clear the enemy had lost sight of them. They kept up a good pace.

"Fucking comms are dead!" Gil hissed, tearing off the headset.

"Mine too. We're on our own now."

"Not that we could have trusted the extraction zone anyhow. How far up the chain do you think we're compromised?"

Dragunov paused atop a small boulder, checking their six. "Impossible to know. It only takes one rat to spoil the pantry. Strange . . . they're not following."

"Probably looking for our bodies. Don't worry, they'll be hot on our asses soon enough."

"I'm not so sure," Dragunov muttered. "Let's keep moving. We've got a long way to go before we get to friendly ground."

They didn't cover more than a few hundred meters before both men were cut down by a burst from a suppressed AK-105.

54

THE PENTAGON

The president of the United States, along with General William Couture, Chief of Staff Glen Brooks, the secretary of defense, and assorted members of the Joint Chiefs, sat before a pair of giant high-definition television screens in Satellite Command Center 4, watching on helplessly as Gil and Dragunov walked unwittingly into the L-shaped ambush. The white heat signatures of thirty-five Chechen bushwhackers were visible to all.

"My God," the president muttered, his palms sweating. "Can't they see them?"

"Apparently not," Couture said, clenching and unclenching his teeth. "If they're not using thermal night vision, they may not see them until they're right on top of them. It depends on how well hidden the enemy is, sir."

One of the two figures reached out and touched the other on the shoulder, halting their advance.

"There! They see them!" Brooks piped up.

"For all the good it's going to do them," muttered one of the Joint Chiefs.

They watched as Dragunov pointed out the enemy positions over Gil's shoulder, with everyone in the room guessing that it was Gil doing the pointing. The figures then lowered themselves to the ground and were in the process of backing away when all hell broke loose on the screen.

The president watched the hot tracer rounds zip across the screen, the flares going off, followed by the explosions of 40 mm grenades and men thrown dead against the ground.

"Holy Jesus," he said, getting to his feet and making it so Couture had to push back from the table to see. "We're going to lose him this time."

Couture nodded, silently agreeing with the commander in chief that no one was likely to survive such a hailstorm of lead.

Brooks, who had never experienced more during his time in the Teams than a limited exchange of fire over a couple hundred meters, was filled with a mixture of dread and awe. He was sure he was witnessing the final moments of a fellow SEAL.

The RPG detonated against the tree in a white flash, temporarily obscuring their view of the battle, and everyone held his breath. A few seconds later, they saw that Gil and Dragunov had successfully broken off contact with the enemy, and they released a collective sigh.

"How the hell did they manage that?" the president wondered.

Couture frowned as he watched Gil and Dragunov run for their lives. "Shithouse luck, sir."

The president wiped the sweat from his brow. "My

God. Look at them go." He watched them run for almost three hundred meters over rugged forest terrain. Then both men suddenly went down.

"They're hit!" Couture exclaimed, looking across the room at the air force liaison officer. "Tighten that frame, Major!" He pointed to the other screen. "And pull that one back. Try and find who shot them."

One camera zoomed in; the other pulled back.

"They're moving," someone said. "They're still alive!"

"But who the hell shot them?" Couture asked in frustration. He was on his feet and stepping closer to the wide-angle television screen. "There aren't any heat signatures for more than three hundred yards."

"Maybe it was a booby trap," Brooks ventured.

Couture shook his head. "We'd have seen an explosion."

"There!" someone said, pointing at a brief, partial heat signature of a human form fifty or sixty yards west of where Gil and Dragunov were now dragging themselves to cover behind some rocks. The partial signature disappeared again almost as suddenly as it had appeared.

"Shit, that's a sniper in a shielded ghillie suit."

"What's that?" the president asked.

"A camouflaged cloak made of heat-absorbent material," Couture replied. "Whoever we just saw, Mr. President, he knew someone might be watching from above, and he's taken steps against being picked up on infrared."

Brooks snapped the pencil he'd been twiddling in his fingers. "Five'll get you ten it's Kovalenko. This op was compromised before they ever left Moscow."

The president's eyes were fixed to the screen. "Can someone please tighten the shot? I'd like to see what our men are doing behind those rocks."

"Whatever they're doing," Couture said, "they'd better do it fast because here come those mean little bastards from the ambush."

The president glanced at the other screen, where more than twenty human heat signatures were sweeping quickly westward toward Gil's position. "I'm not going to lie," he muttered, overawed by what he was seeing. "I'd be terrified. Hell, I'm terrified just watching it." He met Couture's sympathetic gaze. "Any chance they'll surrender, General?"

Couture shook his head. "Men like Gil Shannon and Ivan Dragunov don't even know the meaning of the word, Mr. President."

The president turned to Brooks. "Get Bob Pope on the phone. We need to find out if Moscow's watching this and whether or not they intend to provide any support."

55

THE CAUCASUS MOUNTAINS

Dokka Umarov's nephew Lom had been in command of the ambush, and Lom was furious with his men for having allowed the Russian and the American to escape. He drove them hard through the rugged forest, giving orders on the move for them to keep an even dispersal and not to let the enemy slip through their line. Their Spetsnaz ally Kovalenko was supposed to be out there somewhere blocking the avenue of retreat, but Lom took little comfort in this. The ambush had been deployed perfectly, yet it had failed, and the responsibility for that failure lay on his head. He'd sent a runner to Umarov's camp for more men, but his uncle would not arrive in time. The only way for Lom to reclaim some modicum of his honor would be to catch and kill his prey before they either blundered into Kovalenko's path or escaped altogether.

Lom and his force had so far covered almost three hundred meters, and there was still no sign of their quarry.

They were not likely to have fled north because the forest ended where the high country began, and there would be little or no cover above the tree line, where the going would be far more treacherous. Retreat to the south was even less likely because of the way the terrain dropped off into a steep canyon from which there would be almost no escape.

"Keep your eyes open!" he hissed. "They cannot be far now."

A grenade exploded forty meters to the north, and there was a wicked exchange of rifle fire.

"Move!" Lom shouted. "They're trying to break through our line!" The last thing he needed was for the enemy to break into his rear and wind up making contact with his uncle's force. That would be too shameful to endure.

His men up the line were shouting back and forth, confused over the enemy's location, unable to see much by the faint light of the moon.

Another grenade exploded as Lom arrived on the scene, and this time body parts flew through the air. There was a second savage exchange of machine-gun fire, and an errant round snapped through Lom's upper arm, grazing the bone. He gnashed his teeth against the pain, vaulting a fallen tree and screaming for his men to fill the gap where the grenade had blown a hole in their line.

A dark figure slammed into him from his blindside, moving fast, and sent him sprawling face-first into a boulder, mashing his nose and breaking his front teeth off at the gum line. He was lifting himself up when a second figure stomped on his head and leapt over the boulder, leaving him too dazed to rise again.

He was unsure of how much time had passed when one of his men sat him up against the rock and poured water onto his face.

"What! Where are they?" he said with a lisp.

"They got through," the man said. "I've sent another runner to link up with Dokka. Our man knows the forest, and he should get there ahead of them."

A hooded figure in a ghillie suit appeared like an apparition, throwing back the hood to reveal his face in the moonlight. "Who's responsible for this unholy mess?"

Lom instantly recognized him as Sasha Kovalenko. "I am," he croaked.

Kovalenko glanced around, hearing the moans of the casualties all around them. "Two wounded men just went through your line like shit through a goose! You'll be lucky if your uncle doesn't string you up by the balls." He jerked the rifle from Lom's hands and gave it back to the other man, saying to him, "Round up the men who are still whole and form on me. We're moving out in two minutes."

The man left to do as he'd been told, and Kovalenko turned back to Lom, asking disgustedly, "Can you still fight, little girl, or do you plan on spending the rest of your miserable life sucking cock with that pretty new mouth of yours?"

Lom was so ashamed and infuriated that his eyes filled with tears. "I can fight." he said, lisping grotesquely.

"We'll see." Kovalenko shoved him aside. "Find a rifle and try to keep up."

Two hundred yards east, Gil and Dragunov stopped to lick their wounds beneath an overhang.

"It won't take them long to regroup," Dragunov said, sweat streaming down his head from the pain in his testicles. He held a penlight as Gil unbuttoned his trousers to get a look at his groin wound.

"We hit 'em pretty fuckin' hard," Gil said, using his knife to cut away Dragunov's blood-soaked underwear. "It looks like you're in luck here, partner. The scrotum's torn open but your balls are still in there. These thigh wounds are superficial."

Gil wiped his bloody hands on Dragunov's pants and sat back to begin shrugging out of his harness and body armor. "I don't know if *I* got that lucky."

Dragunov buttoned his trousers and helped Gil shed his gear. The American had a number of small holes in his abdomen where Kovalenko's 5.45 mm rounds had defeated his armor, but the rounds had fragmented, and it looked like the fragments had embedded themselves in Gil's abdominal muscles—painful but not life threatening.

"That was Kovalenko who hit us back there," he said. "It was a setup from the beginning."

"Aye," Dragunov said. "And he'll be coming. We're not dead because he didn't expect us to come running at him like that, but we have to be very careful now. There is a reason he's called the Wolf."

"Maybe we should stay put, lay for him here."

Dragunov shook his head. "If it was only him, I'd agree, but this is Umarov's territory. More men will be coming soon. Our only chance is to keep moving east."

"Deeper into Umarov's territory?"

"Kovalenko and the others are blocking the west. The north and south are impassable. That leaves the east."

"Shitty and shittier," Gil muttered. "Look, we should hold here. Let Kovalenko and the others pass us by, then get back on a westerly heading."

"The others may pass us by—but *he* won't!"

"You're sure of that?"

Dragunov picked up Gil's helmet and gave it to him. "We're not in Sicily now. This forest is his home. He grew up in these mountains, and he'll know what we're up to.

I've fought on his side too many times not to know his instincts, but listen: it will be daylight soon, and three thousand meters east of here is a valley where we can draw him into the open—catch him in a cross fire. If we're both manning a rifle, one of us should live long enough to get off a shot."

Gil looked at him while putting on his helmet. "And you don't think he'll figure out what we're up to?"

Dragunov chuckled. "Of course he'll figure it out, but a fox driven before the hounds has only so many options— and running toward the hounds is never one of them."

Gil felt a spasm in his gut, wincing as he lowered the NVGs over his eyes. "I can't argue with good Russian logic."

56

BETHESDA NAVAL HOSPITAL,
Bethesda, Maryland

"I understand that," Pope said patiently, speaking with his opposite number in the Moscow bureau of the GRU, Bureau Chief Galkin. "But we're watching them on satellite in real time, and they're in serious trouble. You're telling me your people don't have a visual on them?"

"I am not authorized to answer that question one way or another," Galkin said. "What I can say is that we have received no request for assistance."

Pope had one eye on his laptop and saw Gil and Dragunov slowly emerging from their hide. He had already known that Russian spy satellites for that part of the world were tasked over Ukraine, where the fighting had intensified over recent months.

"Do you have any assets available to provide them support?" he asked.

"There is a helicopter available for emergency evacuation," the Russian answered. "But so far we have received no such request."

Pope was also aware that much of Russia's military assets, too, had been sent to Ukraine, and that it had recently lost a pair of Hind helicopters during a mission to kill Dokka Umarov. He was beginning to doubt their willingness to risk another helo pulling Gil and Dragunov out of the fire.

"Have you attempted to contact them?"

Galkin hesitated. Then he said, "Not recently."

"I see," Pope said, putting it together. "You're no longer in contact with them, are you? You've lost contact with them altogether."

Galkin let out a sigh. "If they're as heavily engaged as you say, Mr. Pope, it's no surprise we haven't heard from them."

Pope felt his pulse quicken, piqued by the inanity of the remark. "I would say the exact opposite was true, Mr. Galkin. I don't know Ivan Dragunov, but I know Gil Shannon, and I've been watching this battle very closely. Believe me, if our man could request support, he would do exactly that. It's obvious from the way they're moving that both men are wounded."

"I understand your distress," Galkin said, "but how can we possibly organize an evacuation if we are unable to communicate with them?"

"You could insert another team."

"Out of the question," Galkin said. "We just lost one of our best Spetsnaz teams in that region two days ago, and judging from what you've apparently seen tonight, this mission is completely compromised. To send another team in there now would be suicide."

After another couple minutes of chasing Galkin around the bush, Pope ended the call knowing little more than he had before picking up the phone.

He looked at the computer, watching Gil and Dragunov stalking through the Caucasus, and then turned to agent Mariana Mederos, who had just arrived from Mexico. "You look tired."

"It's late," she replied irritably, secretly intrigued by what was taking place on the computer screen. "Why wasn't I told that Crosswhite was in Mexico to do your wet work?"

Pope couldn't help chuckling at her choice of words. "What did you think he was there for?"

"My security."

"He was there for both," Pope said. "Crosswhite is what we call a pipe hitter."

"I know what a pipe hitter is," she said pugnaciously. "What I *don't* know is why I was there. Crosswhite could have conducted the interview just as easily as me—even easier. You didn't have to make me a party to murder."

Pope gazed at her. Mederos was pretty, and her anger only increased the severity of her beauty. "You were there because I needed Castañeda's full cooperation—and he has a thing for you."

She didn't immediately respond to that, wondering how Pope had known.

"I'm an asset manager, Mariana. That's all the director of the CIA is, an asset manager. You're an asset, Crosswhite's an asset . . . and Castañeda's an asset. It's my job to utilize the agency's assets however I can."

"What if there's an inquiry?" she snapped. "What if I'm called to testify?"

"There won't be any of that."

"What if there is? What if I'm offered some kind of immunity?"

Pope shrugged. "Then I suppose you'll have to follow your conscience."

She stared at him, disliking him for putting her in a compromising position. "I want you to know that I don't trust you anymore. I did before, but now I don't."

He smiled at her. "Good for you," Pope said gently. "You've clung to that innocence long enough. Now I need you to go to Havana. Crosswhite is already there."

Her eyes widened. "I was just in Mexico City. Why couldn't you send me direct?"

"Because you needed to get that business about Hagen off your chest," Pope said. "And I need you to have a clear head when you get to Havana. The CIA has assets in Cuba, but every one of them has been compromised, and Crosswhite is entirely on his own there."

"He's there for more wet work, I assume?"

Pope grinned. "He's not down there collecting for the Red Cross."

She frowned. "How many targets?"

"Peterson and Walton." Pope handed her a yellow envelope. "For your travel expenses."

She tucked the envelope under her arm, her anger beginning to abate. "I thought Walton ran off to the Arab Emirates."

"He did, and he sold them a rather comprehensive dossier on our operations in Eastern Europe. Lives will be lost because of what he's done. Now he's en route to Havana, where Peterson and the rest of their rogue faction think they're beyond my reach."

"This is beginning to sound personal to me."

Pope glanced around his hospital room. "I didn't put myself in here."

"So Crosswhite's carrying out your personal vendetta . . . and you're using me to help him do it."

"Crosswhite is hunting a pair of traitors who have gotten innocent people killed, and who will continue to get innocent people killed until they're stopped. The fact that I'll take personal satisfaction in their misfortune is a bonus. You're going to Havana only as backup. Unless something goes wrong, there won't be reason for you to even leave your hotel, so sit by the pool and enjoy yourself. Get a massage. There's a lot of money in that envelope, and I'm not asking for any receipts."

"Feels a lot like a bribe."

Pope suddenly became very serious. "You'll *think* bribe, Mariana, if something goes wrong and Crosswhite needs you to get directly involved. Now, stop your pouting. You're a valuable operative, and it's time to act like one. The world gets more dangerous every day, and a strong stomach is required."

57

THE CAUCASUS MOUNTAINS

Dragunov was on point, keeping close to the northern tree line as they moved eastward. He suspected that more Chechens were on the way, and that he and Gil would be intercepted before they made it to open country. But by sticking to the edge of the forest, he hoped to avoid being caught up in another tiger sweep.

He had torn a strip from his *shemagh* and used it to tie his injured testicles against his leg, but they had worked loose and were once again rubbing painfully back and forth. At least he could no longer feel wet blood running down his legs. This told him the bleeding had stopped, and he was grateful for that.

A stick snapped at their two o'clock, fifty yards out, and both men froze. The first signs of daybreak were beginning to show in the sky, and they were still a full click from the valley, where they hoped to draw Kovalenko into the open.

They took cover and scanned the forest through their NVGs, watching a long skirmish line of men materialize gradually out of its black depths. Two Chechens came directly toward them at the extreme right flank of the tiger sweep, lagging slightly behind the rest due to the extra-rocky terrain inside the tree line, where small avalanches of football- and basketball-sized rocks had been accumulating for centuries.

Gil drew his knife, and Dragunov followed suit. If either Chechen made a sound, the two compatriots would quickly find themselves cornered with nowhere to run but over the open rocks at the base of the mountain. There they would be picked off at the enemy's leisure.

Dragunov moved forward to take cover behind a thick tree. The pair of Chechens were not walking directly abreast but were moving almost single file, with fifteen feet between them, and Dragunov knew he would have to take the one in back before Gil could take out the man in front.

He kept low as the first of the Chechens brushed past the tree with his AK-47 slung lazily over his shoulder. Then he stood and readied himself for the second one to pass.

Gil crouched in the rocks, watching the first Chechen coming directly at him. If Dragunov couldn't take his man first, they were in big trouble because Gil wouldn't be able to afford the luxury of waiting; he would have to act the second the Chechen drew within striking distance. His Chechen came on steadily, but Dragunov's man stopped to take a leak on the tree. Gil braced himself, waiting until the last possible instant before coming off the ground like a striking anaconda, ramming the knife up through the bottom of the Chechen's jaw to sever the brain stem. He stood with the Chechen twitching in his arms, while Dragunov's man finished taking a pee.

Dragunov held his breath until the man walked past, buttoning his fly. Then he stepped out and grabbed him from behind, cupping his hand over the Chechen's mouth and stabbing the blade into the base of his skull.

Both men lowered their kills to the ground and moved out, cutting deeper into the forest away from the rocks, where the going would be faster. They covered a little over a hundred yards before sweeping around a formation of boulders and running smack into five Chechens left behind on the chance that Gil and Dragunov managed to slip through the skirmish line undetected.

A wild melee ensued.

Dragunov was struck in the head with the barrel of an AK-47, and his face was torn open along the cheekbone. He reeled backward against the boulder, and the Chechen's rifle went off in his face. Had his eyes not been closed, the muzzle blast would have blinded him. As it was, the bullet creased the side of his head and took off part of his ear.

Gil managed to shoot the Chechen off of him before he was struck on the breastplate by a five-round burst that knocked him off his feet. He landed on his back, and the Chechen stood over him, banging the heel of his hand against the receiver of his jammed AK-47. Gil squeezed the trigger on his AN-94 and emptied the magazine, killing his attacker and one other man. He scrambled back to his feet and was immediately tackled by a man who was either too panicked or too inexperienced to unsling his rifle.

Dragunov grabbed the barrel of the Chechen's AK-47, managing to deflect it and avoid taking a burst of fire to the belly. The Chechen twisted the rifle free of his grasp, and Dragunov delivered him a vicious uppercut that chopped off part of his tongue. The two men fell over in the rocks, slugging away at each other.

Gil was down on his right knee, with his left shoulder braced against a tree, barely maintaining his center of gravity as he tried to get loose from the Chechen, who had him around the waist from behind. The man was bigger and stronger than Gil, but he didn't seem to know what to do beyond wrestling his opponent to the ground. Gil knew if he ended up on the bottom he was finished, but his right arm was caught inside the Chechen's bear hug, so all he could do for the moment was keep his opponent in an awkward headlock with his left arm and hope the guy made a mistake.

Dragunov was shoved over onto his back and took a knee to the groin. Seeing stars, he clamped his teeth down on his attacker's thumb and tried to bite it off. The Chechen flailed around in a desperate bid to keep his thumb, and this allowed Dragunov to use a hip-escape maneuver to slip out from beneath him and finally draw his knife. The Chechen caught Dragunov's knife arm with his free hand and deflected the thrust away from his belly.

Meanwhile, Gil shoved upward with his right leg, using every ounce of strength he had, nearly blowing out his anterior cruciate ligament in the process of forcing himself to his feet. This must have surprised the Chechen, because he seemed to lose focus for a moment. Gil broke free of his grip, twisting into him and jamming both thumbs deep into his eye sockets. The Chechen screamed and grabbed for Gil's arms, but Gil locked his legs around his waist and delivered a nasty head butt. The Chechen's legs gave out, and Gil rode him to the ground, clawing out both of his eyes and then jumping to his feet.

"Now, *fuck* you!" he snarled at his howling opponent, grabbing the AN-94 and jumping to where Dragunov still fought for his life. He stuck the muzzle into the Chechen's side and squeezed the trigger without result. The magazine was empty.

Swearing, Gil drew the knife and rammed it into the side of the Chechen's neck. The Chechen went limp, and Gil stabbed him again for good measure.

Dragunov rolled clear of the body, spitting out the Chechen's thumb and struggling to his feet. Both men were too exhausted to speak, so they bumped each other on the shoulder and took off toward the east. Day was beginning to break. They knew that every Chechen in the world would soon be hot on their heels—and that Kovalenko would be with them.

58

THE PENTAGON

The president of the United States glanced away from the screen to see General Couture lighting up a Pall Mall cigarette with a First Air Cavalry Zippo lighter. They had all seen the melee, and no one in the room could believe that Gil and Dragunov were still alive.

"Is smoking allowed in here, General?"

Couture shook his head. "But you're the only man in the room who outranks me, sir. Would you like me to put it out? It's Shannon's fault. He does this to me every time."

The president had recently given up smoking a pipe at his wife's insistence. "May I have one?"

"Certainly." Couture reached into the arm pocket of his starched, digitally camouflaged ACUs and gave him the red pack of cigarettes.

The president took one and tossed the pack onto the table. "Help yourselves, gentlemen."

Brooks was the first to reach for the pack, and the

president smiled as Couture leaned forward to light his cigarette for him. "I'll make sure to buy you another pack, General."

Couture shook his head. "Won't be necessary, sir."

The room filled slowly with a smoky gray haze as they sat watching Gil and Dragunov make their way through the forest. On the other screen, a force of more than fifty men were chasing after them from the west, easily moving twice as fast.

An aide-de-camp stepped into the room and whispered into Couture's ear.

"Mr. President, Bob Pope on line four, sir."

The president picked up the phone and pressed the button. "This is the president . . . Yes, I saw it. We all did . . . You're kidding me! You mean they have to fight their way back to Moscow on their own? Hold on a second, Robert." The president turned to Couture. "The Russians have fallen out of contact with our men on the ground. Apparently there's no help coming."

Couture snapped his fingers at the air force liaison. "Find our nearest Predator and get it flying in that direction!"

"We can't do that," the president said. "They're in Russia."

"Barely, Mr. President."

"Russia is Russia, General."

"Can Pope get us permission?"

"Robert, can you get us permission for a Predator strike?" The president looked at Couture and then shook his head. "He says he already tried that, and they won't even consider it. Moscow says this is a Russian operation and that Shannon volunteered to operate under Russian command."

Couture sucked from the cigarette in frustration. "How about asking them to send in one of those flying washing machines of theirs?"

The president conferred with Pope. "He says not before first light, and even then he's not sure. The Russians say Umarov has acquired MANPADS. I assume you know what those are. I don't."

"It's a shoulder-fired antiaircraft missile, sir. Does Pope have anything in mind at all?"

"He says not at this time."

"Where the hell is the Russian air force?" asked the air force chief of staff.

"Pope says that's a very good question, General."

"Unbelievable," the air force general muttered. "The mission's a failure, so they're just going to let them die?"

"Pope says it's beginning to look that way," the president said. "Is there anything else you can tell us, Robert?" The president listened and then replied, "Call me the second you learn anything new." He hung up the phone and looked at the men sitting around the table. "Unless one of you has a suggestion that doesn't involve starting World War III, I think President Putin is about to have his revenge for Operation Bunny Ranch."

None of the generals had any ideas, but the president spotted a young air force lieutenant sitting back in the corner in front of a computer with his hand partially raised.

"What is it, son?"

"Well, sir," the lieutenant said. "What about calling Tbilisi for help? The Georgian army has helos on the ground right across the border. If they fly low between the mountains, Russian radar will never even pick them up. And they might not mind invading Russian airspace for twenty minutes or so, given that Russia still occupies Georgian territory in South Ossetia."

The president looked at Couture. "What do you think?"

Couture shrugged. "It can't hurt to ask, sir."

The president grabbed the phone and pressed zero. "This is the president. Get Secretary of State Sapp on the phone immediately. And call the Georgian Embassy. We're going to need to speak with the Georgian ambassador."

59

HAVANA,
Cuba

It was well after midnight, and Paolina was curled up in the crook of Crosswhite's arm, running her fingers through the dark hair on his chest by the light of a candle. He was thinking impossible things about an impossible future in Havana when she raised up onto her elbow and looked into his eyes.

"*Me ves como una puta?*" she asked. Do you see me as a whore?

He combed his fingers through her hair and smiled. "I see you as the most beautiful girl in the world."

She smiled back and kissed him. "How long will you be in Havana?"

He shrugged, the smile plastered to his face. "How long would you like me to be here?"

She curled back up in the crook of his arm. "How long, Daniel?"

"A few days," he said. "Maybe a little longer."

"Will I see you again before you leave?"

"Every night that you're available."

She raised back up, cracking a grin. "Then I'll be available every night."

"Good," he said, pulling her down and kissing her. "You don't have any regular clients that are going to be mad?"

She shook her head, looking sad for the first time. "While you're here, can we pretend there are no other clients . . . that I'm someone else?"

He sat up against the wall and took her into his arms. "I don't want to pretend you're someone else. I want to know you . . . everything about you."

"Will you stay the night?"

"Your father won't be upset if I'm still here in the morning?"

She shook her head. "Not about you. He's never drunk with anyone else who's come here—never made friends."

"This is hard for me. I've never . . ." He shook his head. "It's very different for me."

"I understand. But I have to survive, to help take care of my family."

"It's nothing about you," he said. "It's that I'm embarrassed in front of your parents."

"Okay. But it's not necessary."

They were in the midst of making love a second time when his cellular buzzed on the table beside the bed.

"Shit," he said in English. "Ernesto's the only one with this number." He picked up the phone and said, *"Bueno?"*

"Señor? This is Ernesto."

"Yeah, Ernie. What is it?"

"I told Fernando to keep his eyes open while I was on break. He says two men came to the hotel asking about you. He said they described you and wanted to know if you had checked into the hotel. He said they looked Cuban but spoke with a Miami accent."

"Okay, Ernie. Where are they now?"

"I think maybe they're going to Paolina's house."

Crosswhite got out of bed fast. "Why do you think that?"

"Because they asked where you had gone, and Fernando was afraid to lie to them, so he told them you left in a taxi—but nothing more. Then they asked him where to find the cabstand. I'm sure they are going to question the driver."

"How long ago was that?"

"About ten minutes."

"If you had to guess, Ernie, how much longer before they show up here?"

"At Paolina's? Maybe twenty minutes. Is there anything I can do?"

"Keep your eyes open, buddy, and call me if you hear anything else."

Crosswhite put down the phone and reached for his pants. "You'd better wake your father, sweetheart."

Paolina sat up in the bed. "What's wrong?"

"Wake your father," he said gently. "You all need to go to a neighbor's house for the night. There's very little time."

Paolina left, and Duardo came into the room a minute later looking concerned. "What is going on?"

"I work for the CIA," Crosswhite said. "Two men are coming here to kill me—Americans. They have no interest in your family, but if I'm not here, they'll hurt Paolina to find out where I've gone. You need to take your family to a neighbor's house and let me deal with them when they arrive."

Paolina's father nodded his head solemnly. "I knew you were CIA when I first saw you, but I allowed you to stay. Will they have guns, these men?"

Crosswhite let out a sigh. "I can almost guarantee it."

"I'll send the women to my sister-in-law's house, but I'm staying."

"No, you can't risk your life like that. You don't even know me."

"This is my house," Duardo said, "and you are my guest. I'm staying." He went into the other room, telling his wife to take the children and leave right away.

Paolina came back in two minutes later and put her arms around Crosswhite. "I'm scared for you."

"I'm scared too, but not for myself. You have to go right now." He kissed her hair and held her at arm's length. "I'll be fine. Go now."

She disappeared out the door with her mother and the girls.

Crosswhite stepped into the kitchen, and Duardo appeared from the back of the house holding a fourteen-inch WWII-era M1 rifle bayonet made by Union Fork and Hoe.

"This belonged to my father. He fought in Castro's revolution. The government took away his rifle years ago. If we can kill these two *pendejos*, I have friends who can dispose of the bodies. Calling the police would be very bad for all of us."

"Hopefully, you won't need to get involved." Crosswhite put out his hand. "I probably have a better idea how to use that thing than you do."

"Do you like my daughter?" Duardo asked.

"Yes, I do. It's too bad that—"

"She would make you a good wife; give you beautiful children."

Crosswhite shook his head. "I'm no good for any woman. Can I have the bayonet?"

Duardo took an old M1917 .45 caliber Colt army revolver from beneath his guayabera shirt. "This was my father's too. We're not allowed guns in Cuba, so I've kept it hidden." He handed the revolver to Crosswhite.

Crosswhite opened the gate and saw that it held only five cartridges. "I don't suppose you have the sixth bullet?"

Duardo shook his head. "Those five are all I have—and they're very old."

Crosswhite closed the gate and stuck the revolver down the front of his pants. "If they've been kept dry, they'll be fine."

"So what now?" Duardo asked.

"Have a seat at the table to wait," Crosswhite said. "I'll be in Paolina's room. When they arrive, they'll knock at the door and ask to see her. They'll be polite but firm. All you have to do is let them in and tell them you're going to wake her up. Then go into the back of the house, and I'll handle it from there."

60

HAVANA,
Cuba

Ken Peterson sat talking with a local police captain named Ruiz in his modest house on the outskirts of Havana. They were discussing Peterson's future in Cuba while they awaited confirmation that Crosswhite had been eliminated.

"So I'm going to need police protection," Peterson was saying. "At least for a time."

Ruiz took a drink from his bottle of beer. He had been on the CIA payroll for a number of years, and Peterson had always been his handler. "That is going to be difficult," he said, putting down the bottle. "Police protection has never been part of our deal."

"I understand that," Peterson said. "The CIA wasn't supposed to know that I'm here, but the circumstances have changed."

"Yes, they have," Ruiz said. "For one thing, you no longer have access to that big Yankee expense account."

Peterson frowned. "I have money of my own. I can pay for any services that I need."

Ruiz smiled. "I just want to be clear."

"I'm sure you do," Peterson replied dryly. He was more than a little rattled by Crosswhite's unexpected arrival in Havana. He had planned for it to take Pope at least six months to figure out that he was in Cuba, still another month or two to pinpoint his location, and still another month to get the assets in place for a hit. However, he had woefully underestimated Pope's drive for vengeance. In fact, had it not been for one of Peterson's few remaining allies in Mexico, he would have had no idea that Crosswhite was even coming after him.

Fortunately, there were a number of Miami-born operatives living in and around Havana who didn't know that Peterson had been exiled, so he still had assets of his own to call upon, freelancers that Langley knew nothing about. He had recruited the men himself, and he was their sole contact. The only problem was money. The cost of living in Cuba was cheap, but if Pope was determined to kill him, the cost of simply staying alive might easily get out of control.

His best chance was to have Crosswhite taken out fast, thus sending the message to Pope that Cuba was beyond his jurisdiction. There would be no guarantees, of course, but Pope was more than twenty years his senior, and he was confident that he could outlive the old bastard if he was smart about it. After all, the CIA had tried to kill Fidel Castro a number of times—once even succeeding in getting a female assassin into bed with him—but Castro had lived to the ripe old age of eighty-seven. The simple truth was that the CIA just didn't have a very good track record in Cuba, and this was the reason Peterson had chosen to retire there.

"Will your associate Señor Walton still be joining you?" Ruiz asked.

Ben Walton was another checkmark in the plus column. He was an old CIA hand, and he would have some additional ideas for keeping Pope at bay. He also had money, so if he and Peterson could agree on a way to pool their resources, they would double their chances for the long term.

"Yes," Peterson said. "He arrives in the morning from Spain. He'll be staying with me at least until we can get things arranged between us."

Ruiz took another drink. "Walton will have to pay as well."

"That's understood. You've never had trouble receiving payment, Captain."

"You were never an exile," Ruiz said. "Now you are, so I can extend you no more credit. From now on, our business requires payment up front."

Peterson could feel the walls starting to close in on him, but he reminded himself to look at the positive side. Pope's handpicked assassin would soon be dead, and it would be some time before he could find someone else qualified to penetrate Cuba for a second attempt. In the meantime, he and Walton would formulate a plan to mitigate future threats.

"I kind of like being called an *exile*," he said thoughtfully. "It has an exotic ring to it."

Ruiz snickered. "So does 'hermaphrodite,' but I wouldn't want to be one."

The phone rang in the kitchen, and Peterson went to answer it. *"Digame."*

"It's Roy," said a male voice. That was not, in fact, his name, but he was Peterson's contact in Mexico City.

"What can I do for you, Roy?"

"I thought it might interest you to know that His Majesty has gone off the grid." Roy was referring to Tim Hagen. "Disappeared from his hotel room without a trace."

"Well, that's not surprising. I knew he'd run sooner or later."

"I don't think he ran. I think he was *taken*. One of Pope's pipe hitters was here in the city when he went missing: an ex-Delta operator named Crosswhite."

"Do you have anything else?"

"Only this: Crosswhite was seen in the company of Antonio Castañeda while he was here. There was a female agent with him, but I don't have a name on her yet."

"It's probably Mariana Mederos," Peterson muttered. "Crosswhite's already here in Havana."

"Then Pope is definitely cleaning house," Roy said. "You'd better think about getting the hell out of there."

"There's nowhere else for me to go. All my money is invested here."

"In that case, I wish you luck. You're going to need it."

61

HAVANA,
Cuba

Crosswhite stood watching out the window from Paolina's bedroom as the CIA assassins pulled up in front of the house in their own car. There were three instead of two, and that immediately complicated matters because Crosswhite knew one of them would remain outside to watch the street. As they dismounted the vehicle, it became immediately obvious they were ex-military. All three were of Cuban descent, muscular, confident, and alert, with their hair cut high and tight.

Crosswhite looked at the .45 revolver in his hand. It was far better than nothing, but every round would have to count.

Two of the men stepped up to the house and knocked. Crosswhite went to watch through a crack in the bedroom door as Paolina's father got up from the table.

"Who is it?" he asked in Spanish.

"The police. Open the door."

Duardo opened the door, and the men stepped inside without waiting to be invited. "We need to speak with Paolina," the driver said, his Miami accent obvious.

"May I see some identification?"

The driver lifted his shirt to reveal the butt of a Beretta pistol. "We don't want to hurt her. We need to know about the American she was fucking earlier tonight."

"I'll get her," Duardo said, holding his temper as he turned to leave the kitchen.

One of the men followed him into the other room, and Crosswhite pulled back the hammer on the .45. He stepped into the kitchen and blew the driver's brains all over the wall.

The other man ducked into the bathroom and started firing into the kitchen, sending Crosswhite diving into the corner for cover. The third man, who'd been left outside to watch the street, kicked open the door a second later, and Crosswhite shot him in the chest. He flew backward but did not go down. Crosswhite shot him again, and still he didn't go down.

The man fired a shot and hit Crosswhite inside the left thigh.

Crosswhite fired a third time, hitting him in the base of the throat, and this time the man crumpled to the floor.

"Duardo!" Crosswhite shouted. "You okay?"

"I'm okay!"

Crosswhite grabbed the Beretta from the driver's pants and checked to be sure there was a round in the chamber. "Hey, asshole!" he shouted in English at the man in the bathroom.

"What the fuck you want?"

"Cops are comin'!"

"That's a bigger problem for you than me," the Cuban called back in perfect English. "I got friends inside. You won't last twenty-four hours, white boy."

Crosswhite knew that was probably true. He looked at the floor where the blood was pooling on the tile between his legs. "Throw out your gun, and I'll let you go."

"Fuck you! Throw me *your* gun, and I'll blow your fuckin' brains out with it!"

Crosswhite laughed. "You're a funny motherfucker! I'll remember that when I take a piss on your dead fuckin' body!" He glanced out the open door, knowing he should take off in the car, but he couldn't bring himself to abandon Duardo.

"Hey, where's the little whore?" the Cuban called out.

"Your mama? Last I heard she was still takin' it in the ass for five bucks a carload."

The Cuban laughed. "Stick around, asshole. You'll be takin' it in the ass pretty soon yourself!"

"Listen, I got an idea," Crosswhite said in Spanish. "How about you let my man pass? That way we can all get the fuck outta here before the fuzz shows up."

The Cuban was quiet for a moment. Then he answered in Spanish, "Okay. He can pass."

"Duardo, what do you think?"

"I don't know," Duardo answered. "What do *you* think?"

"He knows if he kills you, I'll never let him out of here, and we'll *both* go to prison. That's all I can promise."

"Get the fuck outta here!" the Cuban said. "I'll catch up to you two *pendejos* another time!"

"Okay, I'm coming out," Duardo said a few seconds later.

As he was passing the bathroom, the Cuban grabbed him from behind, screwing the pistol into his ear. *"Ni una palabra!*" he whispered, using Duardo as a human shield as they approached the kitchen. Not a word!

Duardo opened his hand and let the bayonet slide down out of his shirt sleeve. As they neared the kitchen doorway, he jerked his head away from the pistol and stabbed the blade deep into the Cuban's thigh, striking bone.

The Cuban howled, and Duardo spun around, knocking the gun from his hand and kicking him in the groin. The stricken assassin dropped to his knees, and Crosswhite bound into the room, shooting him in the head with the last round from the .45.

"Well done!" Crosswhite said, patting the older man on the shoulder. He then grew dizzy and dropped down on the couch. "Rum?" he said in English. "Shock."

Duardo didn't speak much English, but he understood "rum," and he understood "shock," because they were essentially the same words in Spanish. He helped Crosswhite back to his feet and grabbed the bottle from the kitchen table on their way to the car.

A few minutes later, they arrived at his sister-in-law's house five blocks away.

"My God!" Olivia cried, seeing the blood as her husband sat Crosswhite down at the kitchen table.

"What happened?" asked Duardo's sister-in-law Carmen.

Duardo began to explain, and Paolina went into the bathroom, coming back out with a box of sanitary napkins.

"Good idea," Crosswhite said, shrugging his trousers down to his knees. "Here, let me grab a couple of those things."

A short time later, he was lying on a bed in the back of the house. The bleeding had stopped, and Paolina sat beside him on the mattress.

Duardo and Olivia were in the kitchen trying to calm Carmen. "What the hell are you going to do with him?" Carmen demanded. "He can't stay here."

"He has to," Duardo said. "We can't give him to the police. He's CIA."

Her eyebrows soared. "I can't have CIA in my house!"

Olivia was concerned too. "Won't the police look for him here?"

"They may," Duardo admitted. "But we have to think of something, because in jail he'll be killed."

Paolina appeared and stood leaning in the kitchen doorway. "Go back to the house, *Papi*. Tell the police the man you stabbed was with me when the others came to kill him. No one has to know an American was ever there."

Carmen looked at her. "You're going to lie to the police for a stranger? For the CIA?"

Paolina looked at her aunt with her soft brown eyes, innocent and guileless. "His name is Daniel."

62

THE CAUCASUS MOUNTAINS

"I think we should make a stand here," Gil said as he and Dragunov stopped to catch their wind. "Hit 'em hard with grenades, then haul ass again before they can maneuver to outflank us. That'll slow their pursuit and get 'em off our ass."

"Maybe, but we give up our lead if we do that." Dragunov was holding his wounded groin, resting with one arm against a tree. It was almost light enough to see without night vision.

"I know, but they're gonna catch us anyhow. This way we can hit 'em on our terms one last time before it gets light. We need to kill some of these fuckers before we enter that valley. If those guys catch us out there in the open, we're fucked."

"I have to tell you," Dragunov said. "My *yaytsa* are killing me. I'm worried if I stop, I won't be able to get moving again."

"You'll get movin' again," Gil said. "If I have to put a foot up your ass."

Dragunov gave him a rueful grin, and they took up firing positions twenty feet apart. They could hear the enemy double-timing it in their direction, calling to one another as they came. It was a dangerous way to hunt the enemy, but without night vision or comms, there was no other way to organize a pursuit. Gil thought briefly of how it must have been for his father in the jungles of Vietnam, operating virtually blind in the night with nothing but a hazy starlight scope and unreliable comms, relying almost entirely upon the warrior instinct for survival.

"No way to have to fight a war," he muttered, pulling the pins on a pair of grenades.

They waited until the Chechens drew within range and then lobbed two grenades apiece into their midst. The grenades detonated on impact, blasting men apart. Chaos ensued, and there was a lot of screaming as the forest erupted in an unholy display of machine-gun fire and tracer rounds. They hurled another pair of grenades each, and the enemy fell back under the bombardment.

Gil ran and grabbed Dragunov by the harness, hauling him up, and the two of them disappeared into the shadows.

DOKKA UMAROV SEETHED with rage over the enemy's cowardly use of hit-and-run tactics.

"On your feet!" he shouted, kicking one of his men in the butt. "They're already off again! Get after them!"

Anzor Basayev, his second in command, appeared at his side. "They'll hit us again, Dokka. We need to be careful, or we'll lose too many men."

"How many grenades do you think they carry?" Umarov said. "At most, they have enough for one more ambush—and it's getting light now. Soon we'll have them in the valley, where they won't be able to hide so well. Now get your unit moving!"

At this moment, the second runner from Lom's group finally caught up to them. He'd gotten lost in the dark and hadn't been able to find them until the sounds of battle told him the way.

"Dokka," he said, his chest heaving. "I was sent to tell you the enemy cut our line and is coming this way. But it looks like they've already cut your line as well."

Umarov bit back the foul remark that came to his tongue. "Where are Kovalenko and my idiot nephew?"

"Lom was wounded in the fight," the runner said. "About Kovalenko, I don't know.

Umarov looked at Basayev. "Do you suppose the Wolf has gotten himself killed?"

"I doubt it," Basayev replied. "Dragunov and the American are running scared for a reason."

Umarov grunted. "Get the men moving, tactical columns."

Despite Umarov's and Basayev's hazing them on, the men were hesitant to move at the same reckless speed they had moved before, and the two leaders were forced to accept it; shouting at them would only continue to alert the enemy.

By the time they covered another couple hundred yards, it had gown light enough to see. A grenade went off at the front of the advance, hurling body parts into the air, and the men dove for cover, pouring fire at the unseen enemy.

"Stop firing!" Umarov screamed, grabbing a man by the jacket and jerking him to his feet. "Stop firing!"

"It was just a booby trap!" Basayev called down the line. "Everyone get up!"

The morale of the men was breaking fast. Umarov could smell the fear among them, and he knew that one more booby trap might be enough to break them for good. There was a commotion in their rear, and he turned to see Lom's group dashing toward them through the forest. He was profoundly pleased to see his nephew, but not for the reasons Lom would have preferred.

"Where the hell have you been, imbecile?"

"They cut our line," Lom slurred, his mouth bloody and grotesque. "We were running to catch up."

Umarov took a quick head count of Lom's men, relieved to see twenty fresh fighters. "Get your men to the front of the line."

Lom went forward with his group, and Umarov saw the positive effect it had on the rest of his men.

"At least the fool is still good for something," he told himself. "Forward now!" he hissed at his men. "Allah has provided!"

"As He will undoubtedly continue to do," said a deep voice from behind.

Umarov turned to see Kovalenko standing beside a tree in his ghillie suit, cradling the ORSIS T-5000 in his arms.

"So the Wolf lives," Umarov said. "I thought they might have killed you."

Kovalenko stepped forward. "They're trying to draw me into the valley. Their plan is to catch me in a cross fire. But they're both wounded, and they have to be wearing down after all they've been through."

Umarov smirked. "You wouldn't know it from the way they continue to fight."

"That's because they're the best the Russians and the Americans have to offer. You can stop trying to catch them now. Maneuver them instead. Let them reach the valley, where we can use your men to flush them out. Once they're forced to expose themselves, I'll finish the job."

"I can't afford to waste my men like that." Umarov shook his head. "Not for two soldiers. I'm tempted to let them escape."

Kovalenko put a hand Umarov's shoulder. "*That* is what you cannot afford to do, old friend."

Umarov stared into Kovalenko's green eyes. "And why not?"

"Because this American will keep coming after us. We threaten their pipeline, remember?"

"Hitting the pipeline is a broken dream now."

"No it's not. Our friends in Moscow have begun to see the light, and if we can remove Dragunov and the American, it will demonstrate our resolve. Even Putin would like to see the pipeline destroyed—particularly since the Americans have chosen to oppose him in Ukraine. And though he could never be a direct party to it, he *could* choose to fight the pipeline's destruction with one hand behind his back—and he could do so without criticism because the pipeline is not his to protect."

"You're saying Moscow is . . . What *are* you saying, Sasha?"

Kovalenko grinned, opening his hand to the morning sky. "I'm saying, where are the Russian helicopters?"

63

THE PENTAGON

"There, right there!" General Couture pointed urgently at the screen, which now showed the battleground in living color by the light of day. "That's the ghost! The guy in the ghillie suit we can barely make out!"

"Gotta be Kovalenko," Brooks said, watching the camouflaged image moving stealthily along through the bare forest.

"Well, he's hell and gone from the bridge crossing, isn't he?" Couture grumbled, getting out of his chair. "'Russian intelligence.' Now, there's an oxymoron if I ever heard one."

The president was at the back of the room, talking on the phone with Secretary of State Sapp, who was at the Georgian ambassador's house trying to arrange for air support from the Georgian army. From the sounds of the conversation, Sapp wasn't making a great deal of headway.

On the other screen, Gil and Kovalenko were approaching the edge of the forest at the opening to the valley.

"God in heaven, where are they going?" wondered the aging secretary of defense. "It's a no-man's-land."

"I'm guessing Shannon's going to try to set up a hide," Brooks said. "All he needs is a few hundred yards of clear killing ground, and he'll pick those Chechens off to the last man."

Couture stepped up to the screen, tapping Kovalenko's image. "Not if *this* son of a bitch has anything to say about it."

"I can't argue with that, Bill. I think we're about to see a real-life sniper duel."

Couture turned to the air force liaison. "Major, get a tight shot of the rifle this man is carrying, and do a screen capture. Then run it past G2—see if they can't figure out what that damn thing is." "G2" was military slang for intelligence.

The president put down the phone and returned to his chair. "The Georgian ambassador is still trying to get his government on board, but it's not looking good. Has Pope called back?"

Couture shook his head.

"Want me to give him a call, sir?" Brooks asked.

"No," the president said. "He'd call if he had anything. There's no point in interrupting him."

Couture smiled inwardly, recalling how distrustful they all had once been of the new CIA director.

The images of seven men appeared at the bottom edge of the screen, hiking north along the bank of a wide mountain stream that cut the valley for which Gil and Dragunov were bound.

"Tighten that up, Major."

The seven looked to be Chechen fighters, heavily loaded with packs, machine guns, and RPGs. They were walking slowly—plodding along—and seemed to have hiked in from a long way off.

"Insurgents," Brooks muttered. "Probably coming up from Azerbaijan."

Couture lit a cigarette and exhaled with a sigh. "Get ready for another gunfight, gentlemen." He clicked the Zippo's lid closed and tucked it into his pocket, muttering to himself, "Okay, Gil. Don't get sloppy now."

64

THE CAUCASUS MOUNTAINS

Gil and Dragunov left the cover of the forest to find the early morning sun shining on their faces. The open valley stretched away to the east, with a shallow mountain stream running through the middle of it toward the south. Ice Age boulders littered the landscape, left behind by receding glaciers ten thousand years earlier. Squat, thick hardwoods dotted the expanse, free to expand their limbs outward instead of having to race for the sky in competition for the sun. Beyond the valley, perhaps a thousand yards, the forest began again, but Gil knew the battle would be decided here. In the valley.

They kept moving, Gil's gaze scanning the terrain for the place he would set up with his rifle.

"There," he said, pointing beyond the stream and up the slope to the east. "See those rocks?"

"A textbook position," Dragunov said.

Gil looked at him. "Which is exactly why we can't set up there."

"Right."

They moved fast down the slope, rounded a copse of trees at the edge of the stream, and came face-to-face with a patrol of seven bearded Chechens.

Everyone froze.

The Chechens were visibly weary from their trek. Six of them stood looking slack jawed, rifles slung, but one of them held his AK-47 by the foregrip in his left hand, his wild eyes scanning the slope behind Gil and Dragunov to see if they were alone.

Everyone knew there was going to be a shoot-out, but neither side knew exactly what it was up against.

"Long walk?" Dragunov asked in Russian.

The man with the AK in his hand nodded. *"Da."*

"Looking for Dokka Umarov?"

The man nodded again.

"He's dead," Dragunov said. "What's left of his force has surrendered to the Spetsnaz. There's no reason for you men to be caught up in it. You should go back to where you came from."

One of the others started to unsling his rifle, but Gil leveled his AN-94 and locked eyes. *"Nyet."*

The Chechen narrowed his gaze but took his hand from the rifle strap.

"The others don't speak Russian," Dragunov said in English. "Ready yourself. I'll take the leader."

Hearing Dragunov speaking English threw the Chechen off, but before he could make heads or tails of it, shots rang out from the edge of the forest, and his friends grabbed for their weapons.

Gil let loose with the AN-94, cutting two of them in half at close range.

Dragunov shot the man with the AK, but the remaining four got their weapons loose. He leapt among them, leveling one with a butt stroke to the jaw. Another spun around and whacked him in the back of the helmet with his AK-47, causing him to stumble toward the stream.

A pair of Chechens danced away into the trees, one of them firing wildly from the hip and hitting Gil on his armor. The other tossed a grenade onto the creek-side shale and dove for cover.

The grenade went off on impact, and Gil was thrown into the water, his legs and one of his arms taking shrapnel and bits of shale. Dragunov was blown over and landed on his butt with a splash, firing a 40 mm grenade into the copse of trees.

Dragunov's aggressor was blown off his feet as well, and he too landed in the water, jumping up and beating Dragunov over the head with a rock, smashing the NVGs still clipped to his helmet.

Gil struggled to rise, his brains scrambled by the blast. He fell over in the water and sighted down the barrel of the AN-94, squeezing off the last two rounds in the magazine and shooting Dragunov's attacker.

With bullets striking the water around him, Dragunov got to his knees, unslinging the SVD sniper rifle from his back and setting up the bipod mounted just forward of the ten-round magazine. He lay belly-down with his eye to the scope, preparing to engage a mob of ten Chechens charging downhill. He shot the leader just above the groin.

Umarov's nephew Lom dropped his rifle and grabbed his gut as he collapsed, summersaulting to a stop.

Dragunov squeezed off another round, hitting his second target in the chest. He fired twice more, shattering a pelvis and blowing away the side of another's head.

His fifth shot shattered a femur; his sixth took off most a shoulder. The four remaining Chechens skidded to a halt and turned tail back toward the tree line. Dragunov shot the seventh in the tail bone, and the remaining three he dead-centered between the shoulder blades.

He slung the empty rifle and grabbed Gil up out of the water. "Can you run?"

"Frog's asshole watertight?" Gil muttered, stumbling on the slippery rocks.

Dragunov didn't know what that meant, but Gil was walking, and that was all that mattered. There was a burst of fire from the copse of trees where he had fired the grenade. He grabbed Gil's rifle from his hands, flicking it toward the trees, and fired another grenade to finish the wounded Chechen.

They ran for the far side of the valley, Gil's mind clearing slowly on the way, and made it to another patch of trees on the upward slope. The two of them sorted themselves out under cover and reloaded their weapons.

"How are your wounds?" Dragunov asked.

Gil gazed at him and shrugged.

Dragunov saw that his eyes were glassed over, the pupils dilated, and reached for his aid kit. "You're concussed." He dug out a dextroamphetamine capsule and a cigarette. "Swallow that and smoke this."

Gil downed the capsule with a swallow from his water tube and poked the cigarette between his lips. "I'm not exactly sure this is how you're supposed to treat a concussion, Ivan."

"Too bad," Dragunov said. "We're going up against Kovalenko, and you need to clear your head."

Gil threw the cigarette down after the first few drags. "That's not helping."

"The amphetamine will take effect within three minutes."

"Feelin' it already," Gil muttered, some of his focus beginning to return. "Gotta love the go pills."

"There are more in your aid kit if anything happens to me," Dragunov muttered, getting to his feet. "Now let's move. We have to displace before they can zero our position."

He took one step and flew back against a tree, letting out a gust of air as though he'd been kicked in the chest by a kangaroo and crumpled to the ground.

Gil sprang forward, pulling him to cover behind a large rock and ripping open his jacket to see the bullet had penetrated the ceramic breast plate. He tore out the plate and checked behind it to see that the projectile had fragmented and that the Kevlar had stopped the fragments, as the system had been designed.

"Wake up!" Gil smacked his face. "Wake up!"

Dragunov opened his eyes. "Stop hitting me."

"You're dead, baby!"

The Russian's eyes grew wide, and he grabbed his chest. "What does that mean?"

Gil sat him up with a grin. "It means our Chechen friend out there thinks he just killed you."

65

BETHESDA NAVAL HOSPITAL,
Bethesda, Maryland

Pope kept one eye on the satellite feed while he spoke on the phone with Mark Vance, ex–Delta Force operator and CEO of the private military company Obsidian Optio. Obsidian deployed private mercenaries around the world, protecting various governmental and corporate interests. Chief among those interests were some of the world's most vulnerable petroleum processing facilities. Gil was on Obsidian's books as an employee but only as cover for a double hit he had carried out on two Al Qaeda terrorists in Morocco the year before.

"You say he's where?" Vance asked.

"Just over the Georgian border into Russia," Pope replied. "The Georgians are refusing to violate Russian airspace to pull him and his Spetsnaz partner out. So I need your people to fly in there and get them."

"What about the Russians?" Vance said. "If the other guy is Spetsnaz, why don't they pull them out?"

"It's political," Pope said. "Putin is making a point that I don't have time to explain."

"Well, Christ, Bob, we can't violate Russian airspace."

"You've got your own helos in Georgia that you're using to patrol the BTC pipeline," Pope said. "All you have to do is send a couple of them north for an hour or so and pull my guys out. Keep them close to the ground, and Russian radar will never even know they're there."

"Bob, that's just not something we can do," Vance insisted. "We can't violate a country's airspace like that."

"You violated Brazilian airspace six months ago when your op to eliminate Joaquín Silva went bad."

"That wasn't us!" Vance said, obviously shocked by Pope's knowledge of the operation. "And I resent the implication, Bob! Goddamnit! We're on a telephone here!"

"It was you," Pope said, his voice rising, "and I have the proof. Now, are you going to help me out, or I am going to share that proof with Brasília? I understand you're about to sign one hell of an account with Telemar communications." Telemar Participações, a $48 billion Brazilian telecommunications company, was the country's third largest corporation. "It'd be a shame," Pope said, "if the Brazilian government prevented that deal from going through."

"Damn you, that's blackmail!" Vance growled.

"It's business," Pope said icily. "And in case you haven't gotten the news yet, I've just been appointed director of the CIA. So if you plan on continuing to do business with me, you'd better find a couple of pilots who know something about flying snake-and-nape, because I've got two men in the Valley of the Shadow badly in need of extraction!"

Vance was quiet for a long moment. "So you're the head motherfucker in charge now," he grumbled.

"That's right," Pope said. "And I understand you've got a Killer Egg stashed east of Tbilisi. You'd better send that along in support of the evac. It's likely to be a hot EZ." Killer Egg was the nickname for a Boeing AH-6 Little Bird helicopter, heavily armed with rockets and Gatling guns.

"You know entirely too much about our operations," Vance said. "How many of your people do you having working on the inside?"

"Are you going to get on the phone to your people in Tbilisi or not?" Pope said. "Time is running out for my men."

"I'll pull them out," Vance growled, "but you can bet your ass I'll be expecting a quid pro quo one day. This could cost us a helluva lot if it goes bad."

"That's why it's so important," Pope said. "I'll have Midori call you immediately with the coordinates and the rest of the particulars."

Pope hung up and called Midori, telling her what he wanted. Then he called the president at the Pentagon. "Mr. President, I've arranged for evac. You don't have to bother with the Georgians anymore."

"Who the hell did you get, Bob?"

"Obsidian Optio."

"Obsidian! How in hell did you get Vance to agree to it?"

"I twisted his arm, Mr. President."

"How'd you—never mind!" the president said. "I don't want to know. Let's just hope they get there in time."

66

THE CAUCASUS MOUNTAINS

After agreeing to separate, Gil left Dragunov and moved carefully from cover to cover toward the south, allowing Kovalenko to catch glimpses of him but not enough to risk getting shot. He knew the Chechen was in the tree line on the far side of the valley, so, relatively speaking, the bullet would take a little bit longer to reach him. This extra bit of time would be measured in tenths of a second, but it was enough for Gil to leap between rocks or trees without having to worry about Kovalenko forcing a shot that could potentially expose his position. The biggest risk was that he might anticipate Gil's movement, firing a split second before he made his dash, thus delivering the round in time to intercept him. For this reason, Gil had to be very careful to keep his movements jerky and unpredictable. It was a dangerous game, and if he played it too long, he would certainly be killed.

The plan was for Gil to draw Umarov's men southeast of Dragunov's position. This would put their backs to Dragunov and allow him to start picking them off without immediate danger from Kovalenko. And this would force Kovalenko to make a choice: either let them escape or begin maneuvering against two different sniper positions at the same time. Gil had no doubt he would choose the latter.

The bulk of Umarov's men had reached the stream by this time, and it was apparent from the size of the force that additional reinforcements had arrived. There were at least a hundred men maneuvering through the trees and around the boulders. The fighters at the front of the advance had spotted Gil's movement, and they took the occasional potshot at him as he darted from cover to cover.

After traveling a few hundred meters around the eastern rim of the valley, Gil was forced to pause, having arrived at a particularly wide gap in the trees, where a large fissure cut down through the slope like a firebreak. The fissure was four feet across and five feet deep. He could leap across it easily, but the jump would give Kovalenko time enough to blow him away. He crouched with his back to the rock and thought about the Chechen sitting in his hide across the valley, undoubtedly licking his chops as he waited for Gil to make the obligatory leap of faith.

He envisioned himself in Kovalenko's position, eye to the scope, watching the left side of the fissure for the first hint of movement, then squeezing the trigger, delivering the bullet at the same instant Gil landed on the far side.

Gil darted halfway from behind the rock and pulled back quickly. A bullet struck the rocky ground on the far side of the fissure, kicking up dust, and Gil lunged forward again, throwing himself across the fissure and diving onto his belly behind another rock. A second bullet nicked the heel of his boot as he pulled his legs to safety.

Kovalenko would be cursing him now, and Gil stuck his middle finger up over the rock for a half second and pulled it back. A third round stuck the rock and ricocheted with a whine.

"Good, you're pissed," Gil muttered. "Wait till you find out Ivan's still alive."

The first group of Umarov's men had arrived within effective AK-47 range about a hundred yards down the slope, and it wasn't more than ten seconds before Dragunov's first shot rang out across the valley, cutting down a man in the midst of shouting orders to pick up the pace.

Gil scrambled from behind the rock into the trees, where the cover was more substantial. Dragunov fired again, and another Chechen toppled over about seventy yards downhill, shot in the small of the back.

Gil hunkered in with his own SVD. He placed the PSO-1's unique T-shaped reticle on the face of the next Chechen in line and squeezed the trigger. The bullet struck the man in the left eye and blew out the back of his head. The body spun a tight pirouette to the ground, and the sight had a chilling effect on the rest of the skirmishers, sending them scrambling for cover behind rocks and in shallow depressions. Nothing demoralized infantry like sniper fire.

Gil now had a good estimate of the angle from which Kovalenko was firing, and he knew he would be safe behind the tree until Kovalenko could displace for a better shot. He concerned himself with a pair of Chechens who'd taken cover in a shallow defilade a hundred yards downslope. The two men were pouring AK-47 fire into the trees off to the left. He placed the reticle on the forehead of the first guy, allowing for the drop of the bullet, and squeezed the trigger, blowing off the top of his head. Then Gil shifted a hair to the right and shot the second one through the center of the face. The head snapped back and then forward again, smacking against the ground.

Another, braver pair of Chechens attempted to maneuver uphill through a dense copse of trees, and Gil was about to squeeze the trigger when Dragunov—who must have worried that Gil couldn't see them—shot one through the pelvis. The Chechen went down screaming, and Gil shot him through the head.

The other guy panicked and darted from the trees on the far left side, where Dragunov would not have a shot at him. Gil led him six inches and squeezed the trigger, hitting him in the left temple and blowing out his eyes. He swung back to the right and shot another man in the face just as he was stealing a peek from behind a boulder. The body fell from behind the rock, and an arm reached out to grab him. Gil shot it off at the elbow.

"Looks like you're gonna need some help with those ketchup bottles from now on, partner."

Bullets splintered the tree limbs just above him, and he marked the shooter two hundred yards downslope behind another rock. The rock wasn't very large, but Gil could see only the barrel of the rifle and the top of the shooter's camouflaged cap. He squeezed the trigger. The round hit the forestock of the AK-47 and ricocheted into the Chechen's eye.

The wounded man jumped up and ran away downhill.

Gil let him go, knowing his bloody retreat would have a detrimental effect on the morale of the men farther downslope.

"Okay," he muttered. "Two more rounds before I take this show back on the road."

A bullet passed through a two-inch gap in the rocks to Gil's right, tearing a chunk from the tree just beyond his nose. It was a round that could have come only from Kovalenko. "Fuck me!" he said, pulling back. "Time to go!"

67

THE CAUCASUS MOUNTAINS

Scanning the tree line to the west in search of Kovalenko, Dragunov spotted Dokka Umarov instead, more than four hundred meters away. The Chechen rebel leader was watching the hunt for the American through a pair of binoculars, with only three men for security. Dragunov knew him from the long beard, and he couldn't believe his luck at suddenly having Russia's most hated enemy in his crosshairs.

Eye to the scope, he placed the crossbar of the T slightly above Umarov's head to allow for the drop of the bullet, expecting a solid torso shot. He was about to squeeze off the round when a .338 Lapua Magnum slammed into his right side, penetrating the side panel of his armor and tumbling as it tore through his abdominal muscles. Dragunov recoiled from the impact, throwing himself downhill to avoid being hit again, rolling into a cleft between the rocks, and gripping his abdomen.

In agony, he dug a fentanyl "lollipop" from his aid kit and stuck it into his mouth for the pain. The fentanyl, seventy-five times more potent than morphine, would take effect within five minutes. Until then he would be a sitting duck for anyone who came to finish him off, so he drew his pistol and waited.

KOVALENKO KNEW THAT Dragunov was severely wounded this time and would die soon. He picked up the ORSIS rifle and pulled back into the forest, where he could maneuver freely without having to worry about the American. He hadn't been able to get a clear sight picture on Gil, so he had fired through a tiny gap in the rocks at five hundred meters, knowing that he would hit close enough to scare the American into displacing. Then he had taken out Dragunov by easily hitting a six-inch gap in the trees from two hundred meters.

Now, with only one sniper to worry about, Kovalenko was free to maneuver south and wait for Gil to expose himself. Since he had forced the American out of his sniper's nest, the Chechen infantry had gained the high ground to Gil's rear. Soon it would be in the trees, where he would no longer enjoy the advantage of firing over hundreds of meters of open killing ground. All Kovalenko had to do was get into position by the time Gil was forced from the trees on the south end of the woods. He picked up the pace until he came to Umarov's position and took cover behind a large pine.

"You shouldn't stand out there exposed like that, Dokka."

"I've told him," said Basayev. "It doesn't do any good."

Umarov took his eyes away from the binoculars and glanced over his shoulder at Kovalenko. "Where have you been?"

"Killing Dragunov."

"Good. Now get ready to kill the American. The wolves are in the trees with him now, and he'll soon be flushed out the other end."

The firing on the far side of the valley picked up, and they could hear the chatter of Gil's AN-94 answering that of numerous AK-47s and RPKs.

"He's falling back fast now," Basayev said. "Running out of cover."

Kovalenko emerged from the trees, shrugging out of the hot ghillie suit down to the waist. He took up a firing position on his belly beside a fallen tree and popped the lens caps on the scope. He was able to catch glimpses of Gil falling back through the trees, but it was obvious that even now Gil was conscious of being under a sniper's watchful eye. He never stopped on the downhill side of a tree or a rock to leave himself exposed but was always careful to keep something between him and the west side of the valley.

"Do you have a shot?" Umarov asked.

"No," Kovalenko said. "He's very good . . . but another sixty seconds, and that won't matter."

"Do you hear that?" Basayev said suddenly, looking up into the sky.

Gil had run out of room to retreat. He took to one knee, his back to the open spaces, and fired the last of his 40 mm grenades. The grenade exploded and took out three men as they maneuvered beneath a jutting rock formation. He assumed that Dragunov must be dead—otherwise the men now chasing him through the trees would never have gained the high ground so quickly—and he assumed equally that Kovalenko would be waiting on the far side of the valley to shoot him the second he broke from the trees.

A look over his shoulder told him the closest possible cover was a blunt outcropping of rock more than fifty yards away. The outcrop would barely conceal him from Kovalenko, much less from the Chechens now pursuing him at such close range.

"End of the fuckin' line," he muttered, smacking a magazine into the AN-94 and flipping the weapon over in his hands. He plucked his only smoke grenade from his harness and pulled the pin, tossing it out in front of him. A thick cloud of green smoke formed quickly and concealed his position from the enemy.

Believing that Gil was using the smoke to cover his retreat over open country, the Chechens charged after him pell-mell and were met by withering fire from Gil's AN-94. He lobbed his last hand grenade into their midst and blew them off their feet. Those who survived fell back through the smoke and continued to fire blindly in his direction.

Gil slapped in his last magazine and readied himself for the smoke to clear, deciding that no way in hell was he going to allow Kovalenko the privilege of delivering the coup de grâce. He would die with the infantry.

THE SKY OVERHEAD was suddenly filled with the whine of a T63-A turboshaft engine. A fast moving black OH-6 Cayuse attack helicopter—the vaunted Killer Egg—swooped in over his position and fired a spread of 70 mm Hydra rockets, decimating the advancing Chechens.

Ex–New Zealand Special Air Service pilot Kip Walker then yanked the stick left, rolling out west over the valley. "That should buy 'im a minute while we 'andle this bloody sniper," he grunted. "I don't want the bloke shooting us in the bloody ass."

"He's up and moving!" said the copilot, watching Kovalenko on the infrared monitor.

The FLIR scope mounted beneath the front of the Killer Egg had picked up the prone sniper as they swept in over the ridge, and Walker had poured on the speed to avoid being hit as they flew across Kovalenko's field of vision. Now they were flying directly at him.

Walker lined up the helo and fired the twin GAU-19 Gatling guns hanging off either side of the aircraft.

Anzor Basayev's body exploded from the hydrostatic shock of the .50 caliber rounds, splattering Umarov with gore as he scrambled into the trees hot on the heels of the fleeing Kovalenko. Another burst from the Gatling guns, and both of Umarov's security men exploded on either side of him. He fell forward onto his face as the Killer Egg swept overhead and banked hard to the south.

Kovalenko stopped short and ran back to help Umarov to his feet. "They have infrared. We have to keep running!"

Walker banked the helo over the valley, checking the infrared to make sure that Gil was still alive and in the same position before firing another spread of rockets into the trees in order to flush dozens of Chechens out into the open. He pulled the stick back and to the left, working the foot pedals to slew the helo around and bring his guns immediately to bear on the enemy below. The adrenaline rush of operating over Russian territory was greater than any he'd ever experienced.

He put the helo down on the deck and squeezed the triggers as he swooped in on the scattered enemy, cutting them apart like a buzz saw.

"Get on the talker to Mason!" he shouted into the headset. "Get the Pum'er in 'ere! We don't wanna be around if the damn Russians show up."

The copilot got on the radio and called in the Puma transport helicopter that was holding station on the far side of the ridge.

Walker dropped the helo back to the deck for a final attack run.

Gil watched the helo mow down the rest of the enemy. Then he ran to grab an AK-47. A lone Chechen stood up from behind a rock, firing an RPK at almost point-blank range. Gil jumped inside the horizontal arch of fire and grabbed the long barrel of the machine gun under his arm, slugging the Chechen in the face and jerking the weapon from his hands.

The Chechen fell back a step and pulled a knife. Gil charged and smashed him over the head with the barrel of the RPK, splitting his skull as another Chechen stepped from behind a tree and shot him in the back. Gil fell forward, catching himself with his hands and grabbed the dead Chechen's knife. He spun around and hurled it. The gunner ducked and fired again, missing as Gil sprang to his feet and rushed him, pulling his own knife.

The Chechen swung his AK like a ball bat and struck Gil a glancing blow across the top of the helmet. Gil slammed into him and drove the knife deep into the guy's side. The Chechen screamed in Gil's face, trying to wrestle free of his grasp. The two fell over as one and rolled downhill, slugging away at each other. They came to a stop against a tree. The Chechen clawed for Gil's eyes, and Gil caught a finger in his teeth and bit down, pulling the knife free and stabbing the man over and over again until he quit moving.

Smelling that the Chechen had soiled himself in death, Gil rolled off and drew his pistol, waiting to see if there were any more holdouts. When he felt confident there were none, he staggered out into the sun to see an all-black twin-engine Puma helicopter setting down on a level patch of ground halfway between him and where he had left Dragunov. Six heavily armed men jumped out of the helo and formed a defensive perimeter, two of them armed with sniper rifles.

The Killer Egg remained on station five hundred feet above, its infrared-detecting eyeball keeping a careful watch on the surrounding terrain.

Gil was trotting toward the Puma when he saw a green cloud of smoke forming in the trees at the north end of the valley.

One of the snipers ran out to meet him. "Chief Shannon? I'm Doug Mason. I was with SEAL Team I from 2010 to 2013."

Gil saw the helo had no markings of any kind, not even a tail number. "Who the hell are you guys?"

"Obsidian Optio. Better load up, Chief. We don't have permission to be here."

Gil pointed north. "That green smoke yonder is my man. He's wounded."

Mason glanced over at the smoke two hundred yards off. "Okay, Chief. We'll get him."

They loaded up, and the Puma flew along the ground, getting as close at it could to Dragunov's position before setting down again. Gil and three other men dismounted and climbed up through the rocks to where Dragunov lay in the sun, soaked in his own blood. He had managed to crawl from the cleft in the rocks, but he hadn't made it very far.

The Russian managed a weak smile. "You're alive."

"So are you." Gil checked his wound and saw that his abdomen was torn open from left to right. "We gotta get you outta here, Ivan."

The four of them lifted him up and carried him down to the helo.

"What about Kovalenko?" Dragunov asked as they hurried along.

"He got away," Gil said. "Unless the helo got him."

They set Dragunov down on the deck of the Puma and climbed in after him. Dragunov grabbed Gil's arm. "Kovalenko wouldn't be killed by a helicopter."

"I know it." Gil saw a pack on the bench seat with a SEAL Team trident sewn to the side of it. "This your kit?" he asked Mason.

"Yeah. Why?"

"Gimme your rifle," he said, grabbing up the pack. "I have a mission to complete."

"What are you talking about? They sent us in to pull you guys outta the fire."

"Well, the fire's out now," Gil said. "And the last thing that fucker will expect is me coming after him."

"What fucker? Chief, you're bleeding!"

"Call Pope and tell him to have me picked up at the bridge crossing into Georgia as originally planned."

Mason was confounded. "What the fuck are you talking about? Who the hell is Pope?"

"Your superiors will know." Gil took the McMillan TAC-338 sniper rifle from Mason's hands.

"That's my personal weapon."

"Good. It should already be sighted in, then. If I get whacked, tell Pope I said to buy you a new one."

"What the fuck?"

"Let's go!" shouted the helo pilot. "We're here too long! We gotta go!"

Gil jumped out, shouldering the pack. "How much food I got in this thing?"

"Three days' rations," Mason said. "You're insane, you know that?"

"We gotta go!" the pilot shouted again, terrified of being caught on the ground by a Russian Hind.

Gil placed a bloody hand on Dragunov's forehead. "I think Putin wants Kovalenko to get away. How about you?"

Dragunov smiled. "Watch yourself. I'm pretty sure he's wearing a leshy suit." A leshy was a mythical Russian beast capable of changing its shape to blend in with the forest.

Gil winked and stepped back from the helo with a wave to Mason, and the Puma lifted into the air. Within sixty seconds, he was all alone in the valley and running up through the rocks to retrieve Dragunov's AN-94, along with his ammo and grenades.

68

THE PENTAGON

"What the—!" Couture bit off the rest of what he was going to say, watching Gil climb up through the rocks toward Dragunov's gear.

The president put a hand on his shoulder. "He's completing the mission, Bill. I warned you he'd find a way to break it off in Putin before this was over."

Couture was almost shaking with frustration. He'd thought the worst was behind them when the Killer Egg swept into the valley, but then everyone had shouted in panic when Gil was jumped in the trees. Then when the Puma finally set down, and infrared confirmed there were no more Chechens within two clicks, he had finally dared to believe it was over.

Now Gil was off and running again, with no definite mission profile, no timetable, and no planned extraction.

"What the hell do we tell the Russians?" Couture said, turning around.

"We tell them nothing more than is necessary," the president said. "We'll brief them on the status of Major Dragunov, but nothing more. Not a word about how he got out of Russia until I've had time to confer with Secretary Sapp."

Then the president turned to Brooks and smiled. "You're awfully quiet, Glen."

Brooks sat back with a glass of water in his hand. "A minute ago, I thought we were clear." He took a drink and set down the glass with a sigh. "Now I don't know what to think."

"At least the helos got in and out of Russian airspace undetected," offered the air force chief of staff.

"The thinnest of silver linings," muttered Couture, staring at the table. Then he laughed sardonically. "I don't know why I'm so stressed. Shannon can't hurt anyone but himself this time."

"You're stressed," the president said, "because you like him. It's impossible not to by this point. He's the kid in class who gets away with anything, and we love him for it." He stood up from the table. "I have to go. Glen and I have business at the White House. I'll be drinking much earlier than usual today if you'll care to join me, General."

An aide de camp came into the room. "I have a private message for you, Mr. President."

"Whisper it in my ear, son."

The aide came forward and spoke softly into the president's ear.

The president looked at him, eyes wide. "That's confirmed?"

"Yes, sir."

The president turned to the Joint Chiefs. "Senator Steve Grieves's limo exploded near the Capitol Building half an hour ago. He's dead—along with his secretary and driver."

Couture looked at the aide. "Car bomb or something else?"

"That hasn't been confirmed, sir, but it looks like a car bomb."

"That's a domestic hit!" blurted the Marine Corps chief of staff. "One of Pope's people over at CIA must have done it." It was no secret that he was not a fan of Pope or the CIA.

"I'd better not hear that remark made in public!" the president snapped. "Is that understood, General?"

The general shrank slightly under the president's ire, aware that he'd spoken out of turn. "Yes, sir. I'm sorry, sir."

"We've got enough goddamn trouble," the president went on, "without wild accusations being thrown around."

Couture glared at the marine general. "We'll handle things here, Mr. President. Call me if you need anything."

The president shook his hand. "Keep me posted, General."

The second the president and Brooks were out of the room, Couture turned on the Marine Corps chief of staff. "What the hell were you thinking, Fred?"

The big bald marine tugged on his jacket. "I'm sorry, Bill. I know everyone around here seems to think Bob Pope is the best thing since shaved pussy these days, but I don't trust the son of a bitch. I never have, and I never will. If you want my resignation, all you need to do is ask."

Couture stared at him. "Your resignation isn't mine to ask for, but you're ordered to watch what you say about the CIA from now on. Understood?"

"Aye, General. It's understood."

69

BETHESDA NAVAL HOSPITAL,
Bethesda, Maryland

Bob Pope had fallen asleep shortly after the helicopter flew off and left Gil behind. He opened his eyes a half hour later to see a barrel-chested doctor with close-cut gray hair standing at the foot of his bed, reading his chart. He glanced over and saw that the door to the room was closed. Then he studied the ID tag hooked to the doctor's pocket. The name didn't match the face on the tag. "Ben Walton, I presume?"

Walton looked up, taking a silenced Walther PPK pistol from inside his white doctor's smock and tossing the chart onto the foot of the bed. "Where's the key?" he asked in his deep voice.

Pope was immediately puzzled. "What key?"

"The key Shannon took from Miller aboard the *Palinouros*."

"I don't have any idea what you're talking about," Pope said. "Shannon hasn't mentioned any key."

"I searched Miller's body myself, along with his cabin. Don't play with me. Shannon has the fucking key."

"I don't doubt that," Pope said, "but he hasn't mentioned it to me."

Walton held the pistol level. "Where is he?"

Pope pointed at the laptop sitting on the adjustable table angled across his bed. "That's him moving through the woods."

Walton stepped around to see the screen more clearly. "Where the hell is that?"

"Somewhere in the Caucasus."

Walton cocked a suspicious eyebrow. "You mean he's still chasing Kovalenko?"

Pope shrugged. "He's a very willful boy. I thought you were headed for Cuba."

"I know you did." Walton smirked. "That's why I'm here. Also, Senator Grieves needed to be dealt with."

"You've already paid him a visit?"

"Yeah." Walton gestured at the red telephone on the table beside the computer. "Nobody's called you on the bat phone yet to tell you about it?"

Pope shook his head.

"Maybe it's because they suspect you had something to do with it."

"I'm sure somebody does." Pope's gaze was set. "If they didn't, I wouldn't be doing my job correctly."

Walton took an empty 100 cc syringe from the pocket of his smock and set it down on the table, with the shiny needle pointing right at Pope. "I want you to inject all that air into your IV line."

Pope looked at the syringe. "And if I don't?"

Walton put the muzzle of the silencer against the side of Pope's head. "Then your brains go all over the wall. Now stop stalling."

Pope reached for the syringe, and Walton took a step back.

"I can't reach the line very well."

Walton stepped around and used his foot to push the IV stand closer to the bed. "Get this heart attack on the road, Bob. You're not stalling your way out of this."

"Did you kill Steiner?" Pope asked, reaching to pull the IV stand closer. "I ask because—"

Walton jammed the muzzle of the silencer back up against Pope's head, saying through gritted teeth, "Do it now, asshole!"

Pope fumbled with the line for a moment. Then he made a sudden grab for the weapon, snatching the muzzle away from his head before Walton could squeeze the trigger.

"Help!" he screamed at the top of his voice, holding onto the gun with both hands, his thumb over the hammer.

Walton twisted the weapon free and shot Pope in the chest as two Secret Service agents burst into to the room. He had time to fire once and miss before they shot him down. He collapsed to the floor between the wall and the bed.

Pope lay back holding his chest. "Goddamn, he got in the same lung." Then he leaned over the rail and vomited onto Walton's legs. "Hey. He's still alive over here."

One of agents came around the bed and kicked Walton's gun across the room.

"Finish him," Pope said. "Finish him before someone comes in."

"I can't do that, Mr. Pope. He's down and disarmed."

Walton looked up at Pope, holding his shoulder and grinning. "Fuck you, Bobby. By the time I get done testifying to Congress, there won't be anything—"

Pope shot him in the forehead with a Glock 26 taken from beneath his blanket.

He looked at the stunned Secret Service agents and put the pistol on the table. Then he sat back and closed his eyes. "Sweet Jesus, if this doesn't hurt worse than it did the first time."

The agents stood looking at each other. "What do we do?" one of them whispered.

"I suggest putting that gun back in his hand," Pope said quietly. "You two are in enough trouble already for letting him get past you." He opened his eyes. "I can make that trouble go away—*or not*. It's your call."

One of the agents retrieved the Walther and dropped it into Walton's lap. Ten seconds later, a pair of hospital cops appeared in the doorway, weapons drawn.

"All clear in here!" said the agent. "Director Pope needs a surgeon! He's been shot!"

70

Crosswhite was still at the house of Duardo's sister-in-law. Agent Mariana Mederos had arrived a half hour earlier, and she stood outside the back bedroom, where Crosswhite sat on the edge of the bed talking with Paolina. His leg wound had been sutured by a doctor that Ernesto had contacted on his behalf, and the pain was being controlled by large doses of ibuprofen and oxycodone. The police had bought Duardo and Paolina's story the night before without bothering to do much of an investigation, and the bodies were removed without a single photograph being taken. In the eyes of the law, it had been a whorehouse brawl that got out of hand, and no one really seemed to care too much about it. The police sergeant told them they'd look for the guy who got away, but everyone knew it was lip service.

"Will you come back?" Paolina asked.

Crosswhite touched her face and kissed her hair. "I don't think that's a good idea."

"For you or for me?" She was on the verge of tears.

"For you."

"That's my decision," she said. "Do you want to come back or not?"

"Of course I do."

She put her hand on his. "Then I want you to."

"I do bad things, Paolina."

"To bad people," she said. "And someone has to, no?"

He sat staring at her soft brown eyes, feeling his throat tighten. "That's what I tell myself, but I don't always believe it anymore."

She kissed him. "Come back, Daniel."

"Okay," he croaked. He cleared his throat. "Mariana, come in here."

Mariana stepped into the room and smiled noncommittally at Paolina.

"Got any money?" he asked her in English.

Paolina understood the word *money*. She touched his arm and shook her head. "I don't want you to pay me."

Crosswhite ignored her. "Got any money? *Real* money?"

Mariana let out a sigh and unshouldered her daypack. "How much is she charging you?"

"Cut the fuckin' attitude, and just gimme some money."

She reached into the bag and handed him a zippered leather pouch.

Crosswhite unzipped it and peeled off five thousand dollars' worth of Ben Franklins.

Paolina's eyes grew huge, and she moved away from him on the bed, shaking her head as the tears began to fall. *"No lo quiero."* I don't want it.

"If something happens to me, I want you well—"

"No lo quiero!"

Crosswhite looked at Mariana. "You're a girl. Help me out here."

Mariana stood chewing the inside of her lip, debating whether or not to get involved in this Shakespearean tragedy. "It's way too much money. She thinks it's a payoff—that you're never coming back."

Crosswhite took Paolina's hand and folded the money into it. "I'm coming back," he told her in Spanish. "I swear it. If I don't, it's because I'm dead."

She hugged him and began to cry, and Mariana left the room.

Paolina's mother was in the salon with four small children, her husband and sister having gone to work.

"You're with the CIA too?" Olivia asked.

Mariana nodded. "I'm not really supposed to tell you that."

Olivia smiled. "You're very uncomfortable here, no?"

"Dan shouldn't have brought this trouble into your lives," Mariana said. "Your daughter thinks she's in love with him." She shook her head. "It's not my business, but you should discourage her."

"We are all in the hands of God," Olivia said. "God brought them together, and only He can take them apart."

Mariana glanced at the crucifix on the wall. She wasn't about to debate a Roman Catholic. "As I said, señora, it's not my business."

Crosswhite came into the room, fastening his belt. "You did a good job with the pants," he said. "I wasn't sure you knew my size."

"Are you ready to go? The cab is waiting."

Crosswhite stepped over to Olivia, offering his hand.

"Señora, I'm indebted to your family. Thank you for not turning me over to the police."

Olivia held onto his hand. "Take care of yourself."

He looked at the toddlers playing on the floor. "Which is Paolina's?"

She indicated the little girl with the darkest skin, and Crosswhite touched the child on the head. "Let's go," he said to Mariana.

They got into the cab, and Mariana put on a pair of Ray-Bans. "So are you planning to get this one killed, too?"

Crosswhite was immediately angered—even with the narcotic in his system—but he kept his composure. "Be glad you're a woman, Mariana. I've knocked a man's teeth out for a fuck of a lot less."

She ignored his threat, entirely unintimidated by him. "What's next?"

"Do you have a room at my hotel?"

"Right next to yours, actually."

"Were you spotted at the airport?"

"No one knew I was coming."

"That's not what the fuck I asked you."

She took off her glasses and looked at him. "Quit talking to me like that, goddamnit!"

"Then lose the self-righteous fucking attitude! We're on the goddamn job here! If you don't get your fucking head in the game, you're gonna get yourself killed— which I don't particularly give a shit about—but you might get me killed along with you, and that I *do* give a shit about!"

The cabbie looked in the mirror. "Everything okay?" he asked in Spanish.

"We're just arguing," Crosswhite said, lowering his voice. "Nobody's gonna get hurt."

The cabbie seemed to accept that and kept driving.

Mariana put her glasses back on and looked out the window. "You should know this is a command performance for me. I don't want to be here."

"Then why are you here?"

"Pope ordered me. I guess there are only so many people in the agency he feels he can trust right now."

Crosswhite grunted. "It's not like him to make such a gross error in judgment."

"You're a bastard."

"You know what?" he said, lighting a cigarette. "You're done here. I don't care if you get back on a plane or hang out at the pool, but you and I are done. You're useless to me."

She looked at him, realizing she'd pushed him too far. He had enough influence with Pope to hurt her career. "Why didn't you tell me what you were going to do to Hagen?"

"Is that was this shit is about? You're still pissed about Hagen?"

"You made me a party to murder," she hissed. "That's *not* why I'm in the CIA!"

Crosswhite didn't have the patience to get into it with her. "Take it up with Pope when you get back to Langley."

"I already did that."

"And?"

"And he said tough shit."

"Then you'd better get used to it. This is the world we work in. If you had any brains, you'd realize you're a member of a club now—a very exclusive club. There aren't too many women who can say that."

She looked out the window. "I can't sleep. I'm having nightmares."

"They'll go away," he said quietly. "The important thing to focus on is *purpose*. What we do is not random; it's not arbitrary. There are very definite reasons for it."

She looked at him. "These men should be put on trial. Pope is having them killed out of vengeance."

"That's one way of looking at it."

"What's the other way?"

"Pope sees the future. And in it, there are bad guys with nukes. So he's adopted a zero-tolerance policy."

"I heard what you said to Paolina. You don't even believe that yourself anymore."

He took a deep drag from the cigarette. "I've got a lotta blood on my hands, Mariana. A little doubt here and there is what keeps me human."

They arrived at the hotel and went up to their rooms, pausing in the hall outside their doors.

"Just hang here at the hotel until mission complete," he said. "We'll keep the argument between us. Pope doesn't need to know." He winked at her. "What happens in Havana and all that shit."

Mariana keyed into her room and closed the door. She stepped into the bathroom, reaching for the light switch, and was slugged in the stomach harder than she had ever been hit in her life. She grabbed her middle and collapsed to her knees, trying to scream, but there wasn't so much as a breath of air left in her lungs.

Someone grabbed her from behind, pressing a strip of duct tape over her mouth and shoving her forward onto the floor. Her hands were quickly bound with a nylon tiedown, and two Cuban men carried her into the other room, tossing her onto the bed. One of them jerked her pants and panties down inside out past her ankles, tying the pant legs in a knot and effectively binding her feet.

Mariana's pain was matched only by her terror. She tried to sob, but the wind was still knocked out of her, and she was having a great deal of trouble breathing through her nose.

"One fucking sound," the man said in English, "and I'll break your fucking neck!"

"I'll call Peterson," said the smaller of the two, taking a cellular from his back pocket.

71

THE CAUCASUS

When Gil came across the ruptured bodies of Anzor Basayev and the other two security men, he recognized Basayev's face from the mission dossier he'd been shown in Moscow, making a mental note to tell someone back in the world that at least one high-priority target had been taken out. A short time later, he picked up what he hoped was Kovalenko's trail, and it didn't take long to determine that he was tracking two men. He stopped to study the separate boot prints, seeing that one of the men had cut a notch into the heel of his left boot, and this was all Gil needed to confirm that the Wolf was still alive. Many soldiers who spent a lot of time operating alone—such as snipers—chose to notch the soles of their boots to help guard against walking in circles or tracking themselves. Gil had never employed the technique himself, thinking he could always notch his boot if and when the circumstances called for it. Otherwise the notch might end up being used to track him, the way he was using it to track Kovalenko now.

With the sun nearing its apex, he moved out.

The bolt-action TAC-338 was slung across his back. Chambered in .338 Lapua Magnum, it was a far superior weapon to the semiauto Dragunov SVD, and the scope was far superior as well: a Nightforce 8-32 x 56 mm. For the first time since mission start, he felt like he was adequately equipped, which was ironic, considering his physical condition. His belly wounds were festering but not particularly painful. The shrapnel wounds from the grenade, however, were hurting like hell and suppurated constantly, making it so that his left sleeve and trouser legs clung annoyingly to his skin.

He estimated that, if need be, he could function in this condition for perhaps another thirty-six hours with the help of the dextroamphetamines. By that time, he would be robbing Peter to pay Paul for each additional hour in the field, growing steadily less effective. Once infection set in and fever took hold, he would have to change his priorities.

Sucking down the last of Dragunov's water on the move, he discarded the water bladder and dug into Mason's rucksack for a pair of high-energy bars, wanting to get some food in his belly before reestablishing contact with the enemy. He wondered idly who had arranged for the Obsidian helos, but the answer was obvious. Pope was watching from above. Always Pope—like the omniscient eye of God.

He imagined everyone back in DC throwing a fit the second they realized he was jumping off the helo to go "rogue" again. How he'd come to hate that word. The simple truth was that he loved to fight, and he no longer made any apology for it. His love for combat had already cost him his marriage, so what was left to lose—other than his life? And that was why he'd gotten off the helo—that and because fuck Sasha Kovalenko. Kovalenko liked to fight, too, and he was damn good at it. Gil realized that he liked being well met, and in the last forty-eight hours, he'd come to understand that combat was a lot like the game of chess: the only real way to improve was to compete against someone better than you.

He set a brisk pace down the mountain, wanting to catch Kovalenko before dark. There was a forest camp to the south near the Georgian border. The camp was controlled by an Umarov ally named Ali Abu Mukhammad. Gil had seen it on a map in the mission dossier, and he remembered it was only a few clicks west of the bridge where he and Dragunov had originally planned on hitting Kovalenko. If the man Kovalenko was traveling with was Dokka Umarov, it was almost a sure bet they were headed to Mukhammad's camp.

The titanium implant in his foot began to give him trouble after the few hundred yards of the downhill grind, so Gil slowed his pace. If the foot gave out on him, he was finished.

He was down on one knee beside a brook, cupping the ice-cold water to his mouth, when an enemy patrol of perhaps a half dozen happened by on the far side, partially obscured by the dense undergrowth that grew at the lower elevation—two different species of rhododendron that kept their leaves year-round. He waited for the patrol to pass, but then a Chechen emerged from a gap in the thicket to his right, no more than fifteen feet away on the opposite bank. Gil dropped flat to the ground and froze like a lizard.

The Chechen knelt and dipped a canteen into the water.

Gil was partially hidden behind a rhododendron, but not well enough to conceal him from a direct look. The rifle was beneath him, attached to the three-point sling, and at such close range, he didn't dare move to draw the pistol.

Another Chechen emerged and knelt beside the first, dipping his canteen as well. Within a half minute, there was a regular canteen-filling convention taking place, with six Chechens kneeling shoulder to shoulder at the water's edge. They were talking in regular voices, entirely unconcerned about their security. Two were smoking cigarettes. This was their territory, and they obviously felt safe. Whether or not they had any knowledge of the battle that had taken place a full click to the north was anybody's guess.

The best clue was that they were all filling two canteens apiece, indicating they had possibly spent the earlier part of day operating in the high country, where water was scarce. It might have even meant they'd been traveling parallel to Gil during his descent, but from the ill-disciplined manner in which they carried on, he doubted it. There was no urgency about them; no sense of vigilance.

As they began standing up to put away their canteens, one of them glanced in Gil's direction, looked away—then did a double take, shouting a warning to his compatriots, pointing with the canteen in his hand instead of grabbing for his AK-47.

Gil ripped a ready-grenade from his harness, the pin pulling automatically as he tore it loose and biffed it into the shallow water. The Chechens who saw the grenade dove for cover; those who didn't were grabbing for their rifles when it exploded.

Two of them were blown apart as Gil rolled to his side, laying down a hail of fire from the AN-94. He killed two more, but the remaining two jumped up and fled through the gap in the rhododendron. He sprang to his feet and gave chase, not wanting to risk them warning Umarov's camp. The Chechens crashed through the undergrowth a few meters ahead of him, just out of view as they followed a narrow deer trail, hoping to get away from Gil and whoever might be with him. They would have surely recognized his Spetsnaz camouflage, and the Spetsnaz were known to operate in wolf packs.

Gil fired at them through the undergrowth. One of them cried out, and Gil heard him go down. He leapt over the body in the trail a second later and bound unexpectedly into a glade; a small clearing in the forest. The other Chechen had vanished into thin air. Gil went immediately to ground and tuned his ears for the slightest hint of movement.

72

HAVANA,
Cuba

Mariana lay on the bed utterly petrified, naked from the waist to her ankles, her hands bound painfully behind her back.

"What did Peterson say?" the big guy asked. He had an old 1911 pistol stuck in the front of his pants.

The smaller guy tucked the cellular into his back pocket. "He wants us to kill them both."

The guy with the gun looked at Mariana lying helpless on the bed, his eyes coming to rest on her pubic mound. "You thinkin' what I'm thinkin'?"

His partner glanced at Mariana and shook his head. "That's not really my thing."

"More for me, then." The big man tossed him the pistol.

"You'd better make it fast." His partner tucked the gun into the small of his back. "We're on the clock, and that prick next door is bad news."

"I won't be long, bro."

Mariana began to sob as the guy dropped his trousers and knee-walked across the bed, grabbing her knees in strong hands and forcing them apart, and then falling on her heavily as he maneuvered between them.

The other guy picked up the remote and turned on the TV to cover Mariana's muffled cries. Then he went into the bathroom and stood peeing into the toilet. He finished and dropped the seat, pushing the button on top of the tank before stepping back into the room. After watching his partner on top of Mariana for a minute or so he decided, Why not? They were going to kill her anyhow. It wasn't like she'd have to live very long with the trauma.

The door to the room burst inward, and he spun around just in time for Crosswhite to grab him behind the neck with both hands, holding him in a Muay Thai clinch and delivering him a vicious knee to the groin. The Cuban's legs buckled beneath him, and Crosswhite snatched the gun from the back of his pants, kicking the door shut with his heel and thrusting the pistol before him as Mariana's rapist was rolling off the bed.

"Freeze, motherfucker!"

The big guy stood beside the bed with his pants down around his ankles, his erection wilting rapidly.

Crosswhite stalked forward and buried the toe of his boot in the guy's groin. The man let out a hideous squeal of pain and dropped to the floor, convulsing and vomiting onto the tile. Crosswhite kicked him in the face and stomped his skull with the heel of his boot. The little guy began get to up, and Crosswhite stalked back across the room to slug him in the side of the head with the pistol. Then he put the pistol under his shirt and grabbed the guy by the hair, giving his head a brutal twist and snapping the neck with a crunch.

He took a folding knife from his pocket and cut Mariana loose.

She leapt off the bed and shuffled into the bathroom with her pants still caught around her feet, slamming the door behind her and retching into the toilet. The shower came on a short time later.

Crosswhite was standing by the door when the big guy began to stir. He walked over and finished him off with a heavy heel to the back of the neck. Then he sat down on the edge of the bed and took out his cellular to call Ernesto the doorman.

Ernesto knocked a few minutes later, and Crosswhite let him into the room.

Ernesto saw the bodies. *"Santo Cielo!* Do you leave dead men everywhere you go, señor?"

"Looks that way," Crosswhite answered glumly, sitting back down on the bed and taking out his cigarettes.

Ernesto looked around for Mariana. "Is the señorita okay?"

Crosswhite shook his head. "I don't think so."

"Do you want me to call the doctor?"

"Maybe, but I don't know yet." He struck a match. "I don't think she needs that kind of a doctor."

Ernesto realized for the first time that one of the dead men's pants was down around his ankles, and his face turned ashen. "Was she . . . was she violated?"

Crosswhite tossed the match onto the floor and breathed smoke from his nostrils. "Yeah."

Ernesto stepped over and spit on the rapist's corpse. *"Coño!"*

"Do you know somebody we can pay to get rid of these bodies, Ernie?"

"Yes, but I think it will be very expensive."

"Expensive I can handle," Crosswhite said. "Cops I can't."

"I'll have Lupita bring her laundry cart. The cart is small, so it will take two trips, and she will want the money right away."

"That's fine. What happens after the laundry carts?"

"I can call my cousin. He has a fish truck. He can give the bodies to the men he buys the fish from, and they can dump the bodies in the ocean."

"You're sure they'll help?"

Ernesto shrugged. "If you will pay, they will help. Money is the law here, señor."

"Okay, Ernie. Better go find Lupita. We're burnin' daylight."

Lupita was a small woman of forty. Her black hair was flecked with gray at the temples and pulled back into a ponytail. She crossed herself when she saw the bodies and then looked at the bathroom, where Mariana was still crying. *"Qué pasó con ella?"*

Ernesto gestured at the half-naked body. *"Fue violada."*

Lupita crossed herself again, muttering, *"Santa Magdalena."*

Crosswhite took $2,000 from the leather pouch and offered it to her.

She tucked the money away inside her shirt without counting to see how much he'd given her.

Crosswhite pulled up the guy's pants, and Ernesto helped him put the body into the cart. Then Ernesto and Lupita rolled the cart away down the hall, returning for the second body fifteen minutes later.

"We're going to need some more money," Ernesto said awkwardly. "A woman in the laundry room saw us hiding the body."

"How much?"

"Five hundred should do nicely, señor."

Crosswhite gave it to him. "Call me when you know how much your cousin and the fishermen are gonna want."

"Very well. I'll call you in half an hour."

Ernesto and Lupita were about to take the second body away when Crosswhite had an alarming thought. He grabbed Ernesto by the throat and shoved him up against the wall. "Why the *fuck* didn't you warn me these guys were in the *fucking* building? You fuckin' me in the ass without a reach-around, Ernie?"

"No, señor. I swear it! I'm not working today. After last night, I didn't think to tell any—" Ernesto began to tremble, and then a look of shame fell over him. "You've made me . . . you've made me urinate in my pants, señor."

Crosswhite let him go and stepped back, seeing that the man had indeed pissed himself. "Sorry about that," he said. But he continued to eye Ernesto with suspicion. "If you're not workin' today, how'd you get here so fast?"

"I live upstairs, señor. I'm the head doorman."

Lupita stood by the door, ready to escape, eyeing Crosswhite with disapproval.

"Okay, look," Crosswhite said in Spanish. "I apologize. I had a bad night, and it's been a very bad morning. I know money doesn't fix everything, but I'll make sure you're both well taken care of when this is over."

Lupita glanced at Ernesto and then said with a glint in her eye, "Money fixes many things, señor."

Crosswhite nodded, putting his hand on Ernesto's shoulder. "If it makes you feel any better, amigo, I shit myself during my first firefight. That's a lot worse."

Ernesto smiled halfheartedly, still very embarrassed. "You're the most frightening man I've ever met, señor. There's no need to doubt my loyalty."

"Listen, don't get the wrong idea now." Crosswhite held up a finger. "If some bastard puts a gun in your face, you tell him whatever he wants to know—understand? I don't want you dying for me. But I don't want you fuckin' me, either. See the difference?"

Ernesto nodded. "I failed to protect you and the señorita, but it won't happen again, señor. You have my word."

73

THE WHITE HOUSE

The president looked up from behind his desk in the Oval Office. "Is he going to live or not?" He was asking about Pope.

"The hospital gives him a ninety percent chance." Brooks took a seat in front of the desk. "They just brought him out of surgery. He's in what they're calling *guarded* condition."

"We sure can't afford to lose him now," the president said, stroking his lower lip. "Walton must've been out of his damn mind. What the hell made him chance something like that?"

Brooks shrugged. "I think your guess is as good as any, sir."

The president shook his head, putting the mystery from his mind. "Has Couture heard anything more about Major Dragunov's condition?"

"Yes, sir. Dragunov's going to be fine. His abdominal

wall was pretty badly torn up, and they had to remove a small portion of his large intestine, but he is expected to make a full recovery. Secretary Sapp is in contact with the Russian ambassador, and Moscow has been advised. To quote Sapp, 'They are intensely curious as to how their man got out of Russia.' At the moment, Dragunov's in a Tbilisi hospital under close guard, which is another embarrassment for Putin—having a top Spetsnaz operative end up under Georgian care."

"And a big risk for the Georgians," the president added. "Imagine if somebody gets in there and kills Dragunov before the Russians can pick him up."

"I'm sure that's why there's the close guard, sir."

"Speaking of which," the president went on, "how the hell did Walton get past the Secret Service?"

Brooks smiled a dry smile. "That's an entirely different can of worms."

The president was not amused. "Spill it."

"One of Walton's specialties was phony identification: passports, driver's licenses. He made himself a doctor's ID tag and used it to get past Pope's guards. Hospital security says the ID is perfect. Even they can't tell it's a phony."

"So the Service agents are in the clear? They followed procedure?"

"Yes and no," Brooks said. "Yes, they're clear. No, they didn't follow procedure."

The president cocked an eyebrow. "How the hell does *that* work?"

"Well, procedure dictated they check the doctor's name against a list of docs cleared to be in Pope's room. Whatever Walton's made-up name was, it wasn't on the list, so they couldn't have checked it. That's enough to establish they didn't follow procedure."

"Then how are they in the clear?"

"Because Pope shot Walton in the head after the agents had already put him down and disarmed him. He had a pistol concealed beneath his blanket. We're still trying to figure out how he got it into the room."

The president stared for a moment. "So the agents are covering for him, or what?"

"Sort of. They were debriefed separately—before they had time to corroborate a story—and they both describe the event the exact same way."

"They obviously had time enough to agree on throwing Pope under the bus," the president muttered.

"The initial debriefing was off the record," Brooks said. "Both agents refused to talk on tape until *after* they were allowed to tell the unfettered version of what took place."

The president sat back. "Sounds like they're offering to keep their mouths shut in exchange for keeping their jobs."

"They haven't been so impertinent as to verbalize it quite that way, but that's what they're hoping for, yes."

"Fine. I'll play ball, but no more high-profile security details for those two jamokes. They can babysit some moron in the witness protection program. Or better yet, they should be chasing counterfeit twenties around the Midwest—somewhere far away from DC."

"I'll pass the word, sir."

"Do that. Now, what about Chief Shannon?"

"Couture says they've projected his movement, and it looks like he's headed for a camp presently under the control of a Dagestani militant named Ali Abu Mukhammad. Mukhammad is rumored to be next in line to take over the Caucasus Emirate if Dokka Umarov is ever killed."

"How many people in this camp?"

"Over two hundred, sir."

The president sucked his teeth. "That's another way of saying Shannon doesn't have a chance." Then he smirked and shook his head. "Which is, of course, exactly why he *does* have a chance." He sat scratching his head. "Give the general my regards and let him know that I won't be coming over to the Pentagon to watch."

"You don't care for the stress, sir?"

"Oh, the stress isn't a problem," the president said. "Stress comes with the job, but this is likely to be Shannon's swan song, and I know how hard it is for the good general to maintain his composure with me in the room."

Brooks pursed his lips. "Then we won't be lending Shannon any support at all?"

"He's still in Russia, Glen. I already took a huge risk to bring him out, and he took a pass. There's nothing more I can do. And with Bob Pope lying in the recovery room?" The president shook his head. "I'm afraid Gil Shannon may well have overplayed his hand this time."

74

THE CAUCASUS MOUNTAINS

Gil heard the safety lever eject from a grenade to his right. He saw the orb flying toward him on an almost level trajectory, and his brain calculated a solution with computerlike speed. The fuse on a Russian grenade was only 3.8 seconds, and after the first 1.8 seconds, it would detonate on impact. So when he reached up, it wasn't to catch it—but to fling it past him. The grenade detonated on the other side of a tree, and he sprang into a crouch, firing a 40 mm grenade into the trunk of a tree on the far side of a rotting log forty feet to his right. The grenade exploded, and the Chechen hiding behind the log was killed by the blast.

Gil knifed him behind the ear to make sure and ran to get back on course for Mukhammad's camp. He was moving fast along a well-worn foot trail when he ran headlong into a patrol of four men running north to investigate the explosions. He shot three of them down, firing from the hip as he charged into the column and taking out the last man with a butt stroke to the face. He kept going, reloading the AN-94 on the run.

There was shouting up ahead. Smoke from a cooking fire drifted through the trees among a number of well-camouflaged lean-tos, where men grabbed for their weapons. This was an Umarov outpost—an outpost not designated on the Russian map—and without a doubt, the garrison would be in radio contact with Mukhammad's main force.

Once again, Gil had lost the element of surprise in his pursuit of Kovalenko.

He lobbed a grenade over the rhododendron as he moved to skirt the encampment. It detonated near the cooking fire, blowing away three men and sowing confusion as everyone in the camp realized the perimeter had been breached. He wanted no part of these people in daylight and needed to break off contact before they realized he was only one man. Taking cover behind a tree, Gil hurled another grenade toward a cluster of men receiving hurried instructions from an officer. They didn't see him, but they spotted the grenade in the air and scattered for cover as it detonated harmlessly on the roof of a lean-to with a radio antenna sticking out of it.

He disappeared down a trail to the south, knowing the dangers of sticking to the trails, but the rhododendron left him no other choice. His only chance was to put as much distance between himself and the outpost as he could, hoping for a break in the rhododendron grove. Gil stopped behind a rock to reload the GP-34 and to attach another hand grenade to the ready-hook on his harness. He heard footfalls coming down the trail and drew the suppressed pistol, aiming over the rock as a man came through the curve in the trail. He shot him in the base of throat, and the guy grabbed his neck, pitching forward off the trail.

Gil got back on the move and after twenty minutes began to believe he may have shaken them, but his fantasies were dispelled the moment he heard the faint rattle of equipment moving parallel to him on the far side of an impenetrable thicket. He slowed and stopped, and the rattling stopped as well. There were at least two men shadowing him, but he didn't have time for a cat-and-mouse game, so he took off running.

The two paths came to an abrupt intersection a hundred feet down the trail, and he slammed broadside into one of the men, sending him flying. The second guy jumped on Gil and knocked him down. Fortunately, the impact knocked the man's AK-47 from his hands, and the guy had to turn around to pick it up. Gil machine-gunned them both from his back and sprang to his feet. There was a burst of fire behind him, and the rounds impacted against the armor panel on his back and sent him sprawling forward. He rolled to his back as the Chechen charged, catching his toe on the nub of a root and stumbling forward off his feet, landing in Gil's guard.

Gil wrapped his legs around the Chechen's waist and grabbed him around the neck with his arm, gouging out the Chechen's eye with the thumb of his free hand. The guy screamed and tore off Gil's helmet, trying to get free. Gil released his guard and performed a hip escape, bashing him in the temple with his knee as he got to his feet. He grabbed the AN-94 and finished him with a rifle butt to the head before taking off again.

There was plenty of shouting to his rear now, and Gil knew that the rest of the outpost wouldn't be more than thirty seconds behind him. He guessed there were a dozen men or so bearing down on him, but who the hell knew? It may as well have been a hundred, because his reserves were spent. Every time his right foot hit the trail, it felt like he was stomping on a bowie knife. His lungs burned with fire, and the calves of his legs were beginning to knot up with lactic acid. He desperately needed a chance to catch his wind, but the hounds never allowed the fox that kind of time.

What was it Dragunov had said the night before, that running back toward the hounds was never an option for the fox?

"Fuck it. Better to meet it head-on than to let 'em run you down."

He turned and charged back up the trail.

A dark figure leapt out of the undergrowth and tackled him. Two more men fell on him a second later and pinned him fast to the ground. Gil screamed and went berserk, slugging away and trying to throw them off, but they were too heavy and too strong. They immobilized him, and one of them sat on his head while his hands were zip-tied behind his back. They dragged him into the undergrowth, and Gil lay on his back watching as six men in black quickly fanned out to either side of the trail with AN-94s.

Thirteen Chechens rounded the bend and were met by a hail of fire. The two men at the front of the column virtually disintegrated. Those to the center were cut down without getting off a shot, and those at the rear turned to run—but they didn't make it far. The forest fell silent, and the men in black rose to their feet, dumping the empty magazines from their rifles.

Gil struggled to sit up as one of them came forward. The man knelt in front of him and lowered a black balaclava to reveal his unshaven visage.

"I am Colonel Yablonsky of the Spetsnaz Spetsgruppa A," he said, his eyes almost black beneath dark eyebrows. "Where is Major Dragunov?"

Gil swallowed. "He was medevac'd out by an American mercenary unit."

Yablonsky said something to his lieutenant in Russian. "When?"

"Around noon."

"Why were you left behind?"

Gil watched as the other Spetsnaz men took up defensive positions. "Because I'm going to kill Dokka Umarov and Sasha Kovalenko. Did Moscow send you in?"

Yablonsky shook his head, looking pensive. "We jumped in on our own—against orders. Dragunov is a good friend."

Gil was exhausted, but he found the energy to smile. "My kinda group."

"How badly is Ivan wounded?"

"Bad enough to take him out of the fight," Gil said, "but he'll survive. He's tough."

"And where exactly are you going?"

"Mukhammad's camp."

Yablonsky spoke again with his lieutenant and then returned his attention to Gil. "Do you know Mukhammad has more than two hundred men in that camp?"

Gil nodded. "It was mentioned, yeah."

"And you're going anyway? In this condition?"

Gil shrugged. "Nothin' better to do out here."

Yablonsky told the lieutenant to cut him loose, and Gil dug a couple of dextroamphetamine capsules from his medical kit.

"Do you really think you're capable of completing such a mission in your condition, Master Chief?"

Gil swallowed the capsules with a gulp of water from the CamelBak inside Mason's rucksack. "Yep."

"One man against two hundred? Two hundred who probably know you're coming?"

Gil smiled. "Well, there's seven of us now, Colonel." He chuckled. "Which cuts the odds to something like twenty-eight to one, doesn't it? Unless you guys are leaving, in which case I'd appreciate some ammo and grenades."

Yablonsky was unsure of what to do.

"You say you guys jumped in here against orders?"

The Russian nodded and stood up. "And by now Moscow will know."

Gil got to his feet slowly, testing his weight on the titanium implant and rubbing his wrists. "I'm not Spetsnaz, Colonel, but with Major Dragunov already out of danger . . . well, I'm guessing it might be a good idea for you guys to take Dokka Umarov's head back to Moscow."

Yablonsky smiled. "Even if we fail, it's a story that will grow in the telling." He looked at his men, saying to them in Russian, "The American has challenged us to help him kill Umarov. Anyone want to refuse?"

No one did.

75

HAVANA,
Cuba

After a couple of hours in the bathroom, Mariana emerged. She glanced at Crosswhite, who sat on the bed in front of the television. Then she leaned against the wall, folding her arms in a protective embrace. "What happened to the—to the bodies?"

Crosswhite lifted the remote and turned off the television. "Ernie's people are taking care of things. Do you need him to call the doctor?"

She pulled her hair back behind her ears and then folded her arms again, sniffling. "Thanks. I'm okay."

"I should have cleared the room. I'm sorry."

She shook her head.

"We'll get you on a plane to Mexico City. I'll meet you there after the mission, and we can get our stories straight. There's no reason for Pope to know about this—unless you want him to. And don't worry, I'll tell him I'm willing to work with you again."

She stepped over to the bed and sat down on the corner of the mattress, keeping her arms folded. "How did you know to come in?"

"It's an old building," he said. "I heard him peeing in the toilet through the wall. It didn't sound right. Then when he dropped the lid to flush, and I knew somebody was over here."

She sat staring at the floor. "I must've washed fifty times. I still feel dirty."

"It's normal," he said.

She looked at him. "I'd like to stay and finish the mission. I'm focused now."

"No. You need to recover from this. You can spend as much time as you need in Mexico City. There's plenty of money, and Pope's been—"

"I need to finish this, Dan. If I go back now, it's like it happened for nothing."

"You might feel that way at the moment, but—"

"Listen to me!" she said. "You didn't just save my life. You stopped him before he could finish—and that means more than you have any idea. I can do this. Please trust me."

He sat thinking things over for a long time. He thought about Sarahi bleeding to death in his arms. He thought about his friend Sandra Brux, raped and brutalized at the hands of the Taliban two years earlier—his failed mission to rescue her—and he thought about Paolina. Did he even dare step into her world? What specters of evil might follow him there?

"Dan?"

He looked at her.

"Let me stay."

"Okay," he said reluctantly. "But you have to follow my every instruction."

"I promise." She stood up. "Think we can get outta this room?"

"Sure."

They slipped into Crosswhite's room, and he gave her a bottle of water from the fridge. "I talked to Midori over the sat phone. Pope's been shot again."

Mariana nearly choked on the water. "What?!"

"Ben Walton walked right into his hospital room and shot him—with two Secret Service agents out in the hall. Believe that shit?"

"By now, I'll believe anything. Is he going to live?"

"Sounds like it." He took the Cuban assassin's cellular from his pocket and dropped it onto the bed. "Midori worked the call list and figured out where to find Peterson. Looks like he bought a small *finca* outside of town last year." A *finca* was an estate. "She's going to email us the sat photos and whatever other intel she can come up with. We'll recon the place later and put together a plan of action."

Mariana capped the water bottle and set it aside, rubbing her hands on her legs. "So what do we do while we're waiting?"

"Dunno. You hungry?"

"Yeah, but can we have Ernesto bring us something? I don't feel like going outside right now. I feel like the whole world will know what happened the second they see me."

"Sure."

Ernesto brought them food from a restaurant down the street, and they sat on the bed eating. When they were finished, the two of them stretched out and lay staring at the ceiling. Crosswhite kept the 1911 beside him on the bed.

Mariana rolled to her side and propped up her head on her hand. "I'm sorry for what I said earlier . . . about getting another one killed. That was a cunt thing to say."

"Forget it. We're in another life now."

"I guess that's true, isn't it? For me, anyhow." She stared into space. "They were absolutely going to kill me. Peterson ordered it. The smaller guy said so."

"Well, we're going to return the favor."

She lifted her head and her eyes filled with tears, her voice shaking as she spoke. "They slugged me in the stomach, and I couldn't even scream for help."

"When he was on top of me . . ." Her voice cracked. "When he was on top of me, I *begged* God for you to come through that door. I've never begged for anything like that in my life . . . but I knew you wouldn't come . . . I *knew* it was impossible.

"But then there you were. I still can't believe it."

He smiled. "Well, I guess that just proves the old saying."

She wiped her nose with the backs of her fingers. "What old saying?"

He looped a lock of hair behind her ear with his finger and then rested his hand on the bed.

"Trust in God and the Eighty-Second Airborne."

76

HAVANA,
Cuba

Peterson was back on the phone with Roy, his Mexico City contact, astounded by the news that Walton had shown up in Maryland and gotten himself killed.

"What do you mean he shot Pope?"

"All I know," Roy said, "is that he walked into Pope's room, shot him, and got gunned down by the Secret Service two seconds later."

"I don't fucking believe it!" Peterson said. "He never said a word about going back to the States."

"Well, it gets even more bizarre than that," Roy said.

"How? What the hell else don't I know?"

"It looks like he probably killed Steve Grieves before he paid Pope a visit. The senator's car blew up down the street from the Capitol less than an hour before Walton showed up at the hospital. So if it wasn't Walton's work, it's one hell of a coincidence."

Peterson stood with his jaw hanging down. "Christ Almighty. I must have been next."

"That's probably a safe bet," Roy said. "It looks like Ben was cleaning house all across the board. You know, I never did think he was all that stable. The guy enjoyed waterboarding people way too much."

"That's why he was taken off the detail," Peterson muttered. "Listen, you're sure he's dead?"

"Yeah, that's confirmed. You don't have to worry about him. How are things going with Crosswhite?"

"Last I heard," Peterson said, "my guys were about to pop the Mederos bitch." He chuckled. "Then they were gonna move against Crosswhite. They weren't supposed to risk a callback unless something went wrong, and I haven't heard from them or Captain Ruiz, so it's looking like everything went according to plan this time—no bodies in the street. I'll get confirmation tomorrow and let you know."

"Do that," Roy said. "I'd like to be able to close the file at my end. Depending on how things work out in the future, I may be able to use your eyes and ears in Havana. Hey, maybe we'll get lucky, and Pope will throw a clot. If he croaks, I might even be able to get you white-listed in a couple of years—get you some room to breathe."

"We can sure as hell hope," Peterson said. "Let me know when you want to do business, and I'll get you my account numbers."

"Okay, but there's no hurry. We're talking eighteen months or so down the road."

They ended the call a couple minutes later, and Peterson stepped to the window for a look down at the street, where two off-duty cops sat in a white car outside the gate to the *finca*. Satisfied that all was in order, he went downstairs, took a small snub-nosed .38 revolver from his back pocket, and set it on a table inside the backdoor.

Then he changed into a pair of shorts and went outside for a swim. It was good to be alive.

77

THE CAUCASUS MOUNTAINS

Gil lay on his belly on a ridge beside Colonel Yablonsky, studying Mukhammad's camp through the scope of the McMillan tactical rifle. At two thousand yards, he couldn't make out much detail, but he could see enough to gain a good idea of its general disposition.

"We may have gotten lucky, Colonel. It doesn't look like they're on a war footing down there." He passed Yablonsky the rifle. "Tell me what you think."

The Russian watched the encampment. "I agree they look very relaxed." He passed back the TAC-338. "But how is it possible they're not expecting you? We know the outpost had a radio. We've been monitoring their traffic for weeks in an attempt to track Umarov's movement."

"I must have blown the radio up before they had a chance to put out a call." He capped the scope fore and aft, and the two men pulled back from the ridge. "Now I just have to get within range and wait for Umarov to show himself."

Yablonsky noted the sniper rifle did not have a suppressor. "And you think we'll be able to escape after you make the shot?"

"Did you guys bring any MON-50s with you?" The MON-50 was the Russian version of the American M18A1 Claymore mine.

"Yes. One each."

"Good. After they run into the second one, they'll slow their pursuit. We only have to outrun them for three thousand meters or so. I'm supposed to have people waiting at the bridge crossing into Georgia."

"My men and I cannot cross into Georgia. Moscow would be very angry."

"But less so if we kill Dokka Umarov, and that's why we're here."

"You don't know my government very well."

Gil chuckled as he got to his feet, slinging the rifle around his back. "I'll bet I know it better than you think I do."

"You'll have to get a lot closer than this. Where do you plan to set up?"

"See that tree yonder?" Gil pointed out a hardwood far off to the southeast, higher than the rest. "It's about eight hundred meters from the camp and should give me a good overview of the target area. If I move out now, I should be in position before the sun begins to set."

Yablonsky stood staring at the tree. "It's completely on the wrong side of the camp. You'll have to run all the way around it to escape."

"I'm not running around anything," Gil said. "The

shortest distance between two points is a straight line, and I've got a bum foot."

The Russian took a pack of cigarettes from his pocket. "You're going to run straight across the camp?"

"More like a zigzag, but yeah." Gil took a knee, bidding Yablonsky to do the same. "Look, Colonel, I can only take one shot from that tree. Any more, and they'll pinpoint my location. That means I'll have to climb down and hunt Kovalenko on the ground. I'd prefer to shoot him first, but both our governments want Umarov dead, so Umarov carries priority.

"If you and your men set up on the west side of the camp and open fire with grenade launchers the second you hear my shot, that will help to cover my position and draw them away from me. Then all you have to do is break contact, fall back through your claymore screen, and haul ass for the bridge."

Yablonsky took a drag from the cigarette he'd lit while Gil was talking. "How will you find Kovalenko in all the confusion?"

"I won't have to." Gil smiled. "He won't be drawn off by the diversion. He'll know I took the shot from the tree, and he'll come after me."

"What makes you so sure?"

Gil borrowed the cigarette and took a drag. "There's no time to explain, but trust me, I know." He gave back the cigarette. "I'll need some help getting up into the tree. After that, I'll give you and your men time to circle around to the other side and get set up. Think you can manage in an hour?"

"If all goes well," Yablonsky said, "but I never count on things going well."

"Me neither."

They arrived at the base of the great tree twenty minutes later. The trunk was close to twenty feet in circumference, and the nearest limb was twenty-five feet off the ground. The Spetsnaz threw a hundred-foot rope over it, and the six of them hoisted Gil. He climbed into the crotch of the tree and pulled the rope up after him, giving them a wave to send them on their way. They disappeared in seconds, and he carefully worked his way another thirty-five feet up into the tree, using a section of the rope to secure himself. Once Gil was sure he wasn't going to fall sixty feet to his death, he unslung the sniper rifle and attached it to the three-point sling, stretching out along a broad limb.

He didn't have a particular fear of heights, but his palms were sweating from the tedious climb, so he pulled on a pair of tight-fitting black leather gloves and pulled the rifle into his shoulder, popping the lens caps for a look at the encampment eight hundred yards away. To his shock, Dokka Umarov was one of the first people who came into focus. The Chechen leader was standing in front a command tent talking with Ali Abu Mukhammad. Umarov was by no means the only man in camp with facial hair, but his long, Jeb Stuart–style beard caused him to stand out.

Gil checked his watch. Only thirty minutes had passed since Yablonsky and his men had moved out. He stretched a patch of panty hose tightly over the end of the scope, fixing it in place with a thick black rubber band. The panty hose would prevent the descending sun from glinting off the lens without significantly reducing resolution of the sight picture. He pulled back the bolt to load a .338 Lapua Magnum into battery. Then he released the five-round magazine and loaded a sixth cartridge to top off the weapon.

Now Gil was ready to do battle. He only had to give the Spetsnaz team time to get into position. He was busy studying Umarov when it occurred to him that he had never fired this particular rifle before. The TAC-338 had an adjustable trigger pull of 2.5 to 4.5 pounds, and there was no way to know if Mason preferred a light or heavy trigger without dry-firing the weapon, so he tucked the magazine into his leg pocket and carefully ejected the leader round. He pushed the bolt forward and pulled the trigger, satisfied to find that the rifle's owner had left it on the factory setting of 3 pounds.

Gil made the weapon ready once more and scanned around for Kovalenko. There were dozens of tents and ramshackle huts, numerous cooking fires, and Gil was wondering why the Russians hadn't bombed the place when—suddenly—he was stunned to see three children chasing after a puppy. Upon closer study, he realized there were at least twenty women in the camp as well, along with a half dozen other children. He guessed they were the families of Chechen insurgents, but it was possible they were Chechen or Ukrainian refugees displaced by a decade of war.

Gil felt bad for the women and children and hoped they wouldn't be hit by the Spetsnaz diversionary barrage, but their ultimate fate was out of his hands.

He spotted Kovalenko coming out of the command tent, and his adrenaline began to surge as the ex-Spetsnaz sniper approached Umarov and Mukhammad. Having all three ducks lined up in a row was almost too much for Gil to take. Then Kovalenko made it worse by putting his arm around Umarov's shoulders, giving Gil a golden opportunity to kill them both with a single shot. All three of them stood laughing in the silence of the rifle scope.

"You motherfucker," Gil muttered to Kovalenko. "You're doin' that to tempt me."

It killed him not being able to squeeze the trigger at such a pristine moment, but breaking with the plan could easily spell his death, as well as the deaths of his Russian allies, so all he could do was watch the clock and hope for an equally pristine shot in twenty-five minutes.

78

HAVANA,
Cuba

Crosswhite and Mariana had borrowed Ernesto's car. Now they sat parked in the shade up the street from Peterson's *finca*, staring at a white Nissan parked outside the gate.

"They're definitely watching the place," Crosswhite said.

"I'll bet they're cops."

He thought it over, deciding, "This isn't all bad. If the prick thinks he needs cops at the gate, he probably doesn't have security inside the house."

"Are you going to have to kill them?"

"Hope not," he muttered. "I plan on living here when this is over, and I don't need any more trouble with the local heat."

"You two barely know each other, Dan."

"That's not a problem for me," he said. "I'm old enough to know what I want. If she decides she doesn't like me a month from now, all she has to do is say so."

"And if you decide you don't want her?"

He turned to look at her. "You've seen her. That's not gonna happen."

Mariana realized that was probably true, admitting to herself that the young Cuban woman was as precious as a woman could be. "If you go back to her, you should leave this life."

"I just might do that."

They sat watching for a while, hidden from view inside the car by the shadow of the tree.

"Any ideas?" she asked.

"Nothing's jumping to mind. Those electrified wires around the top of the wall are a real problem."

"Can't we just cut them?"

"That would almost definitely set off an alarm inside the house."

"What if we pay the cops to leave?"

Crosswhite sat up straight behind the wheel. "You know, with the right pair of cops, that could work."

She smiled. "But are they the right pair of cops?"

"Exactly. If they're not, there's no do-overs. It's off to the clink."

"Unless you shoot them."

He nodded. "Unless I shoot them, and without a silencer, that's a risky proposition at best." He started the car and shifted into drive.

"What are you doing?"

"Fortune favors the bold."

He drove down the block and slowed to a stop alongside the Nissan, smiling at the driver.

"Good afternoon," he said in Spanish, the pistol in his lap.

"Good afternoon," the cop said, very businesslike. "Have you been watching us?"

"No, we've been watching the *finca*," Crosswhite said. "Same as you."

The cop narrowed his gaze. "What's your interest in the *finca*, señor?"

"That's not really important, but I'll tell you this: there's ten thousand dollars in it for both of you if you'll let us inside for a look around." Crosswhite knew they earned less than $2,500 a year.

The cop looked at his partner, and his partner told him to power up the window. They sat talking for a minute, and then the driver put the window back down. "Who are you, señor?"

"I'm the guy with twenty thousand US dollars," Crosswhite said, his gaze set. "And all you gotta do is look the other way while we climb over that gate."

The cop in the passenger seat was obviously ready to jump on the money, but the driver was very hesitant. "You should go back to your country," he said, staring off down the street.

"Look, amigo, my business inside the *finca*, it's between Americans. It doesn't have anything to do with you or your government. But I'll tell you what: my country and your country? Things are changing. Castro's out of power. Pretty soon real business is going to open up again. Why not be in a position to capitalize on it when it happens?"

The cop looked at him. "What does that mean?"

Crosswhite pushed all of his chips forward. "It means I'm going to be around awhile, and I'll be needing things from time to time. Simple things. No blood."

"You're CIA . . . like him inside?"

Crosswhite laughed. "No, amigo. I'm a whole lot worse. I'm a corporate point man. I work for a group of Yankee corporations that are very eager to do business here in Havana. It's only a matter of time before they pressure my government into ending the trade embargo, and when that happens, I'll be needing friends in the police. You can turn me away, but you know and I know the other cops won't."

The driver put the window back up, and the two cops talked for another minute. Then he put the window back down. "If our captain finds out we let you—"

"Your captain won't know anything," Crosswhite said, knowing he had them.

"But if that man in there ends up dead—"

"There's a swimming pool."

"A what?"

"A swimming pool."

The cops looked at each other. "You're going to drown him?"

Crosswhite turned to Mariana, knowing it was time to flash some cash. "Gimme ten grand."

Mariana unzipped the pouch and quickly counted out the money.

Crosswhite put the money in a greasy paper sack from the backseat of Ernesto's car and offered it to the cop. "This is ten thousand. You can have the other half when we come back out."

The driver looked nervously at his partner.

"Take it!" his partner said. "What do we care about a CIA man?"

"No blood!" the driver said in a hushed voice.

"No blood," Crosswhite said, tossing the bag across. Then he looked at Mariana and winked. "We're in."

"Go now," the cop said, waving them off. "Park up the block and walk down to the gate."

Crosswhite pulled off and parked a block away. "You ready?" he said to Mariana.

She nodded. "Scared shitless, but I'm ready."

79

THE CAUCASUS MOUNTAINS

Gil noted that Sasha Kovalenko favored his right leg as he turned to go back into the command tent, wondering what kind of wound he had sustained and when it had happened. Gil's own battered body was still suppurating, his shrapnel wounds burning from the jagged pieces of metal still lodged in his flesh. He popped another dextroamphetamine capsule and gulped water from the CamelBak, knowing he was now robbing Peter to pay Paul.

He whispered to himself, "All you have to do is run three thousand yards, and you're in the clear."

Umarov took a seat on a log near a cooking fire, tussling the curly black hair of a small boy who knelt on the ground playing with a toy airplane. A woman gave Umarov a plate of food, and he sat eating, talking with a number of other men sitting around the fire.

A grenade exploded in the forest to the west, followed

by the distant staccato of machine-gun fire, and every man in the camp sprang into action.

Umarov dropped his plate and stepped over the log, making for the command tent.

Gil put the crosshairs on the back of his head and squeezed the trigger.

Dokka Umarov's head exploded like a watermelon shot off a fence post, and he dropped to the ground. The women screamed, grabbing up the children and running for the huts.

Gil slung the rifle over his back and began working to get his feet back on the ground as fast as possible.

COLONEL YABLONSKY AND his men had been in the process of setting up their claymore screen when a small Chechen patrol stumbled across them. A brief firefight ensued, and all four Chechens were killed, but two of the Spetsnaz were hit with shrapnel, and one was shot through the shoulder blade.

"They'll come fast," Yablonsky said. "We'll hit them hard and fall back through the MON screen."

The Russian MON-50 version of the claymore mine came in two different variants. One variant fired 540 steel ball bearings, the other firing 485 short steel rods, each covering an arc of 54 degrees out to lethal range of fifty meters. Employing trip-wire detonators, the Spetsnaz had placed its mines (three of each variant) roughly thirty meters apart in order to deliver the maximum effect on the Chechen line of advance.

"Did anyone hear the American's rifle?"

"I heard nothing," Yablonsky said. "We have other problems to worry about now."

The six of them formed up by twos and prepared for

the attack. They could hear the Chechens shouting to one another as they came forward through the forest, ramming through rhododendron thickets and firing indiscriminately in an attempt to flush out the enemy. They were at least a hundred strong and moved with all the confidence of a superior force. Ali Abu Mukhammad commanded from the center, well back from the front, surrounded by a personal guard of a dozen devoted men. With Dokka Umarov now dead, he was the new emir of the Caucasus Emirate.

The Spetsnaz let loose with a volley of hand grenades, hurling three apiece before falling back through the claymore screen. The grenades exploded all along the Chechen line, killing or wounding nearly twenty men. Taking up firing positions among the trees, the Russians waited as the Chechens sorted themselves out, shouting for the wounded to be recovered and to close the gaps in the line.

The Chechens drew within range once more, and the Spetsnaz opened up with rifle and grenade fire, killing a dozen more before turning to run. The Chechens saw them and opened fire, dashing after them and directly into the screen of MON-50s.

The mines exploded with devastating effect all along the front of the Chechen advance, killing or wounding at least thirty more men, and bringing the advance to an abrupt halt. Men were screaming everywhere, their bodies shredded.

Mukhammad saw the devastation and called for ten volunteers to continue the pursuit while they waited for the remainder of the camp to arrive.

His personal guards volunteered immediately, but they were denied. Ten former Zapad Spetsnaz men came forward and told Mukhammad they would track down the assassins and kill them. He sent them off at once, turning to ask where the hell Kovalenko was, but no one had seen the Chechen sniper. A search of the dead was carried out, but his body was not found.

SASHA KOVALENKO WAS in the forest on the far side of the camp, perfectly camouflaged in his Russian leshy suit, slithering slowly along the ground at a snail's pace. He could now see the great tree from where he lay, the rope hanging down from the high limb, but there was no sign of the American sniper. He could feel him, however; his combat instincts telling him that Gil had not fled the scene. The rhododendron were not as dense here on the east side of camp, where the elevation was slightly higher, so visibility through the trees was about 60 percent.

Something moved along the forest floor to his right, no more than thirty feet beyond a rhododendron thicket. The sound was slow and deliberate, like that of a man crawling, moving parallel to his position toward the east. Kovalenko realized at once that the American was maneuvering to intercept him at the far end of the thicket.

The movement stopped, and he lay listening for five full minutes before he heard the American move again through the dead leaves. He smiled and moved carefully forward on his elbows and knees, his eyes peering out from within the leshy suit, the suppressed AK-105 cradled carefully in his arms. The ground was cleaner on his side of the thicket, so he made very little discernible sound as he moved.

GIL WASN'T SURE of Kovalenko's position, but he could feel him drawing closer, a kind of ozone slowly pervading the air around him. His arrector pili muscles contracted along his arms and shoulders, tightening his skin into gooseflesh, and he pulled the .338 into his shoulder.

He studied the terrain before him, watching not for the movement of a man but of a segment of the forest. Although highly effective from a static position, a ghillie suit was no more effective in motion than any other type of camouflage. The sound of fighting on the far side of the camp had dropped off immediately after the claymores had detonated, and there hadn't been a shot fired since.

He closed his hand around the end of a one-hundred-foot length of parachute cord taken from Mason's rucksack. The other end of the cord was attached to the rucksack, which he had stashed in the rhododendron thicket a hundred feet out in front of him. The cord was concealed beneath the dead leaves and other forest debris, so it would not be readily visible to anyone who didn't already know it was there. Gil gave the rucksack a slow, steady pull of about three feet, hoping to lure Kovalenko in for the kill shot.

He was very tired, approaching exhaustion, and he was a bit shaky from the amphetamines, so when he first detected Kovalenko's movement in the fading light of the forest, he wasn't sure whether or not his eyes were playing tricks on him. Gil eyed the spot through the scope and finally realized that he was looking at one of the finest ghillie suits he'd ever seen. The Chechen's movement was scarcely faster than that of the minute hand on a clock, and Gil had to blink his eyes to be sure he was seeing what he was seeing. As of yet, he did not have a shot because Kovalenko was belly-down against the ground, and Gil was concealed within a natural depression in the earth, a leafy rhododendron branch dangling overhead. His scope had an untrammeled view of Kovalenko, but the muzzle of the rifle did not. In order to fire now, he would have to raise up onto one knee, and he was not about to give a man like Kovalenko that kind of opportunity.

LISTENING TO THE movement on his right, Kovalenko decided the American must not know his position after all. He was moving too fast and making too much noise, shifting position with impatience. The movement stopped, and Kovalenko knew he had him.

He increased his pace, though only slightly, and over the next twenty minutes, he worked his way to the end of the rhododendron thicket. He shifted his angle of attack to the right, training the AK-105 in the direction he had heard the American's movement. Then he lay motionless.

Ten minutes passed, and finally there was another sign of movement. Kovalenko caught a glimpse of a tan rucksack through the rhododendron and opened fire on full automatic, emptying the magazine and chopping the rhododendron to salad. He quickly reloaded and then got to his feet and stepped into the undergrowth for a look at the body.

The instant he saw the shredded rucksack, he knew he'd been had. He stood waiting for the lights to go out, feeling Gil standing fewer than thirty feet behind him. His hand closed around the grip of the rifle, fingering the trigger.

"You shouldn't wait," he said over his shoulder. "This is no game to play fairly."

Gil had the TAC-338 shouldered, the crosshairs fixed dead center between the Chechen's shoulder blades. "I wanted to say it's been a helluva fight."

Kovalenko nodded. "I watched you in the Panjshir Valley on satellite two years ago. Dragunov was there as well. You were all any of us talked about for weeks."

"You were still with the Spetsnaz then?"

"Yes. Now, before we finish this, I want to ask you a question."

"Ask it."

"What did you do with the key you found aboard the *Palinouros*? The key you took from Miller's body."

"It's in my pocket," Gil said.

Kovalenko chuckled sardonically, shaking his head. "If I were you, I'd wait to find out what that key opened before I gave it to Mr. Pope."

"Why's that?"

Kovalenko whipped around with the AK-105, and Gil shot him through both lungs halfway through the spin, exploding his heart and killing him instantly. The Chechen fell over in the rhododendron, and Gil ran to the body, knifing him under the jaw and quickly shaking him out of the ghillie suit. He put on the suit and grabbed up the suppressed AK, moving out toward the camp, hoping that most of the fighting men had joined in the hunt for Yablonsky and his team.

80

THE PENTAGON

General Couture watched Gil disappear from the infrared screen the second he shrugged into the ghillie suit. He snapped his fingers at an aide de camp. "Get the president on the horn, and tell him that Dokka Umarov is dead. He'll want to inform Putin."

Then he picked up the phone. Mark Vance, the CEO of Obsidian Optio, was waiting on the line. "Mark, I'm gonna need your helos again. Shannon and six Russian Spetsnaz are headed for the bridge in the Sba Mountain Pass. They've got about a hundred Chechen militants hot on their ass, so it's gonna be shittin' and gittin' the whole way."

"Bill, I'm sorry as hell," Vance said, sounding very official, "but I can't send my helos back into Russia. I've already got the Russian ambassador to Turkey on my ass. They know we were in there, and they're hotter than a whore in a peter patch over it."

"They don't need to invade Russian airspace this time, Mark. I just need 'em to stand by on the Georgian side of the bridge. Maybe fire a rocket or two across the river if it becomes necessary."

"Bill, I can't do that!"

"Yes, you can! We just bagged Dokka Umarov, for Christ's sake!"

"What? You're shitting me! That's confirmed?"

"I'm confirming it!" Couture growled. "And now your precious pipeline is safe again. So get those helos inbound!"

"Okay, but if there's any international flack over this, the State Department better cover my ass, and I'm not kidding. We're trying to expand our business into the Russian market."

Couture rolled his eyes. "Your ass will be covered, Mark. Don't worry." He hung up the phone not knowing if it was true or not, and not really caring. Mark Vance was a millionaire many times over. He looked at the White House chief of staff. "We just bagged Dokka fuckin' Umarov, Glen."

Brooks chuckled. "I wonder if Moscow will send us a thank-you note."

The secretary of defense came back into the room. "I was just told that Dokka Umarov is dead. Is that confirmed?"

Couture looked across at the air force liaison. "You got it cued up, Major? Play it for the secretary."

One of the screens blanked out for a moment. Then they watched as Dokka Umarov threw down his plate and stepped over the log. A second later his head exploded, and the body went down in a heap, falling over onto its back to reveal the obliterated face.

"Christ," the secretary said. "All that's left is the goddamn beard! What was Shannon thinking, taking a head shot?"

Couture chuckled. "Well, Mr. Secretary, he was probably thinking he wanted the bastard dead."

81

HAVANA,
Cuba

Crosswhite and Mariana didn't have too much trouble climbing over the gate to the *finca*. He gripped the pistol in his hand as they made their way along the wall around the side of the two-story house. They had studied the satellite photos, and so they knew the general layout as viewed from above. There were bars over the windows, and the drapes were all drawn at ground level. They stopped at the side door, and Crosswhite looked inside. The kitchen was deserted, but the door was made of steel, and the window was equally barred.

"We have to go around back to the patio."

They moved to the end of the house, and Crosswhite stole a look around the corner at the pool. It wasn't large, only about twenty feet long and four deep in the shape of a rectangle. The still blue water shimmered in the sun.

"Will he have a gun in there?" Mariana whispered.

"He's a fool if he doesn't. Wait here." Crosswhite stepped around the corner and onto the patio, keeping close to the wall as he made his way toward the door. He stopped at another barred window. The window was open, and the white drapes blew out through the bars with the breeze, suggesting there were more open windows elsewhere in the house.

A man sneezed just inside and then cleared his throat and sniffed, mumbling something unintelligible before clearing his throat again.

Crosswhite stepped in front of the window and pointed the 1911 pistol through the bars.

Peterson looked up from where he sat in a chair reading a book, his feet propped on a leather hassock four feet away from the window.

"You even twitch," Crosswhite snarled, "and I'll blow your fuckin' brains out."

Peterson turned white, staring at the yawning maw of the .45. "How did you get in here?"

"Apparently I pay a helluva lot better than you do." Crosswhite called for Mariana.

She came around the corner and looked in through the window, her anger and hatred boiling up unexpectedly. "Kill him!"

"Go check the door," Crosswhite said quietly.

She went to the door. "It's locked."

"Look for another way inside."

She slipped around the front. "Everything's locked and barred," she said, coming back around. "It's like a prison."

Crosswhite kept his eyes on Peterson. "Check the balcony."

She stepped back from the house and looked up. "The door to the balcony is open."

"Find a way up there."

She glanced around. "There's no ladder."

"Find a way, Mariana."

She went into the brick pool shed, but there was nothing of use in there either. "There's nothing, Dan."

Crosswhite stayed relaxed, but he knew that sooner or later, Peterson would make a move, and he'd have to make a decision. Firing the gun would be a risk. The cops outside the gate might get the bright idea of coming into the *finca* and killing him and Mariana; stealing the rest of the money and making up whatever story they liked. If the cop behind the wheel wasn't such a cowardly type, Crosswhite would have half expected them to try it anyhow.

"Look for a key," he said.

"Where?"

"How the hell do I know? But there has to be one. You don't risk getting locked out of a fortress like this." He noted the slightest change in Peterson's eyes. "There's a key! Find it." He grinned at the CIA man. "Make a move, fucker. I dare you!"

Peterson just stared back at him.

Mariana searched the patio high and low, running her fingers along window ledges, turning over the patio chairs, and poking around in the flower garden with a fork from the table. She even looked for a loose tile, but there didn't seem to be a key.

"Is there a lot of shit in the shed?" Crosswhite asked.

"Yeah." She went back to the shed and stepped inside, pulling the chain to turn on the light. The little building was crammed with pool chemicals and old bags of flower fertilizer left over from the previous owner. There was broken patio furniture, stacks of spare tile left from when the pool was put in years earlier, and various jars containing odds and ends. On one of the shelves was an old metal tobacco can. She took it down and pried off the lid. It was full of nuts and bolts, but she pushed her finger around in it and couldn't believe her eyes when she found a shiny new key at the bottom.

"I'll be damned."

She went back to Crosswhite, whispering into his ear that she'd found the key.

Crosswhite noted the increasing concern on Peterson's face. "I'm going to give you the gun," he told her, speaking deeply to cover the sound of him engaging the slide lock to safe the weapon. "If he makes a move, you shoot his ass. Is that clear?"

Mariana hesitated.

"I said, Is that clear?"

"Yes!"

"Put the key in my back pocket." She did as he said. "Now stand next to me and take the weapon without moving it off target."

They switched hands carefully, and Crosswhite stood behind her for a moment, helping her to steady the weapon. "I'm going in."

He went to the door, and as he was putting the key into the lock, Peterson made his move.

Mariana pulled the trigger, but the weapon didn't fire. Crosswhite swung the door open and ran inside, tackling Peterson on the tile as he was diving for the table where the .38 revolver sat in the open. He slugged the CIA man in the stomach and then hit him in the throat.

Mariana came running in with the pistol. "I tried to shoot him—I swear to God!"

He stood up and put the .38 in his back pocket. Then he took the .45 and tucked it away beneath his shirt. "Don't worry," he said, touching her shoulder. "You did perfect. I knew he'd make a move as soon as one of us started to open the door, so I put the safety on."

Peterson started to choke and rolled to his side, holding his throat.

"I'd like to say you'll be fine," Crosswhite said, hauling him up by the hair, "but that isn't true." He slugged him in the stomach again and shoved him across the room. "Now I'm gonna tell you a story about a Mexican girl, you piece of shit." He slammed Peterson down into a chair and took the folding knife from his pocket. "Her name was Sarahi, and she was one of the most beautiful women I've ever seen . . ."

Five minutes later, Crosswhite and Mariana stepped out through the gate to the *finca* and walked across the street to where the cops still sat in the car. Crosswhite looked around and handed the cop the rest of their money wrapped in a dish towel.

"We arrived too late," he said, "but I'm a man of my word, so I'm paying you anyhow."

The cops looked at each other. "What are you talking about?"

"He committed suicide," Crosswhite said. "Cut his own carotid artery. It's an ugly scene in there."

"I told you, no blood!" the driver hissed.

"And I just gave you another ten thousand dollars apiece!" Crosswhite hissed back, startling the cop. "The crime scene is perfect—so you make it work!"

They walked off down the street and got into Ernesto's car, driving straight to the airport.

Mariana bought a ticket, and Crosswhite walked her to the security checkpoint. "How soon will you follow after me?" she asked.

He shrugged. "Not before Pope is up and around again. I've got the sat phone, so I'll keep in touch. When you get to Mexico City, don't leave the airport. Get on the first available flight to the US—*any city!*"

She smiled. "Yes, sir."

"You gonna be okay?"

"I think so," she said, feeling suddenly lonely. "I wish you were coming with me."

He shook his head. "I'm not your type, Mariana."

She put her arms around his neck. "Thank you for— for everything."

"There's nothing to thank me for."

He watched her go through the security checkpoint, waved to her a last time, and went back to the car.

An hour later, Paolina opened the door to him, and the smile that spread across her face was like no smile anyone had ever smiled at him before.

"You know that I'm not a saint," he said.

She reached up to touch his face, looking deeply into his eyes. "Every saint has a past, Daniel . . . and every sinner has a future."

82

THE CAUCASUS MOUNTAINS

Gil stalked boldly into the camp, his face concealed by the hood of the ghillie suit, gripping the suppressed AK-105. One of the women pointed and said, "Kovalenko!"

He stopped and knelt at the body of Dokka Umarov, using the knife to cut off one of the thumbs. He stuck the digit into a pocket and kept moving, leaving the women gaping after him.

He reached the far side of the encampment and was approached by six men who had been left behind to look after things. One of them asked where he'd been in a language that Gil did not understand. He gunned them all down at point-blank range, dumping the magazine and reloading the weapon as he slipped back into the forest like a wraith.

He picked up the pace, moving into the Spetsnaz kill zone where the claymores had wreaked their devastation. There were Chechens everywhere tending the wounded.

Cries of agony filled the forest. He spotted Mukhammad conferring with his officers and kept going.

One of the officers spotted him. "Kovalenko!"

Mukhammad turned his head. "Sasha! Come here!"

Gil kept going, his fist closed around the ready-grenade.

"Sasha!"

One of the men started after him, but Mukhammad called him back, telling him to let Kovalenko join the chase if he wanted to.

Gil fell in on the trail of the Chechens who were in pursuit of Yablonsky and his men. The terrain grew increasingly rugged, covered with rocks and strewn with impenetrable thickets of rhododendron that forced everyone to skirt around them. He could tell from the way the ground was torn up that at least fifty men were in on the chase and moving fast.

A thousand meters into the track, he ran into four Chechens who had given up the chase and turned back. One of them had broken his leg in the rocks, and the others were helping him return to camp. They smiled at him in his leshy suit, and he sprayed them with suppressed fire. Then Gil stripped their bodies of grenades and whatever ammo would fit his AK-105 before moving on.

He heard firing in the distance and increased his pace. His bad foot was killing him, but the lead element had made contact with Yablonsky, and time was running out.

COLONEL YABLONSKY FIRED a 40 mm grenade to drive the Zapad men undercover and fell back, helping the man with the shattered shoulder blade who had since been shot through both legs. He could tell from the overly aggressive manner in which the lead element was maneuvering against them that they were Spetsnaz trained, and he cursed them for the traitors they were.

The badly wounded man was firing a pistol because he was no longer in any condition to wield a rifle. "Leave me, Colonel. I'm slowing you down."

Yablonsky propped him against a tree. "You're sure, Maxim?"

"I'll never make it. Leave me a grenade, and I'll make it count."

Yablonsky pulled the pin on a grenade and put it into the younger man's hand. Then he patted him on the face and dashed off to catch up with the other four Spetsnaz men.

Maxim crawled forward on his good arm, gripping the grenade. When the Chechens broke cover, he released the safety lever and counted to two before biffing the grenade in their direction. It detonated on impact and blew three of them off their feet. The others overran him and stabbed him with bayonets before moving on.

Yablonsky heard the blast and rallied his men to make a brief stand. They were running out of 40 mm grenades, but they had to keep the enemy back on its heels as much as possible. They fired a volley, and the last of the Chechen Spetsnaz were blown away by the barrage, giving them a much-needed respite.

"LET'S NOT STOP to watch the birds fuck," Yablonsky said. "The rest are not far behind."

Gil caught up to the tail end of the pursuers. He could hear them crashing through the forest ahead of him, calling out to one another to keep themselves organized. The 40 mm barrage echoed through the trees, and everyone picked up the pace.

He switched the AK-105 to semiauto and shot a straggler in the back, stepping on his head as he dashed over him. He shouldered the rifle and shot another man through the back of the skull.

A Chechen to his left heard the hiss of the rifle and jerked to a stop. "Kovalenko? Is that you?"

Gil shot him through the face and kept moving. He picked off a dozen men in this same manner, shooting them silently from behind, sometimes at ranges of up to forty yards, but a group of seven Chechens got wise to him and stopped to form a rear guard, thinking that one of the Spetsnaz men had slipped through the net and gotten into their rear.

Gil crouched motionless in the rhododendron, looking straight across a small glade at the men waiting in ambush. He was tempted to stand up and pretend to be Kovalenko, but it would only take one of them to call his bluff, so he remained motionless, losing time to the mission as he waited them out.

After almost ten minutes, the Chechens began to grow restless, whispering back and forth across their line. A few minutes after that, all but one of them pulled slowly back and resumed the pursuit.

Gil stayed where he was, watching the spooked Chechen who'd been left behind to cover the rear.

He waited until the man displaced to better cover; then he shouldered the rifle and shot him through the neck.

A hundred yards farther on, Gil came across Maxim's body. He saw the Russian was still alive and knelt to check his wounds. It was obvious the young man didn't have long to live. He put back the hood of the ghillie suit, and the Russian opened his eyes, recognizing Gil.

"Umarov?" he asked.

Gil drew a finger across his throat, and the Spetsnaz man smiled. He died a few moments later, and Gil moved out.

He caught back up to the posse shortly after they'd left the forest to descend into the river valley that led downhill to the west toward the bridge. He took cover in the tree line and picked off eleven of them over open sights before they realized they were being fired upon. When the rest finally did realize what was going on, there was nothing they could do about it. Gil was so well camouflaged, they couldn't tell where the shots were coming from. So they ran. They ran as fast as they could over open terrain—and Gil killed ten more of them before finally tossing aside the AK-105 and unslinging the .338.

He looked through the scope to see thirty more Chechens stretched out along the riverbank in hot pursuit of Yablonsky and his men. The Spetsnaz team was in full sprint for the bridge that still lay five hundred yards ahead. The Chechens fired wildly as they ran, but there were at least five hundred yards between the two parties, and the Chechens were too tired for accurate shooting at that range.

Gil set up the bipod and positioned himself behind the rifle. He shot the man closest to Yablonsky in the small of the back from almost eight hundred yards. Then he worked the bolt and fired again, picking off the next closest man. He shot them off the riverbank one at a time, working his way back.

The Chechens gave up the chase and sought whatever cover they could along the riverbank.

Yablonsky and his men pulled up short, stopping to launch the last of their 40 mm grenades in a high arc, blowing the Chechens off the bank and into the river. Then they watched as the last one was picked off by sniper fire, hearing Gil's shot echoing down through the valley.

The Spetsnaz men held their positions, watching Gil come walking down the side of the mountain carrying the .338 in his right hand, with the ghillie suit draped over his left arm. A French Puma and a heavily armed Cayuse helicopter flew into the valley and hovered high over the southern bridgehead without crossing into Russian airspace.

When Gil finally limped up, he smiled and offered Yablonsky the ghillie suit. "This was Kovalenko's leshy. I thought you might offer it to Putin as a souvenir, with my compliments."

Yablonsky smiled back, accepting the suit and passing it off to one of his men. "Umarov is dead?"

"You bet."

The Russian gestured across the river. "Are those helicopters here for us?"

"They better be," Gil said, setting off for the bridge. "I'm in no shape for walkin' home."

The helos landed as they walked along the bank.

"I got close to Mukhammad," Gil said, "but I didn't have a shot."

"Don't worry about him," Yablonsky said. "He doesn't have the influence that Umarov had. Not yet, at least."

They were met halfway across the bridge by Mason and three other heavily armed men. There was also a civilian among them, a man in his forties with thinning blond hair wearing a North Face jacket.

Gil returned Mason's sniper rifle. "I lost your ruck. I'm sorry."

Mason accepted the weapon. "You brought back the part that counts, Chief."

"Master Chief Shannon," said the civilian. "I'm Parker Smith with the US Embassy in Tbilisi. I was sent by the State Department to debrief you on the elimination of Dokka Umarov. There's some concern that we won't be able to confirm his death because you chose to kill him with a headshot, so I need you to—"

"Give me your hand," Gil said.

"I'm sorry?"

"I said, give me your hand."

Smith was reluctant but did as he was told.

Gil put the thumb of Dokka Umarov into the palm of Smith's hand and closed his fingers tightly over it. "This is all the DNA you and the State Department will need for confirmation. Now fuck off."

Gil turned and limped away toward the waiting helos. "Come on, Colonel. First beer's on me."

Smith opened his hand and turned green, stepping to the side of the bridge and retching over the railing.

EPILOGUE

PARIS,
France

Three months later, Gil and Crosswhite were walking across a self-storage lot on the outskirts of Paris, not far from the rail yard where Gil had his first run-in with Kovalenko.

"So tell me about this girl," Gil said.

Crosswhite took a drag from a cigarette. "Not much to tell."

"I know better than that. You moved to a communist country to be with her, for Christ's sake."

"It's actually not all that communist anymore—just dirt poor."

"So you're not gonna tell me about her?"

"Well, she's a little younger than me."

"How young?"

"Twenty-one."

Gil chuckled. "Twenty-one's a good age."

"She wants to get married soon—have a baby."

"You should do it," Gil said, lighting a cigarette of his own. "Be good for you."

"The idea of havin' a kid scares me," Crosswhite said. "And what happens when you get yourself in another jam? Who's gonna save your ass?"

"Don't use me to try and wriggle out of it," Gil said. "Besides, I was just in another jam. You were nowhere around."

"Yeah, and you damn near died, from what I hear."

"I damn near died the other two times."

Crosswhite stopped and turned to face him. "Fuck is that supposed to mean?"

"Means I think you should get married and have a baby, dumbass. Be good for you."

"Yeah," Crosswhite said with a sigh. "I know it." They set off walking again. "She's Catholic. I gotta start goin' to church on Sundays. I hate fuckin' church."

"Christ, it ain't gonna kill ya," Gil said. "You'll have to stop with the drugs, too."

"Already did. You talk to Marie lately?"

Gil grew immediately sad at the mention of his wife. "She doesn't want me back until I'm out for good. And I just ain't ready to quit."

"You know these young guys comin' up," Crosswhite said. "They're faster, stronger—more dangerous than we are."

"I know it, partner, but I ain't ready."

They stopped in front of the orange overhead door of the storage garage and stood looking at the big white number 9 stenciled on the front of it.

"So what the fuck do you suppose is gonna be in there?" Crosswhite wondered. "A booby trap?"

Gil tossed the cigarette to the ground and stepped on it. "I doubt it."

"You're absolutely positive you don't wanna tell Pope about this first?"

"Yeah." Gil stepped forward and put the key into the lock, giving it a turn. The door went up automatically, and both men stood staring.

"You gotta be shittin' me," Crosswhite said.

The phone rang in Gil's pocket. "Hello?"

"So what's behind door number nine?" Pope asked.

Gil glanced up at the sky, not at all surprised. "I think you'd better get on a plane and come have a look for yourself."

ABOUT THE AUTHORS

Scott McEwen is the number one *New York Times* bestselling coauthor of *American Sniper*, now made into a feature film with Clint Eastwood directing and Bradley Cooper playing Chris Kyle, Navy SEAL, CPO, deceased. Scott also coauthored *Eyes On Target: Inside Stories from the Brotherhood of the U.S. Navy SEALs*. He grew up in the mountains of eastern Oregon, where he became an Eagle Scout, hiking, fishing, and hunting at every opportunity. He obtained his undergraduate degree at Oregon State University and thereafter studied and worked extensively in London, England. Scott practiced law in Southern California before he began writing. Scott works with and provides support for several military charitable organizations, including the Navy SEAL Foundation.

Thomas Koloniar is the author of the postapocalyptic novel *Cannibal Reign* and the coauthor of the national bestseller *Sniper Elite: One-Way Trip* and *Target America*. He holds a bachelor of arts degree in English literature from the University of Akron. A retired police officer from Akron, Ohio, he currently lives in Mexico.

Turn the page for a sneak peek of
the next edge-of-your-seat thriller
in the *Sniper Elite* series:

GHOST SNIPER

BY

SCOTT McEWEN

WITH

THOMAS KOLONIAR

PARIS, FRANCE

Gil Shannon and Daniel Crosswhite walked across a self-storage lot on the outskirts of Paris, not far from the rail yard where Gil had had his first run-in with Chechen Sniper Sasha Kovalenko.

"So tell me about this girl," Gil said.

Crosswhite took a drag from a cigarette. "Not much to tell."

"I know better than that. You moved to a communist country to be with her, for Christ's sake."

"It's actually not all that communist anymore . . . just dirt poor."

"So you're not gonna tell me about her?"

"Well, she's a little younger than me.

"How young?"

"Twenty-one."

Gil chuckled. "Twenty-one's a good age."

"She wants to get married soon . . . have a baby."

"You should do it," Gil said, lighting a cigarette of his own. "Be good for you."

"The idea of havin' a kid scares me . . . and what happens when you get yourself in another jam? Who's gonna save your ass?"

"Don't use me to try and wriggle out of it," Gil said. "Besides, I was just in another jam. You were nowhere around."

"Yeah, and you damn near died from what I hear."

"I damn near died the other two times."

Crosswhite stopped and turned to face him. "Fuck is that supposed to mean?"

"Means I think you should get married and have a baby, dumbass. Be good for you."

"Yeah," Crosswhite said with a sigh. "I know it." They set off walking again. "She's Catholic. I gotta start goin' to church on Sundays. I fuckin' hate church."

"Christ, it ain't gonna kill ya. You'll have to stop with the drugs, too."

"Already did. You talk to Marie lately?"

Gil grew immediately sad at the mention of his wife. "She doesn't want me back until I'm out for good . . . and I just ain't ready to quit."

"You know these young guys comin' up . . . ," Crosswhite said. "They're faster, stronger . . . more dangerous than we are."

"I know it, partner, but I ain't ready."

They stopped in front of the orange overhead door of the storage garage and stood looking at the big white number "9" stenciled on the front of it.

"So what the fuck do you suppose is gonna be in there?" Crosswhite wondered. "A booby trap?"

Gil tossed the cigarette to the ground and stepped on it. "I doubt it."

"You're absolutely positive you don't wanna tell Pope about this first?"

"Yeah." Gil stepped forward and put the key into the lock, giving it turn. The door went up automatically and both men stood staring.

"You gotta be shittin' me," Crosswhite said.

The phone rang in Gil's pocket. "Hello?"

"So what's behind door number nine?" Pope asked.

Gil glanced up at the sky, not at all surprised. "I think you'd better get on a plane and come have a look for yourself."

ROBERT POPE, DIRECTOR of the CIA, arrived in Paris the next day, returning with Gil and Crosswhite to the storage unit.

Gil put the key into the wall and the door went up, revealing numerous ammo and weapons crates stacked at the back. What caught Pope's attention, however, was the wooden workbench against the wall with a large lump sitting on top of it, covered with a green canvas tarp.

"The crates are full," Gil remarked.

"What's under the tarp?" Pope asked.

Grinning, Crosswhite stepped in and pulled the tarp back, revealing two hundred neatly stacked bars of shiny gold bullion. Each bar was stamped "*1000g/999.9 GOLD.*" He watched Pope's eyes for any hint of shock or surprise, but there was none.

"How many bars?" Pope asked.

"Two hundred," Gil replied.

Pope did the math in his head. "That's almost nine million dollars. Close the door and give me the key."

Crosswhite shot a startled glance at Gil then back to Pope. "What the hell are you talking about—*give you the key?*"

Pope didn't reply.

"Come on out," Gil said quietly.

"Hey, this puts us on easy street!" Crosswhite said. "Mission complete. Game over. Winner takes all!"

"This puts us in business," Pope said, his blue eyes piercing. "Now close the door and give me the key."

"Gil, what the fuck?"

Gil turned the key.

The door began to close and Crosswhite quickly stepped out, incredulous. "Don't tell me you're down with this. You're gonna let him take all of it for himself?"

Gil took the key and gave it to Pope. "Let's go. We got a plane to catch."

SIX MONTHS LATER

MEXICO CITY *(DISTRITO FEDERAL)*
08:45 HOURS

CHANCE VAUGHT STOOD in the back hall of the US Embassy in Mexico City talking with Bill Louis, US Ambassador to Mexico. A former Green Beret with eight years of combat experience in Iraq and Afghanistan, he was now working as a special agent with the US Diplomatic Security Service (DSS). Currently, he was the special agent in charge of security for Alice B. Downly, the Director of the Office of National Drug Control Policy (aka Drug Czar).

"So you're telling me we have to run the gauntlet between here and the Mexican Senate building?" Vaught was thirty years old with green eyes and a black goatee set in a Latin visage. "I thought the entire week was scheduled for here in the embassy. What the hell happened?"

"Between you and I?" Louis lowered his voice. "Downly offended the Mexican delegation yesterday—namely Lazaro

Serrano. First by suggesting they allow US Special Forces teams into Mexico to act as advisors in their war against the cartels, and then by implying the teams would operate independently . . . the same way our operatives did down in Colombia back in Pablo Escobar's day."

Vaught rolled his eyes in disbelief. "Comparing Mexico to Colombia . . . very diplomatic." He took a can of Copenhagen tobacco from the cargo pocket of his trousers, putting a dip into his lower lip. He was sure the security at the Mexican Senate building—known in Mexico as *La Casona de Xicoténcatl*—would be tight, but he would have zero control there. Meeting off US embassy grounds was always a cause for heightened anxiety, and it was a growing problem for the DSS all over the globe. After the Bin Laden attacks of 2001, billions of American dollars were spent fortifying US Embassies, making them look more like super max prisons than houses of diplomacy, and many foreign diplomats simply refused to meet in the blocky, fortresslike structures. This forced American diplomats to take meetings in less secure locations—like this morning for example.

"It's only two miles." Louis was a round man in his forties, bald with pale blue eyes. He was fluent in Spanish and understood Mexican culture very well. "They're sending the usual federal escort—two trucks, four motorcycles— and with our three vehicles, that'll be plenty. It's only an eight minute ride."

Vaught had seen the entire world go to hell in eight seconds.

"I'll brief my people and get them ready to roll." His mother was from the state of Jalisco, so he had family in Mexico and grew up speaking the languages of both countries interchangeably. This had enabled him to form an immediate rapport with the ambassador. "I wonder what she plans on asking for today . . . our own airbase right here in DF?"

Louis chuckled as he turned away. "Avenida Reforma is the most direct route. I'll make sure the proper arrangements are made over at the senate building. Let me know if you need anything else."

Vaught assembled the other nine agents of his security team in the motor pool behind the embassy. They were all handpicked, each one a former operator with Special Forces. All of them had seen extended tours of combat. "Here's the deal, guys. Downly managed to piss off the Mexican delegation yesterday, so today they want to meet at the *Xicoténcatl* a couple miles from here." The name was pronounced shēko-TEN-katl. "That's the building were the Mexican Senate meets for those of you who don't *habla*." The others laughed. "They're sending the usual escort, so the run shouldn't take us more than eight minutes, but I want you guys max attentive the entire way. Are we clear?"

There were number of *rogers* and *aye-ayes* in response, depending on the agents' former branch of service, and they broke up to prep the transports, three black Chevy SUVs with bulletproof glass and doors.

Vaught took his number-two man aside, an African American named Uriah Heen, also a former Green Beret. Uriah was younger, just twenty six with a handsome face and slightly pockmarked complexion. "I'm putting Sellers in the lead vehicle with the trio. Jackson and I'll be in the middle with Downly, her two aides, and Ambassador Louis. You'll bring up the rear with the other three, but make sure Bogart's behind the wheel. I want somebody who can drive covering our tail. Clear?"

Uriah gave him a nod. "Clear. How'd Downly screw up?"

Vaught spit tobacco juice onto the concrete, tired of swallowing it. "She suggested setting American A-Teams loose down here to fight the cartels. I guess it went over like a fart at a baptism."

Uriah chuckled, rubbing the back of his shaved head. "Who'd she blow to get this appointment?" Alice Downly was a highly educated, forty year old brunette with a photogenic face and an infectious smile, but she wasn't exactly known for her political acumen around the DC social scene. Her appointment to the office had surprised more than a few people in the know.

Vaught's face tightened. "Secure that shit while we're in-country."

"Roger that." Uriah got serious. "I'll get everybody dialed in." He turned away.

Vaught watched him go. "Hey, Heen."

Uriah paused.

"Don't tell anybody." Vaught's green eyes were smiling. "But I think it must've been the Old Man himself."

Uriah grinned and continued on.

AN HOUR LATER the American delegation loaded into the vehicles and they were off. A Mexican Federal Police four-door pickup truck with four officers led the column, and another truck brought up the rear with two pairs of motorcycles leap frogging from stoplight to stoplight, preventing civilian traffic from cutting through the caravan. The DSS men were dressed in khaki cargo pants, black North Face jackets, ball caps, tactical boots, and Oakley sunglasses. Each carried a concealed Phase-5 Tactical CQC pistol on a single point bungee sling and a Glock 21 for back up. The CQC (close quarter combat) pistol was essentially a snubbed down M4 carbine with a 7.5-inch barrel in .223 caliber. The butt stock was removed, leaving only the buffer tube, which looked something like a padded broom handle that could be braced against the shoulder for greater control. Each weapon held a thirty-round magazine, and each DSS agent concealed an additional four magazines Velcroed to his body armor, armor bolstered by twelve-inch ceramic rifle plates front and back.

The column turned right leaving the Embassy grounds traveling southwest, briefly entering a large rotunda before turning right again to roll west. They made another right at the end of the block, traveling on a northerly heading for a quarter mile before making yet another right and driving two more blocks before finally bearing left around another large rotunda northward and onto the main avenue through Mexico City. The motorcycle cops were skilled at their jobs, herding the traffic away from the caravan much the way horses could be used to herd cattle, and there was never a pause in the column's progress.

Vaught rode shotgun in the center vehicle with Jackson, a former Navy SEAL, in the driver's seat and the four diplomats in the back. "Shit," he muttered watching the motorcycles bear to the right down a single narrow lane, "they're taking us down the lateral." The lateral lane ran parallel to the main avenue, separated by a raised median divider lined with trees, park benches, bus stops, and various concrete stanchions. The purpose of the lateral lane was to allow for traffic not traveling the entire distance of the avenue to turn off without hindering the flow of traffic along the main drag. Vaught didn't like to use the lateral on diplomatic runs because it left the column tightly hemmed in between the median divider on the left side and the buildings on the right, with virtually no route of escape.

He activated his throat mike, talking over the radio net. "Look sharp, people. It's gonna be a little tight for the next half mile." He glanced left at a city bus passing the column on the opposite side of the median divider, and the hair raised up on the back of his neck, the terrified eyes of the passengers in the windows alerting him that something was wrong. He caught a glimpse of a figure in a black ski mask and swung his arm over the back of the seat. "Everybody down! We're gonna be hit!"

Ambassador Louis grabbed Director Downly, pulling her toward the floor. Downly's aides, a man and a woman seated behind them, ducked down with the woman muttering, "Oh my God!"

Vaught was in the midst of barking a warning over the radio when the big green and yellow bus swerved over the median divider, bashing aside a bench full of people and slammed into the Federal Police truck at the head of the column, driving it through the front of an Oxxo convenient store. A rocket powered grenade streaked out of nowhere to strike the lead DSS vehicle in the driver's door, detonating with a horrible explosion that killed all four lead DSS agents instantly.

"Everybody dismount!" Vaught jumped out even before Jackson had the vehicle stopped. He jerked the backdoor open and yanked Louis out by the collar, reaching back inside to grab Downly by the arm and hauling her out so abruptly she didn't even have time to get her feet beneath her. She fell out onto the pavement as another RPG slammed into the driver's door and exploded. Vaught was thrown off his feet by the blast and landed on his back. The SUV burst into flames. Downly's male aide managed to scrabble out with his clothes burning and face covered in blood, but the woman remained inside, already consumed by fire. There was virtually nothing left of Jackson but a set of mangled legs on the floorboard.

Vaught was on his feet in a second, his mind processing the scene with computerlike speed, seeing almost in slow motion the four DSS agents to the rear rapidly dismounting the passenger side of the third vehicle. Another RPG struck the unarmored Federal Police truck at the tail of the column, exploding the fuel tank and tearing the truck apart even as the Federal Police were bailing out, killing them all.

Vaught instinctively traced the contrail of the rocket back along its trajectory. He swung up the CQC pistol and took a knee beside the burning Chevy, firing on three men taking cover near a white van parked on the far side of the avenue across seven lanes of traffic. The rocketeer went down, stitched from the groin up, and his two compatriots opened up with AK-47s.

Vaught rolled behind the burning Chevy as Uriah and the other three agents arrived to provide covering fire. Another fusillade erupted farther up the lane where the bus had slammed into the lead truck. Five masked gunmen where piling out the back of the bus, and people were screaming everywhere, running for cover in all directions as the gunners fired wildly from the hip. Vaught was struck on his body armor and the upper left arm. He knew he had to get his diplomatic charges off the street, but there wasn't any time, and there wasn't anywhere to run if there had been. This was a point blank shoot-out to the death.

Ears ringing, Uriah knelt beside him and they poured on the fire, knocking two of the gunmen off their feet.

"Reloading!" Vaught dumped the empty magazine, taking a fresh one from inside his jacket. Uriah dropped his own empty weapon to draw his Glock 21, firing into the remaining three gunners. Another went down, but not before Uriah took an AK-47 round to the chest plate and fell over backward.

Vaught brought the CQC pistol back up and cut the remaining two men down as they fumbled to reload. Uriah rolled to his feet and helped the other DSS men cover their diplomatic charges. With the storefronts along this block locked up behind metal gates, there was no place to seek shelter. The burning vehicles provided some cover but there was the danger of further explosions.

Three masked motorcyclists zipped past, spraying them with 9 mm fire from Uzi automatic pistols. A DSS agent fell dead with a bullet through the brain. Another was struck in the legs. Downly's male aide crashed to the sidewalk, hit through the liver and spleen. He would bleed out in seconds.

Downly screamed and dropped to her knees beside the aide, covering her head with her hands. The bikes whipped back around in the now empty street and made a second high-speed pass, spraying the scene again with the DSS men returning their fire. Ambassador Louis and another DSS agent went down. Vaught ran out into the street to draw a careful bead on the last rider as they raced away, squeezing the trigger and knocking him off the bike with the last round in the magazine.

The four motorcycle cops suddenly reappeared, speeding past him in hot pursuit of the other two fleeing motorbikes.

"Where the fuck are the cops going?" Uriah screamed. "We need 'em here!"

"It's a goat fuck!" Vaught switched out the magazine as he came back from the street. "The whole thing's a goddamn setup! Help Bogart get Downly off the ground while I check on Clay. We gotta move!"

"To where?"

"Anywhere's better than here!"

Bogart's real name was Stevens, but he looked a lot like Humphrey Bogart, and he was having trouble getting Downly up with one arm, needing to keep the other arm free to shoot. The Drug Czar was completely petrified, refusing to carry her own weight and screaming hysterically with her hands pressed over her ears. Uriah grabbed her other arm, and they hauled her to her feet.

Vaught crouched beside Agent Clay, the DSS man hit in the legs. "Can you move under your own power?"

Clay shook his head, gripping his weapon, eyes searching everywhere, bleeding from both thighs and a knee. "The knee won't support my weight. We're in deep shit here, Chance. Why are all these fucking storefronts locked on a Tuesday?"

Vaught stated the obvious. "To keep us out here on the street." He stood and pulled Clay up onto his better leg. By now the remaining Chevy was also fully engulfed in flames, having been too close to the other burning vehicles. "Let's skirt around the bus and keep moving up the street until we find an open building. We should be hearing sirens anytime now."

"Why aren't we hearing them already?"

"They'll wait until they've gathered a large enough force to handle whatever the hell they think is going on down here."

Clay virtually exploded, spattering Vaught with blood and viscera. Vaught staggered back as the cannon shot echoed up the avenue from down the block.

"Holy fuck—it's a Barrett! Everybody down!"

Hesitating a fraction of a second too long, Bogart was struck in the back by a .50 caliber sniper round weighing

45 grams and traveling at 2800 feet per second. The bullet blasted off his left arm and shoulder, sending the appendage twirling up into the air. He fell on the concrete, locking eyes with Vaught as the life ran out of him. The arm and shoulder landed beside Downly. She shrieked in horror, scrabbling back to her feet and running frantically out into Avenida Reforma.

Vaught and Uriah looked at each other from across the walk, knowing that to go after her was suicide. "Stay down!" Vaught sprang up and gave chase. He was almost half way across the avenue when Downly exploded at the waist, her entrails whirling off in what seemed like all directions as the two severed halves of her hit the pavement in a twisted mess with nothing but her spinal cord holding them together.

Vaught had completely failed in his mission to protect his charges, and he'd lost nearly his entire team in the process. It may not have been through any error of his own, but he was still responsible, and he knew it.

With the image of the bullet's vapor trail—cutting through the morning air faster than the microscopic water molecules could get out of its way—seared into his brain, he now knew where the sniper was. Without pause, he sprinted past Downly's mangled remains toward an abandoned taxi on the far side of the avenue, knowing that to turn back would give the shooter a clear shot at a motionless target, even if only for a fraction of an instant.

He took cover beside the taxi and got on the radio to Uriah. "I know where the fucker's at. He's firing from the rooftop of the glass building on my side of the street at the end of the block on the far corner. He doesn't have an angle on you, so stay put. I'm going after him."

Uriah's reply was immediate: "If he's shooting from

the glass building, he doesn't have an angle on you either. Just stay outta sight and let the local heat handle this!"

They could hear sirens now far up the avenue.

"I'm going after him!" Vaught said. "You stay alive and make sure our people know what happened. Don't let the Mexicans debrief you without somebody from our embassy being there." He double-checked his weapon and jumped into the taxi, speeding off as a dozen federal squad cars and trucks came screaming down the avenue behind him.

Don't miss

GHOST SNIPER

coming soon in hardcover!

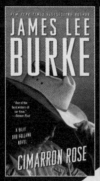

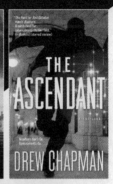
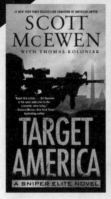